We hope you enjoy this book.
Please return or renew it by the due date.
You can renew it at **www.norfolk.gov.uk/libraries**
or by using our free library app. Otherwise you can
phone **0344 800 8020** - please have your library
card and pin ready.
You can sign up for email reminders too.

ALSO BY MARK EDWARDS

THE
RETREAT
MARK EDWARDS

THOMAS & MERCER

Text copyright © 2018 by Mark Edwards
All rights reserved.

Published by Thomas & Mercer, Seattle

www.apub.com

Amazon, the Amazon logo, and Thomas & Mercer are trademarks of Amazon.com, Inc., or its affiliates.

ISBN-13: 9781477805176
ISBN-10: 1477805176

Cover design by Mark Swan

Printed in the United States of America

Author's Note

This novel is set in North Wales. The town of Beddmawr is fictional but if you want to find where it would exist on a map, it's very close to Llangollen in Denbighshire.

Prologue

It was muddy and windy by the river. At times like this Lily wished they had a dog she could throw sticks for, though Big Cat and Little Cat probably wouldn't approve. She wanted a cute little dog, a pug or something like that. She walked off ahead of Mum and Dad, fantasising about the pug they were going to buy her. She'd call it Sweetie. It would wear a pink collar and win prizes at Crufts and Lily would be on TV, proud and smiling beside her famous pet.

Deep in thought, Lily was hardly aware that her parents were lagging behind. She heard a cry and looked back up the path, along the riverbank. Dad was staring at the water, mouth open like a fish. Mum had her hands on her hips.

They were arguing again.

Mum jabbed a finger towards Dad, whose face had gone pink. Lily realised he wasn't looking into the water but at the edge of the bank, where something metallic lay.

All her hopes of this year being better than the last evaporated. Furious, finding it hard to swallow or even breathe, Lily stomped into the trees where the river curved, so she couldn't see her parents and they couldn't see her. She was sick of the sight of them, and she wished she could disappear, turn into a bird and fly away.

For a moment, she pictured herself diving into the river and drowning herself. Mum couldn't even swim, and Dad was a useless swimmer too. They wouldn't be able to save her and they'd be so sorry, *so sorry.*

She stood there, clenching and unclenching her fists until she realised she was hurting Big Cat. She hugged him and kissed his head, then marched on, along the path to where the trees ended.

She made a decision. As soon as she'd done it she hurried into the bushes that separated the riverbank from the road.

She jumped, as if someone had crept up behind her and shouted 'Boo!'

'What are you doing?' she whispered.

A few moments later, she tried to scream. She'd made a terrible mistake and wished she could rewind time, just a minute or two. She even pictured time running in reverse, sending her back up the path and safely into the arms of Mum and Dad. But it was too late.

'Lily?' She heard Mum calling her name. 'Lily, where are you?'

But she couldn't reply. There was a gag in her mouth and strong arms holding her still. Mum's cries faded into the distance as those strong arms carried her away.

PART ONE

Chapter 1

I crossed the border into Wales shortly after five o'clock, the sun low and muted in a sky the colour of slate. It was raining, but that didn't matter. Because as I hit the crest of a hill, the valley below came into view. And it was *glorious*.

I slowed the car so I could take it in. The flat peaks of the Berwyn mountains framed a green world: patchwork fields dotted with sheep; pretty farmhouses that overlooked rolling fields; trees, some standing proudly alone, others crowded together. And flowing through it all, the River Dee.

This was home.

Why had I waited so long to come back?

When night fell it would all look very different. Then I would probably miss the never-dimming lights of London. But now I wound down the window and let the chill air cleanse me. I was sure that here, finally, I would be able to write again. Rediscover my voice, my inspiration. If I could do that, I was certain all my other worries would dissolve like snowflakes falling into water.

So it was with a great deal of optimism that I steered my car, a white Qashqai, down the hill into the valley. The satnav took me past the small town of Beddmawr – my home town, though it hardly seemed familiar – and into the countryside, down narrow, mud-streaked lanes that skirted the edge of a thick wood. I took a wrong turn, almost ending up in a meadow where sheep grazed, and was forced to back up. This last stretch was beyond the satnav's capabilities. I switched it off and got out of the car, taking advantage of a lull in the rain. The writers' retreat had to be close. In the end, I clambered onto the roof of the car – which I'd bought with my first royalty payment, and which I really ought to treat better – and there it was, standing on a low hill beyond the meadow.

It was a stone house, painted white, with a steep tiled roof. It was bigger and more imposing than I'd expected. The kind of place that looked like it would always be cold inside, no matter how many fires you lit. Behind the house, a steep bank half-protected it from the elements. To either side, woodland stretched as far as I could see.

Something flapped in the branches above my head, startling me and almost making me lose my balance. But I stole another look at the house before I climbed down, and smiled. It was the perfect place to write a scary book.

Back in the car, I headed up a long driveway lined by bare-limbed trees. There was a large barn to the left of the house and, I noticed, a cottage that hid at the rear of the main building like a shy child peeking out from behind its mother's skirt.

The house was even more impressive up close. It was solid. A place that had stood here for, I guessed, two hundred years. The only signs of modernity were a TV aerial on the roof and a child's plastic swing in the garden. Smoke rose from a tall chimney. I wanted to take a good look around but I was tired and hungry, and besides, there would be plenty of time to explore later.

As I removed my small case from the car, the front door opened and a woman stepped out, hugging herself against the cold.

She was about my age – in her early to mid-forties – with long chestnut-brown hair and prominent cheekbones. She was skinny and pale, the kind of person my mum would say would be blown away by a stiff wind, but attractive, a woman who would make me look twice if I spotted her in a bar. She was wearing jeans and a green sweater, with some kind of cashmere wrap over the top. A poncho? She had on a pair of dark-framed glasses that she readjusted as she came towards me.

'Lucas?' she said. 'I'm Julia.'

I shook her hand, which was surprisingly cold. Although her smile was welcoming, she managed to look sad at the same time. There was something in her green eyes, an echo of pain, that made me stop and hold on to her hand for an extra moment. Perhaps sensing that I was studying her, trying to read her, she became businesslike, asking if I had much luggage.

'Just this,' I replied. 'This place is amazing.' I nodded towards the swing. The wind had caught it so it swung slowly to and fro, as if being used by a tired ghost. 'Must be a fantastic place to grow up.'

I knew immediately that my words had stung in some way. She recovered quickly, though, and gestured for me to follow her inside.

'Welcome,' she said, 'to Nyth Bran.'

ɯ

I followed her into a hallway which was painted white with a gallery's worth of traditional pictures on the walls: the local countryside, mountains and horse riders. Crumbling castles and fields of daffodils.

She saw me glance at the paintings. 'They're not really to my taste. But I thought the guests might appreciate it. Rustic Welsh charm.'

'I like them. They remind me of home.'

A raised eyebrow. 'You're from round here?'

'Originally. I was born in Beddmawr but my family moved to Birmingham when I was six. We had pictures just like this in our house.' I nodded at the painting of the daffodils. 'In fact, I'm pretty sure my mum had this exact same picture.'

I smiled, wondering if she still had it, hanging in the villa in the south of Spain.

'How about you?' I asked. She had a faint northern English accent. 'You don't sound Welsh,' I said.

'No, I'm from Manchester originally. Didsbury. We only moved here a few years ago.'

I wondered who she meant by 'we'. The retreat's website listed Julia as the sole proprietor.

'Come into the kitchen,' Julia said. 'It's warmer in there.'

She asked me if I wanted a coffee and I accepted gladly. It was a typical rural kitchen – spacious, with buttery walls, a stone floor and a view of the front garden. I stood by the Aga and rambled on for a minute, telling her about the journey. I hadn't spent time with another human being in days. Julia smiled politely as she waited for the kettle to boil, making the occasional comment. She'd removed her glasses, which had left two little marks on the sides of her nose.

A ginger cat strolled into the kitchen, tail held high, and I stooped to stroke it.

'That's Chesney,' she said, as the cat purred and rubbed his face against my knuckles.

'He's gorgeous. So . . . is it just you and Chesney?'

She turned away from me and lifted the faintly whistling kettle. The cat, detecting a shift in the atmosphere, dashed out of the room.

'Yep,' Julia replied, the gap so long that I'd ceased to expect an answer. 'Just us. And the other guests, of course.'

I looked around, stupidly, as if they might be hiding in the kitchen cupboards.

'They've all gone to the pub,' she said. 'It's become a bit of a tradition, when they finish work for the day. The Miners Arms – it's a couple of miles down the road.'

She handed me my coffee. 'I've got some boring paperwork for you to fill out. How long do you think you'll want to stay?'

'I was hoping to leave it open-ended, if that's okay. I mean, at least a month.'

Her eyebrows shot up. 'A month?'

'Is that okay? I can pay up front.'

'Yes. Sure.'

'I really have to get my stupid book finished.'

Not just finished. Started as well. But I didn't tell her that.

She looked me up and down, like she was seeing me for the first time. At last, she smiled. 'That's absolutely fine, Lucas. Stay as long as you like.'

ᛜ

I spent a while filling out the paperwork and made small talk with Julia while I finished my coffee. Outside, dusk crept up to the windows.

Julia gestured for me to go up the stairs first. In contrast to the immaculate decor on the ground floor, the stair carpet was threadbare and the wallpaper peeled in patches. There were signs that someone had started to decorate this area at some point, but the work had been abandoned.

When we reached the landing Julia said, 'You're on this floor.' I was a little disappointed I wouldn't be at the top of the house, but didn't want to complain.

'Yours is the second door on the left,' Julia said from behind me.

I took hold of the door handle and she yelled, 'Not that one!'

I withdrew my hand as if the handle were red hot. 'Sorry, you said . . .'

'I meant third door. *Third* door. Room Six.' She had her hand on her chest, breathing hard, pink spots on her cheeks. She noticed me staring at her and forced a smile. 'Sorry, that room isn't made up yet. It's a bit of a mess.'

She stepped past me and pushed open the door of Room 6. I followed her inside.

It was an impressive space: wooden floorboards, in better condition than those in the hallway, a neatly made double bed, a wardrobe and dresser. Best of all, there was a huge desk beneath the window with what looked like a comfortable, ergonomic chair. I ran my hand over the desk's smooth oak surface.

'I'm sorry there's no en suite,' Julia said. The pink spots on her cheeks had faded and she was calm again. 'The bathroom is a little way down the hall.'

She stood beside me at the window, so we faced our reflections in the glass. It was dark outside now. No stars or moon. Save for a few lights dotted here and there across the landscape, it was as if the world beyond this house had ceased to exist when the sun went down.

'I'll show you around when you've had a chance to unpack, but you can either write here or in the sitting room, or even in the cottage.'

'Great.'

She produced a room key and laid it on the desk. 'You pretty much have the run of the house, except . . . can I just ask you not to go into the basement. It's not . . . safe.'

'Oh?'

'The stairs need to be repaired.'

'Understood.' I couldn't imagine wanting to go into the basement anyway. I sat at the desk. 'This is wonderful, Julia. How long have you been open?'

'Only a few months. I haven't really got going yet, not properly. I mean, I know a lot of writing retreats have guest authors, classes, et cetera. I'm going to organise all that at some point. For now, this is just a quiet, secluded place for people to come and get their heads down.'

'That's exactly what I'm looking for.' I didn't explain there was another, more specific reason for choosing this particular retreat, so close to where I spent my early childhood. 'Are you an author yourself?'

'Me? No.'

She was about to leave me to it, but hesitated by the door. 'I don't mean to be nosy, but what kind of books do you write?'

'Horror.'

There it was: a faint look of distaste. A reaction I was well used to. 'And is this . . . your first book?'

'No, I've written tons, most of which sold somewhere close to zero copies.'

'Most?'

'Um. The last one did pretty well. It was called *Sweetmeat*.'

She looked blank and I must have appeared disappointed because she said, 'Sorry, I'm not really a big fan of that type of book. I mean, I've read a couple of Stephen Kings but I'm a total wimp.'

I smiled. People were always saying this to me.

'I have enough nightmares as it is.' I could tell she immediately regretted saying this, as she quickly added, 'Anyway, let me leave you in peace. Dinner's at eight, when the others get back from the pub.'

'Great. Thank you.'

She shut the door, leaving me alone at my temporary desk. I stared at the space where she'd been. She was mysterious. A woman with a story. I was looking forward to finding out what it was.

Chapter 2

A clatter of noise came from downstairs: a booming male voice, footsteps, a slamming door. The other guests, back from the pub.

Fellow writers. I instinctively bristled, then chided myself. I had come here not only to get my head down and work, but because I was in need of human company. I had spent too much time on my own since losing Priya. So much time alone that I had begun to talk to next door's cat when she came to visit, and to order parcels from Amazon just so I'd see another human face. I was sure the courier had started to avoid me, tired of making conversation with the crazy guy in Flat 3.

I went downstairs, following the sound of conversation to the dining room.

There were three of them, a man and two women, seated around an oval table. They all looked up as I walked in.

The man was seated on the far left. He was in his late thirties, with a high forehead and a neatly trimmed beard. I recognised him, but couldn't quite place him. Sitting almost on his lap was a young blonde woman with pale eyelashes and a small mouth. Pretty, in that English-rose way, but not my type. On the other side of the table, a woman in her fifties with an expensive-looking haircut was thumbing an iPhone.

The man gestured for me to take a seat.

'So you're the new guy,' he said, sticking out his hand. 'Max Lake. This is Suzi Hastings.' The younger woman mouthed hello.

'And I'm Karen,' the older woman said. 'Karen Holden.'

I'd heard of Max Lake, of course I had. He was a writer of literary fiction who'd been talked about as a kind of *enfant terrible* a decade ago. Now, as far as I could tell, he spent most of his time on Twitter, trying to make every injustice in the world about him. I didn't recognise Suzi's name. A first-time novelist? She and Max were sitting very close together, almost touching. I was sure I'd seen Max mention his wife in an interview – yes, he was wearing a wedding ring – so it would be faintly scandalous if he and Suzi were sleeping together.

I introduced myself as I sat down.

'Lucas Radcliffe as in L. J. Radcliffe?' Karen said. 'Goodness. I loved your book.' As I tried to look modest she turned to the others and asked if they'd read it. They hadn't. 'It's about all these children who disappear and this creature who eats their souls. So deliciously scary. I loved it. It sold squillions as well, didn't it?'

'Yeah, it did okay.' I hated talking about this kind of thing. It made me cringe to my core.

'I heard it was being made into a movie. With Emma Watson?'

'Well. Maybe. But probably not with Emma.'

While looking at Karen, I could feel Max scrutinising me.

'A horror novel, is it?' he asked. 'My agent is always telling me I should write something genre, a thriller or crime novel perhaps, between my proper books. Something to help pay the bills.' He chuckled. 'But I don't know if I could bring myself to stoop to it.'

Before I could respond, Julia entered the room, carrying a plate piled high with bread rolls and a dish of butter. There were a couple of bottles of sparkling water on the table already. She hurried out and returned with four bowls of vegetable soup.

'Smells lovely,' Max said, pouring himself a glass of water.

'Julia, I don't suppose there's any wine, is there?' I asked.

The other three exchanged knowing looks as Julia said, 'Ah, sorry. This is a dry house.'

'That's why we go to the pub every night,' Max said. 'To get our rations.'

A dry house? That wasn't mentioned on the website.

'Would you like a coffee?' she asked.

I told her no, water was fine. The disappointment must have shown because, as Julia left, Karen leaned over and, with a conspiratorial wink, said, 'I've got a bottle of gin in my room if you get desperate later.'

As we ate our starter, I asked Karen and Suzi what kind of stuff they wrote. I was tempted to ask Max too, to prick his ego by pretending I hadn't heard of him.

'I write genre stuff too,' Karen said, with a pointed glance at Max. 'A mystery series and an urban fantasy series.'

'Women bonking billionaire werewolves,' said Max with a smirk. 'She writes a book a month. Can you believe that?'

'Self-published?' I asked Karen, and she nodded enthusiastically.

'Oh yes. I couldn't bear to have people interfere with my work.'

'An editor, for example,' Max said.

She ignored him. 'I like to be in control. And I like the money too.'

I had a horrible feeling they were about to descend into a tedious argument about traditional versus self-publishing, so I cut them off by asking Suzi what she was writing.

Her voice was soft. 'I'm working on my first novel. It's a . . . picaresque, set at a university . . .'

'Not a werewolf in sight,' said Max.

Karen caught my eye. 'There is a lot of bonking, though.'

'Max is helping me with it,' Suzi said. Her face pinked. 'With the writing, I mean.'

Karen chuckled. 'If you say so, dear.'

Suzi was saved from further blushes by the arrival of Julia with our main course, a goat's cheese tart with potatoes and salad. We ate in silence for a few minutes. Suzi still seemed mortified by what she'd said. Karen kept looking at her phone.

'The Wi-Fi here is terrible,' she said, as Max made his excuses and went off to the loo. 'And don't talk to me about the mobile signal. Still, I guess that's what we came here for. Solitude. Time to concentrate.'

'Maybe you can teach me how to write a book in a month,' I said. 'Oh?'

I sighed. 'My deadline is mid-May and everything I've written so far is . . . well, it's shit. It's not scary. It's boring. Boring as hell. I need to start from scratch.'

Karen shrugged. 'Easy. Three thousand words a day, every day, for a month.'

She made it sound so doable. The problem was, I didn't have a story in my head. I barely had an idea. I was too embarrassed to tell anyone, because it sounded like a first-world problem, but I was blocked. Worse than that – paralysed. Soon, everyone would find out that my bestseller was a fluke and I would be exposed as a fraud, vanishing back into obscurity before you could say 'one-hit wonder'.

Like I said, it was a first-world problem. But it was *my* problem.

ω

A week before, I'd called my agent, Jamie, in a panic, telling him we were going to have to give the advance back, that I was washed up, finished.

He told me to calm down.

'You need to go back,' he said. 'Back to the source of your inspiration. Where did the idea for *Sweetmeat* come from?'

'I don't know. A dream.'

He groaned.

'No, really. I woke up one morning with the picture of the creature in my head, and a woman crying because her daughter was missing.

The idea came from my subconscious.' I made a pained noise. 'It's so frustrating. I mean, I've always written. It's always come easily, since I was a kid.'

'Then maybe you need to go right back. You need to fall in love with writing again. Find whatever, or wherever, it was that caused that first spark.'

Wherever. That caught my attention. Although *Sweetmeat* was set in an invented community, it was very much based on the place where I grew up in North Wales. The green, empty landscape, the relentless rain. Dark woods and low mountains; the river where a boy from our school drowned. And boredom – that was a vital ingredient. There was nothing to do, so I'd made stuff up. I started off by drawing and writing comics, then moved on to short stories. I invented whole worlds to entertain myself.

In London, where I'd lived since my early twenties, there was too much to stimulate me on the surface but not enough to stir my deeper imagination. I needed darkness, but lived in a city where lights always shone.

It was time to go back into the dark.

'What are you thinking?' Jamie had asked.

'That it's time to go home,' I replied.

ᚹ

After dinner, while Max and Suzi went upstairs to 'work on her novel', Karen gave me a tour of the house. I didn't know where Julia had gone.

'The rooms are all named after prominent Welsh writers,' Karen pointed out. 'The dining room is the Roberts Room, after Kate Roberts.'

On the opposite side of the hallway to the dining room and kitchen was a decent-sized sitting room, called the Thomas Room, presumably after Dylan. The room was dark and cosy, stuffed full of books, with a library ladder attached to the highest book shelf. There was a utility room, and another large room – the Follett Room – that contained a number of desks with chairs but which appeared unfinished. One wall was only half-painted white and there were no curtains at the window.

Most of the rooms had open fires or log burners, so the smell of woodsmoke permeated the house. It threw me back in time to my childhood, to long, drowsy Sunday afternoons, a black-and-white film on TV, listening to the top forty on the radio, finger poised on the record button. I didn't miss those days but the memory stimulated a nostalgia gland, the sense that life was hurtling by too fast.

'Fancy a ciggie?' Karen asked, a mischievous twinkle in her eye.

'Oh, go on then.'

We went out front – I noticed that she winced slightly as she walked – and she passed me a cigarette. I was strictly a social smoker, but it tasted delicious.

'Max is a terrible literary snob,' she said. 'And a huge narcissist. But he's quite good company.'

'Suzi seems to think so.'

'Good for her.' She lowered her voice. 'Though she is a little weird . . . She asked me to read a few pages. I mean, I'm a woman of the world, I write pretty strong stuff myself. But hers was disturbing. A couple smearing each other with animal blood, using it as a sexual lubricant. Gross, actually. And there's this horrible bit in it with a dead baby in a freezer.' She shuddered.

'Wow.'

'And as for our literary friend, I heard him on the phone to his wife the other day, arguing about money. About whether he should be frittering the last of their cash away on a writing retreat. I think he's going through a sticky patch.'

'His patch is going to get stickier if his wife finds out about him and Suzi.' I frowned. 'Some people just don't appreciate what they've got.'

Karen raised an eyebrow.

I stubbed out my cigarette and reminded myself I'd just met this woman. 'Ignore me. I don't want to come across as judgemental.'

'Oh, me neither.' She gestured at the land around us. 'You know this place used to be a slate mine, a hundred years ago?'

'Interesting.'

She smiled. 'You sound like my daughter when I try to tell her about my youth.'

Back inside, we passed a closed door. Karen noticed how my gaze snagged on it.

'That's the basement,' she said. She leaned forward and whispered in a mock-spooky voice. 'We're not allowed down there.'

'Yes, Julia told me. Something about the stairs being unsafe.'

Karen checked over her shoulder and lowered her voice to a whisper. 'I heard a guest strayed down there once and Julia flipped and chucked them out.'

'Really?'

'Uh-huh. She is a little intense. I like her, but I wouldn't want to get on her bad side. Now, fancy joining me for a small gin?'

I checked my watch. It was only quarter past nine. But I needed to be disciplined if I had any hope of getting this book written, so I said goodnight to Karen and went to my room.

I paused outside the second door along in the hallway, noticing that unlike the other rooms it bore no number. There was Room 5, by the stairs, then this door, then Room 6, which was mine. Standing in the silence, I heard a noise come from inside the numberless room, like a radio turned down low. Looking around to ensure no one was coming, I gently pressed my ear against the painted wood.

Inside the room, someone was singing. A female voice, soft and melodious. I couldn't make out the words, but it sounded like a child's song, a nursery rhyme or lullaby.

I shifted my position and the floorboards creaked beneath me. Abruptly, the singing stopped, and I hurried to my room, hot with guilt, like a Peeping Tom caught in the act.

Chapter 3

I woke up early the next morning, after the best night's sleep I'd had in a long time. It might have been the country air, or the lack of alcohol. After showering in the bathroom along the hallway, I headed to my desk, opening my laptop. Normally, I would spend an hour catching up with Facebook and Twitter, reading the headlines, answering emails from readers. But I had binned the sheet of paper with the Wi-Fi password. I wanted to remain isolated, to go grey. No social media, no email, no Internet till I got this book written. If anyone needed me urgently, they could call.

I opened my work in progress and stared at the blinking cursor. I kept staring. It was too early. I needed caffeine.

Downstairs in the kitchen, I found a pot of coffee and some croissants on a plate with a note saying *Help yourself.* There was no sign of Julia or the other guests, but there was a man in the garden. He was in his sixties, with curly grey hair and red cheeks. He was fiddling with a lawnmower, scraping dried clumps of grass from the rotors and shaking his head.

He looked up and saw me watching him through the window. He raised a hand in greeting, then pointed at the mug in my hand and winked at me.

I didn't want to upset the locals, so I made one and took it out to him.

'Cheers,' he said. 'I take it you're one of Julia's writers?'

'I guess so, yes. I'm Lucas.'

He stuck out a hand. 'Rhodri Wallace.' He nodded towards the house. 'Julia's a lovely lass. I hope this writing retreat thing works out for her, after the time she's had.'

'The time she'd had?'

'You don't know? Well, it's not for me to tell you.'

He returned his attention to the troublesome lawnmower and thanked me for the coffee.

I was about to go when I remembered the singing I'd heard the previous night. 'Are there any children here?' I asked. 'Young girls?'

His face darkened. 'Why do you ask that?'

'I wondered who the garden swing was for, that's all.'

He turned to look at it. Now, in daylight, I could see how rusty it was. How it clearly hadn't been used for a long time.

'That thing needs taking to the tip,' Rhodri said, turning away to indicate our conversation was over.

ʊ

I ate breakfast and knew I should go back to my room, force myself to write. But I still felt uninspired. I had come here to reconnect with the place where I grew up, hadn't I? Outside, the day was clear and bright. I would go for a walk. That was sure to help.

I headed down the drive towards the main road, tossed a coin in my head and turned left. It was cold despite the brightness and I stuck my hands in my coat pockets and put my head down, not really looking where I was going. I headed across a field towards some distant woods. Snowdrops sprouted from the earth, the first harbingers of spring. Birds sang in the trees. It was so peaceful here.

So why did I feel uneasy?

A woman with a spaniel on a lead passed me as I entered the wood. The sight of the dog stirred a memory, which I tried to ignore, exchanging hellos with the woman.

I walked for an hour, still not keeping track of where I was going, failing to drop imaginary breadcrumbs behind me. The path was muddy and I felt foolish in my canvas footwear, but I was determined to keep going. I was lost in thought. But I wasn't thinking about the book I was supposed to be writing. I was thinking about Priya.

We met in our early twenties. Recently, I'd been listening to the radio and the DJ said something about the approaching twentieth anniversary of Radiohead's *OK Computer*. I reeled, unable to believe it had been two decades since Priya and I bought that album. We used to listen to it together all the time. When 'Karma Police' came on the radio, I had to turn it off. It hurt too much.

At the time I'd been working in an office and she worked in my local bookshop. I was in there a lot, one of their best customers, and Priya and I got chatting. She was beautiful and clever and all those things. Funny and sexy and wise. Moody and crazy and restless. She had shiny black hair and little moles that I loved to trace with a finger when we lay in bed.

I told her I was an aspiring writer, and when we started dating, through the period when we moved in together, all of those early years, she supported and encouraged me. When I got my first book deal, she was as ecstatic as I was, possibly more. She told me it didn't matter when my book failed to set the world alight. She counselled me, told me it was all about building an audience – one reader, one book at a time. She calmed me down when my first publisher dumped me. She celebrated again when I got another deal, even though it was tiny. She told me to keep going.

If it weren't for her, I would have given up. One day I was going to make her proud, show her that her faith was justified. I fantasised many times about calling her, giving her good news. The bookshop where she worked had gone bust and she was working in an office, doing a job she hated, surrounded by people she had nothing in common with. I was going to rescue her, rescue us.

But by the time it happened, it was too late. She was already gone.

I stumbled on the path and the shot of adrenaline brought me out of the pit I'd been mentally wallowing in. I looked around. I was in a clearing in the woods, with one path ahead of me and three behind me. I had no idea which way I'd come. I looked for footprints but had mostly been walking slightly to the side of the puddle-strewn path, on the grass, so couldn't see any.

I was lost. I took out my phone, hoping I could find my location on my Maps app, but had no signal. I tried to decide what to do – head back in the direction I'd come from, or plough on. Listening carefully, I thought I could hear traffic in the distance. I decided to carry on.

I passed a stagnant pond, gnats darting about the surface. A dog poop bag hung from a branch. I couldn't be too far from civilisation. As I headed on, the trees thinned and the path became muddier. Within minutes, I was in a large clearing, in a field of overgrown, yellowed grass.

In the centre of this field, which was ringed by trees on all sides, was a dilapidated stone hut. I approached it. The windows were smashed and the wooden front door had half rotted away. I pulled at it, and peered into the hut's interior. A rank, musty smell floated out. The floor was strewn with ancient litter, but apart from that, it was empty. I stepped inside, trying not to breathe through my nose.

Among the rubbish – rusting drinks cans, crushed cigarette packets and a porn mag with curled pages – was something furry. At first I thought it was a dead rat, but peering closer I realised it was a soft toy. It looked old and weather-beaten, the clumpy, damp fur coated with mould. Its glass eyes stared at me until I had to look away.

I closed the door. I had the sensation that fate had brought me here, because suddenly I felt inspired and keen to get back to my desk, an impulse I hadn't felt for a long time.

I was still lost, though. To my right I could hear cars, closer than they'd been before. I headed in that direction and, after tramping through another copse of trees, I found the road. There was no pavement, just a grass verge which was dotted with wild flowers. I was pretty sure the writers' retreat was to the west, so I went that way, keeping to the verge.

Five minutes later, I heard a car behind me. I turned and saw a taxi. Like a chariot sent by the gods. I waved and it pulled over.

The driver wound his window down. 'Need a ride?'

ʊ

It was warm inside the cab, and it smelled of air freshener, the chemical scent a welcome relief after the stink of the abandoned hut.

'What are you doing out here?' the driver asked in his strong Welsh accent. He was about my age, with thinning brown hair.

I told him I'd gone for a walk and lost my bearings.

He laughed. 'Happens a lot. These woods can be deceiving. They all look the same, especially if you're not from round here.'

'I am from here,' I said. 'Well, I used to be.'

'Back visiting relatives, are you?'

'No, I'm staying at Nyth Bran. The writing retreat? Do you know where it is?'

'Oh, I know where it is, all right.' We set off. He drove with one hand low on the wheel and kept looking back over his shoulder at me. I wanted to tell him to keep his eyes on the road.

'So you're a writer,' he said. 'What kind of stuff do you write?'

'Horror.'

'Oh, really? Doing research, were you? Out in the woods?'

'Something like that.'

We passed a squashed badger, lying dead by the roadside.

'My dad's always got his nose in a book,' he said. 'I didn't inherit the reading gene, though. He's always nagging me about it. Maybe I should read one of yours. I love horror movies. The gorier the better.'

'I'll send you one,' I said. 'But only if you promise to read it.'

'Cool. I'd like that.' We passed more roadkill, a rabbit this time. 'So you're staying with Julia Marsh? I was surprised that she hung around. After what happened.'

'What do you mean?'

He flicked his eyes at me in the rear-view mirror. 'Oh, you don't know? It was big news at the time.'

I waited.

'Her husband . . . He drowned in the Dee. Michael. Nice chap, he was.'

'Oh my God.' No wonder Julia looked so haunted. 'When was that?'

He thought about it. 'Two years ago? Terrible, it was. But that wasn't the worst part.'

He stopped, forcing me to ask.

'What was the worst part?'

'Her little girl. She *disappeared*.'

I stared at him.

'They said she drowned like her dad, but they never found her body. The police were there for ages. Frogmen and everything. Terrible. Everybody in town went down to watch. They said she must have been swept along, all the way to Bala.'

That was the lake where the Dee ended up.

'And here we are,' the driver said.

I looked up, confused, expecting to find myself by the banks of Bala Lake. But no, we were at the end of the drive that led to Nyth Bran.

'Can I drop you here, or do you want me to take you up to the front door?'

'Here's fine.'

I got out and found a ten-pound note in my wallet, telling him to keep the change, seeing as he'd rescued me from a long walk.

He nodded thanks and handed me his card. *Olly Jones, Taxi and Chauffeur Service. Short or Long Haul.*

I was about to turn away when he said, 'Some people say that house is cursed.'

'What?'

'Superstitious claptrap. It's all to do with the widow.'

'What?'

The widow? Did he mean Julia?

'Forget I mentioned it. Like I said, it's a load of nonsense.' He started the engine. 'Though you'd be surprised how many folks around here believe in nonsense.'

Chapter 4

I broke my vow not to go online as soon as I got back to my room, retrieving the Wi-Fi password from the wastepaper basket. I went onto Google and searched 'Julia Marsh River Dee'. And there it was, a news story from 8 January 2015.

Girl Still Missing After New Year Tragedy

North Wales Police have called off a search of the River Dee and Bala Lake after the presumed drowning of 8-year-old Lily Marsh on New Year's Day.

Lily had been out walking with her parents on January 1st, along a stretch of the Dee near Beddmawr in Denbighshire.

Her father, Michael Marsh, 42, drowned while trying to rescue his daughter.

According to North Wales Police, Lily had run ahead out of sight. When they caught up, her toy cat was floating in the river, prompting Mr Marsh to jump in.

His wife, Julia, 40, called emergency services, who pulled his body from the water. But emergency services have been unable to recover Lily's body.

The operation involved police divers, the fire service and river rescue teams. But after an extensive search of the river and the four-mile-long Bala Lake, emergency services have been stood down.

A spokesperson for North Wales Police said, 'The search was wrapped up yesterday, but our inquiries are ongoing.'

Michael Marsh was an IT manager who had recently moved to the area from Manchester with his family. Lily attended the local primary school, St Peter's, whose head teacher, Anna Rowland, said, 'This incident has shocked the entire community and we continue to pray for Lily.'

Mr Marsh's funeral takes place today.

Poor, poor Julia. I remembered her yelling, 'Not that room!' The numberless bedroom next to mine must have been Lily's. I shuddered, then realised something. Julia was the mother of a child who had disappeared. What if she found out what *Sweetmeat* was about? Would she chuck me out?

Not for the first time in my life, I felt as if I'd stumbled into the darkness of one of my own stories. Because a river featured heavily in *Sweetmeat* too. A river that stole kids away from their parents.

In my novel, the victims are taken by a supernatural entity, a creature who lives in the woods and feeds on children's souls. That was where the title came from: the creature describes the souls as tasting like sugared fruits or candies. And as he consumes them, he whispers '*Sssssssweetmeat*'.

A river runs through the woods, and in one scene the creature drags a little girl into the water. The heroine is a female cop who is investigating the disappearances of half a dozen kids from a small town in rural England. At the end, she goes down to the river and trades her own soul – 'It's bitter,' complains the creature, as it chokes to death – for those of the children, so they are released to Heaven. But because the detective is killed when she gives up her soul, the fate of these kids remains a mystery.

Not the kind of book Julia would want on her bedside table.

ʊ

I forced myself not to think about Lily Marsh and spent a few hours working on the idea I'd had after stumbling across the rotting hut in the woods. When I came up for air, I was surprised to see it was five in the afternoon. I hadn't been so absorbed by my writing for a long time, and it felt good.

Not long afterwards there was a knock at my door. It was Karen.

'We're heading down to the pub. Fancy joining us?'

I did.

The Miners Arms was on the main road towards Beddmawr. A proper old-fashioned Welsh pub with a roaring fire, horseshoes hanging on the walls and plenty of real ale on tap.

'I'll get the first round,' I said.

A few old men sat propping up the bar and there were two guys playing darts in the corner. They had glanced at us as we entered but lost interest straight away. I guessed they were used to writers coming in. Looking around while I waited to be served, I noticed a creepy painting depicting a woman dressed in red among dark, spiky trees. The woman's

30

face was concealed by shadows, but she stretched out a bony hand as if beckoning the viewer into the picture. It made me shiver.

I bought the drinks and sat at a round table with Karen, Max and Suzi. Karen was as cheerful as she'd been the day before, but Max and Suzi would barely look at each other. A lovers' tiff? Max swiftly downed his pint of bitter and announced he was going to play on the quiz machine. I watched him jabbing at the buttons and swearing under his breath.

'What's up with him?' Karen asked. 'Lost a couple of Twitter followers?'

That made Suzi laugh. She was, I realised, very young. Twenty-three, perhaps? I could hardly remember what it felt like to be her age. I seem to recall I was simultaneously lacking in confidence and thought I knew everything about the world.

'It's nothing,' Suzi said, glancing at me.

Karen spotted the look. 'Do you want Lucas to bugger off to the quiz machine too? So we can talk woman to woman?'

Suzi stared into her glass of white wine. 'No. It's fine. But you both have to promise not to say anything. Okay?'

We promised.

'I know you probably think there's something going on between Max and me, but there isn't. He's married . . . and I would never do that to another woman. I can't bear people who cheat. My mum did it to my dad and it almost destroyed our family. It's disgusting.'

'I believe you,' Karen said.

'Besides, I don't fancy him. He's too . . .'

'Up himself?' Karen offered.

'No. Too short.'

Karen laughed.

'But he has been helping me with my book, giving me lots of advice. I mean, there's been quite a lot of mansplaining going on, but he has been helpful. I keep telling him how grateful I am. And I think – well, I think he got the wrong impression.'

'Did the little bastard make a move on you?' Karen asked.

Suzi took a big gulp of wine and glanced at Max. The pub was growing increasingly noisy as more punters came in after work, and the quiz machine was gurgling and beeping like a crazed robot. He couldn't hear us.

'Last night, after dinner, we went to my room. Just to talk about writing. We were discussing a sex scene I was working on.'

'I see,' Karen said, raising an eyebrow.

'And Max was very enthusiastic about it. He kept going on about how sex is the rawest experience a person can have, that it's a great opportunity to show your character's inner self . . .' She cleared her throat. The skin around her throat had gone pink. 'I could tell he was getting a little, um, overexcited, so I said I was tired and needed to go to sleep.'

'And that's when he made his move?'

'No. Not at all. He said goodnight and left. I got into bed and read for a while, then went to sleep.'

'Right.' Karen furrowed her brow and looked at me. I shrugged.

Suzi had finished her drink now. She held the glass by its stem, rotating it on the spot. 'I woke up an hour or two later. Somebody was coming into my room.'

Karen was all ears.

'The door creaks and I'm a light sleeper anyway, so it woke me up. I sat bolt upright and said, "Who's that?" Immediately the door closed and I heard footsteps going down the hallway. I didn't . . . I couldn't get back to sleep.'

'And you think it was Max?' I said.

She nodded. 'It had to be. I mean, assuming it wasn't one of you two.'

'It definitely wasn't me,' I said.

'Nor me,' said Karen. 'And it doesn't seem like the sort of thing Julia would do. It's pretty obvious to me who it was. Max, feeling all hot and bothered after your sex scene discussion, wanting to discover your "inner self".'

Suzi winced. 'Please.'

'So what did the little bastard have to say for himself?' Karen asked. Across the pub, Max was still bashing at the quiz machine's buttons. He appeared a little happier now, like he was winning. A small crowd had gathered around him.

'I haven't asked him. I was too embarrassed. But I told him I didn't want his help today, that I wanted to work on my own. He's been off with me ever since. Please don't say anything to him. I'm going to ensure I lock my door tonight. It's not like he actually did anything.'

'Hmm,' Karen said.

'I feel a bit sorry for him, too,' Suzi said. 'I think he's having some problems with his marriage.' That echoed what Karen had said the previous evening. 'And his last book didn't do very well.'

'That's no excuse for trying to sneak into a young woman's bedroom,' Karen said, glaring over at him. Max remained oblivious.

'Oh God, I wish I hadn't said anything now,' Suzi said. 'Please don't talk to him about it.' She stood up. 'I need another drink.'

As she went to the bar, I said to Karen, 'Are you going to talk to him?'

'I don't know. I mean, what if Suzi hadn't woken up? What would he have done? Got into bed with her? Raped her? Told her he could help her career if she was nice to him?' She lowered her voice further. 'I'm going to be keeping an eye on him, that's for sure.'

ᙡ

It was dark by the time we got back to the retreat. Julia was standing out front, rattling a silver dish. 'Chesney!' she called. 'Chesney!'

'Cat gone walkabout?' I asked. I needed the loo so had hurried ahead of the others, who were now only halfway up the drive.

She sighed. 'He does it all the time. Disappears for hours, some-times a whole day. It makes me sick with worry.'

I wasn't surprised by her anxiety, not after learning what had happened to Julia. I wondered if Chesney had been Lily's pet. With Michael and Lily gone, the cat was Julia's last link to her family. The cat and the house they lived in.

Julia held her glasses in her hand. She put them on, then took them off again.

'I guess he's got plenty of places to explore around here,' I said. 'Lots of mice to chase.'

'Yeah. Except he's always been a fat, lazy old thing. He never brings mice or birds in. I have no idea where he goes.'

The other writers appeared and Julia put the dish on the ground outside the door.

'He'll come back, though,' she said. 'He always does.'

She stared at the black horizon. I could read her mind. The cat always came back, but she would trade that a thousand times over for a glimpse of her daughter. Should I let her know that I knew? I almost said something, but she turned away before I could speak, and the moment slipped away into the darkness.

Chapter 5

I couldn't stop thinking about what had happened to Lily.

Perhaps if I hadn't written a book about vanishing children, if my imagination didn't tend towards the macabre, the gothic, I might have gone along with the obvious: that Lily had drowned in the river and, for whatever reason, the police couldn't find her body. I wouldn't have seen it as a mystery. But after trying, and failing, to get into my work the following morning, I had an overwhelming compulsion to see the spot where Michael Marsh had drowned. The last place where Lily Marsh had been seen.

There was a map accompanying the article I'd read the day before, showing the stretch of river where the incident had occurred. I copied it into a notebook and went out.

Walking through the thin patch of trees towards the Dee, I tried to convince myself I wasn't a misery tourist, the kind of person who visits a murder scene to see where the carnage happened. I kept telling myself to turn back, go 'home', get on with my book, but my legs had other ideas. They carried me forward until I came out onto a muddy path where the river swept around a bend.

As soon as I stepped onto the path, an image flashed in my mind of this very place. A pebble striking the water. An adult calling out. It stopped me in my tracks.

It had to be a memory from my childhood. And, of course, that made sense. My parents must have brought me here. We'd probably come frequently. But, like so much of my early childhood in Wales, the memory had retreated into a dark, unreachable place.

I consulted the map. Yes, this was where it had happened. It was raining, little icy needles on the back of my neck, and the river was swollen, foaming like a rabid dog. It was easy to see how someone could drown in that churning current as it swept around the corner. Even the strongest swimmer would struggle. A child wouldn't stand a chance.

Tentatively, I made my way down the bank onto some rocks by the water. I found a stone and tossed it in, watching it vanish beneath the opaque surface.

I closed my eyes and imagined a man thrashing in the current, desperate and afraid.

Climbing back onto the bank, I looked around. What else could have happened to Lily if she hadn't drowned? I turned in a slow circle, taking in the landscape. There was no way she could have crossed the river.

This spot was close to the road. Could somebody have been waiting here? An opportunist, spotting a child? I pictured it: he grabbed her and threw her toy cat into the water so her parents would think she'd fallen in, then dragged her back to his car.

But why didn't she scream? Would he have had time to do all that before Julia and Michael caught up? Surely it was too risky.

No. I knew from cops I'd spoken to when researching *Sweetmeat* that the most obvious explanation is almost always the right one. Lily had fallen into the water and drowned. Tragic. But almost certainly a less dreadful fate than what might have happened if someone had taken her.

As I stared into the water, I experienced a prickle on the nape of my neck, the sensation that someone was watching me. I turned and squinted into the bushes. Nothing moved – just the light drumming of raindrops on leaves; a breeze stirring the undergrowth. It was my imagination, that was all. My overdeveloped imagination.

The rain was getting heavier, fat raindrops splatting my sketched map, so I headed back to the house.

ω

The front door of the cottage behind the main house was open and music was coming from within. Curious, I headed over and found Karen inside, working at a little desk in a cosy side room that was named after Bertrand Russell, the radio on. She snapped her laptop shut when she noticed me.

'Lucas! Why aren't you working? Naughty boy.'

I closed the door behind me. 'Have you seen Suzi this morning? Any idea if Max tried to get into her room again last night?'

She turned the radio down. 'No. I saw him, though, on the phone to his wife. Arguing. Again. He told her he's going to stay here for another couple of weeks.' She paused. 'You're a horror writer.'

'I am.'

'Well, I think you'll like this. I had a spooky experience last night.'

'Really?' I pulled up a chair. 'Tell me more.'

'It was about midnight and I couldn't sleep, so I thought I'd sneak down and make myself a snack.' She smiled. 'Don't judge me.'

'I'm not. Sounds like a good idea.'

'It's the country air. It makes me hungry. Anyway, I made myself a cheese sandwich – and yes, I know cheese at bedtime is a bad idea but there was this delicious-smelling cheddar in the fridge which I couldn't resist – and then I heard something. A bang from the hallway. It made me jump out of my skin.'

I pictured it. Karen, about to bite into her sandwich, frozen with her mouth open.

'I went out to investigate.' She shook her head. 'I was carrying the knife I'd used to cut the cheese, trying to kid myself I'm awfully brave. And it was that blasted cat.'

'Oh, good. He came back.'

'Good? The bloody thing nearly gave me a heart attack. Anyway, he shot into the sitting room and I went after him, *here kitty kitty*, all that. Thinking I'd give him a piece of my mind, not that I've got much to spare. Eventually I gave up and went back to the kitchen. And that's when the weird thing happened. My sandwich was gone.'

I laughed. 'Really?'

'Yes! The plate was there, with crumbs on it. But no sandwich.'

'Had you been drinking?' I asked.

'I might have had one or two nips of gin. And a few puffs on a spliff.'

'You were *stoned*?'

'Don't sound so shocked. I smoke it for medicinal purposes.'

I must have looked doubtful because she said, 'No, seriously. I suffer with terrible arthritis, especially in my fingers when I've been writing all day. My knees too. It's awful, but weed helps a lot.'

'Oh, sorry.'

She shook off my apology. 'Anyway, I was *slightly* stoned. But not enough to hallucinate that sandwich. And I hadn't eaten it and forgotten, if that's what you're thinking. My tummy was still rumbling.'

'Hmm.' I tried not to sound too sceptical. 'So what did you do?'

'I made another sandwich.'

I laughed, but Karen wasn't smiling.

'What do you think?' she asked. 'Could it have been a ghost?'

'I've never heard of a ghost stealing someone's supper.'

'Yeah. I guess.'

'Perhaps the cat took it,' I said. 'He might have dragged it off your plate and under a cupboard.'

Or maybe, I thought, *you got stoned, ate it yourself, then forgot.*

'That bloody cat,' she said, then laughed.

I left Karen staring at her laptop and explored the cottage. There was a tiny kitchen, with nothing but a kettle and basic tea-making facilities, a small living room and a toilet. Stairs led up to the second floor, but a chain had been strung across the staircase, barring entry.

There wasn't much else to see, and I really needed to get on with some work, so I left the cottage. I waved goodbye to Karen but she didn't see. She was frowning with concentration. Probably thinking about her missing sandwich.

ʊ

'How's everything going so far?' Julia asked later that afternoon when I popped down to the kitchen to make a coffee. She was leaning against the Aga for warmth, Chesney the cat on the worktop beside her. I was about to repeat Karen's story about the cat and the sandwich when I realised Julia might not appreciate her guests smoking weed in their rooms. If she wouldn't allow alcohol, drugs were almost certainly a no-no, medicinal purposes or not.

'I don't know,' I replied. 'I thought it was going well yesterday but now I'm not so certain. I'm trying not to think about the sand running out of the hourglass.'

'I'm sure you'll get there.'

She tucked a long strand of her chestnut hair behind her ear. Since finding out about Lily, I had been struggling not to look at her with obvious sympathy. She gave off a strong vibe of wanting to be left alone, but I wasn't in a hurry to return to the silence of my room – and, well, I liked Julia. I barely knew anything about her – save what I'd learned from the Internet – but I wanted to know more.

'I was going to make myself a coffee,' I said. 'Would you like one?'

'I don't drink coffee. I'm one of those boring people who only drinks herbal tea.' She nodded at a long line of boxes on the side, chamomile and rooibos and lemon verbena. In fact, she had a mug on the go now.

No alcohol or caffeine. Had she always been clean-living, or was it a recent change?

'What do you think of the retreat so far?' she asked.

'I like it. Though it feels strange being back here. I'm wondering if my Welsh accent will return.'

She smiled. 'Like I said before, I'm going to start organising talks, getting in a resident writer, having discussion groups, when things get going properly,' she said.

'Good idea. Not that I'm into being critiqued by other writers. It's bad enough reading my reviews on Amazon.' The kettle whistled and I lifted it from the hotplate. 'I've been wondering, what made you open a writers' retreat?'

'Money.'

'Always a good reason.'

'The best. I just . . . well, I thought about setting up a bed and breakfast, but then a friend who works in publishing suggested doing this. She said there was a lot of demand for it and I'd meet lots of interesting people.'

'You have friends in publishing?'

'I used to be an illustrator. Children's books. Have you heard of Jackdaw Books? I did a lot of stuff for them.'

I stood with my back to her, stirring milk into my coffee. 'Used to be? What made you stop?'

I was hoping she would mention her husband and daughter but she didn't reply. When I turned around she met my eye and said, 'I looked you up.'

'Oh. Really?'

'Yeah. You didn't tell me you were a bestseller. I read it's being made into a movie.'

I adopted my modest face. 'Hopefully. It's stuck in development hell.'

I paused. It would be easy to carry on the charade and pretend I didn't know about her history. I knew that bringing it up might cause her pain. But I also wanted to be honest. I wasn't going to get a better chance than this.

'I have a confession,' I said.

'Oh?'

'I know . . . I know what happened to you. To your husband and daughter.'

She had been lifting her mug to her lips. Her hand froze and she placed the mug on the counter. It rattled against the Formica. I immediately wished I'd kept quiet.

'Is that why you came here?'

'No, of course not. I only found out yester—'

'You like writing about missing children, don't you? Are you researching a sequel? Are you going to write about how my daughter was eaten by a fucking *monster*?'

She glared at me, then abruptly left the room. I stood there, the cat blinking at me accusingly, stunned by how quickly she'd gone from calm to furious, as if I'd flipped a switch.

After a moment of hesitation I followed her into the sitting room – the Thomas Room, I reminded myself – where she stood by the bookcase, her chest visibly rising and falling, a thunderous expression on her face.

'Julia, I promise I didn't know until yesterday. A taxi driver mentioned it when I said I was staying here.'

She stood with her back to me, staring through the window at the cloud-choked sky. 'And then what did you do? Google me?'

My silence was confirmation.

She turned. 'Do you know how many journalists I had coming here, day after day, week after week? All of them pretending to be

41

concerned, wanting me to give my side of the story. It took months to get rid of them. And now I've got an author staying here who specialises in writing about missing children—'

'I don't specialise in it.'

'I should never have opened this place. I'm not ready.'

She covered her reddening face with her hands. She was silent and I didn't know what to do or say. Eventually, I managed, 'I swear, Julia, that my new book has nothing to do with missing children. I have no interest in writing about you or your family. I feel terribly sorry for you, that's all.'

She shook her head, as if the sight of me made her sick.

'If you want me to go, I will.'

'I think that would be best.'

'Okay.' I felt sick, but what else could I do? 'Now?'

She wouldn't meet my eye. 'You can stay tonight. But first thing tomorrow, I want you to go.'

Chapter 6

I dreamt I was drowning, being dragged to the bottom of a river by clutching hands. All I could see beneath me was hair, swaying like fronds, and I swallowed mouthfuls of dirty black water. I could hear music, muffled and soft. A girl singing on the riverbed, sweet but distorted, the melody bent out of shape.

I woke up gasping – but the singing continued. I lay there, still half in the dream, listening, thinking I must still be asleep. Stupidly, I pinched myself. I was definitely awake.

I got out of bed and pressed my ear to the wall that separated my room from the one Julia had stopped me going into. Lily's room. That's where the singing was coming from, just as before. Now, in the silence of the night, it was clearer – but I couldn't make out the words. I strained to hear and then it struck me. The words weren't in English.

I hadn't studied Welsh since I was five years old but was sure I recognised the first few words. *Un, dau, tri.* One, two, three. The rest of the words, though – and the tune – weren't familiar.

What was a girl doing in Lily's old room, singing in the middle of the night?

I was about to leave my room to investigate further when I realised: it must be Julia. Yes, it sounded like a child singing, but it was conceivable that it was a woman. Or it could even be someone playing a recording . . . That must be it. Perhaps Julia was in there now, listening to a recording of her daughter singing. It was unusual behaviour, but people deal with grief in many different ways.

The singing stopped. I waited for the sound of Julia leaving the room. But all was silent.

Eventually, I got back into bed and pulled the covers up to my chin. I had come up with a solid, rational explanation for what I'd heard, but I was still spooked, and I lay there for hours, the melody from the song repeating inside my head, burrowing deeper into my brain with every loop, until eventually I entered a hypnogogic state where I could hardly tell the difference between imagination and reality. I pictured myself getting out of bed again, crossing the room and touching the wall. It was warm, pulsing, and I became convinced the wall was made of flesh and bone, that the house was alive. I dug my fingernails into the wallpaper and tore holes in the pattern. As the melody from the little girl's song went round and round in my head, blood trickled from beneath my fingers and ran down the walls. The house shuddered as if it were crying.

ꞷ

It didn't take long to gather my stuff and pack my suitcase. Although I felt guilty about looking into what had happened to Julia's daughter and invading her privacy, I also thought I was blameless to some extent. It was, surely, a coincidence that I'd written about the topic that most hurt Julia.

I yawned, exhausted from my disturbed night, haunted by my waking dream. As I checked to see if I'd forgotten anything, I couldn't help but glance over at the walls, expecting to see them bleed. Maybe it was a blessing that I was leaving. One thing had struck me in the morning light: when the house cried in my dream, it had sounded like Priya.

I opened my bedroom door – just as Karen came down the stairs from her room on the top floor.

She spotted my suitcase. 'What's going on?'

'I'm leaving.'

'What? Why?'

Sensing that she would bombard me with difficult questions if I wasn't honest, I gestured for her to come into my room and take a seat. I told her everything, keeping my voice low.

'Oh, that poor woman,' she said. 'I had no idea.'

'Do you remember seeing it on the news at the time?'

'No. I was living in Italy then. It's dreadful. I don't have children but I can imagine . . .' She trailed off. 'It's not right for her to chuck you out, though. I mean, you didn't come here because she had a missing child, did you?'

'Of course not!'

She got up. 'Let me have a word with her. Maybe I can persuade her that you're a good egg, and not a creepy voyeur with a dead child obsession.'

Before I could protest, she left the room. I sat there, feeling like a schoolboy whose mum has gone to talk to the head teacher to plead his case.

Five minutes later, Julia appeared in my doorway.

'Can we have a chat?' she said.

'Of course. Come in.'

She closed the door behind her. Her hair was tied back in a ponytail and, fresh-faced and makeup-free in her baggy jumper and leggings, she looked younger than her age. But she had dark smudges beneath her eyes and her skin was so pale it was almost translucent. She was so thin too, as if grief had melted the meat from her bones.

'Listen, Julia, I promise you I had no idea about Lily before I came here. It's a total coincidence that I wrote a book about . . . missing kids . . . I would never ever dream of exploiting—'

She cut off my babble. 'Lucas.'

'Sorry.'

'No, I'm sorry. I overreacted. You can stay, assuming you still want to.'

'I do.'

'Good. That's settled then. Let's forget it ever happened.'

She went to leave, but I stopped her by saying, 'Do you want to talk about it? About Lily and Michael?'

She focused on a spot on the carpet. 'Not really.'

'I understand. It hurts to talk about it.'

She looked at me curiously and I added, 'I lost someone too, someone I loved, and it still causes me pain just to think about it, let alone talk about it. For you to lose two members of your family . . .'

She shook her head. 'One. Only Michael. I mean, yes, Lily is lost, but she's not dead. I'm sure of it.'

'Oh.'

She made an exasperated gesture. 'Everyone assumes she's dead. The police, all the people in town, my friends. Everyone. But they don't . . .' She sat down on the bed. 'Okay, I'll tell you. But you have to promise you won't put it in a book.'

'On my mother's life.'

'Okay.' She turned her face towards the window. 'It was New Year's Day, two years ago . . .'

ꞷ

The path along the riverbank was slick with mud. It sucked at the soles of Julia's wellies. The wind caught her from behind and she almost lost her footing – heart flipping, arms windmilling – until Michael grabbed her arm.

'Careful.'

'I'm fine.' She wriggled free of his grip and pulled her coat tightly around herself, shivering. She called out to Lily, 'Stay where I can see you!'

Their daughter was a little way ahead. Eight years old and skinny as a snake, the coat she'd got for Christmas unzipped and hanging from her bony shoulders. She'd refused to put on her hat or gloves, insisting she didn't need them. And it was true: Lily was like a human radiator; always had been. On bitter winter nights, when drafts invaded their house – the house that, Michael liked to say, had its own weather system – Julia would steal into Lily's bed and bask in her glow.

Lily was clutching her favourite toy, Big Cat, which she'd had since she was a baby. She raised an arm and carried on along the bank at her own pace. She was at the point where the path descended towards a copse of trees that hugged the bend in the river. She glanced back occasionally, an unreadable expression on her face. Lily had been studying her parents closely today, watching them as if trying to see inside their heads.

Most likely she was watching them because she didn't trust the peace between them.

Julia opened her mouth to call out again, to tell Lily to stay where she could see her, but Michael said, 'Leave her. She's happy.'

'I know. I just don't like her going into the trees on her own.'

'Stop fretting. She'll be fine.'

He put his arms around her and pulled her into a kiss. He still smelled of last night's alcohol and the kiss was brief – but, after a dry spell that had threatened to turn into a drought, it was still something.

Julia made her way down the final stretch of the slippery path, glancing at the river as she went. All that recent rainfall had made the water level rise and it was fast-flowing here, churning white as it swept around the bend. This was a popular spot for white-water rafting, groups of tourists heading downstream from Beddmawr. Julia shivered again and decided her New Year's resolution on the spot: she would conquer her long-held fear and learn to swim.

Lily was still ahead of them, approaching the copse at the bottom of the slope. Julia turned to speak to Michael – and saw him sneak something into his pocket.

47

'What was that?'

'Nothing.'

She stepped closer. 'Show me.'

'Come on, Julia, it was nothing.' He went to move past her but she stepped into his path, making him slip. As he snatched at her arm, she stuck her hand into the pocket of his fleece. He tried to stop her, but she was too fast.

She held up the hip flask. The evidence.

The broken promise.

'It's for the cold,' he began, before trailing off. She expected him to be apologetic, sheepish, but his eyes flashed with defiance. In that moment, he looked just like Lily, when Julia told her to tidy her room or do her homework. I don't have a husband and child, *she thought.* I have two children.

She flung the hip flask with all her strength towards the river. It fell short, landing on the edge of the bank. They both stared after it.

'If you pick it up, that's it,' she said.

'I'm not going to.' But she saw the way his eyes flicked sideways, could see the longing there.

'I'm going to catch up with Lily,' she said. 'We can talk about it when we get home.'

The final part of the path was steep, forcing her to run to avoid slipping again, and she skidded to a halt among the trees. Bare branches, slimy leaf mulch on the ground, more puddles of mud.

But no sign of Lily.

She strode ahead towards the far edge of the copse, aware of her heartbeat accelerating while following a trail of footsteps. Michael was a few steps behind her as Julia called out, 'Lily?'

There was no response. Logic told her she would find Lily just beyond the trees, but logic couldn't quell the cold eddy of fear in her belly.

'Lily,' she called again, trying to keep her voice light. 'We're going to have hot chocolate when we get home.'

And you can watch as much YouTube as you like, *she added silently.*

Julia emerged on the other side of the copse, sure the sky had grown darker during the few minutes she'd been beneath the trees, the clouds more swollen with rain. Ahead, the path rose, steep but not as muddy as before. And the churning in Julia's stomach intensified.

Where was she? Where the hell was Lily?

Julia ran up the slope to a crest that overlooked the river. The water foamed and snapped at the bank. And that was when she saw it, the sight that almost stopped her heart.

Big Cat, floating on the water.

'Michael!'

His name emerged as a scream. She ran back to him, grabbed hold of his arm and pointed at the river, at the black-and-white stuffed toy. He saw it immediately and their eyes locked, mother and father, before he tore off his coat and ran down the bank, across a ledge of flat grey rocks that stretched out to the water. He paused for a second, shouting for their daughter as the river dragged Big Cat beneath its surface.

Michael plunged into the water. Julia had no idea how deep it was, but her husband was swallowed up as if he'd never existed. It must have been only seconds later that his head reappeared, but it felt like forever. Julia paced the bank, wringing her hands and trying to focus on the water, searching among the grey and white for a glimpse of Lily. If she thought throwing herself in would save her daughter, would even give her a tiny chance of survival, she would do it without hesitation. But she was helpless. Useless.

'I can't see her,' Michael called, the panic in his voice reflecting the sick sensation in Julia's stomach. The water rushed around him, crashing over him like waves hitting rocks.

'Keep trying!'

He went under again, then came back to the surface almost immediately, gasping and fighting to stay afloat. The frigid water squeezed the breath from his lungs and his voice was weak as he called out for Lily. He caught Julia's eye and she knew what he was thinking. He was going to give up.

She had to do something.

'Over there!' she yelled, pointing to the centre of the river. 'I saw something.'

He struck out towards where she had pointed, against the current. Water pummelled him and he went under, gulping down air before he kicked out, turning in the water. He was four or five metres from the bank, clearly struggling, fighting the river as it tried to claim him. In her panicked state, Julia imagined creatures beneath the surface, clutching at Michael's ankles, dragging him down. She pictured Lily down there too, wrapped in a river creature's deathly embrace.

Michael was getting weaker – Julia could see it on his face, in his sluggish kick – and a burst of foaming water caught him, sweeping him away from where Julia stood. It didn't cross her mind that he might drown. As a non-swimmer she had an inflated idea of his abilities. All she wanted was for him to keep trying, to find Lily. As he headed for the far bank, submerging for a moment before coming back to the surface, she remembered her phone in her pocket and woke it up with shaking hands, punching 999, yelling at the operator who answered, their calm voice doing nothing to soothe her.

When she looked up, Michael was gone.

Julia dashed down to the edge of the bank, onto the rocks, expecting Michael to emerge, trying not to panic. She swept her gaze along the river, left, then right. Where was he? Where was he? It was cold, so cold on the riverbank, but she barely felt it, in the same way she couldn't feel the tears on her cheeks.

She couldn't feel a thing.

ω

There was silence in the room after she'd finished, the weight of her words thickening the air between us. I groped for something to say, something more than a platitude.

Should I tell her my own story now? Show her that I understood exactly how it felt to have someone you love ripped from your world? For a great boot to stamp on your life?

Julia spoke before I could make up my mind.

'I shouldn't have threatened to chuck you out,' she said. 'But you have to understand it's still raw. All of it.' There was a long pause. I wondered if she knew I might have heard her during the night. I guessed she hadn't thought about it; it seemed she was compelled to spend her nights in Lily's room, communing with her missing daughter, in the same way an alcoholic is drawn to the bottle.

As Julia spoke she twisted her hands together, ignoring a lock of hair that dropped across her eye. 'People think that time heals, that you get over it. But every day for me is like a Groundhog Day, you know? I wake up, missing Lily. A hundred times a day I imagine her coming through the front door. A hundred times a day I blame myself for not keeping a better eye on her. I curse my parents for not forcing me go to swimming lessons. The same things, every single day. And at the end of it, I go to bed missing Lily.'

I didn't know what to say.

She finally brushed the hair away from her eye. 'Of course, there are moments when I almost forget. But then I get this feeling of panic, this knowledge that there's something I'm supposed to be worrying about. Then I remember, and the guilt hits me. Like, how could I forget, even for a second?'

'Oh, Julia.'

I wanted to touch her arm, put a hand on her shoulder, do something to show empathy, an attempt at comfort.

But I sat there, a useless bloke not knowing what to do or say.

'You probably think I should let it go,' she said, shattering the silence. 'My daughter drowned. Move on. She's not going to come back.'

'I don't . . .'

Julia got up and went to the window. It was grim outside again. White mist hung over the distant trees, turning them into ghostly silhouettes. Julia stared into the mist as if she expected – or hoped – to see Lily emerge from it. Her little girl, back from the dead.

'What did the police say?' I asked. 'They must have searched for her . . .' According to Olly the cab driver and the news reports, the river had been swarming with police. But Julia's face told a different story.

'They gave up almost immediately,' she said. 'The investigation is supposedly still open, but I haven't heard anything for over a year. Nobody is actively working on it. They gave up within weeks because they were convinced she drowned.'

'But you . . . are convinced she didn't?'

Her gaze was intense. 'They would have found her body. I'm sure of it.'

'Not necessarily.'

She shook her head. 'I can't believe that she would have been swept along the river that quickly when Big Cat was still there.'

'What do you think happened?'

She didn't hesitate. 'Somebody took her. He was waiting, beyond the trees. Maybe he'd spotted us walking along the path. It could have been opportunistic. Or maybe he followed us there, hoping for a chance to take Lily. A chance we gave him by lagging behind, by not watching her properly.'

In her head, she was back by the river, perhaps imagining a *Sliding Doors* moment, a different path.

'I think someone was following us,' she said.

I studied her. 'What makes you say that?'

'Just . . . It seems beyond even my bad luck that a predator just happened to be out there that day, that he made a decision and acted so quickly. And it's not just that. In the days leading up to Lily's disappearance I had this feeling . . . that we were being watched.'

'What do you mean?'

'Just . . . Have you ever had that sensation? That there are eyes on you, but when you turn round there's nobody there?'

I nodded. I knew that sensation well.

'I still feel like that now,' she said. 'All the time. I think I can see Lily in my peripheral vision, just standing there, watching me. But when I turn, no matter how quickly I move, trying to catch her out, she's never there.'

I understood. I'd had the same sensation, with Priya.

'What else did the police do?' I asked. 'Apart from dragging the river, I mean?'

'I don't know exactly. They looked in the surrounding woods but didn't find anything. They spoke to a few local men who are on the sex offenders register. Put out appeals for witnesses, checked road cameras. But it always felt to me like they were ticking boxes. They thought it was all a waste of time. She had to be in the river.'

'Have you ever considered hiring a private investigator?'

'I wanted to but . . .' She sighed. 'I'm skint. A couple of people started an appeal for funds to help find Lily, but it didn't raise much. The public believed what the police said – that she'd drowned. And another child, a four-year-old girl, vanished at the same time, down in London. Do you remember? Violet something. Her dad was a politician? The press gave all their attention to her. They soon forgot all about Lily. But I'm convinced, Lucas. She's still out there and I won't give up hope. I can't. It's the only thing that keeps me going.' She sighed. 'I've taken up too much of your time. And I need to make breakfast. The others will be wondering what's going on.'

She stood and left the room without looking back.

I crossed to the window. The mist was clearing slowly, bringing the world into focus. In the distance, the river wound, dull and flat, across the landscape.

Was Julia right? Could Lily still be out there somewhere?

Chapter 7

LILY – 2014

'Chesney! Chesneeeey!'

Where *was* that stupid cat?

Lily stood by the back door, calling and calling until she wasn't sure what was her original voice and what was an echo. She was fascinated by echoes. When she was a little kid, like two years ago, Dad made her go trekking up Snowdon. It was boring except for the café at the top where she had an enormous hot chocolate with cream and sprinkles, and, even better, the bit where they stood at the top of the mountain and yelled, 'Hello!', listening to it bounce around and back again.

But Chesney – that stupid, lovely fluff monster – wasn't responding to her voice or its echo.

Lily glanced behind her. Mum was working on her computer and Dad was in his study. She wasn't supposed to go out on her own – even though she wasn't a baby any more – but she really wanted to find Chesney.

She slipped on her trainers and headed over to the cottage. It was locked and she didn't think the cat could have got in there.

She hunted around the garden, making little kissing noises and calling his name. She was getting worried now. What if he'd been run over? Megan said her cat got flattened by a car after falling asleep in the middle of the road. That was the problem with quiet places where there's hardly any traffic. Cats think they can lie down and sleep anywhere. Lily didn't think Chesney was that dumb, though. He was a very special cat; probably the best, cleverest cat in the world. And she loved him. Every night he slept on the end of the bed and she didn't mind him lying across her feet so she couldn't move. It didn't bother her that her sheets were covered in fur and this speckly black stuff that Mum said was 'disgusting flea dirt'.

Sometimes, she thought, he was her best friend. She liked Megan, but Chesney was the only one she could talk to when Mum and Dad were fighting.

Which was pretty much every day at the moment. She heard them at night when they thought she was sleeping, when she was actually under the covers with her iPad, watching her favourite YouTubers. Her mum did most of the shouting, while Dad's voice was a low rumble she couldn't make out. Mum was always going on about 'drinking' and 'being on her own'. Another woman's name came up a lot too, a woman who Dad worked with. Lily had asked him who Lana was once and he went white before saying it was just a woman in his office.

Megan said her mum and dad had argued a lot too. Then they got divorced, when Megan was little. Her dad lived on his own in another town and Megan hardly ever saw him. Now the only man in Megan's life was her grandad.

When Lily thought about her own parents divorcing, she went colder than ice and had to squeeze Chesney really hard to stop herself from crying.

She had reached the edge of the garden and there was still no sign of Chesney. Beyond the fence was a stretch of overgrown grass and long flowers that were probably weeds. Dandelion clocks and stinging nettles.

Dad said there were rabbit warrens in the field, though Lily had never seen any. Maybe that's where Chesney was now. Lying unseen in the long grass, waiting for a bunny to come hopping out of its hole. Lily didn't believe her cat would kill a rabbit – he never brought any gross dead stuff into the house, probably because he knew Mum would freak out – but he probably liked watching them.

Checking no grown-ups were watching, Lily climbed over the low fence into the little meadow.

She hadn't realised how foggy it was until she moved away from the house. The mist hung among the trees like a giant cloud, white and spooky-looking. She imagined it was cold to the touch. There was no way Lily would go into those woods on her own, especially when it was foggy like that.

She didn't want the Widow to get her. Not that she believed . . .

'Lily!'

She almost jumped out of her skin.

'Lily, where are you?' Her mum was starting to sound panicked now and Lily felt the urge to stay hidden. If Mum got really worried then she'd be incredibly relieved when Lily turned up, and she might give her a treat. Maybe she'd feel guilty about working and Lily would be able to persuade her to buy those Heelys she needed.

She crouched in the grass, trying to decide what to do. Her mum's voice grew fainter as she moved away. Lily stood up. She felt mean but was also worried that Mum might be angry with her. She walked back towards the fence – and saw a movement out of the corner of her eye. *Chesney?* She whirled around.

A shape vanished into the trees and was swallowed by the fog.

It was too big to be Chesney.

Too big and person-shaped.

Lily bolted, scrambling over the fence and catching her finger on a jagged piece of wood. It dug into her flesh, a splinter that brought forth a drop of blood. Ow, it really hurt and now she had tears in her eyes.

Through the wet blur, she took another look back towards the woods. There was nothing there. Had she imagined it?

The Widow. Opening her gigantic black mouth to call Lily's name.

She didn't wait around to find out. She sprinted across the garden, calling, 'Mum! Mummy!'

She forgot all about the cat.

Chapter 8

Julia might not have been able to afford to hire a private investigator, but I could. I'd recently received another large royalty payment for *Sweetmeat* and had very little to spend it on.

What would she think? Would she think I was interfering? Going too far? She'd already almost thrown me out and it would be foolish to risk that happening again, but it wouldn't hurt to make enquiries, would it? If I got anywhere, I would tell Julia.

That's what I told myself, anyway.

When I was researching *Sweetmeat*, I befriended a private detective called Edward Rooney. He had been briefly famous because of his involvement in a weird case involving Romanian criminals and babies, which was why I'd contacted him. I wanted to know how he would go about tracking a missing person. He was a nice guy, haunted by the things he'd seen, but willing to help – for a fee.

Worried that Julia might overhear me, I took my mobile to the edge of the garden.

Edward's assistant, Sophie, answered and transferred me across.

'Lucas!' he exclaimed. 'Or should I say "acclaimed novelist L. J. Radcliffe"?'

'I don't know about acclaimed.'

'Ah, don't be modest, man. I read it. Bloody brilliant. So what can I do for you?'

I explained that I was helping out a friend and was hoping to get some advice. Then I detailed everything I knew about Lily's disappearance and the subsequent investigation.

'The police have given up, apparently, convinced Lily drowned. But Julia doesn't believe they did everything they could to find her, that they gave up too easily. She can't afford to hire someone so I offered to help out.'

I cleared my throat. It was a white lie.

It was quiet on Edward's end of the line. Eventually, he said, 'You should save your money.'

'Why do you say that?'

'Because in cases like this, when it involves kids, the police always pull out all the stops. Especially if the parents are nice and middle-class. I don't think an investigator would be able to find out any more than the police did, and it's just going to stir up all the hope in your friend's heart again.'

I thought about it. 'But if we can set Julia's mind at rest, so she knows the police explored every avenue . . .'

He sighed. 'All right. You're not going to let this go, are you?'

'I don't want to.'

'Okay. Look, I'm busy at the moment. There's no way I can schlep all the way to Wales. But I do know someone who lives in Telford, just across the border. Let me text you her number.'

'Okay,' I said. I have to admit I was disappointed.

Edward's text arrived a minute later.

I looked up at Nyth Bran and shivered as I remembered my half-dream, the bleeding walls, the sense that the house was alive.

I ought to be in there, writing. The problem was, I had an itch now. I wanted to know what had happened to Lily, and not just because I couldn't resist a mystery. I imagined myself finding her, bringing her to Julia, the tears and the joy that would follow. Even if the chance of that happening was a thousand to one, the image was powerful enough to compel me to do something.

I called the number Edward had sent me.

ω

Zara Sullivan wasn't busy. In fact, she told me she could meet me in Beddmawr in two hours. While we were on the phone, she looked up cafés in the town on TripAdvisor and told me she'd be at Rhiannon's Café at one o'clock.

'I'll be wearing a red baseball cap,' she said, then hung up.

I stared at my phone. Was she for real? Or was Edward playing a joke on me?

I arrived at the café five minutes late. It was the kind of place I'd usually avoid, chintzy and dimly lit, all pots of tea and scones, frequented and staffed almost exclusively by the over-sixties. There were a number of paintings on the walls depicting mining scenes: men heading down the pit, women with babes in arms watching them go. Among these, the same picture that hung in the pub. The woman in red among the trees.

Sitting in the corner with a pot of tea before her was a woman in a red baseball cap. She took it off as I approached and shook out her hair, which was blonde and stringy, hanging around a moon-shaped face. It was hard to tell how old she was – somewhere between thirty and forty, though she was dressed like a teenager in a black puffa jacket. She really didn't look like a private detective, but then everyone said I – with my reddish hair and 'friendly' face – didn't look like a horror novelist.

'I listened to your book on the drive here,' she said. 'The first hour of it, anyway. Not bad.'

'Er . . . thanks.'

'I'm sure the more you write, the better you'll get.' She raised a hand and beckoned over the waitress, a spritely woman in her seventies. I ordered coffee.

'Let's discuss terms,' Zara said, not wasting any time. Her hourly rate was more than I'd expected, but still reasonable. 'I could travel in from Telford every day, but it would be easier for me to stay here,' she said. 'If you're willing to pay. I like to immerse myself, get to know the locals.'

'That's fine.'

'Luckily, I have an FWB in the police in Wrexham.' That was the nearest large town, where the investigation into Lily's disappearance would have been centred.

'FWB?'

'Uh-huh. A friend with benefits. More than one benefit, in this case.' She grinned and slurped her tea. 'Have a Welshcake. They're scrummy.'

Producing a notebook from her messenger bag, she said, 'Right. Can you tell me everything you know?'

'Before I start, there's one condition. I don't want Julia Marsh finding out I've hired you to do this. I'll tell her if you find anything but I don't want to get her hopes up. So you need to be discreet.'

'Discretion is my middle name.' She readied her pencil over her pad and raised her eyebrows.

The café was busy but the hubbub masked our words as I told her what I knew.

She wrote it all down, then closed her notepad. 'Okay. I'll call you tomorrow with a progress report.' She stuck out her hand. It was sticky with cake residue. 'Let's find out what happened to little Lily.'

ʙ

I spent the afternoon working on my novel. It was about a father who believes the world is coming to an end. He takes his family – his wife and daughter – to live in a shack in the middle of a forest, away from danger. The twist is that the world really is ending, a plague is sweeping across the planet, turning people into hungry monsters (I avoided using the word 'zombies'). And these monsters begin to close in on the family in the woods . . .

After dinner, I went into the Thomas Room to find something to read. Julia had an impressive collection of books – mostly classics and contemporary literature, with the occasional thriller dotted around the shelves. I could see a line of brightly coloured spines on the top shelf.

Intrigued, I climbed the library ladder and saw that most of these books bore the Jackdaw logo. That was the publisher Julia had done most of her work for. Standing on the middle rung, I took down a book called *Twelve Little Beasties*. It was, indeed, illustrated by Julia Marsh, a parade of comical monsters in bright colours. I was impressed. Julia was talented. If she'd stopped work, that only compounded the tragedy of what had happened to her.

At the end of the shelf, a book with a tatty spine stuck out at an angle. Feeling compelled to straighten it, I pulled it out and found an illustrated edition of Edward Lear's poem 'The Owl and the Pussycat'.

The book looked old and I wondered if it had belonged to Julia when she was a child. I turned to the first page to see if there was an inscription, but the title page had been torn out.

I flicked through the book, and something fell to the ground beneath me. I descended the ladder and picked it up. It was a faded Polaroid of a couple: a tall, skinny man in his forties standing stiffly beside a shorter woman. Despite their late-seventies/early-eighties haircuts and clothes, they reminded me of the couple in that painting *American Gothic*. I studied the photo, trying to work out where it had been taken, but the background was too dark, the colours muted and blurred.

'What have you got there?'

It was Max, coming into the room with Suzi. They appeared to have made up. I slipped the Polaroid back into the book and stuck it between two books on the nearest shelf.

'Nothing.'

Max eyed the bookcase. 'I'm sure if we pushed this in the right place it would rotate to reveal a secret passageway,' he said. 'It's that kind of house.'

'Like something from The Famous Five,' added Suzi.

'No, creepier than that,' said Max. 'Like something from one of Lucas's books.'

They sat on the sofa and I perched on the armchair opposite.

'Someone told me this house is cursed.' I explained what the taxi driver had said.

Max's eyes shone. 'How exciting. I love stories like that. Modern folklore. A friend of mine comes from Hastings, where Aleister Crowley lived. Apparently, he cursed the town so it's impossible to leave unless you take a pebble from the beach with you. Nonsense, obviously. But fun.'

'Where's Karen?' I asked.

'I think she went up for a smoke.'

'Maybe we should join her,' Suzi said.

'Good idea. What do you think, Lucas? Shall we go and see if Karen's willing to share her stash?'

He was so naff, but I nodded. 'Why not?'

Upstairs, Max knocked lightly on Karen's door. I was a little embarrassed. We were acting like a group of naughty schoolchildren, sneaking around the dorm.

I wasn't expecting to hear a gasp of fear from inside the room.

'Leave me alone!' Karen cried.

Max and I exchanged a worried glance.

'Karen?' I said through the door. 'It's Lucas. Are you okay?'

I heard footsteps, then the key turning in the lock. Karen pulled open the door and stuck her head out, looking left and right.

'Come in,' she hissed.

We trooped into the room. Karen had retreated to the edge of her bed, clenching her fists. The window was open but the room stank of cannabis. Karen's pupils were huge, dilated like black pools.

'Shut the door,' she said. 'Lock it.'

Suzi sat beside her. 'What's the matter?'

'Somebody was trying to get into my room.'

Automatically, I looked at Max.

'Hey! It wasn't me,' he said.

'No,' said Suzi. 'He's been with me the whole time.'

'Karen,' Max said, 'are you sure you didn't imagine it? What exactly are you smoking?' There was a little bag on the bedside table. Max picked it up and held it to the light, as if he'd be able to tell how strong it was.

Karen continued to stare into space. 'They whispered something through the door.'

'Really? What did they say?'

'*You're not welcome here.*'

We all looked at each other.

'Male or female?' I asked, thinking about the singing I'd heard.

But Karen appeared to have gone into a stupor, staring in terror at the door. Her face was as pale as the moon that shone through the window.

'I'm going to be sick.' She rushed from the room and we heard her running down the hall towards the bathroom.

'She's stoned, that's all,' Max said. 'Pulling a – what do you call it? A whiteout?'

'A whitey,' I said.

But Suzi had gone almost as pale as Karen. '*I* wasn't high when someone tried to get into *my* room.'

'I told you,' said Max, 'it wasn't me.' He seemed concerned for a moment, then laughed. 'It's the curse. The ghost of the dead miner. Wooo!'

'Oh, shut up, Max.' But Suzi laughed too.

'Are you sure it's not you doing it?' Max said, and I was so deep in thought that it took a moment to realise he was talking to me. 'Maybe you're conducting research for your next book. Some kind of meta-experiment.'

'I was downstairs with you, remember?'

'Hmm. Well, anyway. It's all quite exciting, isn't it?'

We left Karen's room. Max headed back downstairs, and Suzi said she would wait to check that Karen was okay.

I went to my room. The most likely explanation was that Karen was stoned and imagining things, almost certainly triggered by what had happened to Suzi. And Max was lying – he had tried to get into Suzi's room but wouldn't admit it. It was all perfectly rational.

So why did I lie in bed, unable to sleep again, imagining a figure on the other side of my door, trying to get in?

You're not welcome here.

I finally went to sleep with those words echoing in my head.

Chapter 9

The atmosphere at breakfast was subdued. Karen seemed embarrassed by the incident the previous night and still looked a little green around the gills. Max tapped at his phone throughout, apparently conducting a Twitter spat with someone who'd made an ill-judged joke about depression. Suzi hadn't come down; I guessed she was still asleep, or working in her room.

I took my used breakfast things into the kitchen, where Julia was stacking the dishwasher, the cat snaking around her ankles.

It was another cold day, frost sparkling on the lawn. Rhodri was in the garden, fixing a section of fencing that had blown down in the strong winds the previous week.

'Did he come with the house?' I asked, nodding towards Rhodri.

'Huh? Oh, you mean did he work here before we moved in? Apparently so. He introduced himself to Michael as soon as we got here, but Michael told him we wouldn't need his help because he was determined to do all that stuff himself. That was part of the appeal of coming here.' She closed the dishwasher. 'He had so many plans for this place.' Her eyes shone with emotion.

Rhodri must have sensed us watching him, as he raised a hand before turning back to the fence.

'What was the previous owner like?' I asked, thinking of the Polaroid I'd found the night before.

'I have no idea. An old woman lived here. When she died she left the house to a children's charity. We bought it from them at auction.'

On my way up to my room, my mobile rang. It was Zara.

'I met up with my friend last night.' I assumed she meant the one with benefits. I hoped she wasn't going to add condoms to her expenses. 'He told me a few interesting things. Very interesting things indeed.'

ʊ

I agreed to meet Zara by the river, at the spot where Lily had gone missing. I found her sitting on a fallen tree trunk, smoking a cigarette and gazing out at the water. Mist hung low among the shrubbery on the opposite bank.

'My policeman friend remembers the case very well,' Zara said, stubbing out her cigarette and slipping the butt into a little plastic bag. 'He repeated what you already told me. That they were initially convinced she fell into the river. They spent a lot of money searching. They had helicopters out, frogmen, the whole works. You name it. All without success.'

'I knew all that,' I said.

'But what do you know about bodies in water? You wrote a book about it, didn't you? I'm assuming you did lots of research.'

I avoided her eyes. 'Hmm. A bit.'

'Ha. Well, my friend explained it to me. When someone drowns, the air in their lungs is replaced with water, which makes them sink. They stay underwater for a while. And assuming nothing eats them, the bacteria and enzymes in their chest and gut start to produce gas. Methane, carbon dioxide, some other gas that I can't remember the name of.'

'And the gas makes them float to the surface.'

'Exactly.' She produced a Mars bar from her coat pocket and unwrapped it. 'Want a bit?'

'This conversation isn't giving me much of an appetite.'

She snorted and sang a jingle from our childhood. '*A Mars a day . . . makes your teeth rot away.* Where was I? Oh yes. Lily Marsh didn't float. The police were convinced she would pop to the surface of the lake. But they waited and they waited. And still no sign of little Lily.'

I stared at her.

'Now, there's nothing in that lake that could have eaten her up. No monsters living in the woods round here, Mr Radcliffe. So if she did go in the water, she must have been weighed down – which didn't fit with her supposed accidental drowning – or she got caught on something under the water.'

'*Supposed* accidental drowning?'

'Yes. If she was weighed down, it must have been murder. But that didn't fit either, because her body would almost certainly be on the riverbed, not in the lake.'

A pair of moorhens drifted by.

'When Lily's body didn't appear, the police turned their attention to the mother.'

I was shocked. 'To Julia?'

'Uh-huh. Think about it. There were no witnesses, other than Mrs Marsh. They only had her word for what happened. My friend said her distress seemed genuine, but maybe it was an accident, one that she tried to cover up.'

'What kind of accident?'

The world around us was eerily quiet and still. A songbird called out from a tree above our heads. The water made a rushing sound as it rounded the bend. Apart from that, all was silent.

Zara crumpled her chocolate wrapper and stuck it in the pocket of her puffa jacket. 'Julia admitted to the police that all was not well in the Marsh household. She had to, because they'd had a massive row in the supermarket just before Christmas. In the alcohol aisle. The police found a witness who reported seeing Julia yelling at Michael about the amount of booze he'd put in the trolley. Something about broken promises, about Christmas being ruined. Lily was there, watching.'

I thought about Julia's alcohol ban at the retreat. Had Michael Marsh been an alcoholic?

'When they did the autopsy, the pathologist found high levels of alcohol in Mr Marsh's blood. So he'd been drinking that day. Here's a theory: what if Julia and Michael had another huge row when they were down by the river, and she pushed him in?'

I thought about it. 'That's possible, I suppose. But what about Lily?'

'The police thought maybe Julia chucked Lily in too, because she was the only witness.'

'That's ludicrous!'

'Or maybe she planned to kill them all, including herself. Murder-suicide. But she chickened out when it was her turn. Or how about this? Julia pushed her hubby into the water and their daughter jumped in to try to save him. Julia can't swim, so she couldn't do anything to help.'

The bird in the tree had stopped singing.

'But that still doesn't answer the question: what happened to Lily's body?'

Zara shrugged. 'That's where the police got stuck too. They had cadaver dogs out searching the woods, looking for a grave, thinking that if Lily didn't drown maybe Julia killed her and buried her somewhere. They searched the house too.'

'So Julia knew she was a suspect?'

'I guess they used the old "exploring every avenue" line. But they didn't find anything, and Julia never slipped up. So they went back to square one. The most likely explanation was that it all happened exactly as Julia described, and Lily's body is stuck somewhere at the bottom of Bala Lake.'

I mulled over what Zara had told me. Could Julia be responsible? No, I was sure her distress was genuine – and it wasn't guilt. Unless she was the world's greatest actress – a psychopath – she genuinely didn't know what had happened to her daughter.

'So, basically,' I said, 'you haven't really made any progress.'

'Except I've done what you asked. Checked the police took it seriously, that they did indeed pull out all the stops. Maybe, Lucas, it's one of those mysteries that will never be solved. Like the *Mary Celeste*, or those UFO nuts who may or may not have jumped off Beachy Head a few years ago.'

I blinked at her.

'So what do you want me to do?' she asked.

I stood up and paced around the copse, hoping the movement of my feet would trigger my brain.

'Did the police interview local sex offenders? Paedophiles?'

'Yep. It's a small community. There weren't that many guys for them to talk to, but they got them all in, checked their alibis, searched their houses. *Nada*.'

'Maybe they didn't search hard enough. Especially if they were fixated on this theory that Julia was responsible or it was an accident.'

Again, she shrugged. 'That's possible. You want me to do some digging?'

'I do.'

She pushed herself to her feet. 'All right, then. Digging I shall do.'

We headed up towards the road where Zara's car was parked. The mist had cleared and the sun had come out, bathing the landscape in buttery, early-spring light. Zara paused to take it in, then looked at me.

'So, you come from round here originally?' she said. 'I'm curious. You hardly know this Julia woman, do you? Why are you trying to help her?'

I was taken aback by her directness. 'I feel bad for her. I want to help.'

'You sure that's all it is?'

We reached Zara's car, a ten-year-old Honda. Inside, it was littered with fast-food containers and sweet wrappers.

'I'm not sure what you mean,' I said.

'Oh, nothing. It's just . . .' She laughed. 'Sorry, I know I can be overly frank sometimes. But I've seen photos of Julia Marsh. She's a good-looking woman.'

'And you think I'm helping her as a way of getting her into bed?'

She unlocked her car. 'Hey, I don't mean to offend you. But there's a certain kind of man who can't resist a damsel in distress. And by "certain kind of man" I mean one with blood in his veins and a dick between his legs.' She chuckled as she got into the car.

She wound down the window. 'I'll see what I can find out about the local kiddy fiddlers and call you tomorrow.'

She drove off, leaving me squinting into the sun and wondering. Was she right? Did I have an ulterior motive? Zara was correct about one thing: Julia was attractive – but it was despite the mask of pain she wore, not because of it. And I didn't fancy her.

I felt uncomfortable, though, as I walked back to the house, and I made up my mind. I would give Zara another twenty-four hours. If she didn't find out anything interesting – and it seemed unlikely that she would – I'd give up, put my head down and finish my book without any further distractions.

Chapter 10

Julia was in the garden, talking to Rhodri, who was showing her the mended fence panel. He took his tools over to the shed and Julia waved at me as I walked up the driveway towards her. She was wearing an old-looking top and gardening gloves, hair scraped back, glasses on.

She looked lovely.

I mentally kicked myself. Yes, she was attractive, but I *didn't* fancy her. It was Zara's fault for putting the idea in my head.

'Been for a stroll?' she asked.

I had the horrible sense she could read my mind. Flustered, I said, 'Yeah. Just trying to get the mental cogs turning.'

'Where did you go?'

I hesitated.

'It's all right,' she said. 'I can hear the word "river" without having a meltdown.'

Rhodri came over, nodding at me. 'Gorgeous day, isn't it? Julia told me you come from round these parts. What are your parents' names?'

'Carol and David Radcliffe.'

'You're joking. David Radcliffe, the solicitor?'

'That's right. You knew him?'

He seemed slightly stunned. 'I know everyone around here. It's been a bloody long time, though. What are they up to these days?'

'They retired to Spain,' I replied.

He whistled. 'All right for some. Well, give them my regards when you speak to them.' He pointed at the flowerbeds. 'What are you planning to do here, Julia?'

'Weeding mainly. And I was thinking of moving those peonies.'

'What? You can't do that!' He acted as if she'd said she was going to pour petrol on the earth and set it aflame.

'Why not?'

'It's bad luck,' he replied. 'If you move peonies, a woodpecker will come and peck out your eyes.'

Julia laughed, but Rhodri looked deadly serious. 'Please don't move them, Julia.'

'Okay.'

He nodded, satisfied, and headed off to the shed.

Julia and I exchanged an amused look. 'Well, I guess the peonies do look all right where they are.'

'I should probably tell him my dad passed away,' I said.

'Oh. I'm sorry. Did it happen recently?' I must have cringed because she added, 'Don't worry, if you'd rather not talk about it.'

'No, it's fine. It's healthy to talk about it, isn't it? It was five years ago now. Pancreatic cancer. He died three weeks after getting the diagnosis.'

'How awful.'

I scraped at the ground with the toe of my shoe. 'Apparently, with pancreatic cancer there are no symptoms until it's too late. The good thing is that he didn't suffer for long.'

'How's your mum?' Julia asked.

'She's okay. She lives in Spain, so I don't see her much. She's fine, though. She's one of those women who just gets on with it, whatever shit life throws at her. She's always been like that.'

I could tell Julia was thinking about herself, the shit life had thrown at *her* and her reaction. I was about to change the subject when Karen emerged from the house, carrying her laptop. She saw us and came over.

'I was just going to the cottage to do some work,' she said.

We exchanged a few pleasantries about the weather, then she said, 'I saw the new guest earlier. So now there are five of us.'

Julia looked puzzled. 'Another guest?'

'Yeah. I got up at six, and when I came down to make coffee I saw them in the dining room.'

'We don't have any other guests,' Julia said. 'Just you and Lucas, Max and Suzi.'

Karen opened her mouth, then closed it again. 'Oh.'

'Were they male or female?' I asked.

'Female. I think. They had their back to me and I only got a brief glimpse. But I thought it was a woman.'

'You must have imagined it,' Julia said.

Karen seemed troubled by this. 'That's really strange. I'm sure I saw someone.'

'Perhaps it was Suzi,' I offered.

'No, I'm pretty certain she was still in bed.' She chewed a thumbnail. 'I suppose I must have still been a little . . .'

She stopped herself, but Julia laughed.

'Stoned? I'm not completely wet behind the ears, Karen. I can smell it in your room. I was going to ask you to do it outside. There are certain boring regulations I have to follow. Sorry to be a massive killjoy.'

'No, I'm sorry.' Karen cringed. 'So now I feel like a naughty schoolgirl who's been caught smoking out the window. I'd better get on.' She headed over to the cottage.

'That's all I need,' Julia said. 'People seeing things. You should all lay off the weed.' She tugged at her gardening gloves. 'I'd better get on.'

I was going to defend Karen, but Julia had already knelt by the flowerbed and picked up the little fork. She jabbed it into the dirt, grabbing handfuls of weeds and yanking them from the earth. A strand of hair fell over her face and she pushed it away with a gloved fist before attacking the flowerbed again.

She caught me watching her and I looked away, embarrassed. I'd been imagining her taking off those gloves and laying her hands on me. Inviting me to lie down on the grass with her.

I walked back to the house on shaky legs, face burning. Not because I thought it was wrong, per se, to be attracted to Julia or to fantasise about her.

No. It was because it felt like a betrayal.

ᗡ

'What are you up to today?'

'Nothing special. I'm just going to carry on making notes for this new idea.'

'The Sweetmeat *one? It sounds good.'*

Priya kissed me goodbye and said something else, but I wasn't really listening. My mind had already strayed to my book, to this idea that wouldn't work, that I was on the verge of abandoning, along with my whole writing 'career'. The ideas, the words wouldn't come, and half an hour after Priya left for work, I put the TV on, pretending to hope it might stimulate my brain.

I was watching a phone-in about neighbours from hell when the land-line rang. It was Priya's boss at the insurance company.

'I just wanted to check that Priya's okay,' she said. 'You're supposed to call in if you're sick. It's an important rule.'

'But she left for work . . .' I checked the time. 'Almost three hours ago.'

I hung up and tried her number. It went straight to voicemail. I texted her, asking her to call me urgently, and tried to phone her again. There was a knot in my stomach that grew bigger with every passing second.

She cycled to work every morning, even though I told her it was dangerous, that the roads in London were insane and choked with rage-filled lunatics. She always laughed off my concerns.

'It's the most exciting part of my day,' she said.

Once, I would have said, 'What, more exciting than coming home to me?' But I knew the answer. I knew that coming home to her morose, waster, has-been boyfriend was probably something she dreaded. She had been coming home later and later recently, going out for drinks with her colleagues frequently, going to bed early. Our sex life was in a coma. It was all my fault, but I was unable to do anything about it. I was in a pit, wallowing in self-pity, and I wanted to dig myself out but the shovel was too heavy, my limbs too weak. Everything was too much effort.

Now, though, as I continually redialled Priya's number, fear jerked me to life like a defibrillator.

I knew the route Priya took to work. Through the park and down a maze of backstreets before crossing the Thames and hitting the manic main roads of North London. I called the police and the hospital. They told me not to worry. It had only been a few hours.

But I knew. Something terrible had happened.

I was about to go out to look for her when an idea struck me. Priya's iPhone. I knew her Apple password, so quickly opened the Find My iPhone app and logged in as her. A map appeared on the screen, a blue dot pulsing and telling me that her phone was on a quiet street between Clapham and Battersea. It wasn't moving.

I almost caused an accident on the Elephant and Castle roundabout, driving across two lanes in my haste to get to that motionless blue dot. Horns sounded. A woman gave me the finger. I checked the map as I rounded Clapham Common, turning off into the leafy residential streets that Priya and I had wandered together numerous times. One day we were going to buy a place around here and raise a family. One day, when I was a bestselling author and we had enough money.

I found the place where the blue spot pulsed on the map and pulled over. There was no sign of Priya or her phone. There was a shabby mansion block on one side of the road. On the other, a jumble of run-down houses and a dry-cleaners that had gone out of business. A railway bridge crossed the road a little way ahead, covered with graffiti; there was a pile of fly-tipped junk on the pavement. Gentrification hadn't quite reached this section of the street.

I opened the Find My iPhone app and hit 'Play Sound'. At that moment, a car went by, but when it had receded into the distance I heard it. A faint pulsing up ahead, near the bridge.

I saw the phone first. It was lying beside a pair of wheeled Biffa bins, to the left of the pile of rubbish. I approached the phone slowly, and then I saw the wheel of a bicycle protruding from behind the bin. The sun was out but I couldn't feel it. Right then, I didn't think I'd ever be warm again.

Priya's body against the brick wall, next to her bike, both of them concealed from view by the bins. There was blood on her face and her left leg was twisted beneath her. Later – after someone heard me yelling and called the police, after the ambulance arrived, after they took her away – a kind young policewoman told me they believed Priya was the victim of a hit and run, that whoever had knocked her off her bike had stopped and dragged her from the street before driving away.

'We'll find them,' she said, as if that would make it all right. As if that would make me and all the other people who loved Priya – her mum and dad, her sister, her best friend, her aunts and uncles and cousins – feel better. As if there could be justice.

Chapter 11

I woke up with a hangover.

I had been drunk when I got back to my room. Mid-afternoon, unable to work, I'd gone to the Miners Arms. I didn't remember seeing any of my fellow writers. I had a blurry memory of chatting to Rhodri about my dad and how I hadn't inherited his practical genes. He seemed to find this hilarious, although most of the conversation was a blur. I told him about Priya too. I remembered getting angry and tearful – and, wincing, I shoved the recollection back beneath the blanket of my hangover.

Eventually I dragged myself out of bed and into the shower. Feeling better, I grabbed a coffee from the kitchen and went back to my room. I badly needed to get some writing done. I hadn't added anything to my word count the day before. Time was running out.

I opened my laptop and found my work in progress open on the screen. As always, I started to read over the previous chapter before writing anything new.

The men went from house to house, looking for the right one. The one whose name was called. A girl or boy who no one would miss very much. They searched the land until they found that child. They knew it was the only way to save the skins they'd made. The child cried until she was an empty well with no more tears to cry. But nobody else cried. Nobody cared

— except for one man, who wrapped her in his strong arms and whispered with his lips against her hair. Whispered that . . .

It ended abruptly, the sentence unfinished. I read over it again, perplexed. I had absolutely no memory of writing these words. Had I done it when I got back from the pub? I tried to peer through the haze of my hangover. I had a vague memory of sitting at my laptop when I got back, but was sure I'd just spent a few minutes checking my emails and Facebook.

But I really didn't remember working on my book. And these words didn't sound like mine. The voice was different. It didn't fit into the novel, either.

I was clearly a bad writer when I was drunk.

And I wasn't very good hung over, either. I attempted to work on my story, but it was no use. After trying to construct the same sentence three times, I gave up and went back to bed.

ш

My phone woke me. It was dark outside and I couldn't make sense of it, until I realised I must have slept through and wasted a whole day. I grabbed my phone. It was six thirty.

'Lucas?' It was Zara and she was whispering. 'Can you meet?'

'Yeah. Sure. Have you found anything?'

'I'll tell you when I see you.'

Thirty minutes later, still a little groggy, I entered the Miners Arms. A few eyebrows went up when I walked in, the kind of looks that said 'Back again?' Oh God, I hoped I hadn't done anything too embarrassing the night before.

'Lucas! We're over here.'

It was Max, Suzi and Karen. Shit, I'd forgotten they'd be here. And there, sitting on her own in the corner, was Zara.

Max got to his feet, intercepting me. 'What are you drinking? We were wondering where you'd got to. Been hard at work?'

'Something like that.'

'We're just talking about all the weird stuff that's been going on in the house. Karen found a dead sparrow in her bedroom today and totally freaked out. I mean, obviously it was that bloody cat, but she's going on about how it's a bad omen.' He rolled his eyes. 'Anyway, what are you drinking? A pint?'

Out of the corner of my eye, I could see Zara watching me.

'Sorry, mate,' I said. My tongue felt sluggish; how much had I drunk last night? 'I'm, um, meeting an old friend. From when I was a kid.'

Max looked around. 'Oh, right. Of course, you were born here, weren't you?' He snickered. 'That's probably why you're so weird.'

'Huh?'

He clapped me on the shoulder. 'Just kidding, obviously.'

I could feel his eyes on my back as I threaded my way between the tables to Zara. She sat hunched, a pint in front of her, cap pulled so low it touched her eyebrows.

'You look rough,' she said.

'Thanks.'

'You're welcome. Not drinking?'

I groaned.

'Ah.' She fiddled with her beer mat and opened her mouth a couple of times, like she couldn't figure out how to get started.

'Have you found something out?' I asked. 'About Lily?'

'Kind of. Well. Rumours. Rumours about this place.' Her eyes flicked from side to side and she shuffled closer to the table as if she were afraid of being overheard. 'One of the things you quickly discover in this job is that if you want to learn about a place, you should talk to a librarian. Not because they've read a lot of books or any of that old guff – no offence – but because they know the local people, they see the stuff they're looking up, they overhear whispered conversations.'

'Sounds sensible.' I rubbed my forehead. I should have taken some painkillers before coming out.

'So that's where I went. Except the staff there were young library assistants, none of them with much knowledge of the town at all. To cut a long story short, I found out the librarian who worked there for donkey's years retired a couple of years ago. And an old dear who was in there gathering a huge pile of crime novels told me he could almost always be found at the chess club.'

I nodded for her to continue.

ʊ

Beddmawr Chess Club was based in a grand Victorian house near the centre of town, just across from the river. Zara paused on the bridge and found herself hypnotised by the swirling water beneath. A nutcase paddled beneath her in a kayak, which made her shiver. You wouldn't catch her doing that, no way. The only place she liked to get her thrills was between the sheets.

She buzzed the door of the chess club building and went inside.

She found Malcolm Jones seated at a chess table, sipping a cup of tea. The seat opposite was free and she gestured to it.

'Go ahead,' he said.

He had the lovely, lilting accent of the region, along with a good head of white hair and sharp eyes. He was sharply dressed too, in a tweed jacket that had been around so long it had come back into fashion.

He started to set up the pieces and she realised he thought she wanted a game.

'Oh. I was just hoping to ask you a few questions,' she said, introducing herself.

'We can play while we talk,' he said.

'But I haven't played in years.'

'I'm sure it will come back to you. Ready?'

'Oh, go on then.'

Malcolm moved his first pawn and said, 'So what did you want to talk to me about?'

She asked him if he remembered Lily Marsh and her father's death by drowning.

'Of course. Dreadful, dreadful. They never found her, did they? I understood that she drowned too.'

'Probably. The only other possibility is that someone took her. I know the police spoke to all the known sex offenders in the area . . .'

Malcolm moved his knight. Was it Zara's imagination or did his hand tremble as he lifted the piece? Perhaps she had imagined it, because his voice was steady. 'And you're wondering about the unknown ones? I was the librarian here for forty years. I must have heard things. Rumours. That's what you're thinking, yes?'

'You read my mind.'

'You're looking in the wrong place.'

Zara had been about to move another pawn. The rules had indeed come back to her, though she was still unsure what the horses – the knights – did. She paused, waiting to see what Malcolm said next.

'Some people think she was taken by the Widow,' he said.

She stared at him, then laughed nervously. 'What are you talking about?'

'No one else has told you the story of our local witch?' he asked.

'No. I'm not from round here.'

'Ah. Well, people don't talk about it so much any more. Not openly, anyway.' He nodded at the board. It was her move. She moved her queen onto a central square and he captured it.

'Bad move,' he said.

'You were telling me about this witch . . .'

'Ah, yes. Well, people don't talk about her these days. Except children. We had a children's section at the library. It's remarkable how many children's books are about witches. The children loved drawing them too, black cats and cauldrons. Spiky trees, a hut in the woods.'

Zara couldn't see how this connected to what had happened to Lily. 'Witches were just clever women that men couldn't tame, weren't they? Women who wouldn't conform. We learned about it at school. I suppose they drowned witches round here?'

'Surprisingly not. There were very few witch trials in Wales. A few cases in Flintshire. But most of that went on in England.' He licked his lips. 'In fact, I don't really know when or how the legend started. The first mention of the Red Widow is in a testimony from the early nineteenth century. It's still in the library if you're interested. Fascinating stuff. According to legend—'

'Malcolm! Are you going to introduce me to your young friend?'

Another man had appeared at Malcolm's shoulder. He was about seventy, completely bald, with hooded eyes. His lips curled back to reveal a set of crooked teeth.

Malcolm's shoulders were stiff with tension. Before speaking, he took a sip from his cup of tea. 'This is Zara . . .'

'Sullivan.' She instantly regretted telling this man her surname. Ridiculous. But she felt like a girl breaking her mother's golden rule. Never speak to strangers. Never tell them your name.

'We're in the middle of a game,' Malcolm said.

'Marvellous.' The bald man reached over and moved one of Malcolm's pieces on the board. 'Checkmate.'

Zara said, 'Oh. Damn.'

'You should give her more of a chance, Malcolm,' the man said. 'My dear, do you mind if I muscle in? I've been waiting to play Malcolm all afternoon.'

'Of course.'

Reluctantly, she got up. She handed Malcolm her card and noticed the bald man watching as Malcolm tucked it into the pocket of his tweed jacket.

'Perhaps we could play another time.'

As she left the chess club, she glanced over her shoulder. The bald man was watching her. And Malcolm had gone as white as the milk in his stone-cold tea.

Chapter 12

'Hang on,' I said, when Zara had finished talking. 'Did Malcolm Jones actually tell you anything useful?'

'He was about to tell me about the Red Widow, before the bald guy, the one with the teeth like tombstones, interrupted us.'

'Zara, I know I'm not at my sharpest today but I don't get it. How are these children's stories relevant?'

She deflated. 'I don't know. It was the way he said "you're looking in the wrong place" when I asked him about sex offenders. I'm sure he knows something. But when the bald guy came along, Malcolm clammed up.'

We both fell silent. My headache had intensified and I was finding it hard to think straight.

'So what do you want to do next?' I asked.

'I want to talk to Malcolm Jones again. I'm sure he knows something. Maybe he felt that he couldn't tell me straight so he was going to wrap it up in an old story. People do that sometimes.'

Across the pub, the other writers were getting up to go. I realised I was starving and the thought of dinner back at the retreat made my stomach growl.

I was sceptical about Malcolm Jones and disappointed that Zara hadn't discovered anything more concrete. But I figured it was worth letting her have one more day before giving up and accepting Lily was gone.

'I'll call you again tomorrow,' I said.

I headed over to join the other writers. On my way past the bar I spotted the painting that had caught my attention on my first visit here. The woman in red, beckoning onlookers into the trees. The Red Widow? Staring at the painting I felt a peculiar sensation, as if I were being pulled into the wood, the temperature around me dropping, and I was sure the woman in red whispered something to me, words spoken in another language. I took a step closer, raised a hand to touch the figure, convinced that she shrunk away from my fingers, sliding back into the wood, retreating as the trees formed a guard around her . . .

'Lucas?'

I jumped.

'Are you all right?' It was Karen. She turned her head to scrutinise the painting, which now looked perfectly normal. Nothing shifted, no one whispered. 'Big fan of amateur art, are you? We're about to head back to the retreat for dinner.'

Outside, Karen fell into step beside me. To either side of us, trees formed black, jagged shapes against a bruised, purplish sky, just like in the painting. Winter was clinging on – but only just. A few steps ahead, Max and Suzi were deep in conversation.

'How are you?' I asked.

'Not great, to be honest.'

I waited for her to elaborate.

'I know it's stupid, that it was the dope making me hear things, but I feel uneasy in my room now. I didn't sleep at all last night. I lay there with the covers over my head like some stupid kid, convinced there was someone outside the door, watching and listening.'

I was going to tell her about the singing I'd heard but realised it would only make her more freaked out. I was sure that it had been Julia grieving in her daughter's room, but Karen might not accept that simple explanation. I didn't want her packing up and leaving. She was the only author here I really got along with.

'Sometimes,' she went on, 'I'm convinced someone's been in my room during the day. Like, things have been moved. Or there's a strange smell in the air.'

'What kind of smell?'

'It sounds stupid, but . . . the smell of fear. A kind of sour, sweaty odour.' She paused. 'Maybe it's me. Maybe I'm sniffing out my own stress.'

'That sounds . . . plausible.'

She laughed. 'I really do need to lay off the weed, don't I?'

'Maybe until you go home.'

She sighed deeply and twisted her hands together. Then she said, 'What if it's not the weed? What if the house really is haunted? In a way, I hope it is. I'd like it if a ghostly apparition appeared one night while we were eating dinner. A woman in white walking through the walls.'

I had a flash from my dream: a trickle of blood running down the wallpaper. I shuddered, but Karen didn't notice.

'Yeah, if a ghost did appear,' she said, 'at least then it would prove I'm not going mad.'

ꟺ

Entering the house, it was immediately clear that something was not right.

Normally at this time, the place would be alive with the smell of cooking, the warm scent of meat or cheese, of herbs and spices, wafting from the kitchen. But the lights were out and there was no sign of Julia.

Max stomped into the kitchen and turned on the light.

'What's going on?'

He stared at the Aga as if food might magically appear. There were some dishes and cutlery in the sink, and a faint, sweet odour hanging in the air, but dinner definitely wasn't on its way.

'Where is she? I'm starving. If I'd known she wasn't going to make us dinner I'd have got something in the pub.'

Max was clearly one of those people who loses the plot when their blood sugar is low.

'Calm down,' I said. 'Something must have happened.'

'Do you think she's okay?' Suzi asked.

Julia's room was on the top floor of the house. Suzi and Karen went up to look for her while Max and I remained downstairs.

'I wonder if any pizza places deliver out here,' Max said.

I wasn't in the mood to humour him. 'You're unbelievably selfish.'

'What? It's part of what we pay for here. Meals provided. It's in the contract . . .'

'Oh, shut up. What if Julia's had an accident? You're going to feel pretty stupid if they find her lying unconscious in her room.'

He grunted. 'She's probably gone out.'

Perhaps it was because I was worried about Julia, and my head was still throbbing so I was irritable, but I snapped, 'While we're on the subject of you being a massive dickhead, what's going on with you and Suzi? It's obvious you fancy her.'

He was speechless.

'You're married, aren't you? Do you love your wife? Do you value your relationship? Maybe you should appreciate what you've got.'

Max's mouth was still flapping when Suzi and Karen reappeared. 'She's not up there,' Suzi said.

'Her room was kind of a mess,' Karen added in a quiet voice.

'Does anyone have her mobile number?' I asked.

We all looked at each other. The website only listed the landline number for the retreat.

'I didn't see her before I came to the pub,' I said.

'Me neither,' Karen responded, and the others murmured in agreement.

I went to the front window and peered into the darkness. Julia's car was parked in its usual spot. Then I noticed something. 'There's light coming from the cottage.'

'It looks like candlelight,' Suzi said.

She was right. The light was yellow and weak, flickering behind a downstairs window.

'Come on then,' Max said, heading for the front door.

I stopped him. 'No, you wait here. The last thing we want is for you to go charging in there complaining about your empty belly. One of the women should go.'

'How sexist,' Max protested.

'Shut up, Max,' said Karen. She and Suzi exchanged a glance. Karen had gone pale. 'I don't know if I feel brave enough to go,' she said. 'It's creepy. What if she's . . . dead or something? I couldn't cope with finding her body.'

'Dead? What makes you—' I sighed. 'All right. I'll go.'

As I crossed the garden, Karen's words rang in my ears. What on earth made her think Julia might be dead? It was stupid. But by the time I reached the cottage I was bracing myself to find something awful. In my increasingly fevered imagination, Julia had committed suicide, unable to cope with the loss of her daughter any longer. I would find her hanging from a beam, or slumped on the floor with an empty bottle of pills beside her.

I didn't think I'd be able to cope with finding another dead body. Especially not Julia's.

'Julia?' I said as I opened the front door. 'Are you there?'

No response.

The candlelight was coming from the little dining room next to the kitchen. The door was shut. I tapped at it lightly and said her name again. Still no answer.

I went in.

It was almost dark in the room. Julia sat at the dining table. In front of her was a cake, covered with lit candles. She didn't look up when I entered, just continued to stare at the cake. The yellow light touched the tear tracks on her cheeks.

'Julia,' I said. I was whispering. 'Are you all right?'

'She was here,' she said.

'Who?'

She lifted her face towards me. 'Lily.'

I didn't know what to say. I pulled a chair out from the table, the scrape on the stone floor making me wince, and sat beside her. It was bitterly cold in the room but Julia seemed oblivious to it.

'It's her birthday today,' she said. 'She's eleven. She was so looking forward to it – we promised when she turned eleven she could have her ears pierced.'

I counted the eleven candles on the cake. It was round, with pink frosting. Lily's name had been written on the surface in white icing.

'She grew out of pink years ago,' Julia said. 'But it still makes me think of her. When she was little.'

'What did you mean when you said she was here?' I asked, still speaking quietly.

She wasn't looking at me any more; she stared at the cake, at the candles, the tiny flames reflected in her eyes. 'I brought this cake over here because . . . I thought it would be private. Just me and her. I was going to light the candles, sing "Happy Birthday", cut the cake. Just spend some time alone, thinking about her, you know?'

I nodded.

'I lit the candles then realised I didn't have a knife. There aren't any knives in the kitchen here so I went back to the house to get one. And when I got back, the candles had been blown out.' She looked at me. There was yearning in that look. A yearning for it to be true. To be believed. But my first thought was that it must have been the wind.

She read my mind. 'There's no wind in this room. No breeze. She was here. She came to blow out her candles.'

'You mean . . .' I could hardly bring myself to complete the sentence. 'You mean her ghost?'

It was as if I'd slapped her. 'She's not dead!'

The sudden rise in volume, the raw emotion in her voice, made me flinch. As if *I'd* been slapped. And then she started to cry – great, rasping sobs, her whole body shaking as she twisted her hands together and whispered, between gasps, 'She's alive, she's alive, she's alive.'

I put my arms around her. It was instinct, the need to comfort her. She was stiff at first and I almost pulled away, but then she relaxed, letting me hold her, and the trembling of her shoulders subsided as she pressed her face against my chest and I gently rubbed her back, shushing her and letting her cry.

When she eventually lifted her head, the front of my sweater was wet. 'I'm sorry,' she said.

'Don't apologise.'

She found a tissue and blew her nose, wiped at her eyes with the backs of her hands. 'Oh God, I'm a mess. I'm such a mess. What must you think of me?'

'I think you're a mother who misses her daughter,' I said. 'That's all.'

She took a deep breath and gathered herself. She was embarrassed now, refusing to look me in the eye. She stood up, went to the sink and splashed some cold water on her face.

She sat back down. 'It probably was the wind. Or candles . . . sometimes candles go out on their own, don't they?'

'I think so.'

To be honest, that seemed unlikely. The most likely explanation, surely, was that Julia had forgotten to light them in the first place, had simply imagined herself doing it. I did that sort of thing all the time. And Julia, in her heightened state of emotion, was more susceptible to confusion, to forgetting, than most.

'Do you want to blow the candles out now? And sing "Happy Birthday", like you planned?'

'Yes. Yes, I do.'

I went to get up. 'I'll leave you in peace.'

She grabbed my hand. 'No, Lucas, please stay. It's sad if it's just me on my own.' She laughed.

'Okay.'

She began singing and I joined in.

'Happy birthday to you . . . Happy birthday, dear Lily . . .'

Julia blew out the candles and cut three slices. Julia placed one in front of me and encouraged me to take a bite.

'Mmm. It's really nice.'

Her slice remained uneaten in front of her, as did the third slice, which she placed on the opposite side of the table. Lily's piece.

I waited to see if Julia would mention singing in Lily's room. I didn't want to bring it up because it felt like an invasion of her privacy.

'Oh God, I bet the others are moaning about not having any dinner, aren't they?' she said. 'What shall I do?'

'Let them eat cake?'

That made her laugh.

'Look,' I said. 'I'll drive into town, pick up a takeaway.'

'Thank you, Lucas.'

'Are you going to come back over to the house?' I asked.

She stayed in her seat. 'I think I'll stay here a while.'

'Okay.'

I backed out of the room, my eyes lingering on that uneaten third slice of birthday cake, on the extinguished candles. I thought about what Karen had said earlier about the house being haunted and the strange smell that hung in her room, but nothing – no number of strange occurrences – would make me believe in ghosts. I didn't believe Lily had turned up to blow out her birthday candles. That didn't make any sense. Julia must have forgotten to light the candles in the first place. It was the only logical explanation.

Chapter 13

LILY – 2014

So far, this was the best birthday ever. Lily had a card that said *It's great when you're eight!* and Mum and Dad had bought her the best present she'd ever had: a new bike to replace the one she'd had when she first learned to ride. Back then, Dad had taken her to a field near their old house and taught her how to keep her balance, not letting her give up. It was one of her happiest memories.

She stood in the park in town, holding the bike by its saddle, just looking at it. It was green – her favourite colour – and there were streamers attached to the handlebars. There was a gift tag attached too, which said, *Happy Birthday Lily. All our love, Mum and Dad xxxx.* It was awesome.

'So,' Mum said. 'Are you going to ride it?'

'I guess.'

'Go on then.'

Mum made a fuss about whether the saddle was too high and double-checked the brakes, while Dad rolled his eyes. That was typical. They had to argue about everything, even today, the most important day of the year. Lily had been watching them closely lately because they hadn't had any of their big massive rows about Dad's drinking, but they made comments to each other all the time. *Snip snip*, like two pairs of scissors having a fight. Dad was always rolling his eyes when Mum's back was turned. And Mum said Dad was something-aggressive.

They still loved each other, though. They had to.

And they loved her. This morning, they'd both come into Lily's room with her cards and presents and Dad had given her a big cuddle and told her how happy she made him, and how she was his princess. It was slightly embarrassing, and he smelled a bit weird, like mouldy potatoes or something, but it was still nice.

'Why don't you do a circuit of the green?' Mum said. 'We'll be able to see you.'

Lily climbed onto the bike. It was a little bit high and the saddle dug into her bottom, but if she stood on tiptoes it didn't fall over. It was a cold day and Mum said she needed to wear gloves, but she had taken off her coat because she was hot. The helmet on her head made her hot too, but she definitely wasn't allowed to take that off.

'Thank you for my bike,' she said, grinning at them. She licked the big gap in her front teeth.

'You're very welcome, sweetheart,' said Mum.

She pushed off, wobbling at first, almost tilting over before getting her balance. And then she was heading down the path. The bike was smooth and fast. She loved it! She gathered pace as she went round the first bend, and kept going, cruising all the way around the green.

She passed Mum and Dad, and shouted that she was going to do another circuit.

Now she was in the swing of it, her mind wandered. It had only been a couple of weeks since she'd gone into the field behind their house, searching for the cat. Chesney, it turned out, had been curled up underneath her bed, safe and sound. But Lily had a bad dream that night. She dreamt she was being chased through the woods, a witch calling her name.

'I only want a taste,' the witch said. 'Just a little taste.'

When she'd told Megan at school about the shape she'd seen in the fog, Megan said it might have been the Widow, but then Charlotte, who was the nosiest girl in their whole class, had butted in and said it was probably a Stranger.

'A Stranger?' Lily asked.

'Yeah. You know . . .' Charlotte pointed to a poster on the wall which showed a picture of a grey van with the words *STRANGER DANGER! NEVER GO WITH SOMEONE YOU DON'T KNOW.*

'A Stranger watching my house?'

Lily shivered. She had only the vaguest idea of what Strangers did. All she knew was that they took kids and did things to them. She didn't know what kinds of things. Bad things. That was all she knew.

'It's okay,' Charlotte said. 'As long as you don't talk to Strangers, they can't get you.'

A squirrel dashed across the path in front of her bike. Instinctively, she yanked the handles to the left and the bike swung onto the green and hit the stump of a tree.

She lost control and fell off.

It didn't hurt, not really, but she lay there dazed for a minute, like a cartoon character with stars whirling round its head.

And then a shadow fell over her. It was a man. He had a bald head and his teeth were all crooked and horrible.

'Are you all right, lass?' he said.

She lay on her back, frozen with fear. A Stranger. A Stranger was trying to make her talk to him. He reached out a hand and she understood that he wanted her to take it so he could help her up, but she couldn't move.

He crouched beside her. She could see right up his hairy nose.

'What's your name?' he said.

She still couldn't speak or move. Where were Mum and Dad? What were they doing? Had they left her alone with this Stranger?

He reached out a fat-fingered hand towards the handlebars of her fallen bike, and read the gift tag.

'Lily,' he said. 'That's a lovely name. Lily.'

At that moment, she heard her mum's voice, and her dad's, and there they were, next to her, eyes full of worry.

'I think she's fine,' said the Stranger. 'Just a little bump, that's all.'

'Thank you,' said her mum, for some reason, and the Stranger walked away. Mum was fussing over her, helping her sit up, and Dad was checking the bike, making sure the wheels hadn't buckled or something.

Neither of them saw the Stranger look over his shoulder and wink at her.

Chapter 14

My parents moved to Spain ten years ago, shortly after they retired. A lovely whitewashed villa in Alicante, a short walk from the Mediterranean. Mum was always telling me I should go out there, spend some time in the sun – after all, it wasn't as if I had an office job – and I thought about it often. The problem was, Britain's gloom suited my writing, and hot weather made me torpid and lazy.

I had been out there only once since my dad's funeral. I'd been shocked when Mum told me the cremation was going to take place in Spain, but she insisted it was where he was happiest. Dad wanted his ashes scattered over a warm sea, somewhere beautiful. It made sense, even if it meant the ceremony was sparsely attended – just immediate family and a few of their ex-pat mates. I was less surprised when Mum told me she was staying in Spain. 'Why would I come back to rainy Britain? I intend to stay here till I'm too old to look after myself. At which point I'll chuck myself off a cliff.'

She was like that, my mum.

These days, we mostly spoke via Skype. Unlike the stereotype of people in their seventies, she was au fait with technology. She ran a group on Facebook for crafting enthusiasts, knitters and embroiderers, and was on Instagram and Twitter. She was always Instagramming photos of her latest creations.

The night before, I had gone to sleep thinking about Julia and Lily, along with what Zara had told me about the local legend. Now, as sunlight filled the room, I opened Skype and saw that Mum was online. I hit the call button and her tanned face appeared on the screen.

'Lucas! Speak of the devil! I was just talking about you with Jean.' Jean was Mum's closest neighbour. 'She wants to know when your next book's out. She loved *Sweetmeat*, though she said it gave her the willies.'

'Have you read it yet?'

Mum was usually my number-one fan, but *Sweetmeat* had come out just after Dad's death. She'd told me she couldn't handle anything darker than a Jilly Cooper but that she'd read it eventually.

'I will. Soon. You look pale. Are you eating properly?'

'Yes, Mum.'

She worried about me, especially since Priya's death. 'Where are you? That doesn't look like your flat.'

'I'm in Beddmawr.'

The look on her face was priceless. 'You're joking.'

'Just outside Beddmawr, actually. A place called Nyth Bran.'

'Where the old mine used to be?'

'Yes. It's a writers' retreat now. I'm here trying to finish my new book. "Trying" being the operative word.'

I had expected her to be pleased that I had returned to the place where I was born, especially as it was her home town, but she frowned. 'Well. I never expected you to go back there.'

'Why not?'

She seemed flustered, which was unusual for her. In that moment, she seemed older, giving me a glimpse of what she might be like in a decade or two. 'You were so young when we left there, I didn't think you'd remember it. Not properly, anyway. As soon as we moved to Birmingham, it was as if Beddmawr never existed.'

'That's the thing. I don't remember it. Hardly any of it. I have the occasional flash of memory. But most of it's lost.'

She sipped from a glass of water. 'That's normal. I don't remember the first six or seven years of my life either. And Beddmawr is hardly the most memorable place.'

Keen to get the conversation back on track, I said, 'There's a guy here, a handyman, who remembers you. Rhodri Wallace.'

'Wallace? It doesn't ring a bell. But it was a long time ago, Lucas. All I remember of those days is looking after you. Oh, you were a difficult child. Did I tell you that you used to come into our bed every night till you were five?'

'Only about a thousand times.'

'I was so exhausted all the time, it's a miracle I can remember anything about that period. It's a great fuzzy blur.' She took another sip of water. 'My goodness, it's hot here today. You should come over, treat this place as a writing retreat, get some vitamin D while you're here . . .'

Was I imagining it, or was she deliberately trying to change the subject from her home town? Thinking about it, she hardly ever mentioned the place. She never had done. Apart from the paintings of Wales that hung on her wall, and her lingering accent, she hardly acknowledged the old country. Why had I never noticed that before?

I was trying to think of a way of broaching this topic when she said, 'I wonder if they ever found that little girl?'

Shocked, I said, 'What little girl?'

'I can't remember her name but I saw it on the news a couple of years ago. They thought she fell into the Dee.'

'Lily Marsh.'

Now it was her turn to look surprised. 'Oh, you heard about it too.'

I lowered my voice, worried that Julia might overhear. 'Yes, I know about it. And no, she hasn't been found.'

Mum shook her head. 'Terrible. I couldn't believe it when I saw it had happened again.'

'What?'

The picture was growing fuzzier, the connection breaking up. My mother's face was pixelated. I wished I could pull her through the screen so I could talk to her properly.

'You won't remember. You were too little. A little girl went missing in Beddmawr when we still lived there.'

'When did this happen?' I asked.

'Shortly before we moved away. Around 1980?'

I made a note in the pad on my desk.

'It was terrible,' she went on. 'They never found her or the person who took her.' The picture was really breaking up now.

'What was her name?'

'I can't remember. Oh, what was it? I'm sure she lived in the children's home, didn't have any parents . . .'

The picture froze, my mother on-screen with her mouth half-open.

'Mum, can you still hear me?'

Bad connection appeared on screen and the call ended. I tried to reconnect but it rang out. This happened sometimes. The Internet in Mum's villa was painfully unreliable.

I went to Google and typed in 'missing child Beddmawr 1980'. There were no results, presumably because news websites hadn't existed in those days. Some newspapers have searchable archives online, but a lot of them are hidden behind paywalls and aren't indexed by search engines.

Still, I thought it shouldn't be too hard to find out.

I called Zara's mobile. It rang half a dozen times, then went to voicemail. I left a brief message asking her to call me back, but as I did so I wondered if all this was a distraction. Surely the disappearance of a child over thirty years ago couldn't be connected to what had happened to Lily? If there was a serial child abductor or murderer out there, there certainly wouldn't be such a long gap between his crimes.

Even so, I felt uneasy, and it took me a minute to realise why. I had written a book about children going missing, and the landscape in that book was eerily similar to the landscape of Beddmawr. I had been six in 1980. The adults around me must have talked about a child going missing. They had probably said something about it at school too. I had no memory of it, but it was feasible that my subconscious had retained and – eventually – leaked this information into my novel.

But that didn't help with the investigation into what had happened to Lily. After singing 'Happy Birthday' with Julia the night before, I wanted to help her more than ever. But I hadn't actually got anywhere, not really.

The truth was, I was stuck. And if Zara didn't call me with some groundbreaking news soon, I figured it was time to give up and go back to the most obvious solution.

Lily had drowned. End of story.

ω

I spent the afternoon working on my novel, immersing myself in the new world I was creating. It was hard going. The cries of missing children kept piercing the surface, echoing through the text, trying to drown out the story I wanted to tell. I had situated my fictional family in the hut in the middle of the woods, with monsters closing in. A stranger had joined them, a young woman who tried to persuade them they needed to go somewhere safer, somewhere far away.

I kept being drawn back to the section I couldn't remember writing, the part about people going door to door looking for a child. Had I come up with a brilliant idea while drunk; an idea that had died during the night? I tried to dig into my memory but it was exhausting.

Every so often, I checked my phone. There was no word from Zara. I tried to call her but she didn't answer.

At around four, I looked out through the window and saw Karen in the front garden, pacing about with her back to me. She was gesticulating as if she were having a conversation with someone. I thought perhaps she was on the phone, using an earpiece. Or maybe she was speaking dialogue from her book aloud. I knew a few writers who did that. She seemed agitated, anyway, but I decided to leave her be. No doubt she would tell me all about it over dinner. I had decided not to go to the pub this evening; I'd had enough of Max and needed a break from him, plus I was still off alcohol. At forty-two, my hangovers lingered for days, and the black hole in my memory from my evening in the pub made me uneasy. The guilt and the fear, they called it, and I was suffering from it big time.

At seven I went down for dinner. Max and Suzi were at the table, chatting.

'Where's Karen?' I asked.

Max ignored me. I guessed he was still sulking after I'd had a go at him, last night before I'd found Julia with the birthday cake.

'We haven't seen her,' Suzi said.

Julia came into the dining room with a couple of bottles of mineral water. She gave me a little smile, then said, 'Karen told me she's not feeling well, so she's having an early night.'

After dinner, I went back to my room to work, then went to bed.

Yet again, I couldn't sleep. I kept thinking about Zara, wondering why she hadn't called me back and wasn't answering her phone. Then I started thinking about Julia and Lily and my book, a jumble of thoughts going round and round like clothes in a tumble dryer.

It must have been 1 a.m. when I eventually drifted into sleep.

I was immediately woken by a scream.

Chapter 15

I jumped out of bed and pulled on some trousers. I was sure the scream had come from upstairs.

My first thought was that something terrible had happened to Julia. I took the stairs two at a time, panting as I reached the landing. With every step, I saw flashes:

Priya, with her scraped and bloody face.

Lily, arms windmilling as she fell with a splash into the river.

Blood oozing from a hole in my bedroom wall.

Julia was there on the landing, wearing a dressing gown, her hair sticking out at crazy angles.

'Are you all right?' I panted. 'I heard a scream and thought . . .'

She looked me up and down. I must have looked wild-haired too. And wild-eyed. 'It wasn't me,' she said. 'I think it came from Karen's room.'

Suzi's door, which was opposite Karen's, opened and she emerged, wearing a pair of pink silk pyjamas. A moment later, Max stuck his head out of the same door, saw us all standing there and quickly vanished. Suzi blushed.

Gently, Julia tapped on Karen's door. 'Karen? Are you okay?'

A high-pitched yell came from inside the room, followed by banging and another scream, one that started anguished and ended with fury.

The door was unlocked and Julia opened it and rushed inside, Suzi and I following.

Both doors of Karen's wardrobe stood wide open and I couldn't see Karen at first. But then I heard her shout, 'Where are you? Where the fuck are you?' A pair of trousers flew across the room, landing on the bed, followed by a black shoe. As we entered the room we saw Karen, leaning into the wardrobe and yelling as if she'd discovered Narnia but the door to the magical kingdom had slammed shut.

Julia tried to take Karen's arm, but Karen shook her off and carried on rifling through the wardrobe, chucking stuff behind her like a crazed poltergeist. A coat hanger missed my ear by an inch.

'Do something,' Suzi said, and I stepped forward.

'Karen,' I said, 'what is it? What are you looking for?'

She didn't seem to notice me, so I said it again. I put a hand on her shoulder and she went stiff, then turned and stared at me with wild eyes. Her body was rigid, as if she were afraid to breathe; her knuckles were white where she gripped a coat she'd been about to chuck across the bedroom.

'They were in here,' she whispered. 'I heard them.'

'What did they say?'

She didn't respond. But at least she'd stopped pulling items out of the wardrobe.

'Come on,' I said. 'Why don't you sit down?'

She allowed me to lead her over to the bed, where she sat, grabbing the quilt and pulling it over her. She hugged herself, her breathing harsh and ragged. I nodded at Julia and Suzi, indicating that I needed them to give us space, and they moved over towards the window.

'She was in there,' Karen said, barely audible.

'In the wardrobe?'

She grabbed hold of my arm. Her pupils were dilated, wide and black, big enough to drown in. Her fingernails dug into my forearm.

'Or the ceiling. Or maybe she's under the bed.' She jerked forward but I held her back.

'Would you like me to check?' I asked.

She nodded and I got down on my hands and knees, making a great show of peering beneath the bed.

'There's no one there.'

'Are you sure?'

'Absolutely.'

I sat up and rubbed my bare arms. I couldn't see anything sinister in the room, but I could feel it. Something. A presence, lurking out of sight. The sensation of being watched. Just like in my dream, I had the sense that the house was alive, breathing. Waiting.

'I'm just going to have a chat with Julia, okay?' I said to Karen, who stared at me as if I'd spoken a foreign language.

I gestured for Julia to follow me out of the room. Suzi came too. We stood in the hallway, talking in whispers.

'It's like she's having a bad trip,' I said.

'From cannabis? Is that possible?'

'I don't know. I've heard about people lacing cannabis with all sorts of stuff,' I said. 'LSD, maybe. It's not really my area of expertise.'

'It could be a panic attack,' Julia said.

'She looks utterly terrified,' said Suzi. 'Like the other night, when she heard that voice.'

'What are you talking about?' Julia asked. 'What voice?'

'Maybe we should call an ambulance,' I said, ignoring Julia's exasperated look.

'I'll do it.' Suzi went into her room to find her phone.

Karen made a groaning noise and Julia hurried in, leaving me on my own for a moment until Max came out of Suzi's room, wearing a dressing gown. 'What's going on?' he said. 'Is Karen demonstrating why you shouldn't do drugs again?'

'Why do you have to be such a twat?'

'Whatever. I'm going back to bed.'

'Your own?'

'We were working. Not that it's any of your business.'

He was right. It wasn't. But I was sick of the sight of Max, and was pleased when he wandered away, yawning and scratching his scalp.

'Lucas. Can you come back in here?' It was Julia.

In the bedroom, Karen was horizontal, pulling the quilt half over her face and peeking out. The terror seemed to have subsided a little but there was an emptiness to her gaze now, as if part of her mind had been torn away.

'She's been talking,' Julia said in a quiet voice. 'But none of it makes any sense.'

'What did she say?'

'She's now saying she thinks there was someone in the ceiling. And they were whispering to her.'

'In or *on* the ceiling?' The latter, I thought, was a fairly common drug-induced hallucination. At least it was in the films I'd seen.

'She definitely said *in*.'

I moved closer to Karen. 'What did they say to you, Karen?' I asked gently.

She pulled the quilt an inch higher, so it was level with the bridge of her nose. '*You're not welcome here.*'

'The same as last time.'

'Last time?' said Julia.

'It happened before,' I explained, 'a couple of days ago.'

'It was a girl,' Karen whispered.

'A girl?' Julia had gone pale.

'Did she say anything else?' I was reluctant to quiz Karen too much in case it prompted another episode. How long would it be before the ambulance got here? There was no hospital in town so it was going to have come from – I guessed – Wrexham.

Karen shook her head, her wide eyes fixed on me.

'Just *you're not welcome here*?'

Karen nodded and I thought she was about to close her eyes. They flickered, and she said, 'And she was singing.'

Julia leaned in closer. 'Singing? Singing what?'

Now Karen did close her eyes. The room was silent for a minute, so quiet I thought I could hear all three of our hearts beating, Karen's loudest of all.

'I couldn't understand it,' Karen whispered.

'Because it was in another language?' I asked.

Julia spun round to stare at me. And then we heard a noise from above.

Bang. Bang.

Karen pulled the quilt fully over her head and Julia looked as if she were about to faint. We both stared at the ceiling.

The noise came again.

'What's up there?' I asked.

Julia didn't take her eyes off the ceiling. The plaster was cracked in places and cobwebs clung to the corners.

'The attic,' Julia said.

'Has it been converted? Is there a room up there?'

'No. There are a few boards down, but it's just used to store junk.'

I went out into the hallway. There was a chair near the top of the stairs. I fetched it and stood beneath the hatch to the attic.

Julia came out of Karen's room. 'What are you doing?'

'I want to set everyone's mind at rest. Prove there's no one up there.'

I tugged at the hatch and, with a sudden jerk and a blast of dust that filled my eyes, it came free.

There was a metal ladder, also furry with dust, and stiff and reluctant to shift. But I managed to pull it down.

'Is there a light up here?' I asked.

'No. Hang on.' She fetched her phone from her room, switched on the flashlight and handed it to me. 'Use this.'

I climbed the ladder and stuck my head through the gap. Holding Julia's phone up, I could make out the shapes of boxes, some pots of paint, a water tank.

'Can you see anything?' Julia asked from below. I glanced down and saw that Suzi had come out of her room now and was beside Julia, looking up at me.

'No. Just a load of old boxes. Hang on.'

I heaved myself up into the attic and shone the flashlight around. It was cavernous, much bigger than I'd expected. I knelt on the boards and peered into the gloom. There was a strange smell in the room, like sweat, but I couldn't tell if it was my own. I could feel a draft too, chilly air touching my face. Perhaps there was a small hole in the roof.

I crawled further into the attic.

'Oh shit!' I shouted.

From below, Julia gasped. 'What is it?'

'Sorry. Sorry, I put my hand on something disgusting.' I shone the light at it and almost vomited. It was a mouse trap, the corpse of a long-dead rat rotting beneath the metal bar. I was worried there might be untriggered traps lying around, so was more careful where I put my hands.

I moved further into the attic until I was, I estimated, directly above Karen's bed, the place where we'd heard the creak. Just beyond was a water tank, and more piles of boxes. The draft was stronger here. I looked around, trying to locate its source, guessing a tile must have fallen off the roof.

I lifted my head towards the cold stream of air.

Something touched my face – a flutter, the brush of something dry and leathery. I shouted out and threw myself across the space, away from whatever it was that had touched me. I put my head down, curled into a ball, convinced something was about to grab me, something I didn't believe in, something that couldn't exist. A ghost. A monster, hunched in the corner. '*Sweeeetmeeeeat!*' it whispered, and the shadows in the corner of the loft stirred and shifted, and the creature lifted its face towards me.

Priya's bloody face.

Priya's sightless eyes.

I put my head down and repeated to myself, 'It's not real, it's not real, it's not real.'

'Lucas? What's going on?' Julia called up from below.

I lifted my head and raised my phone so the beam of light illuminated the corner. There was nothing there.

Of course there was nothing there.

I angled the beam of light towards the roof. At the same time, Julia climbed the ladder and her head appeared through the hatch. 'What's going on? What happened?'

I laughed, aware that there was a hint of hysteria, a top note of madness in my laughter. But as Julia watched, eyes wide and fearful, I got up onto my knees and raised the flashlight higher.

A shadow flitted above us.

'You've got bats,' I said.

ω

Julia and I sat at the kitchen table, two mugs of tea between us. The ambulance had been and gone, leaving Karen upstairs. She had calmed down and fallen asleep, and the paramedics thought she would be better off staying where she was, rather than being taken to hospital.

'Maybe she just needs to go home, see her doctor,' said one of the paramedics. 'Don't let her smoke anything.'

Now, Julia said, 'She asked me to move her to a different room but I didn't get round to it.'

'I don't think it would have made any difference. Perhaps she wouldn't have heard the bats if she was in a different room, but . . .' I shrugged.

'Do you think she'll be okay?'

'I don't know. I hope so. Like the paramedic said, she probably just needs to find some other way to manage her arthritis. She should probably get that cannabis analysed, see if it has been laced with something. Though it might just be really strong skunk. I've never done it, but I've heard the stuff that's around now is much more potent than when I was a student and smoking joints.'

It was black beyond the kitchen window. Julia hugged herself. She had tied back her hair and pulled on a black sweater with sleeves that came over her hands. It was warm in the kitchen, thanks to the Aga. Chesney sat beneath the table, purring loudly.

'So you think she heard the bats, got scared, and then the weed kicked in, made her start imagining things?' Julia said.

'Yeah. I guess.'

'But the things she heard . . .'

'*You're not welcome here*? Maybe that's how she feels. It could be to do with her status as a writer. Authors like Max look down on self-published writers. He's said a lot of horrible, snobbish things about Karen's books. She seems really confident in daylight, but every author I know is a mess of self-doubt and insecurities.'

'And what about the singing?' she asked. She looked at me suspiciously. 'You seemed to know something about it.'

I paused. I had assumed it had been Julia singing in Lily's room. But now . . .

'I've heard someone singing here too.'

'What? Where?'

'It was coming from the room next to mine. I assume it used to be Lily's, didn't it?'

'It *is* Lily's.'

'Oh . . . Of course. Sorry.' I took a sip of tea. It was almost cold. 'I heard singing a couple of times. I thought it was you.'

She stared at me. It wasn't the first time I'd seen Julia go pale. But now she had gone an even whiter shade.

'I haven't been in Lily's room since you got here,' she said. 'I certainly haven't been in there, singing.'

She got up from the table and crossed to the warmth of the Aga. 'What was the song?' she asked. 'You said something about it being in a foreign language.'

'I'm pretty sure it was Welsh. I only recognised the first few words. *Un, dau, tri.*'

'What about the tune? Do you remember it?'

I did. The melody, simple as it was, had burrowed into my brain the second time I'd heard it. Overcoming my embarrassment, I hummed it now.

Julia's eyes grew wide with recognition. When I'd finished, which took less than a minute, she opened her mouth and sang. Her voice was clear and tuneful.

> Un, dau, tri
> Mn yn dal y pry
> Pry wedi marw
> Mam yn crio'n arw.

'It's a traditional Welsh song,' she said. 'Lily learned it at school after we moved here. She used to sing it all the time. She brought home the translation too.'

'What does it mean?'

She pressed herself closer to the Aga. '*One two three, Mum caught a fly, the fly has died, Mum cries terribly* . . . It's about a woman losing a child.'

'Oh my God.'

'Though, specifically, it's about having a miscarriage. Mum caught a fly is a way of saying she's pregnant. But, Lucas, the meaning of the song isn't what's important here. Both you and Karen heard it.' Julia stared into the space between us, at the dancing motes of dust. She lifted a trembling hand to brush hair from her eyes. 'Does that mean Lily's dead? That you heard her spirit?'

I got up from the table. 'No. There has to be a rational explanation.'

'Because Lily's not dead.'

'And because ghosts aren't real.'

I stood close to her, so close I could see the pink threads in her eyes, the dry spots on her lips. She was tired, run-down. Still beautiful – but in pain, caught between a need to grieve and a refusal to do so. Trapped in a desperate limbo.

The rational explanation had to be that I'd been right all along. It had been Julia singing, but she either didn't remember or refused to admit it. Probably the former. I wasn't going to accuse her of that, though.

'Let me think,' I said, stalling for time. 'Maybe . . . maybe it's me. I went to school here. I probably learned that song too, so it would be buried deep in my subconscious.'

She made a sceptical noise.

'No, it's true.' I remembered the conversation with my mum, but didn't want to go into the details right now. 'I've been sleeping badly, having weird dreams. Maybe the song was part of a dream. And I've been singing it to myself ever since, like in the shower. Karen could have overheard me, and when her bad trip kicked off she imagined herself hearing the song.'

'You mean like a group hallucination?'

'More like a chain.'

She thought about it. 'I don't know . . .'

'It makes more sense than it being a ghost,' I said. 'Julia, there's always a rational explanation. This makes sense.'

I waited to see if she would buy it. I really didn't want to tell her I thought it was her. Eventually, she nodded.

'I'll talk to Karen about it in the morning,' she said.

Chapter 16

LILY – 2014

Megan's house was small but cosy. She had a black Labrador called Barney who was lovely, though he kept letting out rancid farts that made Lily and Megan squeal with horror.

'I'm going to take him to the vet if he doesn't stop,' said Megan's mum, who was really pretty and trendy. She was fun, too. She knew all about YouTube and had the radio playing in the kitchen, singing along when Little Mix came on. She poured glasses of ice-cold Coke for Lily and Megan and carried the drinks into the front room, where they were playing a video game on Megan's Xbox.

As soon as Megan's mum left the room, Megan said, 'Danny lent me this new game. Do you want to play it?'

Danny was a boy in their class. Danny was always going on about playing Call of Duty and watching gross stuff online with his older brother. 'What kind of game?'

Megan whispered, 'It's a scary game. I'm not supposed to play it, so if you hear Mum coming, yell.'

Lily shifted uncomfortably on the carpet as Megan located the game. Over by the fireplace, the dog made a groaning noise and Lily braced herself for the stink.

It was the start of the school summer holidays, the best six weeks of the year, and Lily and Megan were on what the grown-ups referred to as a playdate. Dad had dropped Lily off earlier, telling her to be good. 'Don't go off on your own,' he'd said.

'I know, I know. And don't talk to Strangers.'

'Don't worry, Mr Marsh,' Megan had said. 'We're just going to play in the garden. I've got a pack of water balloons.'

But after soaking each other with the balloons and drying off in the hot sun, they'd come inside and now they were doing what Mum said Lily was *always* doing, like it was the worst thing in the world: staring at a screen. It was massively unfair because Mum and Dad were constantly looking at their phones, even when they were supposed to be talking to each other.

Megan put on a horror-movie voice and said, 'Are you *prepared* to be *scared*?'

Lily found herself looking at a big house surrounded by winter trees. The graphics were pretty basic but effective.

'It looks like your house, doesn't it?' Megan said. 'Out there in the woods.'

'Don't say that.'

Spooky music played and Lily realised she was holding her breath as their character entered the house.

'What's in there?' she asked.

Megan's voice was hushed. 'Bloody Mary.'

'Oh God. I'm freaking out.'

Megan laughed. 'You're such a baby.'

'Shut up! No I'm not.'

On-screen, they crept through a series of empty corridors, into dark rooms filled with blocky furniture. Megan said, 'If Mary catches you she takes you into her world.'

Lily swallowed. 'What's in her world?'

Megan smiled at her. 'Freaky stuff. Time moves backwards. There are people with zips for mouths and black holes where their eyes should be. And you'll never see your mum and dad again.'

'I don't like it,' Lily said.

'You really are a wimp.'

Megan concentrated on the game for a while, eyes stretched wide, and then suddenly a dark figure jumped out at them. Bloody Mary. Megan and Lily both screamed.

Footsteps came towards the room. Megan lunged for the Xbox, turning it off before the door opened.

'What's going on?' Megan's mum asked.

'Nothing, Mum. Just Barney. He did the grossest fart ever.'

The dog rolled an eye towards them, as if he knew he was being blamed for something he hadn't done.

Megan's mum pulled him to his feet. 'Come on, you horrible mutt. You can go in the garden for a bit. Leave these poor girls alone.'

Lily felt guilty after Megan's mum and the dog had gone. Poor Barney.

Megan waited till she heard the back door open, then said, 'Have you ever done the Bloody Mary thing? You know, said her name three times in the mirror.'

'No way.'

'Shall we do it now?'

Lily had gone cold all over.

'Come on, scaredy-cat. It'll be fun.'

'Megan! No way.'

An annoyed look appeared on Megan's face and Lily was worried she wouldn't want to be her friend any more.

She was about to say okay, she'd do it, when Megan laughed and said, 'Only kidding. Everyone knows Bloody Mary's not real, anyway.' She paused. 'Unlike the Red Widow.'

The moment of relief Lily had felt was blasted away. 'What do you mean?'

Megan's voice dropped to a whisper. 'The Widow. She's real. I heard my grandad talking about her.'

'She can't be real.'

'She *is*. My grandad said she's lived around here for hundreds of years. She can't die. She's . . . what's the word?'

'Immortal?'

'Yeah. That's it. And you know she feeds on children? It's the children's blood that makes the Widow live forever.'

Lily stared at her friend, expecting her to burst into laughter and yell, 'Pranked!' But Megan's expression remained deadly serious, even a little scared. And that made Lily feel scared too, even if it was obvious the Widow didn't really exist.

They were silent for a minute. Lily wanted to go out in the garden, into the sunshine, to play with the dog and forget all about the stupid Widow and Bloody Mary and scary video games. She wanted to go home and give Chesney a big squeeze and see her mum.

They climbed up to the treehouse and Barney ran around at the foot of the tree, barking. They chucked water balloons down and he chased them, getting splashed and jumping in the air, but always coming back for more. It was hilarious. Lily forgot all about the scary stuff Megan had been talking about indoors.

Megan's mum came out into the garden.

'Girls, it's teatime. Go and wash your hands. And Megan, Grandad's here.'

'Great!' Megan climbed out of the tree and Lily followed.

There was a little bathroom just inside the house. The girls went in to wash their hands, then Lily followed Megan to the kitchen, where lunch was laid out: sandwiches and crisps and slices of cucumber; beakers of orange squash. Lily hadn't realised how hungry she was. Megan's big brother, Jake, was there already, putting his fingers all over the crisps.

Jake was fourteen but, according to Megan, was like a five-year-old on the inside. Not long after Lily met Megan, she'd witnessed her friend fight another girl who called Jake 'retarded'. Seeing the way Megan stuck up for her brother made Lily wish she had a sibling, someone she could look after. But how was that ever going to happen if her parents didn't like each other any more?

'Tuck in,' said Megan's mum.

As Lily concentrated on what food to choose – avoiding the crisps because she had a thing about food other people had touched – Megan shouted, 'Grandad!'

Lily looked up as Megan threw herself into the arms of a stocky bald man who'd come into the kitchen. He gave Megan a hug and whirled her round, laughing, then saw Lily. He put Megan down.

'Hello,' he said.

Lily stared at him. She knew him. He was the man who'd tried to help her when she fell off her bike. The man with crooked teeth.

The Stranger.

Chapter 17

Karen stood on the doorstep of the retreat with her suitcase at her feet. The sun was out for the first time in months, and the breeze was soft against my face. Spring was finally here.

'Are you sure you don't want to stay?' I asked.

'I can't. Not after last night.' She hung her head. 'I'm so embarrassed.'

'Don't be. So what are you going to do?'

She lifted a shoulder. 'Just go home, see the doctor, flush my stash down the toilet. Finish my goddamn book. Maybe the countryside doesn't suit me. I need to be surrounded by people. The nights are too quiet here and my brain is too noisy.'

'I get that.'

The taxi trundled up the driveway towards us. It was the same car, the same driver, who'd given me a lift when I got lost in the woods. Olly, that was his name. He got out and hefted Karen's bag into the boot, nodding at me and muttering, 'All right?'

'Did Julia talk to you about last night?' I asked Karen.

'She tried. She asked me if I'd ever heard you singing this weird song. Something about a fly.'

'And what did you say?'

'That I couldn't remember, but it was possible.'

That was good.

'We'd better get a move on if you're going to make your train,' Olly said. I gave Karen a quick hug and watched her go. Now, unless another writer turned up, it was going to be just me and the lovebirds. That was another thing that made me wonder. Less than a week ago, Suzi had been upset with Max for trying to get into her room, and now she was inviting him in. What happened? Had he worn her down? Perhaps her original protests had been exaggerated.

As Max had reminded me, it was none of my business.

I went inside and found Julia in her usual spot by the Aga, phone to her ear. She finished her conversation and sighed.

'That was the National Bat Helpline. They said it's quite unusual to find a bat in the attic at this time of year. But if you have a bat roost, as it seems I do, you have to leave well alone. It's illegal to disturb them.' A little smile. 'I'm actually quite happy about them being there. It's cool, isn't it? It's nice to give them a home.'

She drummed her fingers on the table.

'Have you heard any other noises coming from Lily's room?' she asked.

'No.' I watched as she chewed her lip. She was a mess of tics and visible tension. 'Julia, did you see a counsellor after Lily disappeared? It might help . . .'

She reacted angrily. 'The police offered a grief counsellor. I reminded them that there's no proof she's dead.'

'But—'

'I know. I know Michael is dead and I should have seen a counsellor to talk about losing him, but I couldn't. I knew they'd want to talk to me about Lily, that they'd try to make me accept that she was dead too. So I didn't go. I couldn't.'

I nodded. I wasn't sure if she was right about what the counsellor might do – the one I'd seen had mainly listened and given me a chance to talk – but I understood that it was complicated. She couldn't separate what had happened to Michael from what might have happened to Lily.

It seemed as if Lily's disappearance had robbed Julia of the ability to deal with her husband's death.

'Come with me,' she said, getting up.

A minute later, we stood outside Lily's bedroom. Julia opened the door and gestured for me to follow her inside. As she stepped across the threshold, her breathing became noticeably heavier. She held a hand against her chest, and I could imagine her heart thumping beneath her palm. She clenched her jaw, as if fighting against physical pain.

'It's exactly as it was the day she disappeared,' she said.

It was a typical little girl's room. Pink curtains, open to let in the morning light. A single bed against the wall, covered with a purple-and-white bedspread, little cushions propped up against the headboard. A dressing table covered with trinkets. Little dresses hung from a rail. A bookcase bearing novels by authors like Roald Dahl and David Walliams, along with a book about folk tales that caught my eye. On the wall, a 2014 Taylor Swift calendar, along with posters featuring fresh-faced stars I didn't recognise.

'Most of them are YouTubers,' Julia said. 'Michael was always complaining about how much time she spent watching videos.'

I noticed an iPad on the bedside table.

'I come in here every couple of weeks to charge it. I know she'll want to watch it when she comes home. She'll have a lot to catch up on.'

There was a huge pile of cuddly toys in the corner, every animal imaginable. On top of the pile was a large black-and-white cat, a smile sewn onto its face.

'That's Big Cat,' Julia said.

I sucked in a breath. 'The one that was in the river?'

She nodded. 'The police kept him for a while, but they let me have him back.' She picked the toy up, pressed her nose against its scruffy fur. 'He still smells of the river.'

She set it back on top of the pile.

'Lily loved cats,' she said. 'She was obsessed with them from the first moment she saw one, when she was a baby. It was actually her first word. Not "Mummy" or "Daddy" . . . "Cat". And she always had two toys she loved more than anything. I think she might have loved them even more than she adored Chesney. Big Cat and Little Cat.'

I looked around.

'Little Cat was in her coat pocket when she vanished. I think . . . I'm sure she still has him with her.' Julia's eyes shone and she had to take a moment to compose herself. 'I hope he's looking after her.'

'I'm sure he is.'

She sat down on the bed. 'Do you think I'm crazy?'

'Crazy? Of course not.'

'I'm sure most people think I am. They think I should clear out this room, move on, but I can't.' She was trembling, one of her knees jerking up and down, her heel tapping against the floor.

Tears rolled down her cheeks. There was a box of tissues by the bed. I plucked one out and handed it to her. I wanted to put my arms around her, to comfort her – a basic human response – but had no idea if it would be welcomed.

When the tears had abated, I said, 'I understand why you leave this room as it is.'

'You do?'

I wanted to tell her that I understood because, even knowing Priya was dead, it had taken months for me to gather the strength to put away her things. Even now, they were all in boxes. I couldn't take that final step – to remove her possessions from the flat. But I didn't think now was the time to bring it up. This conversation was about Julia and Lily.

I also couldn't tell her about my investigation into Lily's disappearance. Not yet, when there was nothing concrete to share.

'If I knew she was dead,' Julia said, 'I could . . . take action . . .'

I wasn't sure what she meant by that, but nodded.

'But I'm stuck.' She looked up at me, eyes pink and sore. 'It's like I dived into that river two years ago. And I'm still under the water, holding my breath.'

ω

I went back to my room, feeling helpless and useless, wishing there was something I could do to help Julia, knowing only one thing would actually work: finding out what had happened to Lily. And that reminded me – Zara still hadn't called me back or responded to my messages. The notification beneath my last message said *Delivered*, not *Read*. When had I last heard from her? Time was beginning to blur, but it was the day before yesterday, in the pub.

I called her, and again she didn't answer. What was going on? Had she given up? She could at least have the decency to answer my calls.

I ought to be writing my novel, but there was no way I could concentrate now.

I grabbed my car keys. I was going to look for Zara.

Chapter 18

I pulled up outside the Apple Tree bed and breakfast, where Zara was staying. It was a few streets back from the river on a long, quiet road with plenty of parking spaces. An elderly woman struggled home with bags of heavy shopping. A young father pushed a buggy containing a sleeping toddler. They were the only people around. The town had an abandoned feel to it, like there had been an evacuation. On a nearby lamp post, a tatty paper sign appealed for the return of a missing cat. *Last seen 23rd June 2015*. Two years ago. I hadn't seen any posters about Lily. Maybe that was because everyone assumed she had drowned.

I rang the bell and a woman in her sixties answered.

'Are you after a room?' she asked. Her hair was dyed auburn and a cross hung around her neck on a gold chain.

'I was actually looking for a friend of mine. Zara Sullivan. I believe she's staying here.'

'Come on in,' she said. I followed her into a cosy sitting room. A little dog with grey fur snoozed on the sofa. It lifted its head to regard me, then went back to sleep, snoring gently.

'I'm Shirley and this is Oscar,' she said.

A painting of Christ hung above the fireplace. On another wall, a tapestry with a quote from the Bible: *Hate what is evil; cling to what is good.*

'Romans 12:9,' she said. 'Are you a believer, Mr . . . ?'

'Radcliffe.'

She peered at me. Her eyes were milky, unfocused. Cataracts. 'Radcliffe. You're not David's son, are you?'

Of course. She was the same age as my parents. 'Yes. Yes, I am.'

'Well, look at you. All grown-up. And very handsome too. Not that I'm surprised – your father was always a very good-looking man. How is he?'

'He passed away,' I said.

Her face crumpled. 'What happened?'

'Cancer.'

'Oh.' Her hand went to the cross around her neck. 'So he was the first.'

'The first?' I asked, but there was no response. 'Shirley?'

She fell into an armchair, still gripping the cross with one hand. She stared into space, into the past.

'Are you all right, Mum?'

The voice from the doorway made me jump. It was a woman in her early forties with curly reddish hair. She wore jeans and a tight black T-shirt. She was curvy with long limbs, pale skin and, strikingly, a tattoo of a red rose on her upper arm, the petals disappearing beneath her sleeve. She laughed, which made her look even more attractive. 'Sorry, didn't mean to startle you.'

Shirley snapped out of her trance. 'My apologies. I was taking a trip down memory lane. This is my daughter, Heledd.'

'Pleased to meet you,' I said.

'What about your mum?' Shirley asked me. 'Is she in good health?'

'She's great.' I explained how she and Dad had moved to Spain before he died, and that Mum was still out there.

'They got away,' Shirley said. 'From this place, I mean. It used to be a thriving town, you know. The Apple Tree was always full up, but these days I can go weeks without anyone coming to stay. It's not surprising, I suppose. Sad, but not surprising. It's a punishment.'

Before I could ask what that meant, Heledd rolled her eyes. She crouched beside Shirley, laying a hand on the arm of the chair. 'It's not that bad. We get by, don't we, Mum?'

Shirley patted her hand. 'I don't know what I'd do without you. My angel.' Her eyes brimmed with tears. 'It's been quite a week for terrible news. First Malcolm, then this.'

'Malcolm Jones? The librarian?'

'Did you know him?' Heledd asked in a surprised tone.

'No. Well, not really. Sorry, what do you mean, *did* I know him? Has something happened?'

'It was his heart,' Shirley said, laying a hand across her own, as if checking it was still beating. 'He's suffered with a heart condition for years so it wasn't a terrible shock. Dreadful, though. He was a good man, but he'll be with Sylvia now.'

I assumed that was his wife.

'When did it happen?' I asked.

'Only yesterday.' Shirley patted her daughter's hand again. 'How is Olly coping?'

'He's okay.'

Shirley nodded. 'He's a good lad. Like his father.' She turned to me. 'I keep hoping Olly will make an honest woman of her.'

Olly? That was the name of the taxi driver. Olly Jones. So he was Malcolm's son, and here was his girlfriend. It was a small town, all right, with a limited dating pool. But now, hearing about Malcolm's death, I was even more keen to talk to Zara.

'So, my friend, Zara. Is she here?'

The dog jumped onto Shirley's lap and she ran a hand along its flank. She'd retreated inside her head again. Away with the fairies, as my mum would say.

'Zara Sullivan?' Heledd said. 'She's gone.'

Her words didn't sink in immediately. 'Gone?'

'Yes, she went yesterday. Packed up, paid her bill and went.'

'But . . . *I* was supposed to be paying for the room. Did she leave a message?'

'No, she said something about her business here being done.'

I swore under my breath. How could she abandon the investigation without telling me? She was eccentric, sure, but I hadn't taken her for a flake. Maybe she'd paid for the room herself because she felt guilty, and she wasn't answering her phone simply because she didn't want an argument with a disappointed client.

But then I thought about how oddly she'd behaved in the pub the other evening, and how jumpy she'd seemed. Had something scared her away?

'How did she seem yesterday?' I asked.

Heledd took a seat on the sofa and crossed her legs. One Converse-clad foot bounced up and down. 'This is very intriguing. What do you mean?'

'Was she acting nervously, or was she relaxed?'

'She seemed absolutely fine to me. She came down for breakfast, ate three rounds of toast and we made small talk. She told me all about a case she'd once worked, something about a guy who went missing. They eventually found him chained up in a sex dungeon. He'd paid the dominatrix to keep him as her slave. We had a giggle over it.'

'She didn't say anything about the case she was working here?'

'No. Just something about hitting a dead end.'

'And you're sure she didn't seem scared?'

'I'm sure. Why, is there something she should have been scared of?'

'I don't know.'

I said goodbye to Shirley, and Heledd saw me out. As I was about to leave, something occurred to me.

'What did your mum mean when she said "it's a punishment"?'

'Who knows? Mum's always talking about sin and divine retribution. Devils with red-hot pokers. I spent my childhood being warned that if I didn't clear my plate or tidy my room I'd be punished by God. Or worse.'

'The Devil, you mean?'

'Oh no. Not *him*.'

She closed the door.

ʊ

Now what? I needed to know if Zara had discovered anything else. Had she met with Malcolm Jones before he died?

I tried calling Zara's office number, but there was no answer. I sent an email from my phone, asking her to call me.

A minute later, my phone pinged.

It was Zara, replying.

> Hey Lucas. Really sorry, but I decided to head home. I wasn't getting anywhere and I couldn't stand being in that B&B a moment longer.
>
> Don't worry about my fee. I didn't get anywhere and don't think anyone ever will. That girl is long gone. It's a total waste of time looking for her. Sorry again! Zara

Damn. So was that it? The end of the investigation? It was hard to accept that it was all over, just like that, even though a voice in my ear whispered that it was a good thing, that I was wasting time on a wild goose chase.

The voice also reminded me that I needed to get back to the retreat, do some work. I still had over three-quarters of my novel to write, and I was never going to get it done if I didn't buckle down to it. I'd been ignoring emails from my agent and editor, both asking when I expected to be finished. I needed to do what I'd originally come here for.

I was desperate to help Julia. But I had no idea what to do next, or who to talk to.

Chapter 19

LILY – 2014

.

Halfway through tea, Megan's grandad narrowed his eyes at her and said, 'Where do I know you from?'

Lily took a sip of orange squash. She found it hard to reply – it was like there was something stuck in her throat – and she had to take another sip before the words could get through. 'In the park. You helped me when I fell off my bike.'

He clapped his hands together. 'Of course! Well I never.'

'What a coincidence,' said Megan's mum, smiling at Lily.

'It is a small town,' Megan's grandad said. 'We all know each other. Although I haven't met your parents properly yet, Lily. What do they do? For a job, I mean.'

Megan's grandad had a crumb stuck to his lower lip which wobbled when he spoke. Lily stared at it, convinced it would drop at any second, but it clung on.

'My mum's an illustrator and my dad does stuff with computers.'

His eyebrows arched up towards his shiny head. 'What would you like to be when you grow up?'

She shrugged. She hated it when grown-ups asked that. 'I haven't figured it out yet.'

'I want to be a pop star,' Megan said. 'I'm going to be in a group and I'll be famous.' She broke into song and her grandad beamed, his eyes shining with love and pride, until Megan's mum told her to be quiet and eat her tea.

This meal was stretching on forever. Lily really wanted to get away from Megan's grandad. She didn't know why, but it was as if she were allergic to him in the same way she was allergic to lambswool, which made her skin prickle and break out in a rash. She had seen how Chesney reacted when a dog walked past, his back going up and his tail getting fat. That's how Megan's grandad made her feel, even though he'd helped her in the park and he was being nice to her now and Megan clearly thought he was the bee's knees.

Megan's mum's phone rang. She took it over to the back door to talk to whoever it was. When the call ended, she came back and said, 'Lily, that was your mum. She's not going to be able to pick you up.'

'Sleepover!' yelled Megan.

Lily ignored her. 'Why not? Has something happened?'

Megan's mum put a hand on Lily's arm. 'Relax. It's nothing bad. There's something wrong with the car, that's all. She asked if I can run you home.'

'Sleepover?' Megan tried again.

'Megan, Lily hasn't got any of her stuff with her. And we have to go out first thing tomorrow.' She looked at Jake, whose face was covered in jam and peanut butter, his clothes like the 'before' in an advert for washing powder.

'I can take her home,' Megan's grandad said.

No no no!

'Oh, could you? That would be so helpful.'

'It's no bother.' He grinned at Lily with his mouthful of crooked teeth. 'No bother at all.'

ʊ

131

Megan's grandad had a grey car that was spotless inside, cleaner than her parents' car had ever been. Lily sat in the front passenger seat on Megan's booster. It was incredibly annoying that she still had to sit on a booster despite being eight. She wound down the window to say goodbye.

'I really wanted to have a sleepover,' Megan said.

'Next time,' said her mum.

'So you live at Nyth Bran?' Megan's grandad said once they were on the main road. It was still bright and warm outside, the summer evening stretching on forever. But it was hot and stuffy in the car and Lily felt sick.

'Uh-huh.'

'Do you know what Nyth Bran means, Lily?'

'Nest of the crow.'

'That's right. I'm impressed.'

'My mum told me.'

He kept looking at her instead of the road. He mainly concentrated on her face, but sometimes his gaze slipped further down to her bare legs. It filled her with a peculiar sensation, like millions of little worms wriggling under her skin.

'Did you have fun today, with Megan? She told me you were playing her new computer game.'

She nodded.

'I don't understand the appeal of those things, myself. Give me a game of chess any day. Do you play chess, Lily?'

'Yeah. My dad taught me.'

'That's marvellous. Maybe you can give me a game sometime, though you have to give me a chance.'

He hissed with laughter.

'So, how long have you lived here, Lily?'

He was one of those grown-ups who always said your name, even when you were the only other person around. Like he had to keep saying it or he'd forget what it was.

'Since last September.'

'Oh, not long. That'll be why I don't know your family. They keep themselves to themselves, don't they?'

She had no idea what to say to that.

'Where did you live before?'

'Manchester.'

'United fan, are you?' He showed her his crooked teeth again. They were yellow too. He must have a rubbish dentist. Or maybe he never cleaned them. His eyes, which were also a bit yellowy where they ought to be white, roamed down to her legs again.

'City,' she managed.

He started going on about how different it must be living here after growing up in a big city. It was such a familiar topic that it calmed her a little. She stopped gripping the seat so tightly, and noticed how her hands had made sweaty marks on the black leather.

'Dangerous places, cities . . .' Megan's grandad said.

They were halfway there now. Five more minutes and she'd be home.

'Still, it can be dangerous around here too,' he said.

'Because of the witch?' she whispered.

His eyes flicked sideways and she could tell he was mulling over what to say. There was no other traffic on the road but they were going slowly, as if he didn't want to take her home anytime soon. A smile crept over his dry lips, which he kept licking between sentences.

'A little girl disappeared around here,' he said. 'A long time ago now. Over thirty years. She lived at St Mary's children's home, in town.'

Lily could hardly breathe. 'What was her name?'

'Carys.'

He kept grinning and Lily realised something. He was one of those grown-ups who enjoyed scaring children. That was why he told Megan stories about the Widow. He got some kind of weird thrill out of it.

That didn't make what he was saying any less frightening, though.

'What happened to her?'

'That's the thing. Nobody knows. She was never found. And you know what? She wasn't the first.'

There was a long, long silence, which stretched out until they reached the driveway to Lily's house. She exhaled with relief and fiddled with the door handle, desperate to get out. Megan's grandad's jaw muscles flexed like he was chewing over something, and the way he stared ahead, it was as if he wasn't seeing the road – he was seeing something inside his head.

'Here we are, Lily,' he said as they pulled up outside the house.

'Thank you.'

'I'm sure I'll see you again soon.'

She opened the door and was so keen to get away she almost fell out of the car. Behind her, Mum came out of the house, raising a hand to thank Megan's grandad. He waved back.

Lily was about to shut the car door when he leaned over and said, in a hushed voice, 'Lily. Be careful, yes?'

She watched him drive away, trying hard not to throw up.

PART TWO

Chapter 20

Over the next week or so, I settled into a routine, the kind I'd envisioned when I booked a place at the retreat. Each morning I rose at dawn to write, fuelled by coffee, hardly seeing the rain that, day after day, beat against the window. My novel had taken on a momentum of its own, the threads of the story knitting together, and I was able to email my agent and publisher to tell them the book would be a couple of weeks late, but no more.

I didn't see much of Julia during this quiet period, except at mealtimes or when I popped outside for some air. I didn't see much of Max or Suzi either. They had both announced they had extended their stays as they were making such good progress on their novels – there was clearly something in the air – but I wasn't sure if they were still sleeping together. I didn't really care.

I didn't hear any singing that week. No mysterious passages appeared in my novel. There may have been events I was unaware of – I was so buried in my work a headless horseman could have ridden through the kitchen downstairs and I wouldn't have known about it – but, as I recall, the week passed without incident.

Then a new guest arrived. And everything changed.

ᴡ

I skipped dinner because I was deep in a chapter and not particularly hungry, but went downstairs at around eight to get a drink. There was a hubbub coming from the Thomas Room, including a voice I didn't recognise.

Julia was in the kitchen. When I'd seen her during the past week she'd been withdrawn and businesslike, and I suspected she felt awkward after crying in my presence, exposing her emotions. She had wrapped a cloak of self-preservation around herself again. Now I felt awkward too, and found myself tiptoeing around her. There had been a moment when I thought that we would, at the least, become friends. But that moment appeared to have passed. I'd allowed it to happen. Partly it was because I didn't know how to help her – now I'd given up on my secret quest to find Lily – but there was something else. Guilt.

I was pretty sure Priya would have liked Julia. I was less sure she would want me to start any kind of relationship with her. Even thinking Julia was attractive felt like a betrayal. And the whole thing was one-sided anyway, I reminded myself. Julia didn't like me in that way. I was being ridiculous even thinking about it.

Julia smiled at me. 'Lucas. You missed dinner. Do you want anything?'

'I'm fine, thanks.'

A burst of male laughter came from the Thomas Room.

'A new guest,' she said. 'You should go and meet her. She's quite a character.' She rolled her eyes and laughed, a slightly giddy laugh. I did a double take. Had she been drinking? Surely not.

She busied herself stacking the dishwasher.

'Do you want a hand?' I asked.

'No, go and meet the new guest.'

A fire burned in the hearth, bathing the room in a warm, flickering light. Max was on the sofa, with Suzi beside him.

Another woman sat in the armchair opposite. I guessed she was in her fifties. She had a dark Louise Brooks bob and wore several heavy necklaces. She was watching Max with an earnest, slightly perplexed expression.

As I came into the room, Max said, 'Ah, the reclusive horror writer. Lucas, this is Ursula.'

'Ursula Clarke,' she said in a moneyed voice. Her name rang a vague bell, but she clearly expected me to have heard of her.

They were, I realised, holding wine glasses. A half-empty bottle stood on the coffee table. Had Julia rescinded the alcohol ban? It seemed as if my guess that Julia was tipsy had been correct after all.

'Ursula wrote *The Spirit's Whisper*,' Max said, with a little smirk. When Ursula wasn't looking, he winked at Suzi, who didn't respond. She was studying Ursula with interest.

'Oh, I've heard of that,' I said. 'It was a huge bestseller, wasn't it?'

'A million copies sold,' Ursula replied, faux-nonchalantly.

'Ten years ago,' Max said.

Ursula's jaw tightened and I felt a wave of sympathy. She was in the exact situation I dreaded: a flash of success followed by years of obscurity. The curse of the one-hit wonder.

'Remind me what it was about?' I said. 'Sorry, I have a terrible memory.'

'It was about my relationship with my spirit guide,' Ursula said. 'How she counselled me, told me secrets, helped show me the way towards wealth and happiness.'

'I have an agent for all that,' laughed Max.

Ursula wasn't amused.

'I'm used to mockery,' she said.

'I think it sounds fascinating.' I sat down. Of course, I actually thought it was a load of hokum, but I wanted to get one over on Max and, like I said, I felt sorry for Ursula. 'Tell me about it.'

'You might need a drink first,' said Max, pouring one for me. He handed me the glass and I took a sip. Red wine, thick and delicious.

'What happened to the booze ban?' I asked.

'I don't know.' Max scratched his head. 'We came down for dinner tonight and there it was. Like a wonderful apparition.'

Ursula made a little *hem-hem* noise in her throat. 'I think you might have me to thank. Julia told me about the dry nature of this place when I called to enquire about booking. I told her how absurd it was. A place for writers with no alcohol? I said if she wanted this to be a viable business she needed to get down to the nearest wine merchant, pronto.'

Max raised his glass. 'A toast to Ursula.'

Suzi raised hers too. I didn't join in. As pleased as I was to have a glass of wine in my hand, I was the only one who suspected why Julia had an aversion to drink.

'Anyway, Lucas, I was about to tell you about spirit guides.' Ursula put down her glass and sat back.

'All of us, even Max here, have a spirit guide. Someone who watches over us and helps us on our journey through this life. Tell me, Lucas, do you ever feel as if someone is watching you, looking after you? Perhaps you glimpse a presence sometimes, when you're dreaming or in moments of high emotion.'

Her words made my skin prickle. Because sometimes I did feel as if I were being watched, especially since Priya's death. Especially, in fact, since I'd come here.

She went on. 'Some people, such as myself, are unusually sensitive. We are able to communicate directly with our guide. She tells me if someone has plans to harm me, and she tells me who I can trust. She also helps me communicate with the deceased too, so they can pass on their wisdom.'

'Does she have a name?' I asked.

'Of course. Phoebe.'

'And did Phoebe used to be . . . a flesh-and-blood person?'

'Oh yes. But hundreds of years ago.' She smiled, although there was a hint of sadness there, as if Ursula were talking about an old friend she hadn't seen for a long time.

'The good news,' she said, 'is that Heaven is real. As soon as I realised that, I no longer feared death – and I truly started to live.'

She allowed me to top up her wine glass along with my own. At the same time, Julia put her head around the door and said goodnight. As I heard her go up the stairs, it hit me, right in the stomach. I missed her. Missed the connection we'd made.

Ursula noticed. 'You like her, don't you?'

I winced, but Max and Suzi hadn't heard, as far as I could tell.

'A lot of men are drawn to women with emotional pain,' she said.

I cut her off. I wasn't that type of man. 'No. It's her inner strength that I like.'

'Oh, so you *do* like her.'

She grinned, and I couldn't help but smile too. 'I like her. But that doesn't mean I *like* her.'

Ursula leaned forward. Her mouth was stained red from the wine. 'You can't fool me,' she said. 'Remember. I see things.'

'Is that how you know she's in pain? Because your spirit guide told you?'

She smiled. 'Actually, it was a taxi driver.'

Ursula waited until Julia's footsteps were no longer audible and said, 'The cabbie who brought me here from the station told me all about what happened to Julia's husband and daughter.'

The others were tuned in now. Max looked as if he were watching a news bulletin announcing that a UFO had landed in Trafalgar Square.

'What did he tell you?' I asked.

Ursula repeated pretty much what Olly, the taxi driver, had told me. 'And they never found her,' she said in a theatrical whisper.

'Oh, poor Julia,' said Suzi.

'Hang on,' said Max to me. 'You knew about this?'

'The same taxi driver told me.'

'And you didn't share?'

'Why should I? I don't think it's right to gossip about Julia's pain.'

Ursula flapped a hand. 'Nonsense. It's not gossip. As Max says, it's sharing. People should be more open with one another. How else are we ever supposed to understand our fellows?'

'Are you quoting from your book?' I asked.

Suzi was staring into space. 'Maybe that's what Karen heard,' she said. 'The little girl's ghost.'

They both looked at Ursula, as if she might know the answer. She was loving it. Before I could interject, she said, 'It's possible. Spirits can become trapped in this realm . . . It could be that she is kept here by her mother's pain, unable to enter Heaven.'

'Oh my God,' I said to Max and Suzi. 'Do you really believe all this?'

'No, of course not,' Max said. 'Sorry, Ursula.'

'This whole thing is making me sick,' I said. 'Can you imagine what Julia's been through? Watching her husband drown? Not knowing what happened to Lily? That's why—' I stopped myself in the nick of time.

'Why what?' Max asked.

'Nothing. But please, can we stop talking about ghosts and spirits?'

'Want to save it for your books, eh? I understand.' Max's smile was condescending.

I stood up and my head span. I must have had more to drink than I realised. 'I'm going to bed,' I announced.

'Watch out for ghosts and ghoulies,' Max laughed as I exited the room.

I showed him my middle finger.

I went into the kitchen to get a glass of water. When I came out, I could hear Ursula talking, loud and indiscreet.

'It is possible,' she said. 'Perhaps Lily's spirit is with us. And maybe she doesn't want us here. She wants to be alone with her mother.'

.

Chapter 21

I jerked awake. It was pitch-black in the room, the kind of darkness you never get in cities, and my heart was pounding as if I'd awoken from a nightmare I couldn't remember. I squinted into the blackness, unable to see anything except spots of colour, indeterminate shapes shifting and blurring. But I was convinced someone else was in the room.

'Hello?' I said, my voice louder than I'd intended.

Someone was breathing on the far side of the bedroom. I was sure of it. I could smell something too. Dirt, or sweat. Fear.

I groped for my phone, which I was certain I'd left on the bedside table. I couldn't find it. I tried to locate the lamp, blind in the utter darkness. Finally, my fingers found the plastic switch and I pressed it.

Nothing happened.

For a moment, I was paralysed, willing my useless eyes to adjust. The air around me was dark grey now. And I was certain there was a darker shape across the room.

A person. Watching me.

The bedroom door opened with a click. Oh Jesus, there *was* someone there. Immediately, it closed again.

I jumped out of bed, found the light switch on the wall. The sudden light dazzled me, burning my retinas. Recovering, I stared at the door. Was the intruder still there, on the other side? I hadn't heard footsteps moving away. I was dressed in nothing but my underwear. I pulled a T-shirt over my head and opened the door.

The hallway was illuminated by watery moonlight that crept through the window at the far end. There was no one in sight. I hesitated. Which way had they gone? I stood between the two staircases, made a choice and headed down.

A clattering came from the kitchen. I froze for a minute. Did I need a weapon? There was a poker by the fireplace in the Thomas Room. I could go in there, grab that, then . . .

Before I could make my mind up, someone came out of the kitchen.

Suzi. She gasped, slapping a hand against her chest. 'Lucas. What are you doing? You nearly scared me to death.'

She was fully dressed, holding a mug of tea or coffee in her other hand. Some of it had sloshed over the edge of the mug when she'd seen me. She noticed what had happened and hurried back into the kitchen, returning with a cloth.

'What are you doing up?' I asked.

'I haven't been to sleep yet,' she said. 'And no, before you ask, I wasn't with Max.'

'It's none of my business.'

'True. Anyway, I was working. What are *you* doing up?'

I dodged the question. 'Did you see anyone come down here?'

'No. Although I might not have heard them because the kettle was boiling right next to me. Why?'

'Hang on.' I ran back up the stairs, and continued to the next floor. I checked both ends of the hallway, even poking my head into the broom closet. I glanced up at the attic. There was no way someone could have got up there without making a great commotion getting the ladder down. Whoever it was had vanished. They must have snuck out the front door and would be long gone now.

I went back to the ground floor and joined Suzi in the kitchen.

'Are you going to tell me what's going on?' she asked. 'Like why you're walking around in your boxer shorts?'

'There was someone in my room.'

Her eyes widened. 'What? Are you sure?'

'My door opened and closed. I heard them leave the room.'

'Are you sure you weren't dreaming?'

'I'm certain.'

She looked at me sceptically and I caught sight of my reflection in the window. My hair was sticking up in a mad-professor style. I could smell the alcohol on my breath too.

'You were pretty het up when you went to bed,' she said. 'That happens to me sometimes. If I go to bed angry or upset I have bad dreams.'

'It felt real,' I insisted.

'Well . . . is there anything missing from your room?' she asked.

I went upstairs, Suzi following, and entered my room. Had anything gone? My laptop was still on the desk, my notebook beside it.

'I had a pen, right here,' I said.

'I mislay pens all the time,' Suzi said.

'No, you don't understand. This was a special pen. I always know exactly where it is.'

Priya had given it to me for my birthday, shortly before I started to make notes for *Sweetmeat*. It was the last thing she ever gave me. It wasn't hugely expensive, but it was valuable to me, and not just because she had given it to me. I'd used it to rough out the outline of my breakout book. I might pride myself on being a rationalist but I was superstitious about this pen. It was my equivalent of Samson's hair. The thought of losing it made me go cold.

'Hang on,' I said, noticing the absence of something else. 'Where's my phone?'

It wasn't on the bedside table. I checked between the table and the bed. It wasn't there. I looked in the pocket of my jeans, where I sometimes left it. I pulled the quilt off and lifted the pillows. I was convinced

I was going to find it, and that Suzi would think I'd imagined the whole thing. But the phone was nowhere to be seen. I half pulled the room apart, searching for it and the pen.

'See,' I said. 'They've gone. Pen and phone. Someone's taken them. Now do you believe me?'

She scanned the room, very slowly, and wrapped her arms around herself. 'I believe you,' she said with the smallest shudder in her voice. 'But who?'

'I don't know.'

Her eyes widened. 'What if Ursula's right?'

I scoffed. 'What? You think a ghost took my stuff?'

She sat on my bed. It was 3 a.m. The world outside was silent. I'd woken up convinced someone was in my room, after spending the evening talking to someone about spirits and ghosts. Over the past couple of weeks I had heard nocturnal singing from the room next door, birthday candles had extinguished themselves, Karen had fled this place after hearing a voice threatening her, and Suzi had experienced someone trying to open her door. It was hard to remain wholly rational.

'I must admit,' Suzi said, 'I'm feeling pretty freaked out right now.'

'Listen. Ghosts don't steal people's phones.' I sat beside her on the bed. 'Also, why would a spirit need to open and close the door? They'd just drift right through it, wouldn't they?'

That elicited a smile. 'True. It's just . . . everything Ursula says, about spirit guides and Heaven. Wouldn't it be amazing if it was true? It's like . . . if Julia believed in Heaven, maybe she would be able to accept that Lily isn't coming back.'

The adrenaline drained from my system and I yawned.

'I should let you sleep,' Suzi said.

'I don't think I'll sleep now.'

She looked at me. 'I can stay if you want.' Hurriedly, she added, 'I mean, to keep you company.'

'It's okay,' I said, not sure if I was relieved or disappointed that she wasn't offering to sleep with me. This was a very confusing night. 'I might try to get some writing done. I should take advantage of the mood.'

'Sure.' She got up. Hesitated. 'I was thinking. Maybe we should ask Ursula to talk to Julia. It might comfort her.'

'I really don't think so. She's never going to accept that Lily is dead. Not unless she sees proof.'

Suzi said goodnight and left me alone in the silence. I lay down, intending to rest my eyes for a minute before starting work.

ʊ

Sunlight dragged me from sleep. Groggy and hung over, I got dressed and headed outside, hoping a kick of cold air might make me feel more human.

Ursula was in the front garden, by the fence that Rhodri had fixed, wearing an expensive-looking red coat. She saw me and waved me over, smiling broadly. It was a bright, mild morning. Low clouds hung over the distant mountains, and the trees in Julia's garden were alive with blossom. Birds passed overhead, returning from hotter climes. Apart from their calls, a hush hung over the land.

'Such a wonderful place, isn't it?' Ursula said. She was, I noticed, almost shaking, giving off the air of someone who'd just won the lottery. 'I knew it . . . I knew if I came somewhere quiet, away from the city . . .'

'Sorry, you've lost me,' I said.

Her eyes shone. 'Last night. Phoebe spoke to me. Oh, it was so wonderful to hear her again! I thought I'd lost my gift, that I was being punished for sharing the secret with the world and benefitting materially from it.' She grabbed my wrist. 'But she's back. She's back!'

For a moment I thought she was about to fall to her knees and raise her face to the sky, to give thanks. Despite my cynicism about such things, her excitement was contagious.

147

But then she said, 'Phoebe told me about you, Lucas. About your loss.'
I stared at her.

'You deserve to be happy, and maybe you could make Julia happy too.'

'How do you know about . . . ?' I stopped myself. Perhaps she didn't really know anything, but was fishing, making guesses like those self-proclaimed clairvoyants who make broad statements and convince their victims they have real insight.

Then again, she might have found a story about Priya online. I had forbidden my publicist from telling anyone about my girlfriend's death because I didn't want it to look like I was capitalising on tragedy. I'd worried it might leak, that a journalist would find out and write a story: *TRAGIC PAST OF BESTSELLING AUTHOR*. But, fortunately, the press weren't interested in authors and books, not unless your name was J. K. Rowling. The only explanation, if she wasn't guessing, was that she'd called her agent or publisher and asked about me.

It made me feel violated.

'I don't have time for this,' I said.

I half-jogged back to the house, Ursula's words ringing in my ears. Suddenly, I had a bad feeling about her coming here. I muttered a curse to myself as I entered the kitchen.

'Are you all right?'

It was Julia. She was seated at the breakfast bar, writing in a black ledger. I couldn't think of a suitable response. I didn't want to worry her by telling her about my nocturnal intruder. And I definitely didn't want to recount my conversation with Ursula.

She filled the silence. 'You seem a bit out of it.'

'Do I? I didn't sleep well, and I can't find my phone. I feel lost without it.'

'I'm sure it will turn up.' She carried on making notes for a minute, then said, 'I saw you in the garden, talking to Ursula. I told you she was a character.'

'That's one way of putting it.'

'You don't like her?'

I hesitated before saying, 'I felt sorry for her at first. But now I think . . . well, I think she's dangerous.'

Julia put down her pen, which I squinted at to check it wasn't mine. 'That's a bit extreme, isn't it?'

'No. She—'

'Hang on, she's coming.'

Ursula entered the kitchen. 'Has the kettle just boiled? I could murder a chamomile.'

Julia smiled at my grimace. 'Coming right up.' She reached for a box of herbal teabags. 'I've got some biscuits here somewhere. Shortbread.' She opened a cupboard and frowned. 'That's weird.'

'Can't you find them?'

'No. They were definitely here yesterday. Maybe one of the guests took them.' She tutted. 'Someone's been helping themselves to my tampons out of the bathroom too.' She picked the teabags up again.

I was about to tell Julia about Karen's missing sandwich when Ursula said, 'I just saw a little girl outside.'

Julia dropped the box of teabags. They scattered over the counter. 'What did you say?' All the colour had drained from her face.

Ursula gestured towards the window. 'There was a little girl, just beyond that field beside the house, on the edge of the woods.'

'How old was she?' Julia said. 'What did she look like?'

'Well, my eyesight isn't what it used to be . . .'

'Tell me!'

'About ten, I think. Brown hair. Skinny as a pole.'

Julia dashed out of the kitchen and through the front door. Ursula stared after her, then turned to me.

'What the hell are you up to?' I demanded.

'I'm not up to anything, dear. Simply reporting what I saw.'

I shook my head, then followed Julia out the door. I found her standing by the fence at the far end of the garden, gazing across the field of overgrown grass.

'Lily was always searching for Chesney in this field,' she said. 'Michael told her something about there being rabbits here – not that I've ever seen one – and Lily became convinced it was Chesney's hunting ground.'

'This is what I mean about Ursula being dangerous,' I said. 'She's trying to fill your head with nonsense about spirits and apparitions.'

Julia hoisted herself onto the fence, swinging a leg over.

'What are you doing?'

'I'm going to look in the woods.'

'Julia . . .'

She turned to me, and her expression told me there was no point arguing. 'What if she saw Lily? What if she's out there . . . too scared, for whatever reason, to come to the house? Or maybe she was about to come back and Ursula frightened her off?'

She was over the fence now, making her way through the grass towards the line of trees. I sighed and climbed after her. The grass clutched at my ankles and the ground squelched, still wet from all the rain that had fallen the previous week.

I caught up with Julia, who stood on a little path just inside the wood. 'Lily!' she called. 'Lily? Are you there? Sweetheart, it's me, it's Mummy.'

'Julia, there's no one here,' I said. 'It's Ursula. She's trying to mess with your head. You should tell her to leave right now.'

She wasn't listening. She stared into the trees, fresh tears on her cheeks. I was furious with Ursula. What was she playing at?

'She was here,' Julia said, her voice thick with distress. 'I can feel it. I can feel *her*.' And then she smiled. The hope in her eyes broke my heart. 'She's alive, Lucas. She's really alive.'

She embraced me, her face against my chest, hot tears soaking through my shirt. I held her and let her cry for a minute until she pulled away, wiping her cheeks with her sleeves.

'Oh God, I'm such a state, I'm so embarrassing,' she said.

What was I supposed to do? Insist that Ursula had been lying? Tell her Lily had to be dead, that there was no way she could be standing here watching the house? I couldn't do it.

'She must be hungry,' Julia said. 'I should bring some food, leave it here. Some warm clothes too. And a note, telling her not to be afraid. Yes. Yes, that's what I'll do.'

She ran out of the woods, back into the field and towards the house.

Looking at the trees all around me I made a silent vow. If I couldn't persuade Julia to kick Ursula out, I had to do what I could to limit the damage.

'Ursula,' I said to myself, 'I'm watching you.'

Chapter 22

Ursula was nowhere to be seen when I got back to the house. I figured she'd gone back to her room.

Julia was in the kitchen, filling a basket with snacks and fruit. She made a cheese sandwich and wrapped it in cling film. It was all very Little Red Riding Hood.

'Won't it get eaten by animals?' I said.

She stared at the basket. 'You're right. I need something more secure. Like a metal box, with a key. I don't have anything like that.'

'Julia, do you really . . . Do you really think Lily could be living wild in the woods?'

She lay her hands flat on the counter, as if stopping herself from falling.

'If there's a chance . . . even the remotest chance . . .'

'Ursula was lying. I don't know why, but—'

'I was not lying.'

I whirled around. Ursula stood in the kitchen doorway. She still wore her red coat even though it was warm in the house. Maybe she was one of those people who is always cold. Thin skin, weak blood. Anger bubbled up in me and I was about to give her a piece of my mind when she produced a mobile phone – one of those large iPhones – and said, 'Look. I took a picture. You didn't give me a chance to show it to you.'

Julia began trembling as Ursula unlocked the phone and located the photos app.

'There. See.'

I couldn't believe it, but there it was. A picture of the edge of the woods where Julia and I had just stood. And in front of the trees, facing the camera, was a child.

'I'm afraid it's not very clear,' Ursula said, as Julia took the phone from her and zoomed in on the figure. It was a girl with long brown hair. She was wearing a blue coat and jeans.

'Is it . . . ?' I could hardly bring myself to say it. 'Is it Lily?'

'I can't tell. I want it to be her so much that I'm seeing her. But I don't know. I don't know.'

'Let's plug it into a computer,' I said. 'Make it bigger.'

I ran upstairs and grabbed my laptop, along with the USB cable I used to charge my missing phone. Back in the kitchen, I plugged Ursula's phone in and navigated through a series of permissions messages. Finally, I was able to import the photo.

It appeared full-size on the screen. It was a top-of-the-range laptop with a retina screen so the photo appeared bright and vivid. It was a little out of focus, but we were able to zoom in on the girl's face so her features were visible enough to identify her.

'It's not Lily,' Julia said, the disappointment making her voice tremble.

I put my hand on her shoulder, which drew a knowing look from Ursula.

'But I know her,' Julia said, staring at the picture. 'It's Lily's friend, Megan. Her family lives on the other side of the woods.'

She grabbed her car keys from the hook on the wall.

'Where are you going?' I asked.

'To talk to her. I want to know what she was doing.' She left the kitchen, then turned back. 'Come on. Bring your laptop.'

ω

'Do you feel bad now?' Julia asked as she drove onto the main road.

'About accusing Ursula of lying? A bit. I still think she's dangerous, though.'

She laughed. She seemed a little giddy. 'You don't get on with many people, do you?'

'What do you mean by that?'

'Oh, just that I know you don't like Max. And you've taken an instant dislike to Ursula. Also, I read an interview with you online, and you were doing the whole Greta Garbo "I want to be alone" thing.'

'I don't think my ironic sense of humour comes across in interviews.' I paused. 'Wait, you were reading an interview with me?'

Did I imagine it, or did she go a very pale shade of pink? 'I . . . um . . . I like to keep up with what my guests are up to.'

'Right.'

Neither of us could think what to say. Eventually Julia said, 'You must think I'm losing it. After what happened earlier . . .'

'Of course I don't. It's totally understandable.'

'It was a bit bonkers, though, wasn't it? My plan to leave a picnic in the woods?'

We headed west, skirting the edge of the woods. This was close to where I'd found the creepy hut and been picked up by that gossiping taxi driver. We were driving in a loop, so it was a lot further by car than it would be on foot.

'Here we are.'

Julia pulled into a little housing estate comprising twenty or thirty houses which looked like they'd been built in the last decade or so. Neat square lawns, wide pavements, trampolines in half the gardens. An estate designed for young families. Julia pulled up outside Number 22, which was one of the largest houses, positioned in front of the woods that stretched all the way to the retreat.

Julia rang the doorbell.

'Hi, Wendy,' she said to the woman who answered the door. She was in her late thirties, slim and wearing a slogan T-shirt. A black Labrador was trying to get past her. She grabbed its collar and held it back.

'Julia. This is . . . a surprise.' She gave me a quizzical look, eyes dropping to the laptop under my arm, then invited us in, saying, 'Get down, Barney' to the dog, which leapt about trying to give both Julia and me a hug. Wendy finally shut Barney in the kitchen and invited us into the living room.

'Is Megan around?' Julia asked.

'She's in her bedroom. Is everything all right?' She kept glancing at me, clearly trying to figure out who I was.

'I wanted to ask her something.'

Wendy gave Julia a curious look, then gestured for us to take a seat, though neither of us sat down. Wendy left the room, calling Megan's name up the stairs. Getting no reply, she went up, her footsteps echoing behind her.

Julia paced the room, chewing her thumbnail, giving off waves of nervous energy. I examined the framed pictures on the mantelpiece. Wendy had two kids, Megan and an older son. Next, I examined the bookcase, something I do whenever I visit someone's house. I can't help it. If I enter a house with no books it makes me uneasy. I wonder what's wrong with the people who live there.

I was drawn past the paperback bestsellers to a book I recognised. *Folk Tales and Urban Myths.* I'd seen this book recently, but where? I took it down and flicked through it. It was a kids' book, full of stories about legends like Bloody Mary and the Beast of Bodmin Moor. It went back further, describing how communities would live in terror of witches and werewolves, night demons and weeping women. The illustrations were vivid and creepy.

'Lily's got that book,' Julia said. 'I have no idea where it came from. She just brought it home one day.'

That was where I'd seen it. Lily's bedroom.

I replaced the book on the shelf as Wendy came back into the room, followed by the girl from Ursula's photograph.

'Hi, Megan,' Julia said.

'Hi, Mrs Marsh.' The girl fidgeted awkwardly, sucking on a strand of hair. She perched on the edge of the sofa, both legs jiggling up and down as if her body couldn't contain all its energy. She couldn't make eye contact with Julia.

'How are you?'

Megan shrugged. 'Good, thanks.'

'Were you outside my house earlier?' Julia asked.

Megan dipped her chin and didn't answer. She stared at a stain on the carpet as if it might contain the answer to the meaning of life. Finally, after her mum said her name, Megan said, 'Yeah.'

'What were you doing there?'

Megan stuck out her bottom lip. 'Just looking.'

'At the house?'

She nodded, and then the lip she'd been sticking out trembled. 'I wasn't doing anything wrong. It's just . . . sometimes I miss Lily. I like looking at your house and remembering.'

'Oh, sweetheart,' Julia said.

Wendy swooped in and folded her daughter up in her arms. 'You're upsetting her,' she said to Julia.

'I didn't mean to. I'm sorry. I thought . . . It's stupid, but I had this idea that Megan might know something.'

'About Lily?' Wendy shook her head. 'It was two years ago.'

'I thought maybe she knew something and was coming to tell me.'

'What's going on?' A male voice came from the doorway.

'Grandad!' Megan extricated herself from her mum's arms and leapt across to the man who'd entered the room, flinging her arms around him. He was completely bald and in his sixties.

'What's the matter, angel?' he asked Megan.

Before Megan could reply, Wendy told him what had happened.

'There's no law against her going into the woods, is there?' he said. His teeth pointed in half a dozen directions. I did a double take. He stared back at me with evident hostility.

Was this the man Zara had encountered at the chess club?

'We're all very sorry about what happened, Mrs Marsh,' the bald man said. 'But that doesn't mean you can come here upsetting my granddaughter.'

I didn't like his hostile tone.

'With respect,' I said, 'Julia was upset when she saw Megan.'

'And you are?'

'Lucas Radcliffe,' I replied.

'He's a writer,' Julia said. Wendy looked confused, so Julia added, 'I've turned the house into a writers' retreat.'

The bald man narrowed his eyes at me. It suddenly struck me that, if this was the man Zara had encountered at the chess club, there was a chance he knew I had hired her. And Julia didn't know about that.

We needed to get out of there before he let the cat out of that particular bag.

'It must bring it all back,' Wendy said, giving me a temporary reprieve. 'I'm so sorry, Julia. I wish there was something we could do.'

'But there isn't,' said Megan's grandad, still training his hostile gaze on me. 'Let me show you out.'

We went back out to the car. Julia was fully deflated now.

'I feel sick,' she said. 'Do you mind driving?'

She handed me the keys and I got into the driver's seat.

'What's Megan's grandad's name?' I asked. 'Do you know?'

'Glynn Collins. Why?'

'Oh, I just thought I recognised him, that's all.'

'He's well known around here,' Julia said. 'A pillar of the community. I remember he offered to take Michael out for a drink, introduce him to some of the other local men, but Michael wasn't into that kind of thing.'

'What do you mean?'

'You know. Men's clubs. Groups of blokes who think women only have legs to get from the kitchen to the bedroom. Michael had his faults, but being a rampant misogynist wasn't one of them. Glynn asked him if he wanted to join the local chess club and Michael went along to take a look, but said it wasn't his scene. Apart from a receptionist, there were no women, just a lot of old blokes.'

As we were about to drive off, something caught my eye. There was somebody in the upstairs window, watching us. The teenage boy whose photo was on the mantelpiece.

Julia followed my gaze. 'That's Jake. Megan's brother. He's very sweet.'

The boy stood up and pressed the tips of his fingers against the glass.

'It's been hard for Wendy,' Julia said. 'Apparently Jake has the mental age of a five- or six-year-old.'

'A kind of Peter Pan.'

'I guess that's one way of looking at it. Can we go home?'

'Yes, of course, sorry.'

I raised my eyes to Jake once more. He was mouthing something, but I was unable to read his lips. He was pointing too, at the woods beyond the house. I concentrated on his mouth, trying to figure out what he was saying. It looked like one word, over and over.

It looked like 'Lily'. And then, as I stared at him, he said another word. It looked like 'window'.

No, not 'window'. *Widow*. He was saying 'widow'.

Chapter 23

LILY – 2014

Dad came into Lily's room and said six words that stabbed her in the heart with an icicle.

'Megan's grandad is taking you out.'

She stared at him.

'Nice of him, huh?' Dad said. 'He called and said he was taking Megan to the adventure playground and Megan asked if you could go too. He's going to pick you up in fifteen minutes so you'd better get a wriggle on and get dressed.' He sighed as he rummaged through her chest of drawers. 'Goodness, Lily, it's a mess in your room. Where are your leggings?'

'I feel sick,' she said. 'I think I've got a temperature.'

He felt her forehead. 'You seem fine to me. Come on. Don't be a malingerer.'

'A what?'

Huffing and sighing, she dressed and waited for Megan and her grandad to arrive. As long as she stuck close to Megan, as long as she wasn't left alone with Mr Collins, it should be okay.

Mum had gone into Wrexham today, because she had an appointment, so Dad was looking after her. As Lily brushed her hair, she tried to put her fear of Megan's grandad out of her mind, but that only freed up space for her other worries to creep into. Her worries about Mum and Dad.

Mum seemed sad at the moment. She'd had a summer cold for weeks and complained about being tired all the time. Quite often, Lily would walk into the room and Mum would be sitting there, staring into space, and she wouldn't respond unless Lily said her name really loud or got right up in her face. Dad said she was a zombie and Mum narrowed her eyes at him and said it was all his fault.

Lily didn't know whose side to take. She didn't want to take anyone's side. She thought maybe her parents needed a date night, which was something Megan's mum and stepdad did – even though the thought of them kissing and being lovey-dovey made her want to vomit – but there was no one around to babysit. The whole thing was like horrible homework that the teacher hadn't explained properly.

Megan and her grandad turned up and they went out. The two girls sat in the back seat and Megan talked non-stop about her brother and YouTube and the Bloody Mary video game. Lily tuned out and concentrated on Mr Collins. She could only see the back of his head, and his eyes in the rear-view mirror. He concentrated on driving, humming along with some rubbish old music on the radio.

She relaxed until he said, 'Everything all right, Lily?'

He had caught her staring at him. Her ears burned and she shrank back into her seat, not speaking until they got to the adventure playground.

The playground was massive. There was a chute slide and rope bridges strung between trees and even a flying fox. Lily started to relax, until a horrible boy, who was part of a group of annoying kids who kept hogging the slide, shoved her out of the way.

'Hey!'

When the boy reached the bottom of the slide, Megan's grandad went up and whispered something in his ear. The boy went white and he kept out of Lily and Megan's way after that.

Maybe Mr Collins wasn't so bad after all. He bought them ice creams too, and slushies. Mum never let Lily drink slushies because she said they contained 'more Es than a rave party', whatever that meant. But Megan's grandad clearly wasn't one of those grown-ups who was obsessed with looking after your teeth.

Back in the car, he said, 'I need to go into town before I take you home, Lily. I've texted your dad and he said it's fine.'

'Okay.'

As they approached Beddmawr, Mr Collins suddenly got this look in his eye – that 'I like scaring kids' look – and said, 'Did I ever tell you girls where the Red Widow came from?'

Megan sat up. 'No! Tell us, Grandad.'

Lily shrank back in her seat. She really didn't want to hear it.

'Lily, you'll be interested in this. Did you know your house is built on the site of an old slate mine?'

She'd heard her parents talking about it before. Slate was basically a kind of rock. Once upon a very boring time, lots of people had spent their whole lives digging it up and using it to build roofs.

'Yes, Mr Collins,' she said.

He grunted happily. 'That mine opened two hundred years ago, you know.'

'When you were a boy,' said Megan.

'Very funny. Now, slate mining was a dangerous business . . .'

Lily's mind wandered off to something more interesting. Her attention drifted through the window and across the fields to her house and, more specifically, her kitchen. What would it be tonight? She fancied burgers, or maybe pizza, or pasta . . .

'And he was crushed to death.'

Her attention snapped back to Mr Collins.

'Terrible business,' he said. 'And most terrible of all for Dafydd's wife. She was pregnant, and they say the shock made her lose her baby.' He shook his head. 'The world was a cruel place back then, girls. None of the mollycoddling that goes on now. Dafydd's wife, whose name was Rhiannon, didn't just lose her baby – she lost her home. She was starving, alone, penniless. And now homeless.'

'So she went to live under the bridge,' Megan said. 'You've told me that part before.'

'Ah, but Lily hasn't heard the story.'

Megan frowned and nodded. She clearly took the story very seriously.

'Poor Rhiannon made a home under a bridge. She was a very pretty woman with all this black hair. One morning, a young man from the mine went down to the river and saw a dozen dead fish floating on the water, with Rhiannon standing by the bank. He ran back to tell the other men and that's when they decided. She must have killed the fish using witchcraft. And do you know what happened then?'

Megan's eyes were wide and round.

'The men formed a gang and drove her into the woods,' she said.

'Exactly. They were going to burn her but they were afraid to get too near her. Instead, they banished her, thinking she'd die in the woods anyway.'

'Were there wolves?' Lily asked.

'No. They died out four hundred years ago. But it was cold and inhospitable and there was nothing to eat.' He cleared his throat. They were almost in town now. 'As she headed into the woods, Rhiannon called out a curse. She said that if the townsfolk didn't bring her a child as a sacrifice, she would come into town and choose one. Do you know what happened next?'

'Tell us, Grandad.' Megan's voice had dropped to a whisper.

Mr Collins's eyes sparkled. 'The people ignored her warning. But a week later, something terrible happened.'

They had stopped at a traffic light and he turned round in his seat, the seatbelt straining against his belly. 'The prettiest girl in the town disappeared. A girl as pretty as you two. She was eight years old, out running an errand for her mother. And she never came home. The townsfolk searched the woods, and guess what they found?'

'What, Grandad?'

'A pile of bones at the foot of a tree. Among the bones was a necklace the pretty young girl had been wearing.'

Lily closed her eyes, imagining it. The girl's mum and dad, crying over the bones, crying and wishing they hadn't ignored the Widow's demands.

Mr Collins showed his horrible teeth. 'The best part is, it's all true.'

Lily turned to look at Megan, expecting to exchange a smile about the scary but silly story – as if it were true! – but Megan looked as serious as she did when their teacher told them Important Facts.

They parked near the river – the same river where the witch had killed those fish – and Megan's grandad went into an old building, leaving the radio on for them. He came out ten minutes later and they saw him go into the bookshop next door. When he got back to the car, he handed each of them a paper bag. Inside each was the same book: *Folk Tales and Urban Myths*.

'You'll enjoy that, girls,' he said. 'Right, Lily, we'd better get you home.'

Lily opened the book and immediately recoiled from a gruesome drawing of a werewolf munching on a sheep's belly. She snapped it shut. Next to her, Megan leafed through hers, exclaiming 'Awesome!' and 'Oh my God!'

Lily looked up and saw Mr Collins watching her in the rear-view mirror. A shiver ran from her toes to the hair on her head and she closed her eyes.

She kept them shut all the way home.

Chapter 24

The next morning, I worked on my novel for a couple of hours, although I found it hard to concentrate. I spent more time staring out the window than I did looking at the screen. My mind kept returning to what I'd seen at Megan's house. Her brother, Jake, pointing towards the woods, the same woods I was staring at now.

Widow.

My mind flashed back to the time I'd explored the woods and found that strange little hut.

There had been a soft toy inside, hadn't there? At the time I hadn't even known about Lily's disappearance, so hadn't thought anything of it. I knew now that Lily's soft toy, Big Cat, had been found in the river. But had someone abducted her, kept her there in that hut and given her a toy to pacify her? It didn't quite add up, because surely the police must have checked that hut, but I could no longer work. I was compelled to go and have another look.

It took thirty minutes to retrace my steps and locate the clearing and the stone hut. A group of magpies hopped about in the long, damp grass, chattering to one another. A light drizzle soaked my clothes and face, the weather so dismal it was actually a relief to take shelter in the grim, litter-strewn interior of the hut.

I had forgotten how dilapidated it was. The door was rotten and the windows smashed. Not a great place to keep a child prisoner, although the abductor could have tied or chained her up. I could imagine local teenagers coming here to take drugs or have sex, or both, although the creepiness of the place might deter them. The image of a little girl sitting here, shivering with fear and cold, played out in my mind.

The soft toy was nowhere to be seen. I poked at the litter with my shoe. I was sure it had been in this spot beside the bench.

Had someone been back and taken it?

If someone had abducted Lily and kept her in this hut, surely they wouldn't have been foolish enough to leave a toy here in the first place? The likelihood was that it had been here for many years. Perhaps a visiting teenager had taken it, or chucked it outside. Maybe a dog had been in and carried it off. There were multiple possible explanations, all of which had nothing to do with Lily.

Disappointed, I left the hut – and glimpsed a figure on the far side of the field, directly opposite the spot where I'd entered the clearing. Beyond this field was another part of the woods. The person vanished into the trees.

They had been wearing a red coat.

Ursula? What was she doing out here?

I hurried across the field, scaring the magpies, which scattered and flew towards high branches. I counted them. Seven. How did the rhyme go? *Seven for a secret never to be told.*

Not the most auspicious sign.

I reached the spot where I'd seen Ursula vanish into the trees. She was probably just out for a walk, exploring the area. Or maybe, I thought sarcastically, her spirit guide was leading her. It still seemed odd, though, that she would come out here in the drizzle, so far from the house. I couldn't resist the urge to follow and see what she was up to. I headed into the woods after her.

I could see her in her red coat just up ahead, walking unhurriedly along the path. She had her back to me and hadn't seen me, as far as I could tell. She had her hood up to protect her from the rain, and she held out a hand, touching the trunks of trees as she passed. Perhaps she was communing with them.

The path forked ahead of her and she swerved left. I followed, but found myself confronted by a huge puddle of black mud. I skirted around it. As I trod back onto the path, I realised I'd lost sight of her. I increased my pace and turned left at the fork. There she was, heading into a thick tangle of vegetation, pushing through sideways, away from the path. That seemed like a strange thing to do. Had she spotted something on the other side? The bushes obscured her and I hung back for a second before following. Brambles clawed at my coat and a wren popped out of the bushes, startling me. I made an *aah!* sound, my voice shattering the peace of the woods. Ursula must have heard me, but she didn't stop moving.

I hurried to catch up, wondering why she didn't stop to wait for me. It was as if she were trying to get away. I glimpsed her red coat through the trees ahead, then she disappeared behind another wall of vegetation. I jogged along the path to the spot where I'd last seen her.

She had vanished.

I walked quickly up the path, which branched off in three directions, checking the ground for footprints, but found nothing. The ground was harder and drier here, beneath the canopy formed by the trees. I chose the middle path and walked for another few minutes. There was no sound except birdsong. And now I was at a dead end formed of impassable blackberry bushes.

I swore out loud.

I'd lost her.

Chapter 25

On my way back to Nyth Bran, I thought more about our visit to Megan's house, and what Jake had been trying to tell us. I needed to talk to him, and had an idea about how this could be achieved. Remembering the route Julia had taken to his house, I changed direction and followed the road towards the estate where Jake and Megan lived.

I hoped Jake's mum, Wendy, would be amenable. Julia had told me that after her divorce, Wendy had started using her maiden name, Collins, again. She had a new partner now, and the kids' dad lived in another part of the country.

'It was a painful divorce,' Julia had said. 'He was a bastard. I think he used to hit her. I heard that Glynn found out and threatened him, told him if he wanted to keep possession of his balls he had better leave town.'

'Glynn's a hard man?'

'Yeah. Plus he knows a lot of people.'

After that first visit to the Collins house, I'd looked Glynn up on Google.

He matched Zara's description of the man she'd met at the chess club, the one who'd made her – and Malcolm Jones – so uneasy. Of course, there were plenty of men around with bald heads and bad teeth, but I had a strong feeling it was him, and thought it shouldn't be hard to confirm. I just needed to check if he was a member of the chess club.

There was very little information about him online. There was an article from the local newspaper about how he and a group of handymen had rebuilt a widow's cottage after it suffered heavy storm damage. Another news story told how he had helped raise money for the local historical society, along with one Malcolm Jones. There had been talk of opening a museum to teach visitors about the disused mine, but nothing had come of it. And there was an old story about how he had coached the local girls' football team and got them to the final of a regional competition. There he was, in black and white, holding his runner-up medal, surrounded by grinning, muddy girls who would be grown up now.

As Julia had said, Glynn Collins was a pillar of the community. I had only encountered him briefly, but in some ways he reminded me of my dad. A typical bluff Welsh bloke. A man's man, good with his hands, keen on sport and tradition.

I was hoping he wouldn't be at his daughter's house now – but as soon as I turned the corner onto the estate, I saw him. He was standing in the front garden, smoking. I hesitated, wondering if I should come back another time, but it was too late. He had spotted me.

I crossed the road, watching as he discarded his cigarette and folded his arms, doing a good impression of a nightclub bouncer protecting his door.

'Mr Collins,' I said. 'We met yesterday.'

He nodded.

'I was hoping . . .' The way he was looking at me, like I was a rat that had strayed onto his property, made me lose the thread of what I was trying to say. 'I wanted to have a little chat with Jake.'

He took a step towards me. It was a classic intimidating manoeuvre. But I wasn't scared of him. He was, what, twenty-five years older than me, maybe more?

'You're David's son,' he said.

I was momentarily taken aback, but it made sense. Glynn knew everybody in Beddmawr, past and present. He must have been asking around about me, which was interesting. Who had he spoken to? Shirley at the Apple Tree B & B?

'That's right,' I said, expecting him to ask after my dad, bracing myself to deliver the news I hated saying.

But instead Glynn said, 'What do you want with Jake?'

'I'm writing a book,' I said, 'in which some of the characters are teenagers. I need to talk to a couple of teenagers about the language they use, the slang and so on.'

This was the line I'd planned to use on Wendy.

'Jake's not an ordinary teenager,' Glynn said.

'I know that, but—'

'The answer's no.'

'Mr Collins, please.'

I caught a movement above us and looked up. Jake was at his window again, staring down at his grandad and me with saucer eyes. Glynn saw and flapped a meaty hand at his grandson, telling him to get back. Jake gawped at me one last time, then retreated into the shadows.

'Like teenage boys, do you?' Glynn said.

His question was so unexpected that I didn't know what to say for a few seconds. 'What? Of course not.'

'Maybe the papers would like to hear about it, how a famous writer has been harassing a young boy with learning difficulties.'

'That's ridiculous.'

'You just asked me if you could sneak up to his bedroom.'

I stared at him. There was no use arguing. 'Fine. I'll find some other teenagers to talk to for my book.' I turned away.

169

'You do that.' He raised his voice as I walked back across the road, just as a middle-aged couple came out of the nearest house. Glynn shouted, 'Stay away from my grandchildren, pervert!'

The couple's eyes almost popped out of their heads as I hurried away, burning with anger and embarrassment.

ധ

Back in my room at Nyth Bran, I finally calmed down enough to think about my encounter with Glynn rationally. Was he simply being protective of his family? No, I was sure there was more to it. I remembered how on edge Zara had seemed after her encounter with him. Maybe it was just that he was an unpleasant arsehole.

But I wanted to know more about him.

I opened Skype and called my mum.

She answered straight away.

'Darling! How lovely to hear from you. Twice in one month!'

'I've got another question for you about the old days,' I said. 'Do you remember a guy called Glynn Collins?'

'Oh. Yes.' All the warmth left her voice. 'Why are you asking about him?'

'I met him recently. It sounds like you don't think much of him.'

She moved her head and sunshine flooded the screen. It was raining again here, in Wales, and the temptation to fly out to Spain and join her fluttered through my mind.

'No,' Mum said, her voice clipped. 'I was never very keen on him.'

'Why not?' It was always a struggle to get my mother to say a bad word about anyone. 'Did he do something to you?'

'Oh no, he never did anything to *me*. Not directly anyway. He's just . . . well, we used to call them male chauvinist pigs in my day. He was proud of it. He was awful to his wife, Nerys, God rest her soul. He was cruel too. Hard.'

'He seems to dote on his grandchildren,' I said. 'And he looks after Wendy, his daughter.'

'Maybe he's softened with age. But forty years ago, if someone in town had a litter of kittens they didn't want, they'd bring them to Glynn Collins. He was always happy to drown them.'

'Lovely. What did Dad think of him?'

She frowned. 'He was friendly with him. They were part of the Beddmawr Historical Society.' She snorted. 'Just a bunch of blokes meeting in the pub and talking about the good old days, as far as I could tell.'

'Was Malcolm Jones part of the Historical Society too?'

'Yes. He was the chairman, although I was never sure why such a small group needed a chairman!'

'Did you hear that he died?'

On-screen, my mum's hand flew to her mouth. 'Oh no! How did that happen? When?'

'A heart attack, just over a week ago.'

'Oh dear, how dreadful. This is going to start happening more and more as I get older . . .'

I remembered someone else I'd encountered recently. 'Sorry, one more person. Shirley . . . Damn, I don't know her surname. She runs a B & B. The Apple Tree.'

'Shirley Roberts?' She grimaced.

'Didn't you like her either?'

Mum ignored the question, probably because she didn't want to admit it. 'How on earth did you meet her?'

'It's a long story. But was she part of this Historical Society?'

'Oh, goodness, no. Glynn wouldn't let any women join. I told you, he was a chauvinist pig. I think he got her to do some secretarial work, though. In fact, there were rumours he was bonking her behind his wife's back.' She wiped a bead of sweat from her brow. 'Goodness me, Lucas, this was all a long time ago.'

She went quiet for a minute, and I hoped I wasn't bringing back painful memories.

'There was another guy who was part of that group. What was his name?' She tapped the side of her head. 'Albert, that was it. Albert Patterson. Oh!'

'What is it?'

'Albert lived in the house where you're staying. Nyth Bran.'

'Really? Hang on, Mum. Wait there.'

I left the room and ran down the stairs and into the Thomas Room. I scoured the bookcase and found what I was looking for: the battered edition of 'The Owl and the Pussycat'. I pulled out the Polaroid showing the *American Gothic*-style couple and ran back upstairs. I held the photo up to the camera.

'Is this Albert?'

Mum went off to fetch her glasses and peered at the screen. 'Yes, that's him. He was a nice chap. I never understood why he hung around with Glynn Collins. He and Bethan were a sweet couple. They were older than us, no kids. I was always envious of them for living in such a lovely big house and having all that freedom. I wonder what happened to them.'

Julia had told me she had bought the house from a children's charity. I guessed Albert and his wife must have died and, having no family, left the place to charity.

'I feel very sad about Malcolm,' my mum said. 'I wonder if they've had the funeral yet? I must send flowers.'

'Hang on.'

I went on to the local newspaper website, the same one I'd been reading about Glynn Collins on, and clicked through to the Births, Marriages and Deaths section. There it was, the death announcement for Malcolm Jones, beloved father of Olly.

'It's today,' I said. 'This afternoon.'

'I've left it too late.'

'Maybe I could take some flowers along on your behalf.'

'Would you? That would be very kind.'

'No problem.'

I said goodbye and ended the call.

I had an ulterior motive for going, of course. I was quite sure Glynn Collins would be there. It would give me another chance to get a good look at him, because the more I heard about him, the more convinced I became that he was hiding something.

Chapter 26

The funeral was at St Mary's Church near the centre of town, close to the chess club and the library. I hadn't brought any smart clothes with me, not imagining I'd need them, so I popped into one of the few men's clothes shops in Beddmawr and bought a black suit off the peg. It wasn't exactly stylish but it would do. Next, I bought some flowers from the florist next door and wrote a message from my mum and myself. Malcolm's family weren't to know I'd never met him.

Noticing a phone shop across the street, I went in and bought a new iPhone, activating it straight away and then logging in to my Apple account to sync my contacts, emails, etc.

Ten minutes later, I shook off my umbrella and crept into the church, laying the flowers with the others. I sat in a pew near the back. Nobody noticed me; well over a hundred people had turned up, many of them Malcolm's age but quite a few younger people too. I guessed they had once been schoolchildren who he'd inspired through his job as a librarian. I couldn't see Glynn Collins. He was probably near the front.

The service started, the pallbearers carrying the coffin down the aisle. There was Olly Jones, Malcolm's taxi-driving son, sitting next to his girlfriend Heledd. Her mother, Shirley, was just behind them. When I'd met Heledd at the B & B I had been struck by her good looks. Now, seeing her and Olly together, I realised what a mismatched couple they were. He was punching well above his weight, which made me think about that limited dating pool again. In a larger town or city, Heledd wouldn't be going out with an ordinary-looking taxi driver, she would be . . .

I stopped myself. Why was I being so uncharitable? Olly must have hidden depths, a spark I hadn't witnessed yet. And the poor sod had just lost his dad.

It was an emotional ceremony. The vicar spoke warmly about Malcolm and his contribution to the community. Olly got up and read out a eulogy, stopping every few sentences to take a deep, shuddering breath. Afterwards, Heledd leaned her head on his shoulder. I learned from the lady sitting beside me that, after this service, the coffin was being taken to the crematorium.

'He wanted his ashes to be scattered in his garden,' she said. 'Among the daffs and crocuses.'

The service ended. I made my way outside and was pleased to find the rain had stopped. I wasn't sure what to do, but the lady I'd sat next to told me I should come to the wake, which was taking place at Olly's house. 'All are welcome,' she said.

ɯ

An hour and a half later I found myself among a crowd of people, explaining who I was and why I was at the funeral. Malcolm's wife had died a few years before but most of the older people remembered my parents and were touched that I'd come along to represent them. Most of them were fascinated to hear about their move to Spain and to learn that I was a novelist, and I found myself chatting to a group of retired women who wanted to know where I got my ideas from.

I spotted the shining dome of Glynn's head through the crowd. He was talking to another man his age, laughing heartily at something the other guy was saying. Was this another member of the Historical Society? I hung back. I wasn't sure what I was going to say to him. *Why was Malcolm scared of you? Why didn't you want me to talk to Jake?*

A scenario played out in my head. Glynn lurking by the river on that fateful New Year's Day two years ago. Snatching Lily when her parents were out of sight and throwing her toy cat into the water.

Taking her somewhere into the woods. Hiding her in that hut. Doing things to her that I didn't want to picture. Killing her and burying her, his granddaughter's best friend, in the woods.

But what evidence did I have for any of this? I quickly ran through it again. Zara had reported that this man made Malcolm seem afraid while she was quizzing him about Lily's disappearance. The next day, Malcolm died before he could tell Zara any more. It had been a heart attack – but if his heart was weak, perhaps he had been frightened to death, if such a thing was possible.

And in this scenario, Jake had seen or heard something, which was why Glynn didn't want anyone talking to him. What could it have been? A conversation he'd eavesdropped on? Had Jake actually seen Glynn with Lily? Perhaps he witnessed something that happened before Lily's disappearance, during one of the many times Lily had visited the house.

I could go to the police with my suspicions but it seemed extremely unlikely there would be any evidence. Even if the police talked to Jake and he told them something incriminating, it would be easy for Glynn to deny it. How likely were the police to believe the word of a teenage boy with learning difficulties?

As I thought it through, I realised I was getting way ahead of myself, my imagination running away with me as usual. To go to the police now, with my half-baked theories, would be liable to cause nothing but upset to Jake and his family. And if Glynn *was* guilty of something, he would be put on high alert.

I needed to wait, to find out more.

I found myself staring at Glynn, and at that moment the crowd between us shifted and he saw me. He stared back, clearly shocked I was here – shocked and angry. He was about to head over, fists clenched, and I braced myself for a confrontation, when a woman in her fifties stepped into his path and started talking to him. The woman had a cleavage that pinned Glynn to the spot. At the same moment, someone tapped me on the shoulder.

'Lucas. I didn't expect to see you here.'

It was Shirley. She was dressed all in black with a fascinator attached to her head. I couldn't help but stare at it. She had a sherry glass in her hand.

'I'm happy to see you,' I said. 'Can we talk?'

'What about?' She touched the cross around her neck, just as she had the first time we met. She was nervous, and the way she glanced over her shoulder at Glynn told me all I needed to know. She, like Malcolm, was afraid of him.

Jostled by mourners moving through the hallway, and aware of Glynn's proximity, I said, 'Maybe now's not the best time or place. Could I pop round to the Apple Tree later, when this is all over?'

She hesitated, eyes flicking to Glynn once again. He was still talking to the chest of the woman with the cleavage.

'You look so much like your father,' Shirley said. 'When he was your age.'

'Is that a good thing?'

She smiled girlishly. 'Come round at teatime.' She took a sip of her sherry. 'I'd better not have too many of these.'

Heledd appeared by her side. 'Yes, go easy, Mum.' She smiled at me. 'Nice of you to come. Hope you're not going to put us all in a book.'

'Ah, you found out what I do for a living?'

'Olly told me about how he'd helped a stranded novelist and I put two and two together. He said you were going to give him a copy of your book.'

'Oh, yes. I think I said I'd give him one if he promised to read it.'

Heledd laughed. 'I've never known him read anything longer than a text message. But I'd love to read it if you want to drop a copy off at the B & B.'

I was about to explain that I didn't have any books with me in Wales, but she was already steering Shirley away. 'Come on, Mum, the buffet's open. Let's get you something to eat.'

As they stepped out of my path, I saw that Glynn had vanished. And it was time for me to make a move too.

I bumped into Olly by the front door. 'Sorry for your loss,' I said. 'My parents were friends with your dad, so I'm here on their behalf. Hope that's okay.'

'Yeah, of course. Thanks for coming.' He gave me a weak smile. 'Not got lost again recently, I hope.'

His eyes were red, and he looked over my shoulder before I could come up with a response. 'Have you seen Heledd?'

'She was taking her mum to check out the buffet.'

'Sounds right.' He went to move away then stopped, leaning forward and blasting me with warm, beery breath.

'Your family did the right thing, leaving this town,' he said.

He disappeared into the crowd.

ᛟ

I stood outside in the rain. I was desperate to talk to Zara. I wanted to go over the conversation she'd had with Malcolm again, and run my suspicions – I hesitated to call it a theory – past her. There was no one else I could talk to and I needed to know if the whole thing sounded insane.

Once again, I tried calling her mobile and her office number. There was no reply. I checked the time – it was three o'clock. Telford, where Zara was based, was only an hour away by car. I could drive there, talk to her and be back in time to see Shirley. The day was already a complete write-off, work-wise. Fired up and eager to keep up momentum, I hurried back to my car.

The road to Telford was picturesque and traffic was light. The rain had slowed to a light patter. A few months ago I'd watched a documentary about the so-called Shropshire Viper, a serial killer who'd terrorised this part of the world, waking up the county for a while. Now, it had slipped back to sleep.

I hit the M54 outside Telford and followed my satnav's instructions to Zara's office. It was located in an office block which housed half a dozen businesses. Like everything in this new town, it was a modern building with little character, function over form. I parked in the small car park round the back and pressed Zara's buzzer. There was no reply.

Perhaps I shouldn't have expected anything else. After all, she wasn't answering her office phone so why did I think she'd be there? It was so frustrating, though, and as I stood in the rain I thumped my fist against the door, cursing my wasted journey.

'Hey, you'll break that door!'

A young woman with curly blonde hair approached the building, a scowl on her face.

'Who are you and what are you doing?'

'Sorry. I'm trying to get hold of Zara Sullivan.'

The woman was carrying a leather briefcase. I assumed she worked in the building. 'The private detective? I haven't seen her for ages.'

My mouth went dry. 'Really? How long?'

'A couple of weeks, at least. I rent the office next door to hers.' She narrowed her eyes. 'You're not a debt collector, are you?'

'I'm a client.'

She gave me the once-over then said, 'Come inside a minute, I'm getting soaked out here.'

In the lobby, she introduced herself as Samantha and said, 'I'm sure it was two weeks ago. She told me she was off to see someone in Wales about a case. She seemed excited. She's been struggling to find clients recently.' She winced, as if she realised how indiscreet she was being.

'I'm the person she was going to see in Wales,' I said. 'She told me she was coming back. That was just over a week ago.'

'Well, she definitely hasn't been back to the office.' She chewed a fingernail. 'Oh, blimey, you've got me all worried now.'

I was worried too. 'Do you know where she lives?'

'Yeah. She lives with a bloke in Oakengates.'

'A boyfriend?' That was surprising.

Samantha laughed. 'No, he's her GBF.' I must have looked puzzled because she said, 'Gay best friend. Hang on, I've got the address here.' She took out her mobile and looked it up. I copied it into my new phone and thanked her, promising to get Zara to contact her as soon as I found her.

It took only fifteen minutes to get to Oakengates and find the address. Another modern building, this one divided into flats. I pressed the button on the intercom labelled *Zara Sullivan and Dan Kaye* and a man answered. Zara's GBF. I explained that I was looking for his flatmate and he buzzed me up.

He was a short guy, good-looking with a shaved head.

'Zara's in Tenerife,' he said.

'Are you sure?'

He raised an eyebrow. 'Are you a debt collector?'

I was offended. Did I really look like a debt collector? But the fact two people had asked me that made me think Zara must be in some financial difficulty.

I told him the same thing I'd told Samantha.

'She emailed me a week ago to say she'd binned the case she was working on and had decided to get some sun.'

'She didn't phone you?'

He shook his head.

'Didn't you think that was strange? Does she normally email you to tell you things? Has she suddenly taken off on holiday before?'

'Yeah, she has actually. Although the email thing is a bit weird. She usually calls.' He smiled. 'She is quite fond of her own voice.'

Something was definitely wrong. Would Zara have really gone straight from Beddmawr, having abandoned the investigation without telling me, to Tenerife? Without even calling home to pick up a swimsuit? She'd have had to come close to Telford to get to the nearest airport.

'Has she updated Facebook or anything with holiday snaps?' I asked.

'She doesn't use social media,' Dan replied.

'If she went abroad without coming back here, she must have had her passport with her in Wales. Does she usually carry her passport around with her? Do you know where she keeps it? Can you—'

He held up his hands as if warding off an attack. 'Woah woah woah. Give me a chance.'

'Sorry.'

He seemed exasperated. 'Look, I don't know anything about her passport. And I have no idea if you're really who you say you are.'

'I'm not a debt collector . . .'

'Please, shut up. I'm not going to answer any more of your questions. I'm happy to pass a message on but that's it.'

'But—'

'Goodbye.'

He shut the door in my face.

ω

On the way back to my car, I called Edward Rooney, who had originally put me in touch with Zara. Once again, I explained what I knew, adding what Dan had just told me.

'Is there any way you can check if her passport has been used?' I asked.

He blew air into the phone. 'Only the police can do that. And they won't take this seriously. She's a grown woman who emailed her flatmate to say she's going on holiday. You've got absolutely no evidence of foul play.'

'But don't you think it seems weird?'

I could picture him shrugging. 'I expect she has gone off to the Canaries. Can't say I blame her. I'd offer to relieve you of some of your money and look into it – fly out to Tenerife to track her down – but I'm in the middle of a bastard of a case right now. My advice: stop worrying, and finish that bloody book. Okay?'

I hung up. It was just after five. If I didn't get a move on, I'd be late for my rendezvous with Shirley.

Chapter 27

I hit rush hour traffic coming out of Telford. I was hardly in a state to drive, unable to concentrate adequately on the road. I pulled onto a roundabout too early, narrowly avoiding a collision with a BMW, the driver leaning on his horn and gesturing furiously as adrenaline flooded my system.

I parked outside the bed and breakfast and paused before getting out of the car. Black rainclouds obscured the sun, sucking all the colour from the street, but it was dark inside the house. Had Shirley and Heledd not come home?

I rang the bell. The dog barked and ran up to the door, scrabbling at the wood as if it was desperate to get out. I searched my memory banks for its name. Oscar, that was it.

I pushed the letterbox open and said the dog's name, but that made him bark more. I peered through into the gloom. Oscar dashed up and down the hallway, a frantic ball of fur, yapping and making a strangled growling sound in his throat. It looked like Shirley had left him longer than expected and he was desperate for the toilet or food or both. I murmured soothing words, crouched by the door, but it didn't do any good. He grew increasingly frantic, then suddenly vanished from sight. I squinted through the letterbox, searching him out, and as my eyes grew accustomed to the poor light, a shape came into focus at the bottom of the staircase.

It looked like a body.

'Oh . . . fuck.' I grabbed the phone from my pocket and turned the flashlight on, shining it through the narrow gap. The hallway lit up, light bouncing off the walls.

There, lying on her side beneath a framed painting of Christ, was Shirley. One arm was stretched out above her head, and there was a pool of something dark spreading out across the floorboards. Blood.

I called the police.

ω

Beddmawr was too small – in this era of stringent budgets and cuts to public services – to have its own police station, so they had to come from Wrexham. It took thirty minutes, during which time Oscar grew increasingly desperate to get out. I continued to talk to him through the letterbox. His yapping had drawn a number of neighbours from their houses, including a middle-aged man from next door. He was overweight, with florid cheeks and no neck, and moaned about the dog, saying it was drowning out the TV.

'Passed out drunk, has she?' he said. 'I saw her come home earlier. Drunk as a skunk, she was. That thing she had on her head was falling off and she could hardly walk.'

'Was she on her own?' I asked.

'As far as I could tell.'

A pair of cops arrived, followed by an ambulance. A police officer with ginger hair looked through into the hallway, then broke a window to gain access, asking me and the neighbours to keep back. As soon as he opened the door, Oscar came pelting out, spinning in circles as he entered the street, barking and growling. I grabbed his collar and scooped him up, cradling him like a baby, feeling his heart thudding against my palm. As the police entered the house, I could see a trail of bloody paw prints between Shirley's prone figure and the doormat. The paramedics went in and shut the door, as a crowd gathered on the pavement.

I waited with them, still holding Oscar, who had calmed down now.

'Poor little mite,' a grey-haired woman said, offering to take him until Heledd got home, explaining that she lived across the street. I handed him over.

'Oh dear,' said the woman. I followed her gaze. There were smears of blood on the front of my coat, transferred from the dog's paws.

'I wonder where Heledd is,' I said.

'Probably with that boyfriend of hers.' There was disapproval in the woman's voice, as if Olly were a criminal rather than the son of an esteemed librarian.

'Don't you like Olly?' I asked.

She seemed surprised that I'd picked up on her tone. 'I don't know much about him, except he was a bit of a tearaway at school. His dad, Malcolm, was very disappointed he didn't go off to college and ended up driving a taxi. Kids . . .' She tutted.

It was funny hearing her refer to a forty-something man as a kid.

'Anyway, I'd better get this dog inside.' She hurried off across the road.

The other neighbour was telling the policeman who guarded the door about how Shirley had come home inebriated. I heard someone else mutter that 'she liked a drink'. I knew exactly what was going to happen. Everyone would assume she'd fallen down the stairs, pissed. An unfortunate accident. Because nobody else could see the pattern.

The door opened and the paramedics carried Shirley out, zipped into a body bag. The ginger police officer followed them, and as they reached the pavement somebody rushed past me, shoes clacking on the asphalt.

It was Heledd, hurrying across from where she'd parked her car. She stepped in front of the paramedics, eyes darting between her house and the body bag.

'What's going on?' she asked, her voice cracking. She took a step towards her house, stopped, and turned back towards the zipped-up body.

The police officer tried to calm her down, taking her arm and guiding her away while the paramedics carried Shirley into the ambulance. The policeman said something to Heledd that I couldn't hear and she went stiff. A second later, she crumpled to the ground and the paramedics returned and knelt beside her. She was only out for a moment, then she sat up, looking bewildered. The rubberneckers, who had been on the verge of dispersing, crowded around them. It was probably the most exciting thing that had happened around here for a long time.

The red-haired police officer was stood a little way from where Heledd lay, scratching his head. I approached him and told him my name.

'Somebody pushed her down those stairs,' I said.

He regarded me with weary scepticism. 'What makes you say that?'

I opened my mouth. Shut it again. 'It's complicated.'

'Hmm. Well, it looks like an accident to me. Tell me what you saw.'

He made notes as I detailed what I'd found. But when it came to explaining why I thought someone had pushed her, I couldn't do it. I knew how crazy it sounded. I knew how easily my argument could be countered. Malcolm had a heart attack. Zara's gone off on holiday. Shirley got drunk and had an accident. There was no pattern, just unconnected events. There was nothing sinister here. I would be wasting my breath.

I watched the ambulance go, taking Shirley and Heledd with it. As I headed back to my car, I felt eyes on the back of my neck. I turned.

There was no one there.

Chapter 28

The others were eating dinner when I arrived back at the retreat. Max was next to Suzi, with Ursula opposite. I watched them from the doorway for a minute. They were too absorbed in a verbal game of tennis to notice me: Max and Ursula bashed the conversation back and forth while Suzi watched them. I was desperate to talk to someone, but could I take any of my fellow writers into my confidence? I didn't trust Max. Ursula would probably try to tell me an evil spirit was responsible. And as for Suzi . . . well, I still wasn't sure about her relationship with Max.

That left Julia – but the thought of telling her I'd hired a private detective to investigate Lily's disappearance, and informing her the detective hadn't found anything concrete, filled me with dread. On the other hand, I felt closer to her again after the sighting of Megan and trip to her house. Surely Julia would understand my intentions were good and that I'd kept it from her because I didn't want to get her hopes up.

The truth was, I had no idea how she would react. But I made up my mind. I owed it to her to tell her, and to stop keeping secrets. And maybe, just maybe, she could help me figure it all out.

'Hello. I didn't see you sneak in.'

I whirled round. 'Julia.'

'Sorry, didn't mean to make you jump. Do you want dinner?' I floundered, which made her laugh. 'It's all right. You don't have to answer straight away. Oh, I've got something for you.'

I followed her into the kitchen, where she opened a drawer and fished out a small object.

It was the pen Priya had given me. I turned it over in my hands, relief washing over me. I'd convinced myself that I'd lost it. I was tempted to kiss it.

I looked up to see Julia smiling at me. 'Why is it so special?' she asked.

'Because of who gave it to me.'

'Oh?'

Julia didn't know about Priya. Since arriving at the retreat, I hadn't found an opportunity to bring it up – to let her know we had something awful in common – without it seeming as if I was saying 'me too'. Now was the perfect time to tell her, but first I asked, 'Where did you find it?'

She hesitated. 'Do you promise not to cause a scene?'

'What? Did someone have it? Was it Ursula?'

She sighed. 'Calm down, Lucas. No, it wasn't Ursula. I found it in Max's room—'

'What?'

'—when I was changing the bedding, under the pillow.' Before I could get angry, she hurriedly said, 'I already asked him about it. He said he had no idea what it was doing there. He thinks he might have picked it up by mistake the night Ursula arrived. He said he has a couple of similar pens.'

'But why was it under his pillow? Also, I'm sure I didn't take it out of my room.'

'You're not one hundred per cent sure, though, are you?'

I rubbed my forehead. I was mentally exhausted, still shocked by what had happened to Shirley, and Zara's absence was playing on my mind. 'No. I suppose it's possible I brought it downstairs. But what about my phone? I'm sure someone was in my room that night . . .'

Julia tilted her head. 'What? You didn't tell me about that.'

I rubbed my forehead. I was getting confused, forgetting that although I'd told Julia about my things going missing, only Suzi knew about my nocturnal intruder.

'Lucas, are you okay? You look shattered.'

She touched my upper arm and her hand lingered there. It was warm. I had the urge to pull her closer. To kiss her. Take her to bed and lose myself in her. In that moment, despite the exhaustion that threatened to suck me under, there was nothing else I would rather do. And I was sure, from the way she was looking at me, and how she didn't remove her hand, that she could feel it. The air between us was thick, heavy with unspoken words. I lay my hand on top of hers, held her palm against my triceps.

Max came through the door.

'Oops,' he said. 'Didn't mean to interrupt.'

Julia snatched her hand away.

Max saw the pen in my hand. 'Sorry about the weird mistake, old chap. I'm always picking up other people's pens. Terrible habit.'

Everything that had happened today, all the stress, including the shattered sexual tension – it combined to make the room lurch around me. I pointed a finger at Max. 'You took it, you arsehole! You came into my room and stole it!'

He stared at me.

'I bet you've got my phone too, haven't you? Come on, tell me – where is it?'

'I don't know what the hell you're talking about.'

'Have you been going through it?' I jabbed a finger at him. 'Trying to find something you could use against me? Oh Jesus, I bet it was you who told Ursula about Priya. You fucking arsehole!'

Out of the corner of my eye, through a pinkish mist, I could see Julia, her mouth open with shock.

'You're a jealous, snobbish, has-been loser!' I spat.

Max sneered. '*Jealous?* Of the tripe you churn out? You're not even a proper writer. You're just a hack. No one will read your books in five years, but mine will live on long after I'm gone.'

The mist was dark red now. 'After you're gone?' I jabbed a finger at him. 'That might be sooner than you think, you fucking—'

'Lucas!'

It was Julia. She had hold of both my arms now, and held me still like I was a child. 'Calm down.'

I heard Suzi say, 'Has he been drinking?' I hadn't heard her enter the room.

'Come on,' Julia said. 'Let's find you something to eat.'

I shook my head. 'I'm not hungry. I'm going up to my room.'

I could feel them all watching me as I headed up. The walls swam around my head; the stairs felt like they were made of foam.

I fell onto the bed fully dressed and blacked out immediately.

ω

When I came to, it felt as if I'd been sucking cotton wool. It was still dark but I was surprised to find it was only midnight. I'd been asleep for four hours. Now my body clock was going to be really screwed up.

I staggered to the bathroom and drank water from the tap, then splashed some on my face and cleaned my teeth. I could hear voices downstairs. The others were still up. A memory of my argument with Max hit me and I recoiled. Had I really gloated about being a bestseller? Oh God, what a dickish thing to do. I splashed some more water on my face until I was fully awake.

Going down the stairs, I could hear Ursula, her voice echoing through the house. I didn't know who she was talking to. Suddenly,

Julia appeared at the bottom of the staircase. She stopped dead when she saw me.

'Can I talk to you?' I said when I reached her. 'In private?'

She looked left and right, then said, 'Follow me.'

To my surprise, she unlocked the door to the basement.

'I thought guests weren't allowed down here? That it wasn't safe.'

A little smile. 'That's not strictly true, about it being unsafe. I just wanted to keep this space to myself. Now I'm making an exception, just this once.'

I followed her down. I expected to find a dusty room full of cobwebs and junk, old boxes and cracked walls. I thought perhaps there would be a broken stair or exposed wires, something to explain why no one was supposed to come down here.

I couldn't believe what I saw as Julia flicked a switch and a fluorescent strip light juddered to life.

'Welcome to the playroom,' she said.

It was a child's paradise. Bean bags and scatter cushions were heaped on the floor, and there was a comfortable old sofa, in front of which stood a TV and a games console. The walls were brightly coloured, with posters everywhere containing positive messages:

Dream Big

What if I fall? Oh, my darling, but what if you FLY?

There was a huge doll's house and heaps of cuddly toys and board games; colouring books and pens and art equipment; a chalk board and a dressing-up box overflowing with costumes.

'Wow.'

She sat on the sofa, sinking into it. 'This was Lily's favourite room, even more than her bedroom.'

'It's amazing. My God, I wish I'd had something like this when I was a kid.'

Julia picked up a stuffed rabbit and stroked its ears. 'That's why we created it. We wanted Lily to have all the things we didn't. Her den. Her private space. She used to come down here with Megan, or sometimes she'd bring Chesney down here and play with him. And the plan was, if we had another child . . .'

She trailed off, deep in a memory for a few seconds.

'I like coming down here. It doesn't make me feel sad like her bedroom. Sometimes I sit here for hours and think, and it makes me feel . . . peaceful. I know that might sound strange but . . .' She shrugged. 'Now, what did you want to talk to me about?'

I took a deep breath.

'I don't know how you're going to react.'

'Try me.'

'Okay. Do you remember telling me you wished you could afford to hire a private investigator? Well . . .'

I told her everything, starting with hiring Zara. I told her how Zara was confident the police had done all they could. I recounted her meeting with Malcolm at the chess club and our subsequent conversation at the pub.

'And then she vanished,' I said, going on to tell her what had happened today. Along the way, I told her about Glynn Collins and the Historical Society and all the other fragments of information I'd uncovered but failed to piece together. I told her how my mum had told me about another girl going missing thirty-seven years ago, which Julia knew already ('Several people mentioned that to me when Lily vanished, as if it would make me feel better'). I finished by telling her about what I'd found at the bed and breakfast. Shirley, dead.

'That was why I was so shaken when I got home.'

She raised an eyebrow at my use of the word 'home'. But apart from that, she seemed calm, apparently accepting what I was saying. She didn't shout or get angry or act horrified. She listened and absorbed what I had to say, her legs tucked underneath her. A strand of hair kept falling over her left eye. She brushed it away, keeping her gaze focused on me throughout.

When I'd finished, she untucked her legs and sat forward.

'I knew I should have thrown you out when I found out what you write.'

It hadn't been calm acceptance. It was stunned disbelief.

'Julia—'

'Shut up.'

She got to her feet. I went to rise too, but she reached forward and pushed me back onto the sofa. She stood over me.

'How could you?' she yelled. 'How could you hire someone, get them to poke into my business? How . . . ?' She wanted to say more but was choked by anger.

'I didn't want to get your hopes up,' I said.

'Jesus Christ!'

'Not unless I found something. Julia, you said you wished you could afford a detective. I was doing it for you. A favour.'

She had stalked off, a few feet away from me. 'Really? Are you sure you were doing it for me?'

I needed to defend myself. If I sat there and tried to apologise, she would chuck me out, I was sure of it. I stood up.

'Yes, Julia, I was doing it for you. For Lily. I wanted to check the police had done all they could. I saw how distraught you were and wanted to help you.'

'The damsel in distress.'

'Your gender has nothing to do with it.'

'Huh. I bet.'

I shook my head. 'It doesn't, actually.' But I didn't sound very sure, even to myself. If it had been Julia who had drowned, would I have tried to help Michael in the same way? I wanted to believe that I would, but . . .

'Maybe I shouldn't have done it. Like I said, I was only going to tell you if I got anywhere. And I think I have. I've stirred something up, and I'm certain it's related to Lily.'

She stared at me, chest rising and falling. 'But you haven't really got anywhere, have you? It's like . . . a conspiracy theory. A crazy conspiracy theory. You might as well have told me aliens came down and took Lily off in a spaceship.'

'I know how it sounds, Julia. But Glynn Collins . . . Don't you think it's a massive coincidence that within a couple of weeks of my private detective starting to ask questions, two members of that group are dead? And the detective herself is missing?'

'On holiday. And the other two deaths – it's not coincidence, it's a chain. Cause and effect. The visit from Zara caused Malcolm stress and made him have a heart attack. Then what's-her-name, Shirley, died after getting drunk at his funeral.'

'But why was Malcolm stressed?'

'I don't know. Maybe he did know something about this girl who vanished in the eighties. Maybe Malcolm Jones was a paedophile. But that has nothing to do with Lily.'

I thought about it. I had been so focused on Glynn that it hadn't crossed my mind that Malcolm might be guilty of anything more than not exposing Glynn's crimes. Could Julia be right? Was Malcolm the bad guy here?

'But what if Malcolm was still . . . operating two years ago?'

'With a thirty-five-year gap between crimes?'

I stood up, paced the room. At least Julia was engaging with me now and not marching me up the stairs and telling me to pack my bags. 'There could be others we don't know about,' I said. 'Other missing children. Maybe it was Malcolm, or Glynn, or . . .'

The lights went out.

And above our heads, in the belly of the house, a woman screamed.

Chapter 29

LILY – 2014

Mum stuck her head around Lily's bedroom door.

'Megan's coming over. She'll be here in fifteen minutes so you should get dressed and brush your hair.'

'What? Why?' It was Saturday morning and Lily was on her bed, still in her PJs, playing a game on her iPad.

'Megan's mum has been called into work and her stepdad is away on a stag weekend. Jake is coming too.'

Lily made the groaning *uhhh* sound her mum hated so much.

'Just get dressed, okay? And be nice to Jake. He's a lovely boy.'

Fifteen minutes later, tyres crunched on the gravel outside. Lily looked out of her window. Megan and Jake were getting out of a taxi along with the taxi driver, who escorted them to the front door. The bell rang.

By the time Lily got downstairs, Megan and Jake were standing in the hall and Mum was talking to the taxi man. It sounded like he was a neighbour and old friend of Megan's mum's, and he wasn't supposed to be working today but he'd run the kids over as a favour. He had nothing else to do. He winked at Lily over her mum's shoulder.

'Why don't you come in for a cup of tea, er . . . ?'

'Olly. Yeah, thanks, that would be great.'

'Follow me. Lily, why don't you take Megan and Jake down to the playroom? I'll bring you down some drinks and snacks in a bit.'

'Okay.' Lily hesitated. 'Where's Dad?'

Mum's eyes shifted around in that way they did when she wasn't sure what to say. 'He's having a lie-in.'

'Lucky bloke,' said Olly.

'Isn't he just?' She sounded angry, though she was trying to hide it behind the smile she always wore when they had visitors.

Mum and the taxi driver went off to the kitchen and Lily ran down the stairs to the playroom, Megan at her heels, Jake trailing behind.

Megan turned around. 'Hurry up, slowcoach.'

'Sorry, Meg.'

He almost bumped his head on the low ceiling halfway down the stairs. He was growing a moustache. *Bumfluff*, Megan called it.

She rolled her eyes, and Lily, not for the first time, felt sorry for him. Although she often wished she had a brother or sister, she'd hate to be bossed around in the way Megan bossed Jake.

Megan headed straight for the Wii U. 'Want a game of Mario Kart? Bet I can beat you this time.'

Last time Megan had come here she'd moaned that Lily didn't have that Bloody Mary game. Luckily, it wasn't available for the Wii U, so Lily had a good excuse.

As Megan set up the game, Lily turned her head to see what Jake was doing. He was staring at the art supplies. Lily remembered that he was really good at drawing and asked him if he wanted some paper and pens.

'Thanks, Lily.' He settled down on a beanbag with a pad and a pack of colouring pens.

Megan looked over her shoulder. 'Hey, Jake, it's Mum's birthday next week. Make her a card from both of us.'

'Yes, Meg.'

Lily and Megan played Mario Kart. Megan won the first race – thanks to a massively fluky blue shell right at the end – and Lily beat her in the second and third. They were about to start race four when the door at the top of the stairs opened.

'All right, guys?'

It was the taxi driver, carrying a tray with smoothies in cartons and a plate of chocolate chip cookies.

'Yay, snacks!' Megan paused the game. 'Thanks, Olly.'

He said to Lily, 'Your mum asked me to bring these down. She had to take a phone call.'

'Oh, right. Thanks.'

He looked around. 'This is a pretty cool space. What are you playing . . . ? Oh, I love that game. Who's your favourite character? I always play as Bowser. He's heavy but when he gets going – whoosh!' He laughed.

Lily stared at him. Was he like Jake? A little kid trapped in a big body?

'I haven't been to this house for years. My dad had a friend who lived here. Hey, you might have met my dad? He's the town librarian.'

Lily looked at him blankly. She had never been to Beddmawr Library. Why would she need to, when her house was full of books, most of them awesomely boring. Lily liked the books Mum had illustrated, partly because they were all dedicated to her.

Olly crouched down next to Jake. 'What are you drawing, mate?'

Jake, who had finished the birthday card and moved on to something else, showed him the paper.

'Woah, what's this?'

Lily peered over Olly's shoulder. The paper was covered in drawings of bare, spiky trees. At the centre of the drawing was a dark figure with arms and legs like wobbly spaghetti, a long body, and a fat head with cat's eyes. Jake had pressed so hard with the pen while drawing this figure he'd almost gone through the paper.

'It's the Widow,' Jake said in a hushed voice.

Lily expected Olly to laugh, but he didn't. His voice was as serious as Jake's when he replied.

'The Red Widow, eh? My dad told me about her.'

He repeated all the stuff Lily already knew. Even Megan appeared a little bored of the topic, but Jake gawped at Olly as if it was the first time he'd heard it.

Olly looked sidelong at the girls.

'I saw her once,' he said.

That grabbed their attention.

'You didn't,' Megan said.

'I did, actually. When I was about your age. It was just before that little girl disappeared. Carys.'

Lily stared at him, as did Megan and Jake. He settled down on a beanbag.

'I was in the woods, near here, with my friends, building a camp. Parents weren't so paranoid about letting kids out to play on their own in those days. Anyway, we'd built the camp and then one of my friends announced that he needed the loo. A number two.'

Megan giggled.

'Yeah, gross, huh? He went off to do what bears do in the woods, and a minute later he came running back, shouting and screaming, saying someone was chasing him. A woman. And that's when I saw her – between the trees. She had eyes just like that' – he tapped the drawing – 'and they glowed white, like she was blind. I got the impression she was sniffing the air, that she could smell us. Thinking we smelled sweet.'

Megan grabbed Lily's hand and squeezed it. Jake made a low moaning sound.

'And then she pointed at us and said, "It's time."'

There's no such thing, Lily reminded herself. *No such thing.*

'What did you do?' Megan asked.

'What do you think we did? We ran like our bums were on fire.' He laughed and the children stared at him.

'*It's time,*' Megan whispered.

'Yeah,' Olly said. 'Because the witch demands a sacrifice once every thirty-five years, according to the legend. When that little girl Carys vanished, that's what we all thought. The witch took her and gobbled her up.'

It was silent in the playroom. All Lily could hear was Jake's heavy breathing.

Olly looked at each of them in turn.

'You know that happened in 1980,' he said, and Lily realised he was just like Megan's grandad. He enjoyed winding up kids, seeing if they'd believe his scary stories. 'Next year it will be thirty-five years and it will be time again.' He looked at their gaping mouths and saucer eyes. 'She's going to be looking for another child.'

Chapter 30

As soon as we heard the scream, Julia took out her phone and switched on the flashlight, the weak light casting her in a ghostly glow. She headed for the stairs and I followed. I wished I hadn't left my new phone in my room.

It was dark in the hallway too. Somebody appeared in the Thomas Room doorway, a black silhouette. Julia pointed the beam of her phone flashlight at the door. It was Max.

'What was that scream?' Julia asked.

'Suzi. Ursula was in the middle of telling us this really creepy story about a dark spirit – you know, the usual nonsense she comes out with – and suddenly the lights went out. It was brilliant. It was as if she'd staged it.'

Julia stepped into the doorway and shone her light inside. Ursula sat in an armchair, apparently frozen to the spot, holding a glass of wine.

'Where's Suzi now?' I asked.

'She disappeared. I think she was embarrassed. She's gone to her room. Do you think it's a local power cut? Does that happen a lot round here?'

'Not since I've lived here,' Julia replied.

'It might be the fuses,' I said. 'It probably just needs resetting. Where's the box?'

'In the utility room.'

We left Max waiting by the Thomas Room and went through the kitchen to the little room where Julia kept her washing machine and dryer. She shone the flashlight at the fuse box, which was on the wall by the back door. I opened it.

'It's not the switches,' I said. 'It must be a power cut. Have you got any candles?'

'I think so. Hang on . . .' We went back into the kitchen.

If this had happened in my flat in London, we would have been fine. Priya had been obsessed with scented candles and most of them were still around. Sometimes I lit them to remind myself of her, if I was feeling strong enough. The smell of jasmine or cinnamon would always remind me of her. But Julia wasn't into candles. The only candles I'd seen since coming here were the ones on Lily's birthday cake.

She searched through the kitchen drawers. Loads of junk, but no candles.

'I think they're in the cottage,' she said.

Max had come into the kitchen, holding his phone, the flashlight switched on.

'I'll go and fetch them,' I said.

'I'll come too,' said Max.

'There's no need.'

But he was already heading out the back door. Julia handed me the key to the cottage and I went after him.

It was cold outside, and overcast, a few stars peeking through the gaps between the clouds. We only had Max's phone to illuminate the way, but as we moved towards the cottage my eyes started to grow accustomed to the darkness. Black shapes against a grey backdrop.

Max stopped walking.

'What are you doing?' I asked.

'I actually wanted a chance to talk to you,' he said. 'Listen, Lucas, I swear I didn't take your pen on purpose. I actually have no recollection of picking it up but, you know, we'd all had a drink.'

201

I could hardly see his face, but he sounded sincere and my emotions were reverberating from the encounter with Julia. I really didn't want another argument. 'It's okay,' I said. 'I'm sorry about earlier. I'd had a difficult day.'

'I apologise too for what I said. I know it's no excuse but I've been under a lot of stress too. Some marital issues, which is why I'm staying here a little longer. My wife doesn't want me to go home.'

I nodded.

'I didn't sleep with Suzi, though, whatever you think. I'm guilty of many things, but not that.' Again, he sounded sincere.

'I'm sorry if it seemed like I was judging you.'

He laughed. 'I hope no one overhears. They might think we're bonding.'

'Heaven forbid. Come on, we should try to find these candles.'

We headed over to the cottage and I opened the door. Max led the way, going into the kitchen first. I began to look through drawers while Max held the flashlight.

'The power will probably come back on the moment we find them,' he said.

There were no candles in the first drawer, or the second, though I found a cigarette lighter which I pocketed, thinking it would come in handy.

'You know, I kind of wish I wrote horror like you,' Max said. 'Or ghost stories, anyway. Think of all the inspiration I'd have had since coming here. Your creative synapses must be on fire.'

He didn't know the half of it. I was tempted to fill him in, but then he said, 'Something weird happened to me the other night.'

I paused halfway through searching the drawer. 'What?'

'Well, I got up in the middle of the night to go to the loo, and heard someone singing.'

I waited.

'It was a woman. At first I thought it must be Julia, but it didn't sound like it was coming from her bedroom. It sounded like someone was inside the room with me.'

'Was it this song?' I sang a couple of lines of '*Un, dau, tri . . .*'

'Yes, that was it!'

'I've heard it too,' I said. 'So did Karen. It was one of Lily's favourite songs, apparently.'

Max puffed out air. 'That matches what Ursula said . . . You don't believe in ghosts, do you? Even though you write horror?'

'No. I don't.'

I knew we ought to head back to the house, or look elsewhere in the cottage for candles. But Max seemed keen to talk. 'Me neither. Except . . .'

'What?'

'Talking to Ursula, it makes me wonder.'

'Oh, don't you start. She's making it all up.'

He leaned against the worktop, looking out at the night. The clouds had cleared a little, revealing more stars, silvery light glimmering across the lawn, with trees and shrubbery emerging from the darkness.

'She's very convincing,' he said. 'I told her about the singing I heard and she said it could be Lily's ghost, trapped here in this house, unwilling to move on to the next realm because of her mother's unhappiness. Ursula's going to consult her spirit guide. She said . . . Hang on, what was that?'

'What?' I joined him at the window.

'I saw someone. Over there, on the driveway. Look.'

I peered into the darkness. The clouds shifted, revealing the moon.

There was someone standing near the top of the driveway, facing us. It was too dark to make out their features, to even tell if it was a man or a woman. But a suspect immediately came to mind.

Before I could say anything, Max dashed from the kitchen and out of the front door. He called out, 'Hey!'

The person moved, down the driveway, away from the house. Max headed after them. I followed, catching up and falling into step beside him. The figure was running now, only just visible as a flickering shape on the horizon of my vision.

'I don't think it's a power cut,' Max said. 'Look – there's a light on in a house over there, on the hill.' He pointed towards the nearest neighbour.

The person we'd seen on the driveway had stopped running. I couldn't see their face, but I was certain they were watching us, waiting to see what we did. Could it really be Glynn Collins? A knot of fear formed in my stomach. If I was right, he'd already dealt with three people who'd threatened to expose him. I hadn't even stopped to think that I was the obvious next target.

In which case, I was walking straight into his trap.

'Come on,' Max said, and broke into a run. The shadowy figure ran too. I had no choice but to follow.

There were pot holes on the path, and I stumbled into one. Max grabbed my arm to stop me from falling. I glanced across at him and saw that he was grinning. He was enjoying it, like it was a game. He increased his pace, leaping over a huge puddle. I guessed this was an escape from his other worries: money, his career, marital woes. This was a little adventure.

We reached the narrow lane that bisected the trees and stopped. The lane stretched left and right, and directly ahead of us was a copse. The main road was beyond that, and a little further on, the river. Our quarry was no longer in sight.

'Which way did they go?' Max asked.

I held up a finger. 'Listen.'

Rustling came from the copse ahead. 'This way,' I said, jogging into the trees where I was swallowed by darkness. The ground beneath my feet was mulchy, slippery, and I grabbed a skinny tree for support. I waited for Max to catch up, as he was carrying our only source of light. He stopped beside me and swung the phone left and right, light bouncing between the trees like a will-o'-the-wisp. Tentatively, we pushed through the branches, Max swearing as something scratched his face. He lowered the flashlight and I hurried blindly on, the lizard part of my brain screaming at me to get out of these trees, even if greater danger lay further ahead. I was sweating and my heart was beating faster than ever before.

I crashed through the final line of trees and stumbled, my knees hitting the rough tarmac.

Max pulled me to my feet. 'You all right?'

I was too high on adrenaline to feel pain. I heard a twig snap ahead of us. 'I think he's heading to the river.'

Max nodded once, and strode into the final thicket of trees, their branches still bare from winter. I took a deep breath and joined him, pushing through until we emerged on the path that ran alongside the river.

'This is where Julia's husband drowned,' I said in a hushed voice. 'The exact spot.'

The water swept around the bend, sucking in starlight and snuffing it out. A curtain of mist hung over the far bank, casting the trees on that side as shadow play. Max looked around while I stared at the water, then hissed, 'There!'

Max dashed off to the left, vanishing into the copse. I did the same, pushing through into a clearing between a circle of trees. I strained to locate the light from Max's phone. There it was, to the right, dancing among the branches. I drew in a breath, afraid to speak.

I heard Max say, 'Show yourself!' A pause, then, 'What are you doing?'

It seemed he had come face to face with the person we'd been pursuing.

There was a scuffling sound, the crunch of twigs breaking and cracking. A grunt and the sound of something heavy hitting the ground. The spot of light from Max's phone disappeared.

'Max?'

I was frozen to the spot. I muttered to myself, 'Come on, come on, move', and managing to unstick my feet, I started towards the place in the trees where Max had been standing, pulling aside a pair of saplings that guarded the spot.

And then: noise behind me. Footsteps on wet leaves. I started to turn.

An explosion of pain in my head. I fell, blind. Hit the earth.

Darkness.

Chapter 31

I awoke in a world of pain and cold. My eyes opened but I was blind. My lungs tried to suck in air and my body flooded. My arms flailed but there was nothing to hold.

Maybe it only took a second for my brain to make sense of where I was, what was happening, but it felt like much longer. An eternity of confusion. By the time I figured it out, my palms felt solid ground beneath them.

The riverbed.

I was in the water.

The pain in my head was indescribable, like hot knives in grey matter. Inside my head, a wave of blackness tried to drag me under, my brain wanting to shut my body down, but a shred of survival instinct fought against it. I was drowning. Somehow, I marshalled the forces of my body, pushing against the riverbed and kicking upwards, flailing in the black, freezing water, feeling it dragging me back down like a creature—

Sweetmeat, come to me, my sweetmeat . . .

—had hold of my ankles. I screamed an inaudible scream, kicked and pulled, fought to escape this liquid grave. *Give in*, said a voice inside me. *Let go, accept it. Sink into nothingness. No more pain. No more suffering—*

Let me make you better, my sweeeeetmeat . . .

No. I refused to let go. I refused to die.

With the last of my strength, I pushed upwards, towards the stars that shone high above the surface and called to me, told me to keep going, to not give up.

I burst through.

Snapped at the air.

Fought the desperate screaming pain in my skull and kicked towards the bank. I grabbed at weeds that tore away in my hands. To the left, I saw the flat stones on which Julia had stood, unable to save her husband. I dragged myself towards them, finally crawling from the water. Gasping and shivering, I lay on my back on the stones, eyes shut, blackness rushing over me again. I surrendered to it.

ω

'Lucas? Lucas!'

I didn't wake suddenly this time. Darkness slowly retreated. Someone was saying my name.

A warm hand touched my face and something was laid over me.

'Lucas, it's me, Julia.'

My eyes opened and I saw her looking down at me. I tried to speak but my teeth were chattering too much. She held my hand, squeezed it. Above her head, the stars that had saved me.

I realised she had covered my soaking wet body with her coat. I tried to push myself up but a lightning bolt of pain flashed through my skull. I gasped and a look of concern flitted across Julia's face.

'I came looking for you,' she said, 'when you didn't come back from the cottage. What happened? Why were you in the water?'

I tried to speak again, but coughed instead, river water running from my mouth. Julia knelt beside me, gently turning me onto my side so I didn't choke. She repositioned the coat.

'I've called an ambulance,' she said.

I coughed and spluttered again, more water spilling from my lungs. I was trembling all over and didn't think I would ever feel warm again. But I needed to speak, to ask her something.

'Max,' I managed to say. 'Where is he?'

Once again, before she could answer, I blacked out.

ʊ

I woke up in hospital. The pain in my head had subsided – they must have pumped me full of painkillers. I tested my arms and legs, fingers and toes. Everything seemed to work. I was still nauseous, shaky, cold. But I pushed myself into a sitting position, careful not to disturb the tube that ran from a drip into my arm. I gingerly felt the back of my head, which was covered with a bandage. Morning light streamed through the window.

A nurse spotted me and headed over.

'Mr Radcliffe. You need to take it easy.' She had an Eastern European accent and kind eyes.

'Is Julia here?' I asked.

'Is that the woman who found you? She's nearby, don't worry. The doctor's going to want to take a look at you. I'll let him know you're awake.'

She was about to go when I said, 'Wait. Max Lake? Is he here?' I strained to look around the ward but couldn't see him.

She attempted a reassuring smile which didn't quite come off. 'I think the police want to talk to you as soon as the doctor says it's okay.' She hurried away.

The doctor came, gave me the once-over, and told me I was fine but they were going to keep me in for a little while for observation. They were mostly concerned about my head injury.

'It's not as bad as it must have felt,' the doctor said. 'Your skull isn't fractured. We've already carried out an X-ray and scan and there doesn't appear to be any internal damage. You have a tough head, Mr Radcliffe. But we want to monitor you for concussion and so on. There's a risk of a subdural haematoma developing, but I think you're going to be okay.'

'What was I hit with?' I asked.

'Hmm.' He consulted his notes. 'A rock, I think. But the police will be able to tell you more.'

'What about Max Lake? Is he here?'

The doctor frowned. 'Not that I'm aware of.'

Half an hour later I was lying with my eyes closed, replaying what had happened, when I heard someone say my name. I opened my eyes to see a woman with short, dark hair standing over me. She introduced herself as Detective Constable Carla Hawkins.

'Are you feeling up to answering some questions?' she asked, pulling up a plastic chair.

'Of course. But can you answer one of mine first? Max Lake? Where is he? Is he okay?'

She formed a fist with her hand and put it to her lips, clearing her throat. 'I'm afraid Mr Lake's body was recovered from the River Dee early this morning.'

'Oh Jesus.'

I wasn't shocked. Since waking up I had been steeling myself for this news. The same thing that happened to me had clearly happened to Max, except he hadn't managed to get out of the river. Had he even woken up and struggled? I hoped not. Better to be oblivious than to struggle against drowning and fail.

'Were you close?' DC Hawkins asked, studying me, obviously trying to read my face and body language.

'No. I've only known him a couple of weeks. But . . .' Guilt squeezed my insides. 'It's my fault. I brought this upon us, and I'm alive and he's . . . dead.'

'What do you mean, you brought this upon you? Do you know who did this?' She had a notepad ready in her lap, pencil poised.

Just as I had with Julia last night – my God, what a long twenty-four hours it had been – I ran through the whole story, keeping it as succinct as possible. DC Hawkins interrupted every so often to ask questions. I didn't mention any of the weird goings-on at the retreat and I tried to avoid straying into conspiracy theory territory.

At the end, I said, 'It's Glynn Collins. He did this.'

DC Hawkins tapped her pencil slowly on the pad. 'Did you see him?'

'No, it was too dark, but I'm sure it was him. Who else could it be?'

The look she gave me was inscrutable.

'Do you know him?' I asked. My head throbbed and I winced as I spoke. 'Everyone says he's a pillar of the community.'

She shook her head. 'I'm based in Wrexham.'

'One of your colleagues had a relationship with Zara Sullivan, the private detective I hired. I don't know his name but maybe Zara spoke to him between talking to me and disappearing.'

'We'll look into it,' she said.

There was a long silence. I broke it by saying, 'So this is a murder investigation?'

Her expression was grim. 'We don't get many of those around here.'

'Just missing children.'

She stood up. 'Two in forty years. It's hardly an epidemic.' She handed me her card. 'We'll be in touch. If you remember anything else in the meantime, any details that can help us identify your assailant, please call me.'

'What about protection?' I asked. 'For me, I mean. He tried to kill me. What if he comes here to finish the job?'

She spread her palms to indicate that I was surrounded by people. 'You'll be safe here, Mr Radcliffe. Try not to worry.'

ᚹ

I woke up later to find Julia sitting by the bed.

'I brought you some snacks,' she said, gesturing to a couple of bags on the bedside cabinet. 'And some magazines. I brought your phone too.' She handed me the phone I'd bought to replace my lost one. 'How are you feeling?'

'I think I'm in shock. About Max, I mean.'

She brushed a hand across her forehead and sighed. She looked terribly sad. I realised the whole thing must have taken her back to the terrible events two years before, when she watched Michael drown in that same spot.

'Thank you for saving me,' I said. 'I probably would have died of hypothermia if I'd been left there by the river. I expect you were tempted to let me.'

She exhaled. 'I understand why you did it. And I know you were trying to help.'

I smiled at her.

'I'm still angry with you.'

My smile faded.

'But I'm glad you didn't drown.'

I guessed that was the best I was going to get.

'So you didn't see anyone? By the river?' she asked.

I repeated what I'd told DC Hawkins and half expected Julia to be sceptical, as she'd been earlier. But this was different, wasn't it? There was no way this could be put down to natural causes or an innocent explanation. Someone had attacked me. Someone had murdered Max.

'You really think Glynn knows something about Lily?' she asked. Her voice was full of longing and terror.

'Hopefully the police will be talking to him now,' I said. 'Have they been to your house? Did they look at what happened to the electricity?'

'Oh yes, they've been round. Two of them came and interviewed Ursula and Suzi and me, looked around. They took Max's computer. Yours too.'

'What?'

'Sorry, I couldn't stop them. They said they needed to check it. They didn't say why.'

My novel was on that laptop, and although it was backed up to the Cloud I didn't have access to another computer here. Still, it hardly seemed like the most important thing at the moment.

'And the electricity?' I asked.

'It came on before I got back to the house,' she replied. 'I told the police about it and they said they'd look into that too. They're frustratingly vague. They were like this when Lily disappeared.'

My headache was coming back with a vengeance now. My vision was soft around the edges, a steady pain pulsing out from the back of my skull. I needed whatever drugs the doctors were willing to give me.

'How are the others? Suzi and Ursula?'

Julia shook her head. 'Ursula has taken to her bed. I can't get any sense out of her. Suzi . . . well, she's really upset. She locked herself in her room after she heard about Max, but I could hear her crying.'

'Max told me there was nothing going on between them.'

'Did you believe him?'

I thought about it. 'Yeah, I did. God, I'm glad I managed to apologise to him before . . . it happened.'

Julia shifted in her seat. 'Ursula told the police about your argument.'

'Oh, great.'

'It's been like a circus at the house. As well as the police, the media turned up. We've had photographers and video crews outside.' Her face darkened. 'The bastards mentioned Michael and Lily on the news reports. *Tragedy strikes again in beauty spot*, all that bullshit. Apparently, Max's wife is on her way too, to collect his things and see where it happened. I haven't been down to the river, but I've heard it's teeming with rubberneckers.'

Without warning, she grabbed my hand.

'I'm so . . .' She stopped, then forced herself to continue. 'I'm so glad you got out of the water.'

Taken aback, I tried to make light of it. 'Me too.'

'When I saw you lying there, on the stones, I thought you were dead.' To my surprise, tears filled her eyes. She continued to hold my hand, but gazed into space, into the past. 'I don't think . . . I don't think I ever mourned Michael properly. I was so fixated on finding Lily. Even his funeral . . . I was numb. Not able to grieve. I'm told I cried, but I don't remember. I hardly heard a word of the service.'

I squeezed her hand and waited for her to continue.

'I miss him,' she said. 'I was angry with him for a long time, once the numbness passed. Angry for his drinking, blaming him for the argument that meant we weren't watching Lily. Our marriage hadn't been good for a long time and we were probably going to break up. I mean, we'd been in and out of the last-chance saloon a dozen times. He'd promised he was going to give up the booze because it was destroying us . . . But he didn't. And I realised, that day, he never would.' She produced a tissue and blew her nose. 'Five minutes later, he was dead.'

I waited for her to continue.

'There was another thing too . . . Another woman. I never found out for sure, but I think Michael was cheating on me with this woman in his office. Lana. Maybe they were only emotionally involved, I don't know. But there was something going on. He probably would have ended up with her after we split up and I wonder, sometimes, if he kept drinking because he wanted me to chuck him out. It was his passive way of ending our marriage.'

She blew her nose again. 'He loved Lily, though. I guess she's the other reason he hung around.' She wiped the tears from her cheeks and sniffed. 'Oh God, you're lying there with a massive bandage on your head after someone tried to kill you, and here I am, going on about my woes.'

'Julia, don't be silly. It's good. You should talk about it.'

She shuddered. 'I'm scared, Lucas. I can't even express exactly why. But I'm scared.'

I tried to find the right words, but before I could locate them someone said my name. 'Mr Radcliffe?'

It was DC Hawkins. This time she had another cop with her, a middle-aged man in an ageing suit. She introduced him as Detective Inspector Garry Snaith.

He nodded at Julia. 'Mrs Marsh.'

He must have met her at Nyth Bran. I wondered if he'd also been involved in the search for Lily two years ago.

'Do you mind if we have a word with Mr Radcliffe on his own?' he asked.

She was flustered. 'Yes. I mean, no. I need to get back anyway. I'll call you later, Lucas.'

As soon as she'd gone, DC Hawkins said, 'We spoke to Glynn Collins. He was at home all night, with his girlfriend.'

I pushed myself up in the bed. 'Girlfriend?'

DI Snaith smiled. 'Perhaps "lady friend" would be a better term. But yes, seems there's life in the old dog.'

I wondered if this was the woman he'd been talking to at the funeral; the one with the cleavage.

'Mr Collins' lady friend is an insomniac,' Snaith continued. 'She was awake most of the night, with her *gentleman* friend lying beside her, snoring.'

'So whoever attacked you,' Hawkins said. 'It wasn't Glynn Collins.'

Chapter 32

The two detectives stayed for ages, conducting what they called an informal chat. They wanted to know everything about me. Did I have any enemies? Did Max? They'd heard Max and I had a fight yesterday – could I tell them more about that? Why did we decide to follow the person we'd seen down to the river? Had we been drinking?

'Why are you asking if Max had enemies?' I said. 'I told you – I was the target.'

'So why kill Mr Lake?' DC Hawkins asked.

'I think he saw their face.'

As I was answering their questions, my mind whirred. If it wasn't Glynn who attacked me and killed Max, who the hell was it? Did this mean he wasn't responsible for everything else? Had I been completely wrong?

'Are you sure Glynn Collins's lady friend isn't lying for him?' I asked.

'You can never be one hundred per cent,' Snaith responded. 'But she, Margaret, is the ex-wife of one of our retired chief inspectors. He told us she's the most honest woman he's ever met and there's no way she'd protect a criminal. Also, Mr Collins has this app on his phone that records his sleep patterns.'

I nodded. Priya had used one of those.

'He showed it to us. According to this app, he slept like a baby while Margaret tossed and turned beside him.'

'Maybe he has someone helping him,' I said. Even as the words came out I realised how desperate I sounded.

The two detectives exchanged a look. DC Hawkins spoke. 'The two deaths you told us about, Malcolm Jones and Shirley Roberts. There's nothing suspicious about either of them. Mr Jones was taking medication for a heart condition. It appears he forgot to take his tablets.'

That seemed strange to me, but I let her go on. 'And by all accounts, Ms Roberts was inebriated when she left the wake. Those stairs are steep. I don't want to pre-empt the coroner, but there's nothing to indicate it wasn't an accident.'

'So we are looking at the attack on you and Max Lake as an isolated incident,' DI Snaith said.

'But what about Zara Sullivan? Have you tracked her down?'

Again, they exchanged a glance. 'You're a writer, aren't you, Mr Radcliffe?' DC Hawkins said. 'Highly imaginative. Always looking for hidden motives and meanings. Well, let me tell you, as someone who deals with reality every day . . .'

'The simplest explanation for something is almost always the right one.'

She raised an eyebrow. 'Exactly.'

My head was pounding again. I had wanted to talk to them about the strange goings-on at the retreat, but what was the point? They had me marked down as someone who makes shit up: a novelist with an overactive imagination.

A nurse came over. 'I think the patient needs to rest now.'

'Sure.'

The detectives got up, DI Snaith grunting as he rose from his plastic seat. DC Hawkins studied me for a moment and I wished I could read her mind, because I was certain there was suspicion in her eyes.

'We'll talk again,' she said before they walked away.

ʊ

The hospital discharged me the following afternoon. The doctor gave
me a self-help sheet listing symptoms I needed to look out for: drowsiness, poor tolerance of light, feelings of disorientation, confusion. I
tried to make a joke about always feeling confused, but the doctor
wasn't amused.

I didn't want to bother Julia by asking her to pick me up, so I
called Olly Jones. It was a long way for him to come but I thought he'd
appreciate the fare. And it wasn't only that I didn't want to bother Julia.
I wanted to talk to Olly.

'Look at you: the walking wounded,' he said as I approached the
taxi and got into the back seat. It was a lovely day, mild and bright,
and it was warm inside the cab. For the first time in months, I felt the
prickle of sweat beneath my armpits.

'I heard about what happened,' Olly said, starting the engine.
'Shocking. Do you have any idea who did it? Who whacked you over
the head, I mean?'

'No.'

'I bet the police haven't got a bloody clue either, am I right?'

'They don't seem to.'

He turned on to the main road. 'Shocking to think two people,
probably three, have drowned in that same spot in, like, two years.' He
swore at a driver who swerved in front of him. 'That Lily was a lovely
girl, you know. I hope she's still out there somewhere.'

I sat forward. 'You knew her?'

'Yeah. I live a few doors down from her friends, Megan and Jake. I
know their mum pretty well.'

Of course. Everyone round here knows everyone else.

'And my dad was good friends with Wendy's dad. Have you met
Wendy? She's lovely. Plus Megan's a little character and Jake . . . well,
Wendy does a brilliant job with him, considering his issues.' He paused.
'I feel a bit guilty, actually. I told Lily and the others this story about
how I'd seen the Widow when I was a kid. I was just winding them up,

having a laugh, but I think they believed me. I always picture Lily with this frightened look on her face. I should have told her it was a joke.'

I tried to get a grip on the conversation. 'I didn't get a chance to talk to you properly at the funeral. I told you about our dads being friends, didn't I?'

'Yeah.' He laughed. 'Weird to think we might have played together when we were little, before you moved away.'

'I know. So . . . what happened with your dad? Someone told me he had a heart condition.'

'Yeah, and the silly fool forgot to take his medicine.'

I feigned ignorance. 'Surely forgetting for, what, one day wouldn't cause you to have a heart attack? I mean, I'm no expert but . . .'

'No. But the doctor told me he must have been under a lot of stress the day he died. And the fact he'd forgotten the medicine didn't help. God knows what he was stressed about. I mean, he was at home watching TV. I guess he must have been worried about something.'

I felt bad. The topic was clearly distressing Olly. But I pressed on anyway. Despite what the police said, I was still convinced Malcolm's death was connected to everything else.

'Did you see him . . . the day he died, I mean? Did he seem worried?'

'No, I didn't.' He fell quiet. I thought maybe I'd pushed him too far. He was still grieving, the wounds raw. 'I spoke to him on the phone, though, and he was acting a bit weird.'

'What do you mean?'

'Just, you know, being more emotional than normal. He said something about how he'd let my mum down, how it was too late to make amends now. I had no idea what he was going on about. To be honest, I wondered if he'd been drinking. Or if it was, like, the first signs of dementia.' We had stopped at a red light. Olly rubbed his eyes with his fist. 'Then he said something really odd. He asked me if I would forgive him if he'd done something terrible.'

The hairs on my arms were standing on end.

'No, hang on. What he said was, would I forgive him if he'd kept a terrible secret. I asked him what the hell he was talking about and it was like he chickened out, started saying it was nothing to worry about, just the ramblings of an old man.' His jaw was clenched and I was worried Olly was about to start crying. He prevented himself from doing so by changing the subject. 'You're into books and stuff, aren't you? Of course you are. My dad had thousands of the bloody things and I've got no idea what to do with them. Maybe you could pop round, take a look and see if there are any you want. Take them off my hands.'

'That's very kind of you, but maybe you should call a dealer. There might be some valuable books among them.'

'Yeah, that's what Heledd said I should do.' He shook his head. 'It's weird. Both our parents dying within a week of each other. What are the odds, eh? She's got the B & B to sort out and isn't sure if she's going to carry on running it. She's talking about selling it and living on the proceeds. I'm trying to persuade her to move in with me.'

'How long have you and Heledd been together?' I asked.

'Twenty years.'

'What?' I was shocked.

He laughed. 'Including the eighteen-year break in the middle. We were together for a year when we were young. We got back together last year. I finally wore her down.'

'And neither of you have children?'

'I have, but they live in Cardiff with their mum, my ex-wife. Heledd doesn't have kids, though. She says this isn't a good place to raise children.'

The whole thing saddened me. It seemed Heledd had stayed here all these years because of Shirley, and now she was threatening to take off and leave Olly behind.

We drove in silence for a few minutes. We weren't far from the retreat now.

'So you have no idea what secret your dad was talking about?' I asked.

He hesitated, just for a second, before saying no. There was clearly something, perhaps buried deep, a doubt or suspicion. I decided not to push it. He would be thinking about it now. Hopefully it would come to the surface.

'Maybe I will come to take a look at those books,' I said as we pulled up outside Nyth Bran.

'Cool.' He made a telephone sign with his little finger and thumb – *call me* – and drove away.

ʊ

Julia was in the kitchen, sitting at the breakfast counter with a cup of tea, surveying the garden. Dark circles ringed her eyes but the sunlight touched her hair and lit up her face, stopping me in my tracks.

'It's rude to stare,' she said, getting up and coming over. She peered at the bandage on the back of my head. 'Any bits of brain leak out?' she asked.

'No important bits, I don't think.'

'Still got the part that contains your common sense?'

'Oh God, no. That withered and died a long time ago.'

She smiled. 'Coffee?'

'It's okay, I'll make it.'

'If you're sure.' Julia leaned against the counter. As I filled the kettle and placed it on the Aga, she said, 'The police were here again, asking questions.'

'About what?'

'About you.'

I turned from the Aga. 'What kind of questions?'

She cradled her tea. 'They wanted to know about your relationship with Max, how you got on. Snaith had a copy of your novel.'

'*Sweetmeat?*'

'Yeah. He was flicking through it, reading out some of the violent scenes. He asked me if you had shown any signs of aggression since you'd been here. Of course, Ursula had already told them about the time you threatened Max.'

'Jesus. They can't believe that was a real threat, surely? What, do they think I killed Max then hit myself over the head with a rock and jumped in the river? That's nuts.'

'I don't know what they think, Lucas. At least the reporters have gone. There was a house fire in Wrexham, several kids trapped . . . I can't bear to think about it. They've all gone there.'

I finished making the coffee, adding two sugars.

'Where's Ursula now?' I asked.

'In her room. She's talking about leaving in the next couple of days.'

'And Suzi?'

'Same. Looks like you're going to be my only customer, unless you're planning on buggering off too.'

'I doubt the police would let me go, even if I wanted to. But I'm not going anywhere. Assuming that's okay with you?'

She met my eye. 'Of course. I want you to stay.' A wry smile. 'I doubt I'll get any more customers coming here after what happened. Not that it matters, anyway. Maybe the whole thing was a terrible idea. I should start illustrating again. Find work. I've still got contacts.'

The energy seemed to drain from her body.

'It feels pointless. All of it.'

'Julia . . .'

I got up and crossed the kitchen to where she stood. She looked up at me, eyes brimming with tears. I put my hand out, touched her arm. She stepped closer to me. We were inches apart, the silence so heavy between us, the air as thick as tar. She moved closer still.

Time stopped. The world was silent. I touched her cheek and brushed away a tear with my thumb.

She rested her forehead against mine. Beyond the window, a bird called out. Sunshine danced across the kitchen. I closed my eyes and waited for our lips to meet.

Suddenly, I was holding empty air.

I opened my eyes. She was in the doorway, arms wrapped around herself. She was painfully beautiful.

'I'm sorry,' she said as she left the room.

Chapter 33

Drowsiness, poor tolerance of light, feelings of disorientation, confusion. I had the full set, but I didn't think it had anything to do with my head injury. I sat at the desk in my room and tried to figure out what to do next. The police had my laptop so I couldn't work. I thought about calling DC Hawkins and DI Snaith and demanding it back, but I didn't want to face more of their questions. If they suspected me, did I need to get a solicitor? Were they going to bring me in for questioning? Nerves chewed at my stomach.

I opened my phone and caught up on the news. Max got all the headlines, of course. Apparently his last book was now number one on Amazon.

It's what he would have wanted.

My inbox was flooded with emails from my agent and publisher, both of them telling me if I needed more time to finish the book, that was understandable. Finally, a tiny silver lining – though I felt guilty thinking any positive thoughts. I had lots of emails from readers too, hoping this wouldn't delay my next novel, and my Facebook page was abuzz with well-wishers. I left a message letting everyone know I was okay, with a link to a page Max's family had set up for donations to a charity in his name.

I had a knot in my stomach the size of Hawaii. Half of me was afraid that whoever had tried to kill me – and I was sceptical about Glynn Collins's alibi – would come back. The other half wanted him to appear so I could confront him. I would be prepared this time. I parted the curtains and looked out at the darkening landscape. It was silent out there; silent and still. The retreat was locked up and secure. No one could get in.

I made a list in my aching head of things I needed to do. Go and see Olly to talk more about his dad. Try to persuade the police that I wasn't a fantasist. Persuade them to check if Zara's passport had been used.

Persuade them, too, that I hadn't murdered Max.

I was exhausted. I felt it deep in my muscles, and in my soul. I went along to the bathroom and ran a bath. The hot water soothed me, and by the time the water started to cool I was almost asleep. I dragged myself to the bedroom and, still damp, fell naked into bed. Into sleep.

ω

The door clicked open. Someone was in my room. But, unlike before, I had left the curtains parted. By the light of the moon, I could see a silhouette standing by the bed as it appeared to slough off its skin. Something soft hit the floor.

The silhouette slipped under my covers.

'What—' I began.

A finger touched my lips. 'Shush.'

It was Julia. Her mouth met mine and an arm slipped around me. She was naked, her skin cool and soft. I pulled her closer, feeling how her body trembled, breath quickening as she kissed me harder, silky hair falling over my face, tickling me as she pushed herself up, manoeuvring me onto my back. She lay flat upon me, legs stretched out along mine,

225

breasts pressed against my chest, one hand gripping mine against the sheets. Skin against skin. Lips against lips.

Then she was sitting up, astride me, rocking slowly, palms flat on my chest, hair falling forward as her hips moved, back, forth, back, forth. I sat up, kissing her deeply and pulling her against me as she nipped at my lips, raked her fingernails down my back. She pushed herself harder against me and I could sense her frustration, the need for an orgasm, and I turned her over, withdrew and put my head between her legs. I glanced up at her, across the glorious landscape of her flesh, the flush around her collarbone, the increasing rise and fall of her chest, and with my fingers and tongue, I made her come.

A moment later, I was inside her again, and I tried to fight it, to hold back, but she murmured, 'It's okay', and I surrendered, a climax like a series of explosions rippling across my entire body.

She lay with her head on my chest. We didn't speak. A little while later we started kissing again. We kissed for what felt like hours. It felt like a dream, like being outside myself. I know at some point we made each other come again.

I remember hearing someone singing, very faintly in the distance. *Un, dau, tri. Mam yn dal y pry.* I think I tried to remark on it, but my mouth was too tired, my tongue too heavy.

The next thing I knew it was light.

And Julia was gone.

ʊ

I found her in the cottage. She had her hair pinned up and was sorting through some paperwork on the kitchen table. She looked up, and smiled when she saw me.

'Are you looking for breakfast? I'm afraid the schedule's gone to hell.'

'No. Of course not. I . . .' Words failed me. I was as tongue-tied as a love-struck teenager. 'Julia . . .'

She got up from the table and pulled me into a hug, quietening me. It felt very much like a platonic hug.

'Julia . . .' I began again.

'Lucas. Let's not talk about it, okay? It was something I needed, that's all.'

'Oh.'

She laughed. 'Please don't look so disappointed. I really don't want to have a long, awkward conversation about it. It felt like something you needed too. No more than that, and no less. You don't want more than that, surely. I'm a mess, and I get the impression you're not ready to move on.'

Was she right? I didn't know. It had been two years since I lost Priya. I missed her, of course I still missed her. But the pain, which used to be ever present, the overriding emotion that darkened every hour of every day, had dimmed. Now I could go for hours without thinking about her before being shocked out of forgetfulness by guilt.

But I didn't feel guilty about sleeping with Julia. Because I was still here, wasn't I? Still living. Still in need of human warmth and pleasure. Still trying to be happy. I was certain Priya, if she was watching me, wouldn't begrudge me that. I was sure, in fact, she'd be cheering me on.

It was different for Julia, though. I understood that. It was more complex, because of Lily. I could move on, but Julia was in limbo.

She sat back down and I joined her at the table. She pulled the paperwork towards her, arranging it into a pile.

'Do you want to talk about it?' she asked. 'The person you lost . . . I assume it was a girlfriend?'

'Yes. Yes, she was.' And I told her what had happened. My panic when Priya didn't turn up at work. Finding her body. The hit and run.

'The police found the guy who did it a week later. He was some high-ranking council official who'd been visiting his mistress before work. It was an accident – he was racing to get to the office before he was missed – and he panicked, thinking he'd lose his job and his wife and kids . . . I was there in court. He seemed genuinely ashamed, kept saying sorry, but I still hated him. If they told me he'd killed himself I'd be happy.' I looked up at Julia. 'That's terrible, isn't it.'

'No. It's understandable. If someone took Lily, and if I ever find them . . .' She didn't need to complete the sentence but her eyes reflected the hatred I still harboured for the man who killed Priya.

'I was luckier than you,' I said. 'I got closure. And Priya's death had an unexpected effect on me. I thought if anything like that ever happened to me I would fall apart, that writing would be at the bottom of my priority list, but the opposite happened. Priya had been so enthusiastic about *Sweetmeat*, which was an embryonic idea at that point, that I became determined, absolutely driven, to finish it. To make it soar, for her. I guess the aftershock of my dad's death was mixed in with it too, the feeling that I'd never made him proud. So I put everything into that book. Everything. For the first time in my life, it was easy, and I knew it was good.'

'And when it was successful, did it make you feel better? Did you feel like you'd done Priya and your dad proud?'

'Yeah, kind of. It was exciting, exhilarating, but it was also kind of scary. When there's been this thing you've wanted your whole life, and you think: *if this happens, everything will be perfect, I'll be happy at last* . . . You convince yourself it will fix you. And then it happens.'

'And it doesn't fix you.'

'No. I wasn't any happier. It didn't make me any less cut up about losing Priya or my dad. Time was the only thing that could do that.'

She nodded and I went on.

'I was a mess. I'm still a mess. But you know what? I feel different now, after what happened to me and Max. Almost dying . . . It's a massive cliché, but it really fucking focuses the mind. This is my second chance. My chance to get my shit together and be happy.' I was silent for a moment, and she waited for me to continue. 'Getting to know you, Julia, has made me realise I don't have any real problems. Nothing compared to what you've gone through. You're so strong.'

'I'm not strong.'

'No. You are. You really are. You're amazing. I know you don't want any more from me, but I just wanted you to know that I think you're amazing.'

'I'm not . . .' She broke off. 'Hang on, we've got company.'

It was Ursula. She burst into the cottage and came straight into the little kitchen. Her hair was sticking up and there was a bed-crease on the side of her face. She was pale, her expression flicking between anxiety and excitement.

'Are you all right?' Julia asked, standing up.

Ursula swiped at her ear as if a wasp was bothering her. Despite my antipathy towards her, I was concerned. There was clearly something wrong.

'My spirit guide, Phoebe,' she said. 'She spoke to me, during the night.'

My concern evaporated. It was just Ursula, talking her usual nonsense.

'And what did she tell you?'

'First, she told me where to find your phone.'

I glanced at Julia, to see if she was as incredulous as I was. She mainly looked worried.

'Oh?' I said. 'Where is it, then?'

'On the bookshelf in the Thomas Room. I asked my guide exactly where and she sang to me. An old children's nonsense rhyme.'

I stared at her. 'Wait here.'

I left the cottage and hurried over to the main house, going straight into the sitting room. I located 'The Owl and the Pussycat' straight away and pulled it out. I couldn't see my phone, so I pulled out a few more books, revealing a gap at the back of the shelf.

And there it was. My missing phone.

On the way back to the cottage I pressed the home button but the phone was dead. I waved it as I re-entered the cottage kitchen.

'She was right. It was there.' I addressed Ursula: 'You must have taken it, hidden it there.'

'Don't be ridiculous.'

I searched my memory. Could I have put it there, on the shelf, the night Ursula arrived? I had a vague memory of going over to look at the books. It was possible; I could have rested it on the line of books and it might have slipped down behind them. I didn't know what to think.

Julia spoke up. 'Did your spirit guide come to you in the night just to tell you where to find Lucas's phone? Does she do that often? Tell you where to find lost things?'

'Sometimes she does.' She looked meaningfully at Julia. 'You should sit down, dear.'

'I'm okay where I am.'

'Very well. You might find this a little alarming, but I'm going to ask my guide to speak to you directly.'

'You're kidding,' I said. 'Julia, come on. Let's go.'

But she wouldn't move. 'No. I want to see this.'

Ursula drew in a long, deep breath, spread her fingers out on the table and closed her eyes. She was silent for so long that I felt the urge to speak, to ask her what she was playing at. But then she started talking.

Her voice was different, higher and younger. It was faintly absurd, but eerie too. She kept her eyes shut and tilted her head to one side as she spoke.

'Julia, your child is gone. Lily is gone.'

Julia put her hand to her mouth. Ursula tilted her head to the other side.

'But do not worry. She is safe, she is happy. She's in a better place, the best place. I've seen her and spoken to her. She wants you to know that she loves you. Her daddy is with her too and they're happy together, even though they miss you.'

'Julia,' I said, but she shushed me.

Ursula smiled, a ghastly smile that made her, with her white face and voluminous hair, look like a Victorian doll. 'Lily's safe now. You don't need to worry about her any more. You don't need to look for her. She's with Jesus.'

PART THREE

Chapter 34

Ursula's eyes darted around the room, as if she didn't know where she was. She clamped her hand over her mouth. Moving twice as fast as normal, she exited the room, dashing to the toilet. I heard retching, then the toilet flushing and a running tap. When she came back into the kitchen she was as pale as bone, and beads of sweat clung to her brow and upper lip.

She sat down.

'Would you mind fetching me a glass of water?'

Julia was frozen still, unable to take her eyes off Ursula. I found a glass, filled it from the tap and handed it to Ursula. She gulped it down.

'I apologise,' she said. 'This always happens when I channel. Would you mind leaving me for a minute, until I get my strength back.'

I was glad to get out of that room, but Julia was more reluctant.

'She said Lily's with Michael,' Julia said. 'And Jesus.'

Ursula half-smiled. 'Did she? I didn't hear what was said. I was in another place.'

'Come on, Julia,' I said, guiding her from the room. We left the cottage and stepped into the garden. Julia was in a daze. I tried to put my arm around her, but she pushed me away.

'Please, I want to be on my own for a minute.'

'You can't believe that was real, surely?'

'She knew where to find your phone, didn't she?'

I could feel all the warmth between us draining away. I was convinced what Ursula had done was an act. Perhaps she was insane and thought it was real, but the idea that someone could channel a spirit who would talk through them was nonsense. I knew Julia was desperate to believe it, but it was so frustrating. I was surrounded by superstition and irrational beliefs. What next? Was Ursula going to claim that a woodland spirit knocked Max and me over the head with a rock and chucked us in the river?

'She probably hid my phone in the first place so she could set this up. Next she'll be asking you for money in exchange for messages from Lily.'

Julia started towards the house but stopped and whirled round. She jabbed a finger towards me. 'You don't get it, do you? How it feels.'

She thumped her chest with a flat hand.

'You tell me I'm "amazing".' She made air quotes with her fingers. 'For what? Being strong? Holding it together? You have no idea . . .'

Ursula had come out of the cottage and was watching us. Julia ignored her.

'You don't know how much it hurts, Lucas. No idea how many times I've been down to that river and thought about throwing myself in, knowing I'd drown because I'm so weak I can't even swim. If someone showed me proof that Lily was dead, then maybe I'd do it. There'd be nothing to stop me any more. No hope left to keep me alive.' She waved an arm at the house. 'I thought when I opened the retreat it would give me some new purpose. A business to run. Something for me. What a mistake!' She began to laugh, on the edge of hysteria. 'I should have gone with my original idea and opened a boarding kennel. Dogs might be needy and difficult, but my God they're not half as needy as you writers.'

She turned her attention to Ursula, who still loitered by the door of the cottage.

'So what should I do, huh? Are you telling me Lily is dead, one hundred per cent? Should I give up hope? Should I go and throw myself in the river?'

'Julia—'

She cut me dead with a glare and took a step towards the cottage. 'Come on, Ursula. What does your spirit guide say? Does Lily want me with her, now?'

Ursula clung to the door frame. It was scary how much she'd aged almost overnight. 'No, Julia. She doesn't want you to join her. I expect she wants you to find the person who did it to her. The person who killed her.'

Julia and I both stared at her.

'And did your guide give you any clues?' Julia asked, her voice hard and cynical. *At least*, I thought, *she doesn't seem to believe Ursula now.* Her anger had burned away the belief.

'Not yet,' Ursula said.

'Well, give me a call if she does. I want you to go. Pack your bag and go home.'

I couldn't help but smile, until Julia whirled round to point at me. 'You too. All of you.'

She gestured to Suzi, who had appeared by the front door of the house. She looked a mess, pale and shaky. She seemed almost relieved to be given her marching orders. She hung her head and went back inside.

'The police told me I needed to stay nearby,' I said after Suzi had gone, aware of how pathetic that sounded.

'Get a room in town then,' Julia snapped.

She stormed back to the house, leaving Ursula and I alone.

'She doesn't mean it,' Ursula said. 'She'll calm down. She's had a shock, that's all.'

'Yeah, and whose fault is that?' I said, as she followed Julia into the house.

I walked down to the fence and looked out at the surrounding countryside. I touched the bandage on the back of my head. A few hours ago, Julia and I had been in each other's arms. Now she was kicking me out. Maybe, despite the police's instructions not to leave town, I should do as she asked. Go back to London, forget about Julia and Lily and all the rest. Try to forget that someone had attempted to kill me. Finish my novel. Get on with my life.

But I was in too deep now.

My mobile rang in my pocket. It was Olly.

'Hey,' he said. 'Are you busy? Do you want to pop over?'

I was confused. 'To look at your dad's books?'

'No. Well, kind of. It's just . . . I found something that's related to what we were talking about yesterday. I think you should come and take a look.'

ꝏ

Malcolm Jones had lived alone, since his wife died, in a large stone house on the other side of town. It stood alone halfway down a narrow lane. There was an empty pond out front, and vines snaked up the facade, all the way to the guttering on the roof.

Olly let me in. He had the air of someone who hadn't slept much, and the faint whiff of body odour emanated from him. He led me into the kitchen.

Heledd turned around from the sink, where she was washing up. She wore a white T-shirt and her rose tattoo was on display again.

She dried her hands on a tea towel and came over to me. Like Olly, she seemed strained, nervous energy radiating from her. Grief. I recognised it well.

'It was you who found my mum,' she said.

I nodded. 'How are you?'

Olly put his arm around her shoulders. 'We're supporting each other, aren't we?'

'That's right.'

She touched a cross that hung around her neck and I realised it was the necklace Shirley had worn. I looked from Heledd to Olly and back. I was still certain both their parents had been murdered. And that I was partly responsible.

I was groping for something to say – I was wondering if it would be insensitive to ask about the dog – when Olly said, 'Come on, mate, let me show you what I found.'

He led me up to Malcolm's study, leaving his girlfriend in the kitchen. The hallway was full of cardboard boxes where Olly had begun to pack his father's belongings. I squeezed past them into an unexpectedly spacious room dominated by an enormous desk and lined with sturdy bookshelves. There were hundreds, possibly thousands, of books in the study, crammed into every space – ramming the shelves, stacked on the floor and the surface of the desk. A shiny iMac was incongruous among the many dusty volumes.

'This is just the tip of the iceberg,' Olly said. 'There are thousands more downstairs. You'd think he'd get sick of seeing books after spending his working day with them, but I think he was actually addicted to acquiring them. My mum was always moaning at him. "You've got a six-foot pile of books by our bed that you haven't read yet – why do you need to buy more?"'

A section of books on a shelf to my left caught my eye. They were dedicated to folklore, fairy tales and urban legends. One of them was *Folk Tales and Urban Myths*, the book that Lily had owned and that I'd also seen in Megan's house. It was clearly a bestseller around these parts. Beside these were a number of volumes about the history of North Wales and the local area. *A Clean Slate: An Oral History of Quarrying and Mining in Wales*. Hardly the catchiest title. I leafed through it quickly, checking the index for Beddmawr, wondering if there was anything about the former mine on which Julia's house stood. Yes, there it was. The mine had been at the heart of the local community, I read, until it closed in 1946. *There were stories that the wife of a miner who was killed at work placed a curse on the town.* I knew that already, and the book didn't offer any new information.

'What did you want to show me?' I asked.

He hesitated for a second. 'Heledd said I shouldn't tell you, that you'd probably put it in a book or something. But I can trust you, right?'

'Yes. Of course.'

'Good. Because it would be crap if you gave her the opportunity to say "I told you so". There's some stuff about her in there, so she's a bit sensitive about it.'

I still wasn't sure what he was talking about, but said, 'Okay.'

Olly picked up a holdall from the desk chair. 'Let's go downstairs. There's nowhere to sit here.'

Once we were seated in the living room, he said, 'My dad kept a journal. There's one for each year, going back to 1965. They were all on a shelf, in date order. I started to look through them. There's all this stuff about how he met my mum; their early courtship, as he called it. Their wedding. Having me. Loads of stuff about work too, and his colleagues. Plus there are reviews of books he read and films he watched. Quite interesting, if only to me.' He licked his dry lips. 'But I noticed 1980 was missing. And that got me thinking about what he said to me the day he died, about keeping a terrible secret.'

1980. I had been six at the time. It was the year before we left this town and moved to Birmingham. My mum had mentioned 1980 when she told me about the little girl who'd gone missing from the children's home.

Heledd came into the room carrying two mugs of coffee for us. She sat down next to Olly.

He went on. 'You know, it looked like someone had been in there, in his study. The desk drawers were in a mess, like they'd been rifled through. There were books scattered all over the floor. Dad would never have done that. He was obsessed with things being filed correctly. So at first I thought someone must have been in there and taken 1980. Then I remembered.'

I was desperate for him to get to the end of the story.

'Dad had a hidey-hole. It's under the carpet in his bedroom. A loose floorboard. He didn't know that anyone knew about it, but I discovered it when I was a kid, after I peeped in on him once and saw him messing around with the carpet. He used to hide money in there. Other stuff too. A girlie mag.' He laughed. 'I found it when I was nine or ten. I'll never forget it. Those bushes!'

Heledd rolled her eyes.

'Anyway, it was in there, 1980.' He held the book out to me. As I was about to take it, he pulled it back.

'You're the first person who's seen this, apart from me. Even Heledd hasn't read it yet, though I've told her the important stuff. I'm only showing it to you because I think you will be able to help us figure this out. Also . . . well, you'll see in a minute.'

He passed the journal to me, open at a page near the back. I began to read.

Chapter 35

Something dreadful has happened, Malcolm wrote. The date was Thursday, 8 May 1980. *It frightens me to put it down here, but I have to get it on paper. If the knowledge remains confined to my head for another moment, my skull might burst.*

I haven't written in here for a few days, so I need to recap. Let's go back to Monday. The 5th. The Society met, as we always do on a Monday night. We met at the Miners Arms. It was quiet as usual and we took our table in the back.

Glynn had brought Shirley Roberts along, to take notes. I have long suspected that Glynn is the father of Shirley's illegitimate daughter, Heledd. It was a minor scandal when Heledd was born. We don't "do" unmarried mothers around here, and people gossiped and whispered and called Shirley a slut and many other names besides. I admire Shirley for holding her head high. The little girl is six now and Shirley sometimes brings her into the library. A sweet little thing who gravitates towards grown men as if searching for a father. If Glynn is her dad then God help her.

I glanced up at Heledd, wondering if Olly had told her what his dad had written about her. It was awkward, to say the least, reading this speculation in her presence.

I turned the page.

Glynn had an old newspaper with him, yellow and dog-eared. He explained he'd found it when laying a carpet in a house he was doing up. Old newspaper had been put down beneath the underlay. It was dated 1945. The local paper. There would be a copy in the library, stored on microfiche.

Glynn laid it out for us all to see the headline.

POLICE ABANDON SEARCH FOR MISSING GIRL, AGED 5, IN BEDDMAWR.

The report told how the five-year-old daughter of a couple who had recently moved to the area had vanished two weeks before. She was out playing with friends who had ridden off on their bikes, leaving her behind on the edge of the woods. Her name was Glenys Williams. A grainy photo accompanied the report. Little Glenys, on a beach in Llandudno, licking an ice cream on her last family holiday. The police had carried out a search of the woods, with dogs, but were unable to find her.

'This is the interesting part,' Glynn said. 'Listen . . . "Police reported that they had received little help from locals, who seemed resigned to what had happened. A local woman who refused to be named said that it was clear that little Glenys had been sacrificed to keep the other children of the town safe. Police believe the girl must have wandered towards the nearby River Dee and fallen in, although no body has been recovered."'

'I showed it to my mother,' Glynn went on. 'She remembered it happening. And guess what she told me? Thirty-five years before, in 1910, the same thing had happened. She remembered because her own mother, my gran, told her about it. She said it happened every thirty-five years. A child had to be given to the Red Widow, or she would come and take one.'

Glynn went on to tell us that his mother told him the sacrificed child was always one who would be 'less missed' in the community. The witch didn't like sick children – they taste bad – so the local people couldn't give up a child who was likely to die anyway (he said this as if this was a terrible shame). Instead, they chose a child who had been orphaned, or whose parents were new to the area, or a bastard. The Widow particularly liked children with sin in their blood. It was not worth the risk, said Glynn's mother, that the witch would come and take a child from an important family, a son and heir, a child whose death would rock the community.

'Thirty-five years,' Glynn said, looking around the table. 'Nineteen forty-five was thirty-five years ago.'

As if we hadn't all already worked that out.

'It's lucky nobody believes in such superstitious nonsense any more, isn't it?' I said.

I looked around the table at the faces staring back at me.

Glynn. Shirley. Albert. David. All of us in our mid-thirties now, but we've known each other all our lives. We went to the same school. David and I were the studious ones, Albert somewhere near the bottom of the class, Shirley a nervous little thing who followed Glynn around like his pet lamb. Glynn, of course, was the class bully.

Now, Glynn pointed at me.

'How would you feel, Malcolm, if little Olly was taken by the Widow? Shirley, what if Heledd was taken? And you, David, what if the witch came and took away Lucas?'

I gasped and stopped reading, looking up at Olly.

'My dad was there,' I said. 'That's why you wanted me to see this.'

He nodded.

My mouth was dry, fingers trembling as I turned the page.

'I certainly wouldn't want to risk her coming for Wendy,' Glynn said.

I could hardly believe how serious they all looked. As if they believed Glynn and his crazy old mother. As if they actually believed a witch might come into the town in the dead of night and steal their precious children away.

Only Albert, who didn't have any children, looked less afraid.

I banged on the table, startling them from their stupor. 'This is madness,' I said. 'Perhaps, a long time ago, this crime – the crime of taking children into the woods and leaving them to be taken by a non-existent being – happened. Maybe, just maybe, it happened in 1945 too, though I find that hard to believe. It's far more likely that Glenys got lost and fell into the river. An accident, that's all.'

'Except,' Shirley said, speaking for the first time in that meeting. 'All it would take was for one person to believe in the Widow. One person willing to murder little Glenys so there was no risk of their own child being taken.'

I called an end to the meeting. I needed to get out of there, away from the atmosphere that hung over that table. The others lingered behind. I heard them murmuring. Glynn's booming laugh rang out as I left the pub.

I glanced up at Olly and Heledd. We'd each had a parent at that meeting – at least one, in Heledd's case. It felt strange, like a reunion. Glynn's daughter Wendy was the only person missing.

I read on.

Malcolm's journal entry was broken in two. There was a space on the page before the next section began.

I've been staring at this page for fifteen minutes, trying to decide what to write, how to tell the rest of this tale. A large part of me is shouting at me to leave it, that it's too dangerous to record. There will be repercussions. But I have to do it. Damn the consequences.

How brave I sound within the pages of my journal. How brave the coward sounds.

The facts.

Last night, a four-year-old girl went missing from St Mary's children's home. The girl's name is Carys Driscoll. It's all over the radio and local news, and the police are combing the area, trying to find her. Details are patchy, but rumours are running like wildfire through the town. It was all anyone could talk about at the library today, including a young woman who works at the home. She came in to return some books then hung around, a group gathering as she told the tale. I loitered on the edge of the group, the blood in my veins turning to ice as I listened.

Carys Driscoll was put into the care system after her mother, a heroin-addicted punk, died of an overdose when her daughter was three. There has never been a father on the scene. Nobody knows who he is, and the grandparents wanted nothing to do with the child. They have been trying to place her in a foster home or find someone to adopt her but, so far, without luck.

She was last seen at teatime, yesterday evening. Apparently, the children were then allowed outside to play for a little while. A member of staff was supervising them, but one of the children hurt himself and had to be taken inside for first aid. Then the children were called inside.

Nobody noticed Carys was not among them until this morning.

The woman faced down the cries of incredulity in the library with excuses. There are so many children, she said. It was getting dark. Carys was so quiet, 'a little mouse', that she tended to shrink into the background. The staff are overworked and tired. None of the other children said anything.

I am sure heads will roll at St Mary's children's home. But that won't help poor Carys.

All I could think of was the conversation in the Miners Arms on Monday night. The faces of my fellow Society members around the table.

I told my assistant I wasn't feeling well and left the library, leaving the gossips behind. I headed straight to Albert's house. Rhodri Wallace – another old classmate – was in the garden, cutting the hedge. He was a likeable boy at school, good with his hands and popular with the girls. Now he was the most in-demand gardener and handyman in town. He raised a gloved hand when he saw me. His face was as pale and shocked as all the others I'd seen on the way over. I didn't stop to talk to Rhodri – instead, I headed inside.

Albert was as horrified by little Carys's disappearance as I was.

'It has to be a coincidence,' he said.

'Do you really believe that?' said I. 'Two days after our conversation?'

His eyes were wide, disbelieving. If he was acting, he was doing a very good job of it. But maybe it was fear of being exposed. Or fear of Glynn.

'You think one of the others took that child, took her into the woods to be sacrificed to the witch?' He paced the room. 'What does the legend say the witch demanded? What did the townsfolk do in the stories?'

I told him that the child was meant to be secured to a tree in the heart of the woods and left for the witch to take.

Albert nodded. 'You and I know there's no such thing as the Widow. It was less than twenty-four hours ago, so if they did take her and tied her to a tree, she'd still be there. Are the police searching the woods?'

'I don't know. I hear they're organising search parties now.'

He picked up his phone and I asked him what he was doing.

'Calling Glynn.'

'Are you mad? It could have been him.'

'It could have been you,' he said to me. 'It could have been any of us.'

'But you have less reason than the rest of us for doing it. You don't have children. That's why I came here.'

We stared at each other.

'Do you believe in the Widow?' he asked.

'Of course not. Do you?'

'No, I don't. But what did Shirley say? All it takes is for one person to believe. It could have been any of you. Any parent who was trying to protect their child.'

He was right. I knew it wasn't me. I didn't think it was David – he always seemed so rational, had even confessed to being an atheist because he couldn't believe in something for which there was no scientific proof. Glynn was the obvious suspect. I knew he could be cruel, that he was unfaithful and unafraid of violence. I'd seen him square up to men in the pub. At school he was a bully. And his mother – she undoubtedly believed in the old stories. Glynn seemed to believe in them too.

His one redeeming feature was that he doted on his daughter, Wendy.

But would he really take and sacrifice another child because he believed she might be in danger?

'We should go to the police,' Albert said. 'Tell them about our meeting and what Glynn said.'

'Wait. Let me think.'

I imagined myself talking to the police. Accusing my fellow Society member of this terrible crime. The thought of falsely accusing someone filled me with horror.

And there was another reason not to go to the police, of which I am deeply, deeply ashamed. If the police took us seriously, they would want us all to provide alibis, wouldn't they?

I couldn't do it. Because I was out yesterday evening, visiting a friend. And if I was forced to give an alibi, Sylvia would find out.

I read this part out to Olly. He sighed.

'His friend. He mentions her in other parts of the journal. The old bastard was cheating on my mum.'

Just like the man who killed Priya. Men with secrets, flinching from justice. My opinion of Malcolm plummeted.

I read the final paragraphs of the entry.

I persuaded Albert that we should keep quiet. The chances were, I said, none of the members of the Society had taken that girl. It was a coincidence. He agreed. The girl had probably wandered off, he said. She would turn up in a day or two.

But on the way home, I made an anonymous call to the police, from a phone box, advising them to search the woods, to look for signs that Carys had been tied to a tree.

Just in case.

Chapter 36

In the following entry, Malcolm described the next meeting of the Historical Society. All four of them were there, along with Shirley:

We all sat in silence at first, nobody quite daring to speak, shifty eyes flitting around the table. Shirley kept clutching her cross. Albert gave me meaningful glances and David looked green around the gills. The girl still hasn't turned up, though I heard the police had searched the woods and interviewed known sex offenders in the area. The detective in charge of the investigation was quoted in the paper, saying it wasn't helpful that local people kept telling him the girl was taken by the Widow, chosen because no one had given her an offering.

Glynn leaned forward and looked around the table at each of us in turn.

'So,' he stage-whispered. 'Which one of you did it?'

There was a flurry of denials and accusations. It descended into a fierce argument. I couldn't work out if Glynn was acting, cleverly trying to lay the blame at someone's feet. Creating a smokescreen of confusion.

'How about you, Glynn?' I said. 'Was it you?'

He smiled. 'Perhaps what people are saying is right. Perhaps the Widow came into town and took her.'

Absurd. But I couldn't work out if he actually believed that.

I examined each of my so-called friends in turn. Was one of them guilty? More than one, perhaps, working together? What if it was all of them?

Before we wrapped up, Glynn said, 'At least she won't be missed. The girl, I mean. At least the Widow didn't take anyone important.'

The entry ended there. Olly said, 'I flicked ahead, seeing if there were any more references to it. All I know is the girl was never found.'

'What do you think?' I asked. 'Do you think one of them did it?'

He shrugged. 'I have no idea. I know a bloody witch didn't come into town to grab her. But it's a hell of a coincidence, isn't it, if she did just wander off? Did your dad ever say anything about it?'

I set the journal aside, placing it next to my empty coffee cup. 'No. Not that I remember. I mean, I must have heard about the disappearance and the rumours.' I explained the similarities to my novel. 'We moved away in 1981, a year after this happened. Maybe that's why. Maybe my dad wanted to get away.'

Olly's eyes were wide. 'You think it might have been him?'

The very thought made me sick. 'I don't know. It goes against everything I know about him. Did your mum ever mention Carys and what happened?' I asked Heledd.

'No.' She had picked up the journal and was flicking through it, as if the answer to all of this might be contained in its pages. 'At least not in any detail . . . She always said this town wasn't safe for children, that if I ever gave her grandchildren she would worry herself sick about them.'

'But she never elaborated?'

'Hmm?' She was distracted by the journal. 'No. I mean, she told me about the Widow. Every kid around here knows about her. But that's it.'

I got up and went over to the window. The sun was struggling to come out from behind the clouds.

'What are you thinking?' Olly asked.

'I'm thinking that thirty-five years after Carys went missing, history repeated itself. A child was taken. A newcomer to the town, a family that weren't integrated into the community.'

'You think they did it again? With Lily Marsh?'

I paced around. 'It can't be a coincidence. And Glynn Collins is the obvious suspect. Back in 1980 he thought he was protecting Wendy. Or – sorry, Heledd, but I have to say it – Wendy and you.'

She met my eye but didn't say anything.

I had to ask. 'Is Glynn your dad?'

She didn't answer for a few long seconds. 'I don't know. Mum never told me.' She had gone pale and now I felt terrible.

'Let's leave it, eh?' Olly said, putting a protective hand on his girl-friend's shoulder.

'Okay. Yes, I'm sorry. It doesn't matter . . . I mean, it doesn't make any difference to what we're talking about. Glynn could have been protecting Wendy. And maybe . . . maybe this time he was trying to protect his granddaughter, Megan.'

Olly gaped at me.

'Glynn Collins,' he said. 'He's always scared me. Back when I was a kid, I mean.'

Heledd had set the journal aside and was deep in thought, tuned out of the conversation.

'Glynn met Lily through his granddaughter, Megan,' I said. 'She knew him . . . It would have been easy for him to lure her away, maybe tell her she needed to go with him to see something. She would probably have trusted him. Now he's got it in for me too. He knows I've been nosing around.'

The back of my head, where it was still bandaged, was beginning to throb again.

'But he's got a rock-solid alibi for the night I was attacked.'

I thought about that. Was somebody helping him? If so, who?

Olly was agitated. 'You know what I said about keeping all this secret, about protecting our dads' reputations. I think we're beyond that now, aren't we? We should go to the police. Show them the journal.'

'There's no point. Last time I talked to them they dismissed me as a writer with an overactive imagination.'

'Let me do it,' Heledd said. 'I'm local and I got on well with the policeman who was there when Mum died.'

'I bet you did,' Olly muttered, which made Heledd roll her eyes.

'I think it's a good idea,' I said to Olly. 'They might listen to her.'

'I suppose so. Maybe I could come with you?'

She hesitated, and I thought I could tell what she was thinking: that the police would respond better to her solo.

'Perhaps it's best if Heledd goes on her own, in the first instance anyway,' I said.

Olly grunted and we lapsed into silence again. I parted the curtains and peeked out at the street, paranoid that someone was watching us. That Glynn would come here looking for Malcolm's missing journal. Heledd's phone rang and she said, 'Excuse me' before taking it out of the room.

Olly watched her go then picked up the journal, flicked to the relevant entry and tapped the page. 'Something just struck me. Albert Patterson . . . You know he lived at Nyth Bran?'

I nodded, even though it hurt to do so.

'That's a weird bloody connection, isn't it? Lily Marsh disappearing after living in that house. If Albert hadn't died, what, five or six years ago, I'd say *he* was the prime suspect.'

'Plus he didn't have kids, did he? Like your dad said, he had no one to protect from the Widow, so why would he do it? Did you ever meet him?'

I thought about the photo I'd found hidden in the book at the retreat. The tall, skinny man and his stern-faced wife.

'Yeah. I went to his house a couple of times when I was a kid. He was all right, a nice bloke actually. He loved kids, even though he didn't have any of his own. Loved playing with us, keeping us entertained while the other adults stood in the kitchen and chatted about boring stuff.'

Heledd came back in. 'That was the estate agent,' she said to Olly, who nodded.

The pain in my head was getting worse. I stood up. 'I should go.'

'What are you going to do?' Olly asked, showing me to the door.

'I don't know. This headache is making it hard to think straight. But I'll call you later.'

'All right.'

'If you see Glynn, don't say anything to him, okay? Not yet.'

Heledd kissed my cheek as I left. 'I'll let you know what the police say about the journal.'

'Thanks.' They stood side by side, their faces pale with worry. 'Be safe,' I said.

ᴍ

I drove back towards the retreat, a wall of white noise inside my head. Fortunately, the roads were quiet and I was able to drive on autopilot. Halfway back, my phone rang. It was that detective, DC Hawkins. I ignored the call. I didn't feel ready to talk to her yet.

I stopped at a petrol station and bought a pack of extra-strong painkillers, ignoring the warning on the packet and gobbling three. Then I pulled over by the side of the road, killed the engine and closed my eyes. The silence was broken only by the occasional passing car, and the gentle bleating of sheep in an adjacent field. I emptied my mind and waited for the paracetamol to kick in and rub away the sharp edges of my headache.

By the time I reached the retreat I was feeling better. As I went in, I saw Ursula coming down the stairs. She had a sheet of paper in her hand. She looked even more wild-eyed than she had earlier.

'Have you seen Julia?' she demanded.

'I've just got home.'

'You're no use.' She stalked off into the kitchen.

Suzi appeared, carrying her suitcase down the stairs.

'You're going?' I said.

She didn't answer with words, but with a look of panic. She looked dreadful: washed out, her hair lank and with rings around her eyes.

'I saw her,' she said.

'What? Who?'

'Lily. I went for a final walk in the woods, to say goodbye, and I saw her.' She hugged herself. 'She was there in the distance – and then she vanished.'

'What are you talking about?' Goose pimples rippled across my arms.

'It was like . . . like she was made of smoke or mist. She was dressed in red – red like blood. I need to tell Julia.'

She started towards the kitchen. I grabbed her arm. Everyone here was going crazy, haunted by visions in the woods. It had to be group hysteria, a swirl of grief stirred up and encouraged by Ursula. 'No! You are not going to tell Julia—'

'Tell me what?'

Julia appeared at the top of the staircase. She came down towards us.

'Oh, Julia. I saw her. I saw Lily.' Suzi shook me off. 'I saw her ghost.'

I wanted to scream. Julia was staring at Suzi, arms wrapped around herself. I took hold of Suzi's arm again, more gently this time. 'Come on, Suzi. You're clearly in shock after what happened to Max. You should rest . . .'

Then Ursula came out of the kitchen and spotted Julia. 'There you are.'

The wound on the back of my head pulsed.

Ursula flapped the sheet of paper she was holding at Julia. Her eyes bulged.

'My guide . . . she came to me again. She told me where to find proof – proof that Lily has left this realm.'

I stepped between them. 'Julia, don't listen to this. It's insane.'

Julia pushed me aside. 'Shut up, Lucas.' She grabbed the sheet of paper from Ursula's hand.

Suzi had slid down the wall onto the floor and sat there, hugging her knees, rocking back and forth.

'What is this?' Julia asked. I moved behind her and looked over her shoulder, staring at the lines and curves, the crosses and squiggles on the sheet of paper.

'It's a map,' Ursula said. 'I drew you a map.'

Chapter 37

LILY – 2014

Lily sat on her bed, cradling Big Cat in her arms. She held him against her cheek and screwed her eyes shut.

Mum and Dad were fighting again.

'When the hell were you going to tell me?' Mum shouted.

She couldn't make out Dad's reply.

'You're ruining us! Fucking ruining us!'

Lily winced at the swear word. Mum never swore except when she was yelling at Dad. Lily wasn't totally sure what he'd done wrong. Something to do with money and lying and broken promises. The usual stuff they argued about. Lily wished her parents could be more like the ones she saw on TV, parents who cracked jokes and put their arms around each other.

Mum swore again and Lily searched the room for her headphones. Where were they? She remembered: they were in her bag, in the closet downstairs.

She crept out of the room and down the stairs, opening the closet and pulling out her bag. The headphone wires were tangled up. She tried to unknot them, Chesney sitting blinking at her as she grappled with the stupid things. She wanted to ask Mum or Dad to help but they were still screeching at each other. She heard Mum say that name again. *Lana.* Hot tears of frustration burned Lily's cheeks and she chucked the bag and the stupid headphones back into the closet. Chesney jumped down from the windowsill and dashed to the front door, miaowing to be let out.

Lily opened the door and watched him slink across the lawn.

She wished she was free too.

'I've had enough!' Mum yelled.

So had Lily. Closing the door quietly behind her, she slipped out into the garden. She climbed over the fence into the overgrown meadow and entered the woods.

It was still and quiet among the trees. Autumn leaves formed a carpet of red on the path. Lily imagined herself as a movie star, attending the premiere of her new film. Reporters asked her if she would ever forgive her parents, who deeply regretted how they'd behaved now she was a superstar.

She was so engrossed in her fantasy that she wasn't sure if she was going in the right direction. Megan's house wasn't this way, was it? She paused, trying not to panic.

Something moved in the trees.

Lily went absolutely still. *It's just a bird*, she thought. A big bird. Probably a magpie. There were loads of them around here.

Crack.

Lily tried to make her legs move, but it was as if her soles were superglued to the path. Her whole body had gone cold.

It's a crow, it's a crow, she told herself, staring into the thick tangle of branches where the noise had come from, praying that she'd see black feathers, the bird flapping towards the sky.

Instead, she saw a face.

Eyes, peering at her through a gap in the branches.

Lily tore her feet from the path and ran, blindly, realising within seconds she was still heading away from her house, but unable to stop and turn.

It's the Widow! The Widow!

She crashed through low-hanging branches, leaves clawing at her hair, almost slipping over in a muddy puddle that sucked at her Converse. Tears blurred her vision. She could hardly see where she was going. The path branched left and right and she stopped, paralysed, unable to work out which way to go. She could sense the witch behind her. She tensed her shoulders, convinced that at any moment cold, clawed hands would reach out from the bushes and grab her.

In the picture book Megan's grandad had given her, the Widow was a young woman, dressed in red rags. She had long black hair and was as slim as the women on the covers of Mum's workout DVDs. She would be beautiful if it weren't for her face. Her eyes were as black as Big Cat's fur, and her mouth gaped open like a shark's, with long, needle-like teeth. Lily had discussed this with Megan: the Widow would be old now, so old, and the girls imagined her skin would be as wrinkled as a crocodile's. Her lips would be stained with the blood of all the children she'd eaten. Her breath would smell like kids' bones and there would be torn flesh beneath her fingernails.

There was a rustle behind her and Lily gulped down a scream. She ran, heading left along the path, trying not to slip or fall, leaping over a knotty tree root that tried to grab her toes, like it was the witch's helper. Now she imagined the trees had faces, that they were watching her, laughing at her. Why had she left her house? It was all Mum and Dad's fault. Well, when the witch caught her and ate her up and her bones were never found, they'd be sorry, and they'd wish and wish they hadn't fought, that they'd spent their time loving their only daughter instead.

It would almost be worth it.

Just as she had resigned herself to being caught, convinced the trees were closing in on her, forming a wooden cage around her, she saw a clearing up ahead. Light entering the woods; buildings beyond. She sped up and, heart bursting with relief, flew out of the trees onto the estate where Megan lived.

And there was Megan, standing outside her house. Jake was there too. They were playing a game of tag on the front lawn.

Lily ran across the road to them.

'What's the matter?' Megan asked. 'You look like someone's chasing you.'

Lily panted. She couldn't speak for a moment. Her lungs burned and her heart was going *bang bang bang*.

'It's the Widow,' she said. 'I saw her.'

Both Megan and Jake gawped at her.

'What was that?'

Lily spun round. It was Megan's grandad, coming out of the garage. There was another man with him, but he was concealed by shadows.

'Lily saw the Widow,' Megan told him.

'Do your mum and dad know you're here?' asked Mr Collins, ignoring what Megan had said. Lily was surprised. He was acting like she'd said something silly and childish.

She shook her head. 'I ran away.'

'Really? Well, I'm glad you didn't go too far. Do you want to go home? I don't know how long you've been gone, but I'm sure they'll be worried about you.'

Lily tried to stop the tears coming, but she had no control over them. She could feel her face going bright red too. She hated crying. She knew it made her look like an ugly red frog. Everyone was staring at her.

'Tell you what,' said Megan's grandad, handing her a clean handkerchief. His voice was kind. 'You go inside and play with Megan for a little bit and I'll call your parents. How does that sound?'

This time, all she could do was nod.

ꟺ

As soon as Megan shut her bedroom door, she said, 'I can't believe you saw the Widow. What did she look like?' Unbelievably, she sounded jealous.

'I don't want to talk about it.'

'Oh, come on. Don't be a baby. Did she look like she does in the book?'

Lily sat down on Megan's bed and pulled Megan's giant teddy bear towards her. Megan's grandad had bought it for her. It wore a little rosette that said *World's Best Granddaughter*. Lily stifled another sob. She didn't have any grandparents. Maybe if she did she could go and live with them.

'Tell me,' Megan urged. She had found her copy of *Folk Tales and Urban Myths*, which fell open at the page they were always poring over. 'Did she look like this?'

'I only saw her eyes.'

Megan's voice dropped to an awed whisper. 'Were they black?'

'I don't know.'

'What about her skin? Was it all wrinkly? Were her lips stained with blood?'

'I didn't see.'

Megan made a disgusted noise. 'You're useless.'

Anger pulsed at Lily's temples. She was *not* useless. 'I was too busy running to take a proper look.'

'Yeah. A big scaredy-cat. If it had been me—'

'Well, it wasn't you.' Lily cut her off. It had been a terrible day. The worst day of her whole life. She felt a hot bubble of hatred expand inside her. An urge to lash out.

'I didn't see her properly,' Lily said. 'But I heard her.'

Megan's eyes almost popped out of her head. 'What did she say?'

Lily pointed a finger at her best friend's face. 'She said your name. She said *Megan*.'

Later, remembering Megan's look of terror, the way she'd flinched, would make Lily feel bad. But in that moment, it was delicious.

'Lily!' It was Megan's grandad. 'Your dad's here.'

Lily ran down the stairs and out the front door. Dad was talking to Mr Collins, his hands on his hips. He noticed Lily and turned around.

'Oh, sweetheart,' he said, putting his arm around her. 'What are we going to do with you?'

She didn't respond. As Dad took her hand and led her to the car, the other man who'd been in the garage came out, wiping his oily hands on a rag. It was Mr Wallace, the man who did work in their garden sometimes.

'Hi, Rhodri,' Dad said as he unlocked the car.

Rhodri Wallace waved as they drove away, but he wasn't smiling. It was weird. If Lily didn't know better, she'd swear he looked scared.

Chapter 38

It was five thirty. Just two hours of daylight remained. I suggested to Julia that we wait until morning, but she wouldn't hear of it. I didn't even bother trying to persuade her that Ursula's map had to be a con or a fantasy – not after our argument that morning. Julia had to find out for herself. She grabbed a little rucksack and threw in two flashlights, along with a bottle of water and a small pair of shears 'in case we need to cut our way through any overgrown vegetation'.

Ursula had gone back to her room, saying she was too tired to come along, leaving us with the map. It was crudely drawn, like a child's sketch of a pirate treasure map. The retreat was situated at the southern tip of this map. Beyond that were the woods where I'd gone walking that first day. Near the top was a large X which, according to Ursula, indicated where we would find 'the proof'.

Despite my scepticism, it made the hairs on the back of my neck stand up. It was impossible not to get sucked into Ursula's fantasy; the boy in me could not resist a map where X marked the spot.

'Are you sure you want to do this?' I asked Julia a final time. 'It might be more sensible to call the police and let them look.'

'I'm not waiting any longer, Lucas. I need to see. I need to know.'

'I'm coming with you. No arguments, okay?'

She shrugged.

Julia took a photo of the map with her phone, so we had a backup copy. Her hand trembled and it took two attempts to stop the photo from blurring. Two years of bouncing between despair and hope. Two years of grieving with no body to say goodbye to. Two years of believing that Lily was still out there, still alive. It was all there on her face, in the tension that vibrated through her bones. She took a deep breath, filling her lungs, and turned to me.

'Let's go.'

Walking across the garden, I checked back over my shoulder. Ursula was watching from an upstairs window, her face inscrutable. She caught me looking and let the curtain fall back.

ω

The path was dry, cracks snaking through the mud. Blossom coated the branches of the trees near the perimeter of the woods. Catkins hung above our heads and songbirds called out to one another. If it weren't for Julia's brisk pace and the grim determination on her face, this would have felt like a pleasant late-afternoon ramble.

I wanted to talk to Julia, to tell her everything I'd learned from Malcolm's journal, but I needed all my breath to keep up with her. It could wait. I was certain we weren't going to find anything. We'd be home in an hour or two and I could talk to her then. I also wanted to talk to Mum, ask her what she knew about the Historical Society. Surely Dad had said something during that time when Carys Driscoll went missing?

An image came to me: Glynn Collins, thirty-seven years younger, carrying a little girl into these woods. Maybe heading along this very path. Was the story about the Widow a smokescreen, a convenient tale for a paedophile to hide behind? What if seeing Lily playing with his granddaughter had stirred a sick desire in Glynn, a desire that had lain buried for a long time? She looked similar to Carys, though Lily was

263

older. It was easy to imagine. He had got away with it last time. He thought he could do so again.

Before leaving the house, I had sent Olly a text explaining what was going on. He'd replied straight away, telling me Heledd was on her way to the police station with the journal. I was keen to hear about their response.

'What are you thinking about?' Julia asked, slowing down as we approached the edge of the woods. Watery sunshine flowed through the treetops, and light danced on Julia's hair. It was inappropriate to think it right now, but she was beautiful. I knew I could never be satisfied with the single night we'd spent together. But, like all the other things I wanted to say to her, it would have to wait.

'I was thinking about Lily,' I said vaguely. 'I want Ursula to be wrong.'

Julia stopped walking.

'How do you think it feels?' she said. 'Not knowing? Being stuck in limbo?' She looked around, turning her face upwards and shielding her eyes against the light. Branches and twigs formed a lattice against the sky. 'Sometimes I think I can feel her, here. Her presence. If she did die here . . .' She swallowed.

'Julia . . .'

'Quiet. Please. I think a part of her is still here, in these woods. She's there, in the blossom. In the leaves that bud every spring. In the grass that grows on the path. I couldn't feel her before, but now I can.' A tear slid down her cheek. 'She's watching me.'

It was silent all around us. Even the birds had fallen quiet.

'If we find proof, like Ursula says . . . At least then I'll be able to take comfort in knowing she's still here.'

I nodded, afraid of choosing the wrong words.

'And then I'll know it's okay to join her.'

I stared at her. 'You mean . . . take your own life?'

'Why not? I've nothing else to live for. Once I know she's gone, I can be with her. Forever.'

I went cold inside. 'Julia. You can't say that. Lily wouldn't want that.'

I wouldn't want that.

'How do you know what she'd want? You can't save me, Lucas. You've no right to try.'

She went to move on, but I stepped into her path. 'So if we do find evidence today that Lily is dead, you're going to kill yourself? What, are you going to do it right there? In front of me? Have you got a knife in that bag?'

She glared at me.

I ploughed on. 'How are you going to do it? Slash your wrists? Hang yourself from a tree? Oh, I know. You're going to throw yourself into the river. You can't swim. It will be perfect. Kind of poetic. You couldn't save Lily because you can't swim, so you're going to drown yourself. I can see the newspaper headlines now. Maybe I'll write a book about it.'

'Get out of my way.'

She tried to get around me but I grabbed her arm. 'Julia, listen to me . . .'

She punched me in the chest with her free hand. Her fist was sharp and the shock made me step back, but I held on to her.

'Let go of me!' she hissed.

This was getting out of hand. I let go and we both stood there, facing each other, shaking. I didn't know what to do. I was terrified I'd wrecked what remained of our relationship. But it was a sacrifice worth making if it made her reconsider and see sense.

Her face was pink, a tremor of fury coursing through her. I needed to diffuse the tension between us.

'I'd be pretty upset if you killed yourself,' I said, deadpan.

She didn't laugh.

'Okay. *Quite* upset. Although the royalties from my book about you would help ease the pain.'

'You're such a dick.'

She fought the smile that flickered at the edge of her lips.

'Yeah. Maybe I am a dick. But I'm your friend, Julia. And at the risk of getting all serious again, I care about you. Also, I don't believe in spirits or the afterlife or any of that stuff. When you're dead, you're dead. If you kill yourself, you won't be with Lily, you'll just be gone. And the world will be a shittier place.'

She held her head in her hands. 'I can't talk about this any more. We're losing light. We need to press on.'

I studied her face. I had no idea if what I'd said had made any difference, or if she was serious about suicide in the first place. But I made a vow that if we did find proof that Lily was dead – and I didn't believe that would happen today – I would do everything I could to persuade her that it was worth carrying on. That there could be life after death.

ᚹ

We reached the clearing a few minutes later. I figured we only had an hour left until dusk. Julia consulted the map.

'We're right here,' she said, pointing at a spot between the woods. The little run-down hut had been crudely drawn by Ursula, a small square with a pointy roof.

'Have you ever been in that hut?' I asked.

'No, why would I? Don't tell me you have?'

'Actually – a couple of times. My first day, when I came for a walk. Then again, when I saw . . .'

'What?'

I realised I hadn't told Julia about that. 'I saw Ursula come into the woods, the day after she arrived. I wondered what she was up to, so I followed her.'

'And?'

'She vanished.'

'You mean you lost her?'

'It depends how you look at it,' I said.

Julia looked up at the darkening sky. 'We should get going.'

We walked side by side across the field towards the next line of trees. Magpies, perhaps the same ones I'd seen before, watched us go. We were still only a third of the way through the map, and the chances of us getting there and back before it was pitch-black were now close to zero. I explained my concern to Julia.

'I'm not stopping now,' she said. 'We've got the flashlights and the sky is clear so we'll have moonlight. Haven't you ever camped in the woods?'

'No. It's not my thing.'

'You should try it.'

I hesitated before speaking. 'How about we go together? If it's so much fun. This summer, you can show me what it's all about.'

She shook her head. 'You're incorrigible.'

'Yep.'

We entered the next set of woods. It was noticeably darker now. There were noises in the undergrowth, rustling in the bushes. I refused to let it bother me. But when we reached the point where I'd lost Ursula before, I heard a heavier crack behind us and stopped walking.

I listened, gesturing for Julia to stay silent. Nothing.

We pressed on. The woods grew thicker and darker, as the remaining sunlight found it harder to break through the canopy. The path forked several times, but Ursula's map clearly showed us which way to go, though the line of dirt beneath our feet grew increasingly narrow and more overgrown, until we found ourselves stepping over thorny brambles and holding back branches that tried to block our way.

And then we hit a wall: a solid wall of vegetation, dense with prickly leaves. It covered the path and stretched for ten metres in both directions. We would have needed a machete to hack our way through it. We checked the map. We were so close. The X was just beyond this point.

'Shit,' Julia said. 'What are we going to do?'

I eyed a nearby tree.

'Wait there.'

It had been a long time since I climbed a tree. It took all my strength to hoist myself onto a lower branch, but from there it was easier. I picked my way around the trunk, picking out places to put my feet, ducking beneath branches and concentrating so hard that I didn't look until I was halfway up, with a clear view over the barrier that stopped our progress.

I peered into the half-light, rubbing my eyes like a cartoon character as shadows knitted together to form the shape of a building.

'Fuck,' I said, hardly believing what I was seeing.

'What is it?' Julia called up.

I leaned forward, to make sure I wasn't mistaken.

'It's a church,' I said. 'An abandoned church.'

Chapter 39

I climbed down from the tree.

'There's a path that leads around to the church,' I said. 'Follow me. We need to retrace our steps a little.'

We headed back the way we had come, then pushed through the trees until we came to another path that snaked off to the left. I led the way, skirting around the edge of the mass of vegetation. It was getting harder to see. We were, I estimated, twenty minutes from dusk. I could sense nocturnal creatures stirring in their hiding places, ready to emerge when twilight turned to night.

We edged sideways between a pair of spiky bushes. Julia almost slipped and I grabbed her hand, holding on to it for a moment, and then we emerged into a clearing. There it was: a small stone building, with a steeple and arched windows that had been boarded over. Crumbling stone steps, ripped apart by tree roots that broke through like the tentacles of some underground monster, led up to a pair of wooden doors. A metal strip had been nailed across the doors, presumably when this place closed, but at some point it had been ripped open – either by nature or human hands. Ivy had swarmed across every surface of the church like a virus.

'What the hell is a church doing out here?' I asked, looking around. Nature pressed in from all sides, slowly reclaiming this place. One day, the gap would be filled, the building buried, invisible. Bare branches already poked through the church's roof, and green moss coated the walls where ivy didn't cling.

'I've heard about this place,' Julia said. 'It was an estate that's been abandoned for years. An estate with a private chapel. The house will be nearby.'

So a chapel, not a church.

'Michael came out here once to take a look and came back telling me how amazing it was, how exciting it would be to hire an architect and redevelop it, turn it into a wedding venue or something. Of course, he never did anything about it.'

I was frozen to the spot, pulse throbbing in my ears, a shiver running through me as I took in the scene. There was something beautiful about it, and not just in the detail, the curlicues on the pillars either side of the doors, or the rusted bell that hung visible in the broken steeple. It was in the connection to the past. The secret history of this place. It spoke directly to the horror novelist in me, the lover of all things macabre. But more than that, one thought shone through: it was the perfect place to hide a body.

The perfect place to hide a child.

Julia tapped the X on Ursula's map. 'This is definitely the spot.'

She took a deep breath and went up the steps, unhooking the rucksack and taking out one of the flashlights. I followed, catching up as she squeezed through the gap between the doors. It was dark inside, with the windows boarded up, though a few chinks of light entered through cracks in the walls. She turned on the flashlight and placed it on the floor. Darkness turned to gloom.

It was larger than I'd expected, about the size of a school classroom, with an altar at one end and three rows of pews. Everything was blackened by neglect, the smell of damp filling the air. Vines hung from the ceiling. One touched my neck as I turned around, making me tense up so the muscles cramped painfully.

Over in the corner, propped on the floor, was a huge painting of Christ on the cross, turned on its side. I guessed it must have hung here once, but had fallen or been taken down. The frame was cracked and the paintwork was dark with mould. Jesus stared out at us, eyes filled with pain, blood trickling down His forehead.

Julia looked around, peering into nooks, running a hand along the cold walls. She walked over to the altar, peered beneath the pews. She found a Bible, sodden with rainwater and falling apart. A draft blew through the building and made me shiver. My body was telling me to get out, to go somewhere warm and light and modern. Because there was nothing here. No proof that Lily was dead.

I wasn't surprised. Ursula had made it all up.

'We should go,' I said.

'No. There must be something here. Why would she send us here otherwise? How would she even know about this place?'

'I told you, I saw her exploring the woods. She must have found it. I know what's going to happen next, Julia. She'll tell you we must have missed it, that you need her help to find it. And that's when she'll mention money.'

But Julia wasn't listening. She was in the far corner, staring at the painting of Christ. She grabbed hold of one edge and pushed it to one side. It was heavy, the frame made of solid wood, and I went over to help her. We shoved it to the right, the effort making me grunt. I pulled myself up straight and, seeing what the painting had been concealing, said, 'Fuck.'

It was a wooden door. The wood was a little warped in its frame and there was a gouge down the centre, as if it had been swiped at by some giant creature.

I turned to Julia to remark on this find, but she wasn't looking at the door. She was staring open-mouthed at something that lay on the ground in front of it.

She crouched down and picked the object up, then stood, clutching it like an explorer who'd found the Holy Grail.

'It's a cat. It's *Little Cat*.' I gaped at it. The toy Lily had been carrying when she vanished; the other cat left floating in the river. She held it out to me, looking like she was going to throw up. 'Look.'

One side of the toy was matted with a dark, brownish substance. A liquid that had dried and stuck to the cat's fur.

'It's blood, isn't it?' Julia said, her voice catching.

I swallowed. 'You should put it down. The police . . .' They'd want to check it for DNA, wouldn't they? This was evidence.

But Julia wouldn't let go. She held the small soft toy against her chest. Then her attention shifted to the painting. 'What did Ursula say? *She's with Jesus.*'

'You think . . . you think she meant it literally?'

We both stared at the painting of Christ, then at the door it had been concealing. I pulled at it, expecting it to be locked.

It wasn't. It was heavy and stiff, but I pulled it open without too much effort.

'We should call the police,' I said. 'Now.'

I took my phone from my pocket. Unsurprisingly, I had no signal. Not out here, deep in the woods.

Julia got to her feet, still clutching the cat. She went to go through the door.

'Wait.'

I checked behind us; it was almost completely dark outside now. I grabbed the other flashlight from the rucksack and turned it on. The beam was bright, doubling the amount of light in the chapel.

'Let me go first,' I said. 'Just in case.'

In case Lily's body is in there.

Julia was mute as I pulled the door fully open, revealing not a room but a set of stone steps. Steps that led down into the earth.

'A crypt,' I whispered.

'Oh God, what's that smell, Lucas?'

The stench of something rotten wafted up the stairs. Rotten meat. A wave of nausea hit me and I had to rest against the damp wall beside the doorway for a moment.

Julia moved towards the stairs, but I held out an arm to stop her.

'Let me go down first,' I said. 'If Lily's down there . . .'

'I want to see her. I need to see her.'

'No. Julia, please. If she is down there, we don't know . . .' I felt horrible saying it. 'We don't know what state she'll be in.'

'Oh God. Oh God oh God.' She took a step backwards, hugging the filthy, sodden Little Cat.

'I'm going to check it out,' I said. 'Then we're going to leave here, find a house and call the police. Okay?'

'Okay.' She sat down at the end of the nearest pew.

I hefted the flashlight in my hand and, with one last look back at Julia, ducked through the low doorway and started down the stairs. The steps were a little slippery, narrow and steep, so I had to hold on to the wall, shining the flashlight down so I could see where I was treading. As I descended, the smell grew more sickening. I pulled the collar of my coat up over my nose in a vain attempt to block the smell.

I reached the bottom of the stairs.

I was in a narrow room with an arched ceiling, small and cramped. There was a small wooden table at the far end, with a cross hanging above it. I had been afraid there might be coffins down here, family members left behind when the chapel was abandoned, but if there ever were, they must have been removed.

Something lay on the floor in the corner, beside the table.

It was a body. I was certain of it. A body, covered by a thick sheet which was actually, I realised as I inched closer, a heavy, old curtain. The smell was almost unbearable now and I covered my nose and mouth with one palm, laying the flashlight on the ground, the beam pointing at the body beneath its makeshift shroud.

I wanted to bolt from this place, to go and call the police, but I needed to see. Julia would want to know.

I crouched beside the shroud and, after counting to three, pulled it back to reveal a white, moon-shaped face.

I fell back, dropping the flashlight and sending it spinning in a circle. Light danced around the crypt, ramping up my dizziness and nausea. I grabbed the flashlight and got back up onto my haunches, directing the light at the human face.

Her eyes were closed. She looked almost peaceful. But this wasn't a child. It wasn't Lily.

It took a few seconds for my fear-stricken brain to make sense of it, to figure out who I was looking at. And the relief was replaced by guilt. She was here because of me. Because of something I'd started.

Zara.

There was no blood. No visible sign of injury. I had peeled the shroud back just far enough to see the shoulders of her black puffa jacket. I could see her feet too, poking out: trainers with mud creeping up over the soles. I covered her face and stood up.

I heard the door above me open. Julia. I was about to tell her to stay where she was, but before I could speak, she was falling. She fell onto her back, sliding down the stone steps, landing on the hard ground of the crypt and rolling onto her side.

I rushed over to her. She lay panting, looking up at me, wincing with pain.

'Are you okay? Are you hurt?'

She pushed herself to a sitting position, rubbing her back. 'I'm just bruised. I'm okay.' She tried to get to her feet, but her face contorted and she fell back onto her bottom. 'I'll be all right, I just need a minute,' she said. Then she caught sight of the body beneath the shroud. 'Oh!'

'It's okay,' I said hurriedly. 'It's not Lily.'

The meaning of what I'd said sunk in. 'Is it a child?'

'No. Her name's Zara Sullivan.'

'What? You know her?'

'Knew her. She was the private investigator I hired.'

She drew in a breath.

'Why did you come down? I told you . . .'

'What? I didn't *come* down. Didn't you see what happened?' She looked up the staircase and I followed her gaze. The door was shut.

'I was pushed,' she said.

Chapter 40

I climbed the steps as quickly as I could. I grabbed the rusty door handle and rattled it. The door moved an inch but then stopped. There was something blocking it. I pushed harder, but it wouldn't budge. Something was wedging it shut.

I tried not to panic. We were trapped in the crypt of an abandoned chapel, as night was drawing in. Did anyone know we were here? Yes . . . but only Ursula.

Ursula, who had to be in on this. Whatever *this* was.

I banged on the door and called out, 'Hello? Let us out!' I pressed my ear to the wood, but it was too thick to hear anything outside.

I made my way back down the steps to where Julia was sitting, as far from the body as she could get. She had dragged herself across the floor, her face screwed up against the pain in her back. I sat down beside her.

'Tell me what happened,' I said.

'You were taking ages,' she said through gritted teeth. 'I was going out of my mind, sitting up there, waiting for you to tell me if Lily was down here. I couldn't wait any longer so I went to the door, to the top of the steps.'

'And somebody pushed you.'

She nodded. 'I felt hands on my back. Luckily, I managed to twist so I went down on my back rather than face first.'

'Did you see them?'

'No. They must have come into the chapel while I was standing there. They were fast because I was only there a few seconds before they pushed me.'

I searched her eyes. Part of me thought she was lying, that she'd thrown herself down. A scenario played out in my head: Julia had killed Lily. She was responsible for all the weird stuff that had happened in her house. She was the person Max and I had followed down to the river, the person who'd attacked us. None of this had anything to do with what happened thirty-five years ago. Julia was a murderer. She had killed her daughter and her husband. Then Max. Maybe she had killed Zara too after finding out, somehow, that I'd hired her.

'What is it?' she asked. 'Why are you looking at me like that?'

I pinched the bridge of my nose, tried to shake the dark thoughts away. It couldn't be Julia. Not unless she was the greatest actor on earth. Her grief, that was genuine. The way she'd acted when she found the extinguished birthday candles.

Unless she was insane and didn't know what she'd done . . .

I stood up and paced the small space, staying clear of Zara's corpse. I told myself not to be so stupid. It wasn't Julia. She was innocent. I couldn't have misjudged her that badly. Could I?

Julia tried to get to her feet again, but her eyes watered and she swore. 'Ah, my back.'

I looked into her eyes, at the pain there – both physical and emotional – and told myself again that I was being stupid, that she wouldn't have thrown herself down those stairs and hurt herself. This time, I believed it.

'Is the rucksack still up there?' I asked. 'The shears?'

'Yes. I—'

A yell came from above us. Then a series of thumps.

'What the hell?'

Now I believed Julia one hundred per cent. I ran up the stairs and pressed my ear against the door. I could hear scuffling. A voice cried out in pain. Then all went quiet.

Julia called up, 'What's going on?'

I thumped on the door and shouted again. Nothing.

Then somebody screamed. The sound almost sent me hurtling down the stairs. It sounded like it came from inside the chapel, just beyond the door. One thing I was sure of – it was a woman.

'Lucas, please, what's going on?'

I ran back down to Julia, more confident on the slippery steps now, and began to tell her what I'd heard.

She grabbed my arm. 'Lucas.'

'A woman. Who could it be? Ursula. But why—'

'Lucas!'

I shut up.

Julia pointed at the stairs. 'The door. I think someone just opened it.'

'Oh shit, I should have brought a weapon, a knife . . .'

I hesitated, listening for sounds of life above us. It was completely silent. I had to go up, to find out what was going on, even though I knew it could be a trap, was probably a trap. But what else could I do?

Slowly, I crept back up to the door. I turned the handle and pushed it open.

I didn't know where Julia's flashlight was and I'd left mine down with her, so the room was dark. I waited for my eyes to adjust. Shapes sprang out of the darkness. A chair, which had been used to wedge the door shut, lay to my right.

There was somebody on the floor between the pews. They weren't moving.

I crept closer.

They sprang to life.

'Get away from me! Get away!' It was definitely a woman, but it was too dark to see her face, and although I recognised the voice I couldn't place it.

'Who is it?'

I spun round. Julia was in the doorway. She must have dragged herself up the stairs. She was bent almost double from the pain, but managed to lift the flashlight to cast the beam onto the woman on the floor, who was cowering in terror against the altar.

The woman lifted her face towards us.

'What the fuck are—'

She cut me off with a groan.

It was Heledd.

'I saw her!' she babbled, eyes darting around the interior of the chapel. 'She told me to confess my sins. The sins of my father and my mother.' She crossed herself, gazing past us at the painting of Jesus.

I approached her and she shrank away.

'She said . . . she said if I don't confess she'll come back for me.' She began to mutter to herself, her words a rapid blur. It was a prayer. She crossed herself repeatedly. For a confused moment I wondered if Heledd had a twin sister, because this woman seemed so different to the cool, sane woman I'd been talking to just a few hours before. But no, this was definitely Heledd. Two books lay beside her. One was the ruined Bible I'd spotted earlier. The other, clearly identifiable in its brown leather binding, was Malcolm's journal.

'Who told you?' I asked.

Heledd picked up the Bible and held it against herself. 'The witch. The Red Widow.' She pointed towards the door. 'She was here. She told me to confess. The sins of the father and the mother. The sins of the daughter.'

Julia approached her, pointing the flashlight at her face.

'Confess? What did you do?' she demanded. Her voice rose to a shout. '*What did you do?*'

But all Heledd could do was sob.

Chapter 41

LILY – 2014–2015

It had been the worst Christmas ever. Not because the presents Mum and Dad got her were rubbish – Lily got pretty much everything she had asked for, except a new kitten – and not because it rained all day which meant she couldn't go outside to try out her new Heelys. Dinner was nice too. Mum gave her an extra helping of roast potatoes and didn't make her try any sprouts.

All of that was great. Lily's tummy still fizzed with excitement at the *Christmassy-ness* of it all, even though she wasn't a baby who believed in Santa any more, despite Mum's insistence he was real. But what ruined it, what made it the worst Christmas, was the atmosphere between her parents.

Christmas night, Lily went to bed, taking Chesney with her, along with Big Cat and Little Cat, and bit back tears. Her tummy still hurt from eating too much dinner and she couldn't get to sleep. So her brain churned.

There had to be something she could do to make her parents realise how lucky they were. Her attempt to run away had been a massive fail. She hadn't been gone long enough for them to worry. They hadn't even realised she'd left the house! Mum was all fretful and cross when Lily got home, telling her never to do that again. Dad echoed what Mum said and that had been good, seeing them agree about something for a change.

So maybe it hadn't been such a fail after all.

But that had been weeks ago, and as Christmas approached the atmosphere between her parents had become as frosty as the morning grass.

Until today: New Year's Eve. Earlier, Mum and Dad had locked themselves in their room for ages. She could hear them talking and then they'd gone quiet for a while. When they came out they were both smiling and the atmosphere around them had changed. It was amazing. They said she could stay up with them till midnight. But then they'd started watching this programme with all these ancient, boring rock stars, and they were drinking champagne and getting all lovey-dovey, which made her want to vomit. She wanted them to love each other and not argue, but kissing in front of her? That was gross. So she left them to it, went upstairs and Skyped Megan.

They played MovieStarPlanet together for a little while, and then Megan said, 'It's 2015 tomorrow. You know what that means?'

'What?' Lily asked.

'It means it's thirty-five years since the Red Widow last took a child. Since Carys was sacrificed to her.'

Lily remembered that taxi driver, whatever his name was, telling them this.

Megan went on. 'That day you saw her in the woods, she must have been scouting.'

'Scouting?'

'Yeah, you know. Looking for kids. Getting ready.' There was a long pause. 'Did she really say my name?'

Lily hesitated. Megan had asked her this, like, a hundred times since that day. Lily knew she should have confessed straight away that she'd made it up. But there was something thrilling about seeing the fear on Megan's face, and the longer time went on, the harder it became to tell the truth. She didn't want Megan to be mad with her and call her a liar.

'Yeah,' Lily said, and Megan nodded, sadly, as if she really believed her fate was sealed and there was nothing she could do to fight it.

The stupid Red Widow. Since that day in the woods, Lily had become increasingly convinced the witch didn't exist, that she had imagined those eyes watching her, just as she'd once imagined seeing a fairy at the bottom of her garden. Seeing how easily Megan had swallowed the lie about the witch saying her name made Lily realise how she too had been – what was the word? – *gullible*. Childish. It had been a trick of the light, that was all.

'Can we talk about something else?' Lily said. 'I'm so bored of talking about the Widow.'

'Oh. Sorry to be so *boring*.'

'I didn't say you were boring . . .'

But Megan wasn't listening. She scowled into the camera. 'I bet you'd be glad if the Widow took me, wouldn't you?' Megan said.

'What? Don't be stupid. Come on, it's only five minutes until midnight. Let's not argue.'

But it was too late. Megan was in a strop and she refused to say Happy New Year when midnight struck. She muttered goodnight and ended the call.

A few seconds later, Mum came in. Lily quickly slid her iPad under the pillow.

'I'm so sorry,' Mum said. 'I was going to call you down so we could see in the new year together but I lost track of time.'

'That's okay.'

Mum sat on the bed.

'Well, Happy New Year, sweetheart.'

Mum gave her a hug and a kiss on the cheek then said, 'Are you all right?'

'Yeah. Just tired.'

'Me too.' Mum took Lily's hand. 'I know things have been difficult lately, with me and your dad. But it's going to get better from now on. I promise. We love you more than anything.'

The words warmed Lily's insides and she gave Mum another cuddle, and then Dad came in and said, 'Happy New Year!' and they had a group hug. She forgot all about grumpy Megan.

Lily went to sleep feeling happier than she had in ages.

ʊ

The next morning, Mum and Dad looked tired. Dad said he had a headache. But they smiled at each other and Mum didn't flinch when Dad gave her a hug in the kitchen.

Over lunch – soup and crusty bread – Mum said, 'Why don't we go out for a walk? Get some fresh air.'

'Great idea,' said Dad.

Lily groaned. She hated fresh air. She wanted to go to her room to call Megan or watch something on her iPad. But her parents insisted that it would 'do us the world of good'. They decided to go for a walk down by the river, where Lily knew it would be muddy and windy. But, she reminded herself, at least they were in a good mood and getting on well. Maybe things had turned the corner and Mum and Dad weren't going to get divorced and she wouldn't be forced to choose between them. (Not that it would be much of a choice. Mum would win every time.)

As they were about to leave, Mum said, 'Don't forget to put your coat on.'

'But I'm not cold.'

Mum gave her a hug. 'You're like a radiator. How do you do it?'

Lily smiled. 'I've got a warm heart, obviously. Can I bring Big Cat and Little Cat?'

Dad appeared. He'd been looking for his wellies. 'Haven't you outgrown those toys yet?'

Lily scowled and Mum said, 'They're not toys, are they, Lils? They're real.'

That made Dad laugh and Lily said, 'Family hug.' It had been a long time since they'd done this, the three of them standing up and putting their arms around each other, a circle of love and togetherness, and in that moment Lily thought everything was good. This was going to be the best year ever.

Chesney followed them to the edge of the garden and Lily thought he might come with them all the way to the river, but then he got distracted by a bird or something and ran off. She would have to make do with her cuddly cats. She held on to Big Cat, while Little was stuffed into her pocket.

It *was* muddy and windy by the river, just as Lily had suspected. She walked along for a while, fantasising about having a dog. A pug, that's what she really wanted. Then she remembered that last time she'd said she wanted a pug, Dad told her you have to squeeze their bum glands which made all this stuff ooze out that smelled of fish. This was the most disgusting thing Lily had ever heard. Suddenly, she'd gone right off the idea of getting a pug.

And then she heard her parents arguing. Again. She couldn't believe it! So much for this being a happy new year, a fresh start. Mum was jabbing a finger at Dad, who looked both angry and shame-faced.

Lily wanted to scream.

Furious, she stomped off ahead into the trees. She looked back up the path but couldn't see them. They must have stopped walking, too busy arguing to move forward.

Oh God, they were going to split up. She'd probably have to move away. One parent would get her and the other would keep Chesney.

She had to do something.

Think, think. She could make them think she'd disappeared, run away again.

But that hadn't worked last time, had it? She needed to do something more drastic. She could jump into the river . . . No, that was crazy. But what if she made them think she'd drowned? That she was dead? Even if they thought it for a moment, the shock would be so great it would make them see how stupid they were being.

She looked down at Big Cat. Could she do it? She could throw him in, then hide. Wait for her mum and dad to appear, let them panic for a minute, then show herself. She didn't really want to throw Big into that freezing water, but he was only a toy really, wasn't he? They'd be able to get him out with a long stick, she was sure.

She kissed Big Cat then, without thinking about it any more, took a step towards the bank and threw him into the water. He fell short, but rolled across the rocks and, in slow motion, plopped into the river.

She hurried into the bushes – and almost jumped out of her skin.

'What are you doing?' she asked.

And then there was a hand on her mouth, stopping her from screaming or calling out. The hand was replaced by something else. A gag. She tried to run, but strong arms held on to her then dragged her away, through the bushes. She could hear Mum calling her name but she couldn't respond.

She had been stupid – and now she couldn't do a thing to save herself.

Chapter 42

Julia unzipped the rucksack and took out the shears she'd brought with her. She held the tip against the cowering Heledd's throat.

'Tell me what you did to Lily or I'll cut your fucking head off!' she said.

Heledd stared at her, lips trembling but not speaking. I placed a palm on Julia's shoulder, put another hand on her arm, gently lowering it until the shears pointed at the ground.

I tried a gentler approach. I was still finding it hard to separate this shaking, tear-stained Heledd from the calm, intelligent woman I knew. If it wasn't for what she'd said about confessing her sins and those of her parents, I'd find it difficult to believe she was guilty of anything. That and the journal, which she'd brought to this place instead of taking it to the police.

'Did you follow us?' I asked.

She stared at me like a mute, frightened child.

'I told Olly we were coming out here, so I guess he told you, is that right? Or were you planning to come here all along? To destroy this?'

I held up the journal.

'What's that?' Julia asked.

'Olly's dad's journal.' I riffled through the pages of the journal, remembering how Heledd had leafed through it earlier. 'Did you see something in here? Something incriminating?'

She was silent.

'Tell him!' Julia urged, pointing the shears in her direction.

Heledd shrunk back. Finally, she spoke. 'Malcolm . . .' She drew in a breath. 'He found out who my father is . . . Saw him and Mum together. Saw all of us . . .'

'How is that incriminating?'

She didn't reply, so I moved on.

'Your father? Who is he? Glynn?'

Again, she refused to answer. Again, I moved on.

'Heledd, was it you who pushed Julia down the stairs?'

Her eyes darted to Julia then back to me. Then a tiny nod.

'You bitch,' Julia said.

Heledd cowered and I lay a hand on Julia's shoulder until I was sure she wasn't going to use the shears.

'Were you and Ursula working together?' I asked.

Heledd frowned with confusion. 'Ursula?' She genuinely didn't seem to know who that was.

'Did you kill Zara?'

She took a deep breath and closed her eyes. 'I had to . . . She was going to find out.'

I groaned. 'Find out what?'

But she'd clammed up again. Julia paced behind me, a human ball of raging energy. Two years of frustration and anger she had previously directed inwards now threatening to burst out.

I had one more question for Heledd. 'Who did you see? Who scared you?'

But all she would say was, 'The Widow.'

'Let me talk to her,' Julia demanded, pushing in front of me. Heledd looked up at her and I saw something new in her eyes. Sympathy, perhaps. Not the fear or guilt I expected to see there.

Julia took a step towards Heledd, crouching and grabbing the front of her top with one hand, holding the shears in the other.

'Tell me one thing,' she demanded. 'Is Lily alive or dead?'

Heledd answered with a whisper. 'I don't know.'

'Tell me!'

There were tears in Heledd's eyes. 'I don't know. I really don't know.'

'Fuck this!' Julia stood and threw the shears across the empty chapel.

I found the other flashlight and switched it on. 'One of us should go and get the police, and the other should stay here to guard her.'

'I'll go. I might kill her if I'm left alone with her.'

'Are you sure? Is your back okay?'

Julia waved away my concern. 'It's fine. Adrenaline's a powerful painkiller. I think there's a farmhouse not too far away. I'll go there and use their phone.'

'Okay.'

She stopped for a second, taking one last look at Heledd, who appeared to be praying silently.

'She really believes she saw the Widow, doesn't she?'

'It seems that way. She doesn't realise you're much scarier than any witch.'

'Huh.'

She left, leaving me alone with Heledd.

I tried to talk to her again, but she had withdrawn fully now. In the end, I gave up. I sat on one of the pews while she remained in the corner, shivering and hugging herself. I leafed through Malcolm's journal. Heledd must have seen something in it while she was looking through it earlier, something that made her decide she needed to destroy it. It was cold in the chapel; the thought of Zara's body rotting below my feet made it feel even colder. And then, finally, there was commotion outside, lights shining through the woods, and DC Hawkins came through the door.

'Fucking hell. You have a way of attracting drama, don't you?' she said to me.

I shrugged. 'It's a special talent.'

288

A uniformed officer escorted me to the nearest road, where a number of police vehicles were parked. Getting into the car, my phone signal returned and it vibrated in my pocket. It was a voicemail, received at 10.30 p.m., from Olly Jones.

'I'm worried about Heledd. She went out hours ago and hasn't come home.'

I laughed darkly. He was in for a shock.

It was 2 a.m. by the time I got back to the retreat. Julia was already there, the police having sent her home. She sat in the kitchen with a bottle of red wine open before her.

'I'm giving up being teetotal,' she said, pouring me a glass. 'Did Heledd say anything else?'

'No. What about Ursula? Have you spoken to her?'

Julia pulled a disgusted face. 'I've tried. She just rambled on about her spirit guide. But she swears she's never met Heledd.'

She shook her head then picked up her phone.

'Who are you calling?' I asked.

'The police.'

She managed to get through to DC Hawkins, who told her she'd ring her once they'd had a chance to interview Heledd.

'I have to know what she knows about Lily,' Julia said, her voice cracking. The stress of the past few hours had shaken her to her bones, and I went over as soon as she ended the call and put my arms around her. She was stiff at first, before finally relaxing and slumping against me.

We drank the wine together in exhausted silence. Julia kept checking her phone until the battery died. She took it over to the counter and plugged it in.

'You can't sit here all night,' I said.

'I can't go to bed. What if the police call?'

She sat down at the table and lay her head on the smooth surface. I sat beside her and realised, a few minutes later, she had fallen asleep.

I fetched a cushion and gently placed it beneath her head, then crept up to bed.

ω

I was awoken by voices from downstairs. I wasn't sure where I was at first. My body was heavy as lead, brain wrapped in cotton wool. I was naked and the scent on the sheets brought it all back to me. Naked flesh, eyes and hands and tongues. Intense, hungry, cathartic sex. I lay there for a moment, wishing I could remain in this bed, the past and future locked outside, existing only in the present with Julia beside me.

Except I was here and she was somewhere else. I could hear three voices, one deep, another higher. I dressed hurriedly and went downstairs, squinting against the light.

Julia was in the kitchen with DC Hawkins and DI Snaith, steaming mugs of tea before them. They both looked tired. I guessed they'd been up all night. I imagined them being dragged from their beds by the call that led them to me and Heledd in the woods. Any lingering hostility I might have harboured after they regarded me as a suspect crumbled away.

'Mr Radcliffe,' DI Snaith said. Beside him, DC Hawkins's nose wrinkled. I no doubt smelled like I needed a shower.

'What time is it?' I asked.

Julia replied, 'Just gone noon.'

There were dark circles around her eyes and she had pulled her hair back into a tight ponytail. No make-up. She was beautiful.

She shot me a 'stop staring at me' look. 'The detectives are about to tell me what happened with Heledd.'

I sat down and DI Snaith nodded to his colleague, who cleared her throat.

'She's confessed to the attack on you, and to the murders of Max Lake and Zara Sullivan.'

'Oh God.' I put my head in my hands. 'Why did she kill Max?'

'Apparently she was only intending to do away with you, but Max saw her face so he had to go too. And Zara Sullivan – well, Heledd was terrified she was going to find out—'

'That Heledd took Lily?' Julia interrupted.

DI Snaith held up a hand. 'I'll come to that in a minute.'

'But—'

'Please, Mrs Marsh, I need you to be patient, just for a minute.'

I squeezed Julia's hand. It was cold. I turned back to DI Snaith and DC Hawkins.

I kept my voice calm. 'What about Shirley and Malcolm?'

'Malcolm Jones died from his heart condition,' DI Snaith said. 'But Heledd admits to confronting him – threatening him, I should say – the morning before he died, telling him not to talk to Ms Sullivan. It seems likely that the stress of the situation contributed to his death.'

'But it's not something we'll ever be able to prove in court,' DC Hawkins added.

'How did Zara die?' I asked.

'We won't get the coroner's report for a while, but Heledd said she led Zara to the chapel, telling her she had something important to show her, something related to her investigation. She pushed her down the stairs to the crypt. We think she broke both her legs during the fall. And Heledd left her there.'

My whole body went cold. 'Left her to die. Of dehydration?'

The detectives' silence told me I was right. I hung my head, imagining Zara lying there in agony, unable to climb the stairs, cold and growing increasingly thirsty and hungry, her body shutting down. A slow, aware death. It was my greatest nightmare.

I forced myself to shake the image off though I knew it would return, deep in the night. That it would haunt me for the rest of my life.

'So what about Shirley?' I asked. 'Did Heledd confess to killing her?'

DI Snaith replied. 'She says it was an accident. They were arguing at the top of the stairs, after the wake. Heledd was furious that Shirley had agreed to talk to you and she was convinced her mother was going to tell you the truth.'

'What truth?' Julia asked.

'I'll come to that in a second. Heledd said her mother tried to get past her. She was drunk and wanted to lie down before Mr Radcliffe here turned up. Heledd blocked her way, they struggled for a second and Mrs Roberts ended up at the bottom of the stairs with a broken neck. Heledd says she checked her pulse, realised she was dead and fled the scene.'

'That's bullshit,' I said. 'She'd already killed Zara by pushing her down the stairs. It's her MO.'

'Maybe,' DI Snaith said. 'Although she's confessed to the other murders.'

'She keeps talking about needing to confess her sins,' added DC Hawkins.

'And "the sins of the mother and father"?' I asked. 'That's what she was saying last night.'

Snaith nodded. 'Again, I'll come to that. But regarding her mother's death, even though Heledd is clearly terrified, she doesn't seem to regret her mother's death. Her attitude is that her mother was ungrateful for everything Heledd was doing, trying to protect her. She says Mrs Roberts *wanted* to be punished. She wanted to atone before she died so she could, as Heledd puts it, face St Peter at the pearly gates with a clear conscience.'

I was pretty sure I knew, now, what Shirley and Heledd's father had done. But I waited for the detectives to continue.

DC Hawkins said, 'It seems Heledd was far more concerned about protecting her father. Concerned, that was, until the Red Widow told her to confess.' She rolled her eyes.

The hairs stood up on my arms. Whatever DC Hawkins thought about Heledd's sanity, we were so close to the truth.

'Her father?' I braced myself. It had to be Glynn, surely. According to Malcolm's journal, Shirley had been sleeping with him. Glynn had to be guilty of everything, just as I'd suspected. I was itching for the detectives to get to the end of their account. 'Glynn Collins?'

'No. Not Glynn Collins.'

I thought I'd misheard. 'Sorry, did you say *not* Glynn Collins?'

'That's right.'

'Then . . . then who?'

DI Snaith and DC Hawkins exchanged a look, as if they weren't sure if they should tell us.

'Rhodri Wallace,' DI Snaith said.

Julia gasped. 'Oh Jesus!'

'I believe you know him?' DC Hawkins said to Julia.

'He's my handyman. I mean, he's done a lot to help me since we moved here.'

My mind raced ahead, trying to fit it all together. Rhodri was Heledd's dad? He, not Glynn, had been Shirley's lover back in the 1970s?

'So Heledd was protecting Rhodri and her mother . . . because *they* abducted Carys Driscoll. Oh my God, they did it to protect Heledd, didn't they? To save their child from the Widow?'

Julia stared at me, confused, but DI Snaith nodded. 'I'm not sure how you knew that, but that's Heledd's story. Her mother told her the whole thing when she was growing up. I think she wanted Heledd to know how lucky she was. How *blessed*.'

DC Hawkins sighed, and DI Snaith went on to recount what Heledd had told them.

'In 1980 the Widow was due to come to the town to claim a child, unless another child was given to her as an offering. Heledd says that her parents' friend, Glynn Collins, had warned her mother about it at a meeting of the Historical Society.'

I nodded impatiently. 'He found some old newspaper articles.'

'That's right. And Shirley was terrified. She met up with her secret lover, Rhodri, that night, and told him what Glynn had said at the meeting. Of course, they already knew about the legend of the Widow. Everyone in this town is obsessed with it, especially the older generations. Old people and kids.'

I thought about Rhodri and his conviction that a woodpecker would attack Julia if she moved the peonies. Superstition ran through his veins. Shirley must have believed in the Widow too. I guessed they were brought up treating the Widow's existence as a fact, passed down from their parents and grandparents.

'And Heledd,' DC Hawkins said. 'She believes too. She's spent her whole life being told she was saved from the Widow. She's an intelligent woman, though. I'm sure her belief lay dormant for a long time until last night. Now she's absolutely convinced she saw her, that the Widow came into the chapel and told her to confess.'

DC Snaith and DI Hawkins shook their heads in tandem, as if despairing of this place where the locals clung to superstition and crazy legends.

'You were telling us about Shirley and Rhodri,' Julia said.

'Oh yes.' DI Snaith went on. 'According to Heledd, they were terrified the Widow was going to take their love child. I think there was something in the legend about how the witch was more likely to take children born out of wedlock or one whose parents weren't together. So they made up their minds. They would take a child who, according to them, wouldn't be missed. An orphan from the children's home. They would take her into the woods and leave her tied to a tree – which is what they did.'

'But what happened to her? Surely the woods were searched after she went missing?' Julia asked. 'The Widow can't have taken her. She doesn't exist!'

'We don't know that yet,' DC Hawkins said. 'But we've arrested Rhodri Wallace. We're going back to talk to him now. So far, he's keeping schtum. He won't even admit that Heledd is his daughter or that he was sleeping with Shirley all those years ago. I guess he's worried what his wife will say. They just celebrated their fiftieth wedding anniversary.'

So that was why he and Shirley weren't together. He was already married when Heledd was conceived.

'According to Heledd, he lived a double life. Coming to visit her at the bed and breakfast, then going back to his wife and other children. He's maintained a relationship with Heledd in secret all these years. Maybe his wife knows and has been turning a blind eye. I guess we'll find out when we talk to her.' DI Snaith ran a hand over his scalp. 'People and their fucked-up, messy lives. The way Heledd talks about him, it's as if he's some great hero. The man who made huge sacrifices to save her from the Widow, who risked everything each week to visit her. She said she would do anything to protect him. Anything.'

'And that's what she did,' said DC Hawkins.

I got up and crossed the kitchen. 'I don't get why Heledd decided she needed to kill Zara, or why she wanted to kill me. We didn't know anything about what her parents did.'

'But she was terrified you were going to find out. And who knows? Maybe Shirley gave something away to Zara, or Heledd believed she had. It seems she got it into her head that all potential leaks had to be dealt with.'

'What about the journal?' I asked. 'Malcolm found out that Rhodri was Heledd's dad. But he didn't know they took Carys.'

'Apparently not. But Heledd had been brought up to believe it was imperative that no one find out who her dad was, that it would ruin his life if everyone knew he had cheated on his wife. I guess his secrets were mixed up in her mind so she felt she needed to keep all of them.'

Throughout the conversation, Julia had been growing increasingly impatient, fidgeting and tapping her foot against the floor. Finally, she couldn't hold back any longer.

'But what about Lily? What did Heledd tell you about *her*?'

Again, the two detectives looked at one another before DI Snaith spoke. 'Heledd denies any knowledge of what happened to Lily.'

Julia stood up and slapped the counter. 'She must be lying!'

'She's confessed to two murders and the manslaughter of her own mother. She's told us about the abduction of another child, naming her own parents as the perpetrators. She seems utterly terrified of the Widow, as if the witch is going to come for her if she doesn't tell us everything. I'm sorry, Julia, but I don't think she's lying.'

'Then it must be Rhodri. That bastard. He was always around here. He used to tell me how lovely Lily was. I thought he was a nice guy. But he was watching her, wasn't he? Waiting? To do to her what he'd done three decades ago. I bet there are more. And she knew him, she trusted him, would have gone with him if he asked.'

She paced the kitchen, out of breath. I got up, tried to take hold of her, but she pushed me away. She jabbed a finger towards Snaith.

'You have to get him to tell you what he did to Lily. What he did with her. Let me come to the station, put me in a room with him for five minutes. I'll get that bastard to confess.'

Hawkins raised his palms. 'Mrs Marsh . . . I can assure you, we're doing everything we can.'

Julia's face was red. 'Then why the hell are you still here? Why aren't you at the station, getting him to talk? I need to know where my Lily is. I've waited so long. *I can't wait any longer!*'

She stormed from the room, leaving me alone with the cops. My brain was whirring. There were still so many questions – but answers were beginning to form, like silhouettes in the mist.

'We will get to the truth,' DC Hawkins said, picking up her jacket.

I was lost in thought, her voice coming to me as if from a great distance. When I looked up, they were gone.

Chapter 43

I knocked on Julia's bedroom door. 'It's me,' I said.

After a long pause she told me to come in. It was the first time I'd been in here. She was sitting on the double bed, her eyes pink from the tears she'd cried; pink from exhaustion too. I sat beside her and put my arms out. She allowed me to hold her against my chest and I looked around the room. It was full of pictures of Lily – on the walls, on the dresser, frames on every surface. There were photos of Julia with Michael too. On their wedding day. With Lily when she was a toddler. A photo of Michael holding the newborn Lily took pride of place on the dressing table.

I wanted to be able to help her break free of the past, to move on. I knew that if Lily was dead, Julia would never get over that. How could she? But she could still have a life. A good life. Last night, in the woods, she had threatened suicide if she discovered Lily was dead. I was going to do everything in my power to show her that wasn't the right decision.

But first, we had to get to the truth.

'Are you okay to talk?' I asked.

She extricated herself from my grasp, found a tissue and blew her nose. 'Go ahead.'

'Okay. So. There are two things. Last night, at the chapel, we heard a shout, scuffling, like Heledd was fighting with someone. Unless she's completely mad and was fighting with herself, there *was* someone else there.'

'She said it was the Widow.'

'Yes. Except we don't believe in centuries-old witches, do we?'

Belief. That's what this whole screwed-up situation came down to. The power of stories, of superstition and fear.

'So who was it?' I went on.

Julia shook her head.

'Let's look at the second question,' I said. 'Ursula and her map. I believe in spirit guides about as much as I believe in witches. I still think Ursula found Little Cat in that hut and took it to the chapel, with the ultimate plan of getting you to pay her to talk to Lily. Heledd seemed genuine when she said she didn't know Ursula, so I don't think they were working together. There's something else going on here.'

'Like what?'

I got up and crossed to the window, looking out towards the woods. The sky was colourless, the world bleak and grey. Below me, Chesney the cat slunk across the lawn.

'Let's think it through. Heledd came to the chapel to destroy Malcolm's journal because there's something in there she didn't want anyone to see. She was probably planning to move Zara's body too. My guess is that she got a shock when she discovered us there, which is why she pushed you down the stairs and wedged the door shut. She panicked, was trying to work out what to do. Set the chapel on fire, maybe? But then someone came along and caused her to freak out.'

'Ursula?'

I shook my head. 'Surely not. Ursula's too old. Heledd could overpower her easily. And how would Ursula make Heledd think she was the Widow?'

Julia got up and headed to the door.

'What are you doing?'

'Ursula's in the cottage. I'm going to talk to her.'

ω

We entered the cottage. Ursula was at the desk in the Bertrand Russell Room, staring into space, her laptop open but untouched before her. It seemed so long ago since I'd first come here and found Karen writing. Back before the mayhem began.

Ursula jumped up as soon as we entered. 'Have the police gone? What happened? What did you find in the woods?'

'Come off it, Ursula,' Julia said. 'We know you planted Lily's toy cat there.'

She gave us a blank look. It was convincing, I'd give her that. 'I don't know what you're talking about. Was that what you found? Lily's toy? Oh, Julia, I'm so sorry. I hoped Phoebe was wrong . . .'

Julia erupted, sweeping Ursula's laptop off the table. It crashed to the floor.

Ursula's mouth opened, a look of absolute shock. 'Julia, what—'

'Stop lying!' Julia shouted. 'You found that cat and took it there. Lucas saw you, out in the woods.'

Ursula's attention snapped towards me. 'What? He's mistaken.'

'It was two days after you arrived here,' I said. 'I know it was you. You were wearing that red coat.'

Ursula stared at me, then at Julia. 'Don't you remember, Julia? The day after I got here, I told you I'd mislaid my coat. I wore it that morning, took it off when I came inside and couldn't find it later. We searched the house for it – and I still haven't found it.'

'Oh, stop it,' I said. 'You're just making it—'

'She's right.'

I stopped talking.

Julia repeated it. 'She's right. I remember now. We looked for it for ages.'

'You're saying someone took it? That they wore it into the woods? Who? Why?'

Julia had gone pale again. 'Maybe it was all part of a plan.' She sat down opposite Ursula. 'Can you describe the experience when you heard Phoebe talking to you? Was the voice inside your head?'

'I'm not crazy. It was inside the room.'

'A disembodied voice, inside the room? Is that how it usually happens?'

Confusion flickered in Ursula's eyes. 'To be honest . . . Phoebe usually speaks to me in my dreams.' She caught my reaction and said, 'It's all in my book. I'm not making this up.'

Julia said, in a gentle voice, 'But this time you heard the voice when you were awake?'

'Yes. Well, it was during the night. At first I wasn't sure if I was dreaming. But then I realised I was conscious, and my guide was talking to me, that she was there. I was overwhelmed at first. It had been a long time since she'd come to me and I feared she'd deserted me, that my book had made her angry. But here she was, a voice in the dark, but there. Really there. I'd never heard her speak out loud before. In the past, her voice was always inside my head, so I was terribly excited. She told me she had an important message to tell me about Lily.'

'That was the first time she came to you?' Julia said. 'When she told you Lily was with Jesus?'

'That's right.'

'Hang on,' I said. 'You told me your guide spoke to you about my girlfriend, Priya.'

Ursula couldn't meet my eye. 'I wasn't being one hundred per cent honest with you then . . . I asked my agent about you.'

Just as I'd suspected.

'What about the second time Phoebe spoke to you?' Julia asked. 'When you drew the map? Surely you didn't draw it in the dark?'

'No. It was shortly after lunchtime and I was at my desk, writing. I heard a voice behind me. She told me not to turn around, to listen carefully. She said she was going to describe a map to me and that she wanted me to draw it. She described it very clearly. As soon as I'd finished I turned around, hoping to see her, but she wasn't there.'

'Thank you, Ursula.'

Julia got up and, taking hold of my arm, led me out into the garden, shutting the cottage door behind her.

'You remember how Karen said she'd heard a voice, telling her to get out? And you both heard singing. Actually, didn't you say Max heard the singing too?'

'That's right.'

'And then there was the incident with the birthday candles,' she said.

My pulse quickened as I realised what Julia was saying.

'And what about the night you thought someone was in your room?' Julia said.

'When my phone and pen went missing.'

We stared at each other. 'There's been somebody in the house, sneaking around, talking and singing and taking things. Not a ghost. A person. Oh my God . . .'

She ran across the lawn towards the house and I followed her, up the stairs to Room 2: Ursula's room, which was the same room where Karen had slept.

It was a corner room so there were two exterior walls, one of which had a window that looked out over the front garden. Could someone have been outside that window, talking to Ursula, and to Karen before her? I looked out. It was a sheer drop, with no balcony, no surfaces for anyone to stand on. The roof was high above. It wouldn't be possible for anyone to throw their voice from up there into this room.

'The attic,' I said, thinking back to the night when Karen had freaked out and reported hearing someone telling her she wasn't welcome. She'd heard singing too.

I went into the hallway, closing the bedroom door behind me, and pulled down the ladder that led into the attic. I climbed, tentatively putting my head through the gap – not just because I was afraid there might be someone hiding there, but because of the bats. Julia had been instructed to leave them alone.

There was no sign of the bats, though. And there was definitely no one hiding up here.

I pulled myself fully into the loft space and crawled over to the area above Ursula's room and lay on my belly. I spoke, reciting a Halloween rhyme about witches, bats and big black cats in a loud voice. It was the first thing that came into my head. Then I sang several lines from a song. Finally, I tapped on the floor, before heading back down the ladder and into Room 2.

'Did you hear me?' I asked. 'Talking and then singing?'

'No. Maybe very faintly. I heard you knock but that's it.'

I turned my attention to the other exterior wall, which was dominated by the wardrobe. I opened it. It was stuffed full of clothes and had shelves which would make it very difficult for anyone to hide inside. I remembered how we'd found Karen with her head in the wardrobe, as if searching for Narnia.

'Ursula said that when she turned round there was no one there, even though it felt like the voice came from directly behind her.'

I looked at the desk, then at the wardrobe again. 'Help me with this, will you?'

We shoved the wardrobe, which was lighter than it looked, to one side, revealing an expanse of wall that needed a lick of paint. I tapped it. It sounded hollow.

Julia said, 'Wait here', and left the room, returning a minute later with a claw hammer.

'What are you—'

I didn't get to finish the question. She swung the hammer at the wall. It went through like the wall was made of cardboard. Shards of thin plaster landed at my feet. Julia swung again, working at the gap with the head of the hammer to create a large hole. We used our hands to expand the hole, throwing chunks of wall behind us. The dust cleared and Julia said, 'Oh my God.'

There was a space behind the wall, just over two feet wide. A crawl space. Easily large enough for an average-sized person to crouch in. And the plaster was so thin, a voice would be audible through the wall, helped also by a little vent just above the skirting board.

'They've been moving around behind the walls,' Julia said, shuddering.

'But how did they get in there?'

We pulled away more of the wall until there was a hole large enough to enter. I peered in. To the left was a dead end, but the hollow space stretched away to the right, beyond the boundaries of this room. Julia produced her phone, switching on the flashlight, and crawled inside before I could offer to go first.

'Be careful,' I said.

She went off on her hands and knees, calling back after a minute. 'It runs alongside Room One.' That was the room where Suzi had slept. It gave me the creeps, the idea of someone hiding in the walls, listening. But how did they get in?

Julia came crawling back and stuck her head out through the hole. There were specks of plaster in her hair, and a cobweb clung to her shoulder.

'There are steps leading down to the middle floor,' she said.

'You had no idea any of this was here?'

'No, of course not. The police didn't find it either when they searched the house after Lily vanished.'

I was about to accuse the police of incompetence, but why would they have found these hidden spaces if they weren't looking for them?

'I'm going down.' Julia turned back around.

'Wait. Let me go.'

'No. It's my house. I want to do it.' She crawled back through the secret space. As soon as she was out of sight, I ran out of the room and down the stairs to the middle floor, where my room and Lily's old bedroom were located. I could hear movement inside the walls, as Julia descended the hidden steps. I went into Lily's room and waited.

Julia tapped on the wall and I placed a palm against the paintwork, knowing she was on the other side.

'Can you hear me?' she asked.

Her voice was a little muffled but easy to make out. This must have been where the singing I'd heard came from.

'It stops here,' she said. 'Oh, hang on. There's a hatch.'

'A hatch?'

I heard a grunt of exertion, then she called, 'I'm going down.'

Again, I hurried down the stairs to the ground floor. I stood in the main hallway, by the front door. Lily's room was, I was sure, above my head. I could no longer hear Julia. Where the hell was she? I called her name but got no response. Then I heard knocking. It was coming from the Thomas Room.

'Julia?' I called again.

Two knocks on the ceiling. She was above my head. It didn't make sense. But then I stepped back into the doorway and looked into the hallway, then back to the Thomas Room. I had never noticed before, but the ceiling in the Thomas Room was considerably lower.

'Can you hear me?' I shouted.

Her voice came back, but it was too faint to make out what she was saying. And then I heard a thump from the far end of the room. It came from behind the bookcases. I hurried over.

'Hello?'

There was no reply.

My heartbeat accelerated. 'Julia? Hello? Are you all right?'

I was about to run upstairs to enter the crawl space, convinced someone had attacked her, when she spoke and relief flooded my body.

'There's a room,' she called. 'A tiny room. Where am I exactly?'

'Behind the bookcases in the Thomas Room.'

'Jesus Christ. Listen, there are more steps. I'm going down.'

'Julia, are you sure?' This felt bizarre, talking to her through a bookcase. 'Is there anything in the room?'

'There's a glass. A tumbler.'

Someone had been in that little room, with a glass pressed against the wall, listening.

'I'm going down the steps now!' she called. 'Come down to the basement!'

'No, Julia, wait there!' I raised my voice. 'There has to be an exit from the passageway into the house.' I felt along the bookcase, looking for a loose panel.

Then I remembered something. Karen had reported seeing a new guest in the dining room. We thought she'd imagined it – but what if she really had seen someone?

I asked Julia to give me a minute, then went into the dining room. There was a cupboard against the wall where the Roberts Room – the dining room – was joined to the Thomas Room, at about waist height. I crouched and opened the cupboard. Apart from a few ancient phone directories, it was empty. On my hands and knees, I reached through to the back of the cupboard. There was a handle. I pulled it and the back of the cupboard came away.

'I knew it,' I said aloud.

I slithered through on my belly and found Julia staring at me. Her face was smeared with dirt and she was breathing heavily. I entered the little room behind the bookcases, which was too small for me to stretch out my arms, and got to my feet. It was dusty and claustrophobic, the walls furry with ancient cobwebs.

'Let me go first,' I said, pushing past her and going down the steps before she could protest. I had my phone out now as well, filling the space with weak light. Julia followed.

I found myself in a narrow passageway, tall enough to stand in, with bare brick walls on both sides. I tapped the wall to my right. 'This must be the basement. The den.'

I moved slowly through the passageway. It was around eighteen feet long. As I got closer to the end, I slowed, hardly able to believe what I was seeing.

I turned to look at Julia, to make sure she could see it, that I wasn't hallucinating. She could clearly see it too.

It was a door. A solid steel door.

Chapter 44

I placed my hands against the cold metal and pushed. The door didn't budge. I examined it using my phone's flashlight. There was no handle, no keyhole. It had to be bolted on the other side.

'Maybe there's another way in,' I said, keeping my voice low.

Julia was about to bang on the door but I caught her wrist.

'No,' I said. 'The person who's been inside your house could be in there now. If there's another exit, we don't want to alert her. She'll get away.'

'She?'

I put my finger to my lips and squeezed past Julia, leading her back up the steps and into the little room behind the bookcases. We took turns to squeeze through into the dining room. I dusted myself off and did what I always do when I'm trying to think through a problem. I paced.

'It has to be a woman,' I said. 'Ursula's guide's voice was female. The voice I heard singing was female.'

Julia nodded. 'And Heledd was convinced the woman who stopped her last night was the Red Widow.'

'Come on,' I said, hurrying from the room. I thought I knew who she was, the woman who had been haunting Nyth Bran, the uninvited guest, but wanted to be sure before I shared it with Julia. 'The secret room is beyond that door. And I think I know where the other entrance is.'

ᚹ

On the way out, I grabbed a flashlight from the kitchen. It was raining, a light drizzle, but I hardly felt it as I jogged along the path towards the woods, Julia at my heels. I phoned the police station and was told DI Snaith and DC Hawkins were busy. Interviewing Rhodri, I assumed. I left a message, asking them to call me back urgently.

Julia and I passed the clearing with the hut and entered the second set of woods. It was my fourth time here and I was becoming familiar with the landscape.

'Remember I thought I saw Ursula here, wearing her red coat? Well . . . whoever it is who's been in your house, it must have been her,' I said. 'I guess she took a fancy to it. She can't have known I would see her go into the woods and follow her.'

I stopped.

'She vanished somewhere around here. Just before the fork in the path.'

Last time I came here, the branches had been bare, everything frozen in suspended animation, waiting for spring. Now buds sprouted, wild daffodils peeked through the grass, and the undergrowth was even thicker. I stopped and scanned the ground, turning around slowly. Beyond a thick tangle of brambles, twenty feet from where I stood, was an ancient-looking oak tree. I headed over, stomping on nettles and stepping over fallen logs until I reached the tree.

Julia caught up with me. I looked around, searching for the spot where I thought I'd seen the woman in the red coat vanish.

'The entrance . . . It has to be around here somewhere.'

'The entrance to what?'

'To the—' I began, stepping forward, and then I was falling, the ground giving way beneath me.

Julia snatched at my arm, and I twisted, grabbing hold of the ground. Along with damp earth, I got two handfuls of brambles which ripped into my palm. My legs hung in the air beneath me and I kicked out, convinced I was about to fall.

'Pull!' Julia urged, holding on to me with all her strength.

My foot found something beneath it. A protruding tree root. By pushing against it, I was able to drag myself back onto solid earth. I lay on the ground, waiting for my heartbeat to slow down.

'Looks like we found the entrance you were looking for,' Julia said.

I sat up. 'Yeah. I did that deliberately.'

She laughed, and for a wonderful moment the tension dissipated.

I checked my phone. We'd reached the point where my signal was fading, but neither DI Snaith nor DC Hawkins had tried to call me back.

'Do you want to wait for the police?' I asked.

Julia shook her head. 'No. I need to see.'

'I was hoping you'd say that.' I lay on my belly and peered down into the hole, using the flashlight to see beneath me. 'Just as I thought, there's a tunnel. Let me help you down, then I'll follow.'

I lay on my front and Julia lowered herself into the hole, grasping my wrists.

'You ready?' I asked.

She grunted and let go. It was only an eight-foot drop, and she landed on her feet, bending her legs and rolling onto her side like a parachute jumper.

'Right, my turn.'

'Wait, there's a ladder,' she said. She lifted it until its tip emerged beside me, and I climbed down, leaving it where it was. This was obviously how Julia's uninvited guest entered and exited the woods – like on that day she'd vanished before my eyes, when I thought I was following

Ursula. The fact the ladder had been lying on the ground surely meant she was inside now. It was hard for me not to think of it as her lair, and as I thought that an image from my book hit me. The creature, hiding beneath ground, fat and happy from the souls it had consumed. In *Sweetmeat*'s final scenes, my hero trudged through a filthy, sewage-caked tunnel to confront the beast. It sent a chill through me. Life imitating art, again.

Except the tunnel we stood in was, apart from a puddle of rainwater around our feet, dry.

'It must have been part of the mine,' Julia said. The walls were constructed of compacted slate and the tunnel stretched in both directions as far as the eye could see. There were rusted metal tracks set into the ground. I guessed that once this tunnel would have been used to transport carts full of slate towards the town – or maybe towards the estate where we'd found the chapel. That didn't matter right now. What mattered was that I was certain this tunnel ran beneath Julia's house.

The roots of the oak tree, which would have been an acorn when this tunnel was built, hung above our heads. These roots had pushed through the roof of the tunnel and created the hole we'd climbed through. I guessed that, sooner or later, the whole thing would collapse.

I switched on the flashlight.

'You know,' Julia said as we made our way along the tunnel, 'after you leave, I'm always going to associate you with dark, claustrophobic spaces.'

She was trying to keep her voice light, but it cracked towards the end of the sentence.

'Are you sure you want to do this?' I asked.

'Please stop asking.'

'Okay.'

As we trudged through the darkness, with the woods above our heads, I thought about what she'd just said. *After you leave.* Despite everything that had happened here, the prospect of leaving and going home filled me with dread. There was nothing for me there, except an empty flat. Loneliness. Here, with Julia beside me, I felt alive, and maybe that was *because* of everything that had happened since I'd arrived at the retreat. Yes, I felt horribly guilty about what had happened to Zara and Max and the others, and I could foresee a period when I would have to deal with that guilt and the trauma of it all. But now, watching Julia as she walked through the tunnel beside me, I remembered how it felt to be thrilled by someone else's presence.

I didn't want to go home. I wanted to stay here, with her, whatever happened today.

But now was not the right time to tell her that.

As we progressed along the tunnel, we found old pieces of machinery that had been left there to rot. I didn't know what any of it was called. A contraption the size of a fridge-freezer with a metal wheel that had turned brown. An iron bench that had suffered a similar fate. Lurking at the edges of this forgotten place, they made me think of rusting ghosts, the trapped spirits of ancient robots. The woman who became the Widow of legend – her husband had died down here, hadn't he? That made me think of other kinds of ghosts and I reminded myself there was no such thing. I pulled my jacket tighter and increased my pace.

'Surely we must be getting close to the house now,' Julia said after we'd been walking a while.

The tunnel curved around a shallow bend. I thought of the River Dee, somewhere above us, where all this had started – for Julia at least. I sneaked a glance at her. Her jaw was set with determination. Someone had been in her house, on her territory. She hadn't said as much, but I knew she felt violated. Angry. And something else: if the uninvited guest had been living here, roaming the woods, had she seen what had happened to Lily?

And why had she attacked Heledd and opened the door so Julia and I could escape?

We rounded the bend and stopped. It looked like we would be getting answers very soon. A metal ladder attached to the wall led up to a wooden hatch.

Without waiting to argue about who would go first, I started up the ladder. It was slippery, but less rusted than the other metal objects we'd seen down here. I pushed at the hatch. It shifted an inch, then got stuck. I managed to push one edge up, which let through a chink of light.

'It's not locked,' I said. 'But there's something on top of it.'

Holding on to the ladder with one hand, I climbed as high as I could and put my shoulders against the hatch, bent into an awkward, painful position. I pushed. Something scraped against the floor above me. I pushed again, until I was able to lift one side of the hatch, tilting it until whatever was blocking it slid away. One more heave, and I was through.

I pulled myself up through the square gap and gestured for Julia to follow.

We found ourselves in a small chamber with stone walls. The ceiling was low, and I had to stoop slightly so as not to bang my head against the slightly damp ceiling. There was nothing here except a trunk that had been covering the hatch. At one end of the chamber was a solid wooden door. I tried it. It was open.

'Are you ready?' I asked Julia.

She nodded and we went through. I heard Julia catch her breath.

It was an underground apartment. A bedroom. A mattress lay on the floor in one corner, covered with a dirty quilt that looked as if it hadn't been washed in years. Beside the mattress, a chest of drawers, with chipped and faded baby-pink paintwork. A lamp – battery-operated, I guessed – sat on top of it. There was a little porcelain bowl in the corner. It took me a moment to realise what it was – a bedpan. There was another, larger bowl next to that, and a silver tray bearing a bar of soap, a hairbrush, a toothbrush and toothpaste. There was a tap set into the wall. I gave it a quick turn and a trickle of cold water came through.

Julia stood in the centre of this room, her mouth open, looking at the posters on the walls. Pages torn from magazines: Care Bears, a couple of Australian soap opera stars from the late eighties, a boy band. There was a calendar too, dated 2013.

Julia crossed to the little tray of toiletries.

'I *thought* my tampons had been going missing,' she said in a low voice, picking one up. 'This is the brand I use.'

She spotted something else: a cooler, the kind you'd take on a picnic. She lifted the lid. It contained a packet of ham, butter, slices of bread, a few apples.

'All the food that's gone missing,' she said. 'This is where it ended up. But who—?'

She hugged herself, trembling from the shock of discovering that someone had been living under her house, sneaking in and helping herself to things. Lurking in the walls. Listening. Watching.

Had she been there, listening, when Julia and I were in bed together?

I was about to tell her my theory about who it was when we heard a thump. It came from a point ahead of us.

'We should go back up to the house, call the police,' I whispered. I had already checked my phone and, unsurprisingly, found I had no reception down here.

'No,' Julia said. 'I have to see. I *have* to.'

'Okay.' I took a deep breath.

We went through the door at the other end of the room and entered a short passage. At the far end was the metal door that had blocked our entry earlier. Behind us, an alcove. But something else grabbed our attention. Another door set into the stone wall.

Julia approached the door tentatively and turned the handle. It was locked.

To keep us out, or keep someone in?

Heart thumping, I crouched and put my eye to the keyhole. A light was on inside the room. I found myself looking at another mattress on the floor. There was something on the pillow. I blinked several times before I realised what I was looking at.

I stood up so fast that all the blood rushed to my head and I had to grab the handle to stay upright.

Julia was staring at me. 'What is it?'

But all I could do was stare at her, unable to tell her what I'd seen.

Chapter 45

LILY – 2015

Lily felt herself being lifted and slung over someone's shoulder, the person who had grabbed her from behind and gagged her with some kind of cloth, the person whose face she couldn't see. Her arms were pinned by her sides and she tried to bite at the gag, but it was no good. She panicked, unable to breathe properly, before snorting air through her nose. They were heading along the road, away from the river and towards the woods.

Megan hurried along behind. Megan, who had been waiting in the bushes.

Lily knew her parents would have reached the spot where she'd been standing by now, that they'd be panicking, looking for her. They'd see Big Cat in the water and think she'd fallen in. Oh, why did she do that? She was such an idiot.

They reached the woods. She tried to punch the back of the person carrying her but she was too weak, the punches bouncing off, like fleas attacking an elephant. She wanted to scream but the gag prevented her from making any sort of noise except a strangled moan. They kept heading into the woods, along the path until they reached a clearing. There was a scary-looking hut. Lily struggled and felt something drop from her pocket. It was Little Cat. She made a desperate noise, hoping Megan would see that she'd dropped him and pick him up. But Megan stepped over the cat, eyes fixed on the path ahead, and they carried on across the clearing into the next wood.

They headed further along the path. Lily fought back tears, but clung to hope. Megan was here. It had to be some sort of game. A prank. Though she didn't understand why Megan wasn't smiling or laughing. Lily had never seen her friend look so deadly serious.

They stopped by a large tree with a silvery trunk, and the person carrying her dropped her roughly onto the damp ground. Lily stared up at him.

It was Jake.

Megan's big brother was panting with the exertion of carrying her all that way. He looked to Megan, as if waiting for instructions. Lily reminded herself that even though Jake was a lot older and bigger than his sister, inside he was younger. Megan always bossed him around. Lily had no doubt that Megan was in charge here.

With her arms free at last, Lily grabbed the gag and pulled it away from her mouth.

'Don't scream,' Megan said, 'or we'll hurt you.'

This must be what it feels like to be in shock, Lily thought. This was her best friend. But the way Megan was looking at her now, it was as if she hated her.

No, it wasn't hate in her eyes. It was fear. Fear and determination.

'What are you doing?' Lily asked.

'We're saving ourselves.'

'From the Widow,' Jake said.

Lily gawped at him, then at Megan. 'But the Widow isn't real.'

Megan leaned forward, hands on her thighs. 'It's 2015 now. The year of the Widow. She's going to come to town to take a child unless another child is sacrificed. And Grandad said she likes children whose parents aren't together. Like ours. Like *us*.'

Lily couldn't believe what she was hearing. 'Megan, it's not real! It's a made-up story.'

'No. She's real. You saw her, remember? You told me she said my name. She'll come for me, unless I do something about it.'

Lily felt like she'd swallowed a giant ice cube. 'But I made that up.'

'What?'

'I lied! I was trying to scare you.'

Megan put her hands up. 'No. I don't believe you. You're just saying that now to save your skin.'

'Megan, please.' Lily tried to get up from the wet grass but Jake put a strong hand on her shoulder, keeping her down.

Megan said, 'Put the gag back on her.'

Jake grabbed her roughly and pulled the gag back into place, tightening it at the back and pulling it against the edges of her mouth. It hurt. She tried to grab at it but Jake held her arms, trapping them behind her. She thought she was going to wet herself. She wanted her mummy and daddy. Why had she left the riverbank? She should have stayed with them. Even if they didn't love each other any more, they loved *her*. They would protect her. She tried to fight back tears but it was impossible. They rolled down her face and her nose filled with snot, making it even harder to breathe. She sniffed it back, her body shaking, barely able to see through her tears.

'Stop snivelling,' Megan said.

Megan was carrying a rucksack, which she opened. She pulled out a length of brown rope that she tossed to the ground. Then she fished out a pair of handcuffs.

'I got these from my mum's bedroom,' she said, snapping them over Lily's wrists behind her. 'Jake, put her against the tree.'

They wrapped the rope several times around her and the tree trunk. Jake pulled it tight. She heard him grunt with effort.

'Have you done the knots properly?' Megan asked.

'Yeah.'

'Are you sure? She won't escape?'

'They taught us at school. Mr James said I'm really good at it. He gave me a star.'

The little silver handcuffs dug into Lily's bum. She really felt like she was going to wet herself, but she fought to hold it, and to stay calm. There was no such thing as the Widow. Someone would find her and save her and then Megan and Jake would be in so much trouble. They'd probably go to prison and it would serve them right.

'Maybe we should wait,' Jake said. 'Won't the Widow come when it's dark?'

Megan glared at him as if he were the stupidest person on earth. 'Do you want to be here when she comes? She might take one of us instead. She might take all of us! I think she'll come as soon as she smells Lily. It says in *Folk Tales and Urban Myths* that she can smell child meat from a mile away.'

Jake looked around nervously, probably imagining the Widow hiding in the trees, sniffing the air.

Lily tried to speak, but the gag stopped her.

Megan stepped towards her. 'I don't think she'll hurt you. You won't feel much . . .'

'Grandad said it's agony, when she sucks your soul—'

'Shut up, Jake.' Megan touched Lily's arm. 'I'll always remember you, Lily. I'm sorry it had to be you. But Grandad said in the old days the townsfolk would always sacrifice the newcomer. The outsider. It's tradition.'

In that moment, Lily hated Megan. She burned with it. A line Lily had heard in a film played in her head. 'You're going to pay for this.' If it wasn't for the gag she would have spat the line into Megan's face, but all she could do was glare – glare until Megan turned away.

And then she and Jake were heading back along the path, walking quickly. Megan looked back over her shoulder once before they vanished into the trees.

Lily couldn't hold back any longer. She peed herself, and more tears came. She was cold and her wrists hurt and so did her mouth. And she was scared, so scared. She didn't believe in the Widow – she really, really didn't – but what about animals? Rats and foxes and bats. And snakes . . . None of the snakes in Wales were poisonous but she had an image of one slithering up her leg and . . .

She had to shake the image away.

She waited. There was nothing else she could do. Mum and Dad would be looking for her. She guessed they'd search all along the river first. Oh God, if they thought she'd fallen in, maybe they wouldn't look any further. But there were dog walkers, weren't there? Someone would come by. Surely.

She said a silent prayer and dipped her head, closing her eyes. When she next opened them the sun was dipping behind the trees. She must have passed out for a while. Dusk was falling.

She would be stuck here, in the woods, at night. In the dark. And all the animals would come out.

She chewed at the gag, trying to dislodge it or tear it, but it was so tight. She rubbed the back of her head against the tree, hoping she might be able to wear down the knot, or loosen the gag. It was no good.

And then she heard a noise. She jerked her head up. Suddenly, she forgot that bears and wolves didn't live in this country any more. She imagined them circling her, sniffing her out, gathering the courage to come closer.

The trees across the path rustled.

A face peeked out from among the branches.

Lily screamed against the gag as the figure emerged from the trees. She had long black hair and a white face and was wearing a long dress, the kind women wore in the olden days. She looked left and right then crossed the path.

The Red Widow. She was real. She was actually real.

Lily passed out.

When she came to, Lily was lying on a mattress on the floor.

The Widow was sitting by her feet.

Lily screamed and the Widow didn't seem to mind. 'These walls are soundproofed,' she said. 'My father built them so no one would hear me down here.'

Lily moved her hand to her mouth. She was no longer handcuffed – the Widow must have broken them open, perhaps using witch magic – and the gag was gone. Tentatively, she pushed herself up into a sitting position. The Widow had wrinkles on her face – laughter lines, Mum called them – but she was not as ancient as Lily had always imagined the witch to be. Her lips were not stained with children's blood. Her teeth were yellow and kind of mouldy-looking but they weren't pointed.

'Are you going to eat me?' Lily whispered.

That made the Widow laugh. It didn't seem like an evil laugh, the cackle of a witch. It wasn't like her mum's laugh either. It was sharper. A crazy person's laugh.

'I thought the Widow was going to kill me too,' the woman whispered. 'A long, long time ago, when I was even younger than you.'

Lily gaped at her. 'You're not the Widow?'

That laugh again. 'No.'

She got up and turned around, looking down at Lily.

'My name is Carys. Carys Driscoll.'

Chapter 46

LILY – 2015–2017

Carys Driscoll. Lily was sure she'd heard that name before. It took a second, then she remembered: Carys was the little girl who had disappeared thirty-five years ago. That taxi driver had told them about her.

'You're not dead,' Lily breathed. For the first time, she took the room in properly. 'Where are we?'

'This is my home,' Carys said, spreading out her arms. 'I've lived here since I was rescued. Just as I rescued you. If I'd left you there till night-time, the Widow would have come.'

That threw Lily. This woman believed in the witch too?

'Daddy rescued me and kept me safe here. Safe from the Widow. Just as I'm going to do to you. You know, Lily, that once the Widow knows your name, you can never be safe from her? Not until you're all grown-up, like me. Once you bleed, you're safe. Safe from the Widow, anyway.'

She bared her rotten teeth and made a hissing noise.

The woman got up and crossed the room, fetching a bottle of juice. It was the same kind of juice they had at home.

'Here,' she said. 'Drink up.'

'I want my mum and dad.'

Carys smiled sadly. 'Oh, Lily.' She reached out a hand to stroke Lily's hair, and Lily shrank back.

'They'll be worried sick. I need to let them know I'm okay.'

'I'm so sorry to have to tell you this, but they're dead.'

Suddenly, Lily couldn't breathe any more.

'They both jumped into the river, trying to save you. I saw it happen.'

Lily sobbed. She couldn't hold back. Carys watched her, smiling with sympathy. When Lily had finally stopped crying, she said, 'But Mum can't swim. Why would she do that?'

That seemed to surprise the woman, but she shrugged and said, 'She was so desperate to save you. But it's okay, little one. You'll be safe here with me. I'll never let the Widow get you. You can have your own room, your own things. There's a rubbish tip near here, where I'll be able to get you a mattress like this one.' She patted the mattress Lily was lying on, and Lily realised this was Carys's bed.

'You'll like it down here with me,' Carys said. She reached out a long finger and stroked Lily's face. Her fingers were rough, the nails long and sharp. She scratched Lily's cheek. 'And you know, I've been so lonely since *my* daddy and mummy died. Now here we are, two orphans together.'

She smiled. 'You know, I've been watching you for a while, wishing I could talk to you.'

Lily flashed back to that time she was looking for Chesney, when she saw someone standing at the edge of the woods. Carys. It must have been.

'I think we're going to be the best of friends,' Carys said.

She left the room then, and Lily lay down on the bed and cried. It was all her own fault. If she hadn't thrown Big Cat into the river . . .

Then she remembered what Megan and Jake had done, and hatred and anger and fear mixed together until her sobs finally faded.

ʊ

Now, a long time later, those first days with Carys were as hazy as a dream. Lily knew she had cried a lot. She had begged Carys to let her go. If her mum and dad were dead, she needed to go to the funeral. But Carys said it wasn't safe, that Lily couldn't show herself to the Widow. Lily continued to beg. She scratched at the door of her new room – so tiny compared to her big bedroom at home, and the mattress Carys brought her stank like a blocked toilet – and screamed, praying someone would hear her. But they never did.

One day, when Lily hadn't been living there long, Carys ran in, slamming the door behind her.

'The Widow! She heard you. She's looking for you in the woods. You have to be quiet or she's going to come and then she'll kill you and *eat you*!' She shouted the final two words, her face an inch from Lily's.

Terrified, Lily fell silent.

'She's the only one who can hear,' Carys said. 'Her hearing is like a bat's.'

Lily didn't scream or yell any more.

Carys brought her food. Strangely, she knew what kind of stuff Lily liked. She brought all her favourite chocolate bars, snacks and sandwiches. Sometimes she brought cooked meat. When she told Lily it was rabbit, Lily refused to eat it at first. She couldn't eat a bunny! But eventually, hunger got the better of her. Now it was her favourite thing. When she smelled it through the door it made her drool like a dog.

The worst was having to go to the toilet in a pot. It was gross. But Carys took it away every day and brought the pot back clean, along with a bowl of water for Lily to wash in. She had soap too, and shampoo, though the water was always cold. Her new home was cold, just a little warmth seeping in from the ceiling, which was weird, but Carys gave her blankets to huddle under. Carys brought her books too. Often they were damp and yellowed and Lily suspected they'd come from the tip.

She also brought her toys. A cuddly tiger and a camel, which Lily cuddled at night, their bad smell eventually fading. And one day, like a miracle, Carys brought her a surprise.

Little Cat.

'I found him the same day I found you,' Carys said. 'I've been keeping him here, safe. And because you've been such a good girl, I'm going to let you keep him.'

Lily clutched the toy. He smelled damp and there was dirt on his fur. Her tears helped wash it away.

Carys put her face close to Lily's, laying one hand on the cat. 'But if you're bad, I'll take him away and you'll never see him again. Understand?'

'I understand.'

Every day, Carys would let Lily out of her little room into the main part of the underground chamber to exercise for an hour. Together, they jogged on the spot, did star jumps, sometimes threw a ball back and forth. Carys always seemed really happy during this hour, grinning at Lily and squealing with excitement. It made Lily wonder if Carys was like Jake, a kid on the inside. She acted like a child in an adult's body. A child who'd never grown up.

Lily didn't hate Jake. She only hated Megan. Jake had only done what his sister told him to do. When Lily first met Megan and Jake, she was surprised by how compliant he was, his sweet nature making him want to obey his sister, who took full advantage. Megan had needed Jake's physical strength to carry out her plan. Oh, how Lily wished she'd stepped in all those times she'd seen Megan bossing her brother around. She should have told Megan to leave him alone. Now it was too late. Too late to stop Megan.

Megan, who'd betrayed her best friend to save her own skin.

Lily thought back over their friendship. When Lily moved here from Manchester, Megan was the first girl who talked to her. Lily had been so relieved to make a new friend that she ignored Megan's bossiness, her obsession with scary video games and the Widow. She even put up with Megan's creepy grandad. She could almost laugh about that. It wasn't Mr Collins she should have been afraid of. It was his granddaughter.

When Lily closed her eyes and thought about Megan, she felt as if black moths were flapping around in her head. Black moths that beat their wings against her skull, that made her squirm and ache.

If she ever got out of here, she decided, she wouldn't tell anyone that Jake had been involved. It wasn't his fault, after all. He had simply been following his sister's orders. Blaming him wouldn't help to set the moths free.

She would find another way to ensure justice was done.

Six months after Carys had brought her Little Cat, they were exercising when Carys suddenly collapsed, clutching her knee. She lay on the floor, groaning.

'What's wrong?'

Carys screwed up her face. 'I pulled something. Help me up.'

But Lily hesitated, glancing over her shoulder at the door she wasn't allowed through.

'Come on,' Carys hissed, trying to get up but falling back.

Lily didn't stop to think. She pulled the door open and ran through, finding herself in a small room with a wooden chest at its centre. There had to be a way out, surely, but—

Carys lurched into the room, a length of metal pipe in her hand.

'You little bitch!' she yelled, and swung the pipe at Lily's head.

When Lily came to, back in her room, she had a throbbing pain in her head. Worse, Little Cat was gone.

'I warned you,' Carys said later, 'if you were bad, I'd take that cat away. Now he's somewhere you'll never find him. And if you try to escape again, you'll spend the rest of your life in this room.'

She slammed the door.

Lily gave up hope of ever seeing Little Cat again – but then, a few days ago, Carys had appeared with the toy in her hand. Lily jumped up, delighted, until Carys produced a knife. She slashed at the palm of Lily's hand, making her cry out, then grabbed her wrist and pushed Little Cat against the cut. She held him there for a minute before pulling him away, studying him with a smile before she left the room.

ω

That night, nursing her injured hand, Lily thought back to the longest conversation she'd ever had with Carys. It had happened a few months ago. Carys had come into the little room stinking of something familiar. A smell that reminded Lily of her dad. Alcohol. Carys sat on Lily's mattress. She seemed tired and sad. She kept scratching at her arms with her sharp nails.

'Do you miss your mum and dad?' she asked.

Lily didn't know how to reply. She thought she might start crying again, until Carys said, 'I miss my daddy so much. His name was Albert. Albert Patterson. He's the one who saved me from the Widow.'

Lily waited, knowing Carys was about to tell her a story. The woman stared into the corner, her voice dropping so Lily had to strain to hear her.

'Daddy said the people who tried to sacrifice me were friends of his. A man and a lady. I remember the lady – she talked to me at the home, told me she had some kittens and did I want to come and see them?

'Albert saw them taking me into the woods and followed them, just as I did for you.' She smiled, showing her yellow teeth.

'One day, the lady who tried to give me to the witch came to Nyth Bran. I recognised her straight away. The woman with the kittens! She had her daughter with her. The daughter had beautiful red hair. I wished my hair was that colour, so pretty and bright . . . I hid in the walls and watched them.'

Lily swallowed. This 'lady' was Carys's equivalent of Megan. The person who'd tried to give her to the Widow.

'Did you hate her?' Lily whispered. 'For what she did?'

'No, because if she hadn't done it, Daddy wouldn't have found me.'

Lily was astonished. 'But she tried to kill you! Carys, if it wasn't for her you wouldn't have spent your life living down here, in a hole like a . . . like a Hobbit.'

Carys narrowed her eyes. 'What's a Hobbit?'

'See!' Lily exclaimed. 'You don't know anything. Have you ever watched a movie, or TV? Your whole life was stolen from you.'

Carys shook her head. 'No! Daddy hid me from the Widow and looked after me. He said I was his and Mummy's reward, a reward for their patience. They couldn't have children – and then I came along, like a gift. That's why he made these walls soundproof – so when visitors came to the house they wouldn't hear me.'

Lily stared at her. 'I don't understand.'

Carys scratched her arms harder and glared at Lily as if she were stupid. 'Because no one could know I was here, *of course*. Daddy said if they found me they'd take me away. Send me back to the home.' Tears appeared in her eyes. 'I couldn't go back to that place. It was so horrible there. The other children were mean to me and the grown-ups were mean too. The food was disgusting. I was so sad there.'

Her eyes darted from side to side and she leant forward as if she were about to share a big secret. 'Daddy said he would never let me go back to that place, that he would never let anyone find me. He built spaces into the walls of Nyth Bran so I could enter the house without anyone seeing me. He said that if anyone ever came looking for me, there would be places for me to hide. He got the idea from a book, he said, about a little girl in the war who hid from the nasties.'

'The Nazis, you mean? Anne Frank?'

Carys frowned. 'I'm sure he said nasties.'

Something dawned on Lily. 'Wait. Nyth Bran. That's my house!'

'That's right.' Carys pointed to the ceiling. 'It's up there.'

Lily jumped up. She went all dizzy and had to put a hand on the wall to steady herself. 'Who lives there now?'

'Nobody, Lily. *Just us.*'

'Then why can't we go up there, into the house? I want to see it! My things might still be there. My toys and books. My iPad! I can show you things. Videos! Games! I can show you all the things you missed.'

The angry look came back, but there was confusion there too, as if Lily were actually getting through to her, making her see that she hadn't been saved. Her 'Daddy' was *not* a good guy.

'Let me go upstairs, find the iPad, all my other things . . .'

'No! It's all gone. And it's not safe to go up there, not for you. The Widow will see you.'

Lily wanted to wail with frustration. She had to make Carys see that this wasn't right, that she had been wronged. That she didn't need to live underground.

'Where's your . . . daddy now?' she asked after a while.

Carys clenched her fists. 'Daddy got sick. The Big C, they called it. He was sick for ages, and then he died.' Her eyes were watery. 'And then Mummy got sick too, soon after. She said when he died her heart stopped working properly.'

'Then what happened?' Lily asked.

A smile. 'She let me into the house to look after her. It was nice, being able to do that. But then . . . then she changed. She became mean. Nasty.' She screwed up her face and her voice changed. She sounded like a scary witch. '*I never wanted you, never loved you. He loved you more than he loved me. I know what happened when he came down here to see you. You cunt. You little cocksucker.*'

Lily gasped at the bad language.

Carys's voice returned to normal. 'But he never touched me. No man has ever touched me.'

Lily didn't know what to say to that.

328

'Mummy told me that when she died I would have to leave here. She said she was going to leave the house to charity, to atone for all her and Albert's sins. She cried a lot, ranted about how she was going to Hell but at least Albert would be there too. And then one day I went up to see her and she was gone. I waited and waited but she never came back. I began to sleep up there, with the sun coming through the windows, in their big bed. That was when it struck me. If Mummy was dead too, that meant the house was mine. I was their daughter and it rightfully belonged to me.' She almost shouted the last sentence.

'But then people came. A man and a woman, wearing posh clothes. They put up a big sign outside. *For Sale*. I pulled it down but they brought another one. People kept coming to look around the house. Strangers. Nosy parkers. I hid in the walls and I made noises. You should have seen their faces.' She laughed, sounding like a witch again. 'But then I got sick . . . I thought I was going to die. I dreamt that a family had moved in upstairs, a new family with a little girl. And when I woke up the dream had come true.'

She pointed a finger at Lily. 'This house is mine. And your parents stole it.'

Carys stood up and loomed over Lily, raising a hand. Lily pressed her back against the wall, closing her eyes. But nothing happened, and when she opened them again, Carys was smiling.

'I liked your family, Lily. I liked listening to them through the walls. Especially you. I lay in the space by your bedroom, learned the song that you and your mum sang together.'

She sang it now, the song Lily had learned at school, in a surprisingly tuneful, sweet voice that made her sound like a little girl.

Un, dau, tri.
Mam yn dal y pry . . .

329

'I went into the house when you were all out. I liked to stand in the kitchen, imagining myself sharing a pot of tea with your mum. I sat at the dining table, wondering what it would be like to eat dinner with you all. I went into your room and cuddled your toys, pretending we were best friends.' Her smile grew broader. 'That part of my dream came true.'

'We're not best friends,' Lily dared to whisper. She thought about her old best friend, Megan, and her head felt hot.

Carys didn't seem to hear her. 'I was so sad when your dad didn't come home that day, after I brought you here.'

'But you weren't sad about my mum?'

Immediately, from the expression on the woman's face, Lily knew Carys had said something she didn't mean to say.

'My mum? Is she still alive?'

But Carys didn't answer. 'That's enough for now.'

She stood up and left the room, slamming the door behind her. Lily beat on it with her fists. 'Please. Is my mum alive? Where is she?'

But there was no reply.

ᘓ

Last night, a few days after Carys had cut Lily's hand and pressed it against Little Cat, Carys came into the room with a strange expression on her face.

'I saw your mum,' she said.

Lily jumped up. 'What? When?'

'A bad lady tried to hurt her . . . She's much older now but I knew her. I knew who she was! I never forget a face, Lily.' She giggled and Lily wondered if she'd been drinking again. Her eyes were shining with excitement.

'Who are you talking about?' Lily asked.

'Her! The girl with red hair! Her name is Heledd. The daughter of the bad lady who tried to give me to the Widow. She tried to hurt your mummy, Lily.'

Lily fought back tears. Her mum was alive and nearby. But before she could form a question, Carys started to ramble on.

'It was so funny. She thought *I* was the Widow. Imagine that! Because I was wearing my new red coat, the one I took from that crazy lady, the one who believes in spirits.'

Lily had no idea what Carys was talking about.

'And you know what? I remembered what you said – about how Heledd's parents had tried to kill me, and suddenly, *suddenly* I was angry. Angry like I've never been before.' She stood up and began to pace around the tiny room, with crazy eyes, waving her arms around and clenching her fists.

'I told her she should confess. That she should tell the world what her mother and father had done. Confess all their sins! And if she didn't, I would *kill* her.' She cackled, just like Bloody Mary in Megan's video game. 'She believed me. I told her to confess everything.'

Without warning, all the life seemed to leave Carys, like an untied balloon, and she flopped onto the mattress.

'Maybe I shouldn't have done it. Maybe it will lead them to me, to us. But I couldn't stop myself. I thought about her, living her life up there, watching movies and TV and playing games, and I thought about my life down here, living like a mole. I could have killed her, Lily. I should have killed her.'

She rambled on for another minute, making less and less sense.

Finally, Lily said, 'But my mum? Is she okay?'

Carys nodded. 'Oh yes. I saved her.'

Lily couldn't hold back any longer. She jumped up and shouted, 'Mummy! Mum! I'm here!'

Carys watched her. 'She won't hear you. I told you. No sound escapes this place.'

'Mummy!'

Carys grabbed hold of her and raised a hand again. 'Shut up!

Lily didn't want to cry, but she couldn't stop herself. 'Please. Please let me go back and be with her. I don't want to be here any more.' She collapsed on the bed, sobbing.

'Shut up! Stop that, now!' Carys screamed at her, her face as red as blood. 'I told you, you're mine now. And if anyone tries to take you, I'll kill them. I'll kill *you*.'

Carys stood by the door.

'I should never have spoken to Heledd, never told her to confess. They're going to start looking for me again.' She scratched at her arms. 'I need to hide you somewhere better.'

'Why not just let me go?'

'No! Shut up! We're going to leave here, tonight, when it's dark. We'll go somewhere new. Somewhere they'll never find us. So we can be together, you and me, *forever.*'

Chapter 47

'What did you see?' Julia demanded.

'Hold on.'

I crouched by the door again and put my eye to the keyhole. It was so hard to see. But then the person on the mattress shifted, turning over and giving me a good look at her light brown hair. She was small too.

A child.

'Julia,' I said. 'I'm not a hundred per cent sure, so don't freak out, but I think it's a little girl.'

Julia gasped and put her hands over her mouth. 'Lily? You think it's Lily? Oh my God . . .'

She pushed me out of the way and knelt by the keyhole. Her entire body started to shake.

'It's her, it's her.' Her voice caught on the final word, so it became a sob. She stood up and thumped on the door with both fists while I returned to a crouching position and peered back through the keyhole. 'Lily! *Lily*, it's me, it's Mummy, I'm here, sweetheart . . .'

Inside the room, the girl in the bed sat up, blinking with confusion, and then she leapt out of the bed, flying towards the door. It was her. It was definitely Lily.

'Mummy!' She screamed the word and thumped on the door. Julia was pulling at the handle, rattling it, as if she could pull the door from its hinges.

I grabbed her arm. 'Julia, Lily's trying to tell us something.'

Julia fell quiet. Through the door, Lily shouted in a wavering voice. 'The key. She keeps it in the chest by her bed.'

'Who's *she*, sweetheart?' Julia asked, her voice thick, just about managing to hold back the tears. It was a testament to her strength. The emotions coursing through her would have overwhelmed most people. But she was holding it together, at least until she got Lily safely out of here.

'Her name's Carys,' Lily said through the door.

I had been right. Of course it was her. The other little girl who'd gone missing all those years ago. Not a little girl any more. And, like a child who is mistreated, or worse, who passes it on to the next generation, Carys was doing exactly what had been done to her. History repeating.

I had many questions for Lily – not least of which was, where was Carys now? – but first we had to get her out of her cell. I ran back into the other room and pulled open the top drawer of the chest. It was full of underwear. Half of this stuff was probably Julia's, I thought, throwing aside bras and knickers, groping for the key. There was no sign of it.

And then Julia yelled.

I rushed back through the door.

Julia was lying on the floor and the door to Lily's cell stood open. Blood seeped from a wound on Julia's temple. Before I could react, something rushed out of the cell, something that let out an unearthly, violent howl. No, not something – someone. Carys. She must have come in through the house, through the steel door we had been unable to pass.

She smashed into me, knocking me off my feet. I sprawled on the hard floor, banging my head on the concrete. The world went white for a moment. When I came to there was a terrible ringing inside my head – it felt like a bell that had been struck by an iron rod – and Carys was gone. I got to my feet, holding my head, wondering briefly if this second injury would do any permanent damage.

The cell was empty. I took in the dirty mattress, the children's books piled beside it, the bedpan, the stuffed toys. It reminded me of photos I'd seen of the places hostages were kept in the Middle East, albeit a child's version.

'Where is she?'

I whirled round. Julia was getting to her feet and looking around.

'*Where is she?*' she screamed.

We heard a thud. It had come from the room where we'd entered this underground apartment. I rushed towards it, Julia following. The chest had been pushed to one side, exposing the hatch. Ignoring a wave of pain and nausea I bent to open it, lowering myself to drop through it, picking up the flashlight we'd left here when we came through a little earlier. Julia went to follow.

'You should stay here,' I said. 'You're injured.'

'What? Fuck that.'

'But Julia—'

From somewhere below us we heard a child's cry.

'Hurry up or get out of my way!'

There was no point arguing. I climbed down into the tunnel, Julia right behind me, and ran back the way we'd come. Our footsteps echoed around us, making it hard to hear how far ahead of us Carys and Lily were. What did Carys intend to do to her? I didn't have time to think about it. I stuck out an arm and stopped Julia, so we could listen.

Lily cried out, 'Mummy!'

They were just ahead of us. We ran, side by side, around a slight bend, past all the equipment that had been left here to rust. I held the flashlight in front of me, the beam bouncing wildly around the enclosed space. I slowed a little, concentrating on shining the light into the tunnel. And there they were.

Carys must have heard our gaining footsteps as she stopped and turned, realising she couldn't outrun us, not with a child in tow. She was holding Lily by the wrist. There was something in her other hand, but it was too dark to see.

Julia called Lily's name and Lily tried to run towards us, but Carys held tight. We had slowed to a walking pace now and were just seven or eight metres away from them.

Carys pulled Lily closer and grabbed hold of her from behind, so they were both facing us.

'Keep back!' Carys screeched.

She had black hair and, in the flashlight, was as pale as a vampire. It was hardly surprising: she had spent most of her life underground. I imagined her eyes would be attuned to the gloom, far better than mine were anyway. She was thin too, with bulbous, sunken eyes and a face like a skull. She was repugnant, but I felt terribly sorry for her.

Between them – Rhodri and Shirley, and the Pattersons – they had stolen Carys's life from her. They had turned her into this creature. This creature who had raised her hand to reveal what she was holding. A long, thin kitchen knife.

She held it against Lily's throat. 'Keep back,' she hissed. 'She's mine. You can't take her!'

I took a cautious step forward. 'Carys. That's your name, isn't it?'

Her shoulders flinched with surprise.

'We know what happened to you, Carys,' I said, taking another step towards them. Lily was crying now, her young face shining with tears. 'We know about the people who took you from the children's home. One of them is dead and the other is going to go to prison. You don't need to hide any more.'

She was silent, watching me, but the knife didn't move from Lily's throat.

'We know you helped us at the chapel. You saved us, and we're so grateful. But we need you to let Lily go.'

'No. She's mine. Aren't you, Lily? I saved her, so she belongs to me.'

I took another baby step towards her. 'It was Albert, wasn't it? He found you in the woods and brought you here. He and his wife couldn't have children, so they brought you up as their daughter. I understand that. But it's no life for a child, is it, Carys? Children need to live in the sun, to be free. They need friends. They need to go to school and explore the world.' I could hear Julia just behind me, breathing heavily. 'Most of all, Carys, they need their parents. Lily needs her mum.'

'She needs me.'

'She's not yours!'

It was Julia. She stepped forward, both arms held out before her. 'It's okay, Lily, Mummy's here. It's okay.'

'Shut up!' Carys hissed. 'Get back or I'll cut her. I swear, I swear on my daddy's grave.'

'We'll get you help,' I said in a soft voice. 'Find you somewhere to live. A house of your own.'

She stared at me.

'I want my house,' she said.

I thought I understood. 'Nyth Bran? Okay, you can have it, can't she, Julia?'

Julia's eyes darted between Lily and me. 'Yes, of course. You can have anything, Carys. Just let Lily go, please. Don't hurt her.'

'You don't want to hurt her, do you?' I said.

She shook her head, but still didn't lower the knife.

'Come on,' I said. 'We're not angry with you. We're happy you've been looking after Lily, aren't we, Julia?'

Julia forced herself to say, 'That's right.'

Carys looked at me, then at Julia. I could see her thinking, trying to make a decision. I waited, holding my breath, and then Carys relaxed her grip on Lily. Immediately, Lily ducked and scuttled away, towards the wall of the tunnel. And in that moment, Carys appeared to have a change of heart. She darted towards Lily and tried to grab her.

Julia threw herself at Carys.

Terrified she was going to be stabbed, I jumped between them, just as Carys lashed out with the knife. It swept in an arc across my body, slashing my belly just below my rib cage. I cried out with shock and pain, clutching my stomach, blood soaking the front of my shirt. The flashlight fell to the ground but didn't go out.

Carys turned, pointing the knife at Julia, who stood crouched like a cage fighter, fingers outstretched, her own wound weeping blood. No, I realised – not like a cage fighter, like an animal. Mama bear. Claws out. Teeth bared. The two women faced each other, frozen, while Lily watched, eyes wide, mouth open.

There was a rock on the floor by my feet. Still clutching my bleeding stomach, I fell onto my haunches, doubling over as if about to collapse.

I snatched up the rock and threw it with all my remaining strength at Carys.

I had been aiming for her face but it struck her on the chest. She flinched, lowered the hand holding the knife for a split second, but it was enough. Julia leapt at her, pushing her back, slamming Carys's head against the wall. Carys dropped the knife and Julia grabbed her by the throat, holding her, her face inches from Carys's.

'She's not yours,' she hissed. 'She belongs with *me*.'

She grabbed Carys's hair and pulled her head forward before pushing it back, hard, so it smacked against the wall. Carys crumpled to the ground and lay still.

Panting, Julia turned towards her daughter, who stood a metre away, hunched in the shadows. She was so pale, so thin.

But she was alive.

'Lily.'

'Mummy.'

They both sobbed, clutching each other, holding each other so tight I feared their bones might break. I took a step back, wanting to give them space, and watched from a short distance as they held each other, touched each other, repeating one another's names until they ran out of breath.

Chapter 48

Julia came in from the garden, wearing a T-shirt and shorts. Not for the first time I was struck by how beautiful she was, and how lucky I was to have her. Summer sun had lightened her hair a little and she had the first signs of a tan. She'd gained a little weight too, and the circles beneath her eyes were less dark. The past week, I'd noticed she'd been sleeping better, not waking with a gasp from terrible dreams. Her therapist, who was helping her deal with the anger issues that still affected her – sometimes I would see her eyes narrow, jaw muscles clenching, and I knew she was picturing herself hurting Carys – said those emotions might always be inside her. But she was able to cope. In her darkest moments, all she needed to do was hug Lily, smell her hair. Or just look at her. It was important, the therapist said, not to smother her.

'What's she doing?' I asked.

'Playing with Chesney.' She smiled. 'Sometimes I think she missed him more than she missed me.'

'I doubt that.'

She filled a glass with water from the tap. When she turned her arm over I saw the scar from that day four months ago. I had a matching one across my belly. Sometimes, in bed, we would trace our fingers over each other's scars and remind ourselves how fortunate we were.

Julia sat down at the breakfast bar, keeping an eye on Lily through the window as she chased the cat around the garden. Lily was due to start school again soon. Julia was nervous about this, about the idea of Lily being out of her sight, but Lily had insisted that she wanted to go back.

'I want to see my friends again, Mum.'

It had taken weeks to get the full story out of Lily about what had happened. She said she'd been trying to scare her parents, throwing Big Cat into the river and then running away into the woods. That was where Carys had grabbed her. Lily said she'd intended to hide for half an hour, that was all.

The police, and the psychiatrists who'd interviewed Carys extensively, said that she genuinely believed in the Red Widow and that she thought she was protecting Lily. Carys said she'd found Lily tied to a tree, but Lily denied that. The police were sure Carys was getting it all mixed up in her head. Her own abduction, and finding Lily in the woods.

Carys had told the police everything she could remember. How Shirley and Rhodri had taken her from St Mary's children's home into the woods. How she had been convinced the Widow was going to kill and eat her – until Albert, the man she soon called Daddy, 'rescued' her and took her to his nearby house. She described her life there in great detail. According to DI Snaith, she cried when she recounted the death of her 'Daddy', though seemed less upset about the death of Bethan, her 'Mummy'.

People who'd known Albert and Bethan – including my mum and a few older people who still lived in town – talked about a quiet couple who had, for a long time, seemed sad that they couldn't have children. 'But then they seemed to get over it; they were happier, more relaxed.' That was the testimony of the elderly proprietor of Rhiannon's Café, which the couple frequented. 'That would have been in around 1980.'

The year when they finally 'got' the child they'd always yearned for.

It turned out they hadn't been able to adopt through official channels because Albert had a criminal record (he stole a car when he was a young man and crashed it into a shop, leading to a few years in jail). The police theory was that the couple knew they wouldn't be allowed to keep Carys, so they let everyone think the Widow had taken her. Neither Shirley nor Rhodri knew what had happened to the girl they left in the woods. They never knew that Albert had seen them while out walking by the river; that he'd followed them, watching as they tied Carys to a tree. He let them go on thinking the Widow had taken her. It suited Albert and Bethan if the whole world thought Carys was dead.

DI Snaith told me the police psychiatrist had tried to find out if Albert had abused Carys, if they'd had a sexual relationship – either while she was still a child or as an adult. She denied it, but the police weren't sure if she was telling the truth. Perhaps one day she'll reveal all, but now she continues to talk about her 'Daddy' as if he were a saint.

Carys went on to describe how, after the deaths of Albert and Bethan Patterson, she'd continued to 'visit' the house upstairs. She was angry when the Marshes moved into 'her' house, but then learned to like them; she even began to see them as her new family. She liked to listen to Julia and Lily and Michael. After Michael drowned, and while Lily was locked up under the house, Carys was happy with the state of things. She came into the house and took what she needed. She watched Julia as she mourned the loss of her husband and child. Carys said Nyth Bran was her home, but she was happy to share it with Julia . . . until she opened the writers' retreat.

Suddenly, there were strangers traipsing through the house, invading Carys's space. Carys had to get rid of them. She tried to scare them off by making it look as if the house was haunted. I was one of the people she wanted to get rid of. And when she overheard me talking about how I was investigating Lily's disappearance, it became even more imperative to dispose of me.

The rest, we pieced together from both Carys and Heledd's testimonies.

Carys didn't know that Heledd was assisting her in this. Heledd was trying to shut down the investigation into Lily's disappearance because she was worried it would lead to the truth coming out about what had happened with the last little girl who disappeared. And so past and present were coming together to create a perfect storm.

When Carys overheard Ursula talking about spirit guides, her twisted mind came up with what she saw as a good plan: she wanted to convince Julia that Lily was dead. She spoke through the walls and told Ursula that Lily was 'with Jesus', wanting us to believe she had died in the chapel. She told Ursula that Lily had gone to a better place and was happy with her dad. She hoped then that we would stop searching for the truth. She wanted me to leave, and Julia to give up hope of finding Lily alive.

But when we didn't stop, she used Ursula again. She retrieved Little Cat from the hut where she'd hidden it after Lily's escape attempt, made Lily bleed onto its fur and left it in the chapel. Then, through Ursula, she directed us to the chapel, hoping the toy, stained with Lily's blood, would convince us Lily was dead.

She followed us from the house, keen to see if her plan worked. She had no idea Zara's body was in the crypt. And she had no idea Heledd was on her way there too. But when she saw Heledd push Julia down the stairs she was horrified. She attacked Heledd. Carys, in her red coat, sprinting into the chapel. Heledd, already in a state of heightened emotion, was petrified. The Red Widow – in the flesh! Heledd fell to her knees and began to babble, terrified the witch was going to kill her, all these years after her parents had sacrificed another little girl to save her.

And Carys knew who Heledd was. Years before, when Heledd was a teenager, Shirley had brought her to Nyth Bran to visit her old friends Albert and Bethan. When Carys encountered Heledd at the chapel, she flipped.

She had saved our lives and, inadvertently, given herself away.

And that was the end of the story. The police interviewed Rhodri Wallace and he finally confessed to abducting Carys back in 1980 with the help of Shirley Roberts. Rhodri, it turned out, had done some work in the garden of the children's home, which gave him the idea of where to find a child who 'wouldn't be missed'. Rhodri doted on his secret daughter, seeing her as often as he could. Her happiness and well-being made everything he'd done worthwhile. In his mind, it absolved him of all his sins.

Glynn Collins had nothing to do with any of it – apart from scaring Shirley with the story of the Red Widow. He had also told Shirley that someone new – Zara Sullivan – was in town, asking questions, a conversation that Heledd overheard.

So Glynn was indirectly responsible, but not guilty of any crime. I still wondered why he had refused to let me talk to Jake. There was something not quite right about that . . . But after thinking about it for a while I decided he was most likely just being a protective grandfather.

And Heledd? She was in prison, having pleaded guilty to the murders of Zara Sullivan and Max Lake, and the manslaughter of her mother, Shirley Roberts. She denied causing the death of Malcolm Jones, and the CPS had decided to drop that charge, as it was impossible to prove.

All the guilty parties were either dead or locked up. Carys was currently in a secure psychiatric hospital. Nobody yet seemed to know what was going to happen to her.

Personally, despite what she'd done to Lily, I thought Carys deserved to be free, as long as she was kept under observation and was a long way from us. She was a victim herself. She'd spent her whole life living in that dark hole beneath this house, believing wholeheartedly in the Widow. When she took Lily, she genuinely seemed to believe she was harbouring her from the Widow. I imagine that, after a while, she got used to having Lily around, like a pet. And she couldn't let her go because then Carys's secret home beneath Nyth Bran would be revealed.

Didn't Carys deserve to spend some time in the light? I thought about the paragraph Carys had written on my laptop, the words I thought I'd drunk-typed. She had a fascinating story to tell. Maybe, with encouragement and help, she could tell it. She would need a ghost-writer, of course . . .

I didn't think Julia would be too happy about this idea.

'I'm going to see if Lily wants some lunch,' Julia said, kissing me before she left the kitchen.

I looked around. I had fallen on my feet here. Julia and I had decided to make a go of the writers' retreat together. We had our first new intake of guests due at the start of September. I was going to act as a tutor and organise courses for the guests. That would be my job for now. I had abandoned the novel about the family living in the forest. The contract with my publisher had been cancelled – or, at least, put on hold. I would write something again when I was ready. I was thinking about writing something lighter next time. A romantic comedy, perhaps.

'Yeah, right,' Julia said when I told her that.

She was looking for illustrating work again too – she had a meeting coming up with an old contact at Jackdaw Books – and was seeing a grief counsellor. Now Lily was home, Julia was finally able to confront Michael's death. There had been a lot of tears shed during the nights. I think it helped that I had lost someone too – we could share our feelings, talk about our former partners without either of us worrying we had to compete with the dead. I knew there were going to be bumps ahead, but I felt confident we could cope with that.

It was worth trying, anyway.

My phone beeped. It was a message from Karen, who I'd been in regular touch with over the past few months. She'd kicked her heavy weed habit but had been hugely relieved to discover she hadn't been imagining the voices in the walls.

Her message contained a link to a story on the *Bookseller* website: Suzi Hastings had signed a six-figure deal for her debut novel, which was described as 'a highly erotic thriller about an affair between a married writer and a young ingénue, set in a writers' retreat in Wales'.

Looks like they were at it after all! Karen texted.

Either that or Suzi was making it up. Max had sounded so sincere . . . but I guessed we'd never know for certain. It didn't matter anyway, did it? Though I didn't think Max's widow would be too happy about Suzi's book.

As well as Karen, I'd kept in touch with Olly Jones, meeting up with him a few times for a drink. He wasn't driving a taxi any more. Instead, he'd used the money from the sale of his dad's house to set up his own minicab firm. He was the boss now. He told me running his business kept his mind off Heledd and how she'd broken his heart. He insisted he was over her now, but I wasn't fully convinced.

I went over to the window. Chesney had vanished, and Julia and Lily were playing together on the lawn, running through the sprinklers, laughing as the water soaked them. They collapsed into a heap on the grass and Julia threw her arms around her daughter, pulling her close.

I had a feeling there was something Lily wasn't telling us, as if part of her story was missing. But when I said this to Julia she told me not to be stupid. Why would Lily lie? I had no answer to that, but there was something niggling at me.

Now, in Julia's embrace, Lily looked over her shoulder so I could see her face. She wore that expression, the one I caught occasionally when Julia wasn't looking. The smile she wore for her mum slipped away and her brow would furrow, eyes darkening.

I guessed she was remembering her time in that room beneath the basement. She would recover, I was sure, but sometimes her expression frightened me.

Sometimes, like now, she looked murderous.

Epilogue

It was the last day of summer. Tomorrow, Lily would have to go back to school and guests would start arriving at the retreat. Right now, Mum and her new boyfriend Lucas were still in bed, enjoying their last lie-in. Mum would never have let Lily come down to the river on her own. She wouldn't let her go anywhere. And that was fine. Lily didn't want to go anywhere.

But she had unfinished business.

Walking down to the riverbank, she'd thought about Lucas. He seemed all right. He wasn't her dad, but at least he seemed to make Mum happy and they never argued, not seriously anyway. Sometimes, at night, she'd hear them laughing together. Maybe, Lily hoped, he would ask Mum to marry him and Lily could be a bridesmaid. That would be pretty cool. Just as long as he didn't expect her to call him Dad. She already had a dad.

And every time she thought about her father and why he was dead, she felt as if there were a flame inside her that filled her entire body. She tried to hide it from Mum and was sure she had succeeded. But the flame drew the moths: the black moths that came to her in the night, each one representing a dark thought. They landed inside her head and clung there, dozens of them, hundreds. A whole swarm of bad thoughts that wouldn't go away, no matter how hard she tried.

She wondered if this was how Rhiannon, the woman who became the Red Widow, had felt after her husband died. If that was what made her put the curse on the town.

Revenge. That's what the bad thoughts were about.

Revenge for Dad's death. And for the two years she'd spent locked in that room.

She reached the river. It had rained all night and the water was grey and high and choppy, rushing around the bend like it was late for an important date.

Lily pictured Dad drowning in that water and was forced to look back – and there she was, threading her way through the bushes towards her.

'Hi, Megan,' Lily said.

Megan looked nervous, just as she had yesterday. Lily had sneaked through the woods and emerged by Megan's house, hiding and hoping to catch a glimpse of her former best friend. She got lucky. A bus pulled in at the end of the road and Megan got off. She gasped when Lily stepped out of the trees and said hello.

'I want to talk to you,' Lily had said. 'Meet me tomorrow at nine in the morning, okay? Down by the river. I've got something to tell you. Something important.'

Lily knew Megan would come. She was a curious girl. And sure enough, she did. Lily watched her walk across the field, dragging her feet slightly.

'How are you?' Lily asked when Megan reached her. 'How's Jake?'

'He's fine. Not happy about going back to school but, like, who is?'

Lily didn't blame Jake for what had happened. He'd simply been following instructions.

'I'm looking forward to it,' Lily said. 'Even though I've missed, like, nearly three years and am going to be bottom of the class.'

She walked closer to the river, Megan following after a pause.

'I'm . . .' Megan started, before swallowing her words. Finally, she spat it out. 'I'm sorry. I was just . . . I was scared. I really thought the Widow was real. I was a kid, a silly, scared kid. And when they said you'd gone missing, I was convinced. The witch really had got you.'

Lily stared at the water, letting Megan ramble on.

'I felt so guilty, though, especially after— especially after what happened to your dad. I used to watch your house, wishing you were still there. Jake wanted to tell, to confess, but I knew they'd send him to prison. I thought they'd send me to prison too. I was terrified.' She tried to meet Lily's eye. 'I didn't want it to be you, but there was no one else . . . You were the only other kid who didn't live in town, who we could . . .' She trailed off.

'It's okay,' Lily said. 'It all worked out fine in the end.'

Megan stared in that annoying way of hers. Some things never changed.

'You really mean that?'

Lily nodded.

'Is that why . . . ?' Megan's voice dropped to a whisper and she looked around, as if someone might be lurking in the trees, listening. 'Is that why you didn't tell anyone what really happened? Why you didn't tell them about me and Jake?'

'That's right.' The black moths fluttered their wings, ready to take off, to bash and batter the inside of her skull. 'I don't want Jake to go to prison either. And you're too young. You wouldn't be punished.'

Confusion flitted across Megan's face, but Lily smiled. 'You're still my best friend.'

Megan couldn't hide her relief. 'I'll do whatever it takes, Lily, to make it up to you.'

Lily had one more question. 'Does your grandad know what happened?'

Megan looked pained. 'I don't think so. I mean, I've seen him looking at me sometimes, like he's wondering about something. But he's never said anything. And he never will.'

Lily nodded, satisfied, then turned away, still smiling, and said, 'What was that?'

'Huh?'

Lily pointed towards the far bank and moved closer to the river. 'Down in the water, over there. I saw something shining.'

Megan stepped closer to the edge of the riverbank. 'What? Really? I can't see anything.'

Lily pointed towards the far bank. 'Over there. Look.'

Megan stepped closer still to the edge, leaning forward with one hand cupped over her eyes. 'I still can't see it. Are you sure?'

Lily moved behind her former best friend.

'You should be careful what you believe,' she said. And pushed.

She watched Megan thrash in the water for a minute, watched the strong current pull her under, just as it had done to Dad. Megan came to the surface, mouth opening, flapping soundlessly, but only for a moment. The river claimed her.

Glancing around to check no one had seen, Lily headed home, smiling quietly to herself. No one would ever know it wasn't an accident. She rubbed her scalp.

The moths were quiet at last.

Letter from the author

Dear Reader

Thank you so much for reading *The Retreat*. I love hearing from readers and you can email me at markcity@me.com, find me on facebook.com/markedwardsbooks or follow me on Twitter: @mredwards. I've also joined Instagram (@markedwardsauthor) because the world desperately needs more photos of books, cats and dogs . . .

Please note, the rest of this letter contains massive spoilers, so PLEASE don't read it until you've finished the book.

The initial spark for *The Retreat* came from a newspaper article I read a few years ago. A family had been driven out of their home by somebody who believed the house rightfully belonged to them. This led to an idea: a house that was haunted, not by a ghost but by a living person.

I combined this idea with an image that came to me from nowhere: a family, out walking by the river on a winter's day; the parents rounding the corner to discover their daughter missing, and a soft toy being carried away by the churning water.

But what had happened to this girl? And who was haunting the house? It took a while to figure this out.

I have always been fascinated by urban legends and folk tales, by the stories people tell each other. Shortly before starting *The Retreat* I watched a fascinating documentary called *Beware the Slenderman*, about a horrifying case in which two young girls attempted to murder their best friend because an Internet meme told them to. At the same time, my YouTube-addicted son began to ask questions about the Slenderman and my daughter came home from school talking about Bloody Mary.

It struck me that this was what my novel was about: the scary stories we tell each other about 'boogeymen', stories that spread much faster and wider now we have the Internet . . . And it's not only children who believe scary tales. In this world of post-truth politics and 'fake news', it's more important than ever that we think very carefully about what, and who, we believe.

Finally, if you enjoyed this book I hope you will recommend it to a friend. Maybe pass it on to someone who doesn't usually read much. There are few things I like better than receiving a message from a reader whose love of books has been sparked or rekindled by one of my novels. The more people we can turn on to the joy of reading, the better the world will be.

Best wishes
Mark Edwards
www.markedwardsauthor.com

Acknowledgments

Thank you to all the usual suspects, the team of people who are always there for me and help me get my books into the hands of readers:

Emilie, Sana, Hatty, Eoin, Laura, Shona and everyone else at Thomas & Mercer for being fabulous publishers and knowing what authors need (a quick reply to emails and lots of alcohol);

My brilliantly astute agent, Sam Copeland, whose enthusiasm for this book was infectious;

My ridiculously clever and gorgeous wife, Sara, for supporting me in every way and being my first and most critical reader (in a nice way).

A number of people helped specifically with this book. As one of the world's least organised people, I apologise in advance to anyone I've missed out:

Ian Pindar, my editor, for countless wise suggestions and for making the editing of this book seem almost unbelievably straightforward;

The real Heledd Roberts, who not only let me use her name but provided the creepy Welsh song and helped me name the town of Beddmawr, along with Suzanna Salter and Jackie Davies;

All the other members of my Facebook page who volunteered to have characters named after them: Malcolm Jones and Olly Jones (who are not related in real life!), Karen Holden, Ursula Clarke, Garry Snaith and Suzi Hastings. Also, Lily Jenkinson for helping come up with the name of the cat, Chesney, and Julie Baugh for helping me christen some of my other characters;

Everyone else on my Facebook page, Twitter and Instagram for your endless enthusiasm and cheerleading;

My daughters, Ellie and Poppy, for showing such interest in your dad's book, even though you're not allowed to read it yet, and for advising me on words the kids of today would and would not use. I promise not to say 'LOL' or 'true dat' ever again;

Lisa Shakespeare and Rachel Kennedy at Midas PR for helping to spread the word about my books – though I'm still waiting for a feature about Rebel and me in *Your Dog* magazine;

Heather Large and Lisa Williams at the *Express & Star* for all your support;

And finally, my mum – who engendered my love of books and who, unwittingly, started me on this path many years ago by bringing home that James Herbert novel. Thank you not just for that but for all your encouragement and support. I still need to buy you that bungalow . . .

Free *Short Sharp Shockers* Box Set

Join Mark Edwards' Readers' Club and get a free collection of short stories, including 'Kissing Games', 'Consenting Adults' and 'Guardian Angel'.

You will also receive exclusive news and regular giveaways.

Join now at www.markedwardsauthor.com/free.

About the Author

Mark Edwards writes psychological thrillers in which scary things happen to ordinary people, and is inspired by writers such as Stephen King, Ira Levin, Ruth Rendell and Linwood Barclay.

He is the author of three #1 bestsellers: *Follow You Home* (a finalist in the Goodreads Choice Awards 2015), *The Magpies* and *Because She Loves Me*, along with *What You Wish For* and six novels co-written with Louise Voss. All of his books are inspired by real-life experiences.

Originally from the south coast of England, Mark now lives in the West Midlands with his wife, their three children and a ginger cat.

Mark loves hearing from readers and can be contacted via his website, www.markedwardsauthor.com.

Printed in Great Britain
by Amazon